CORNISH FISHERMEN

A
BOOK OF CORNWALL
BY
S. BARING-GOULD
AUTHOR OF "A BOOK OF BRITTANY," "A BOOK OF THE RIVIERA," ETC.

Cornish Fishermen
  From a photograph by the Rev. F. Partridge.

CORNWALL

CHAPTER I.

THE CORNISH SAINTS

A saint or squab pie--The saints belong to five classes--I. The members of the royal Dumnonian family--II. Irish-Welsh colonists--The invasion of Brecknock--Brychan--The invasion of Cornwall and Devon--Murtogh Mac Earca--III. Irish in West Cornwall--IV. Welsh-Breton saints--V. Pure Breton importations--Ecclesiastical colonies--Llans and cells--Tribal organisation--Ecclesiastical also tribal--The sanctuary--How a tribe was recruited--Jurisdiction--What a Celtic monastery was--Rights exercised by the saints--That of ill-wishing--Missionary methods of the Celtic saints--Illand and S. Bridget--The power of the keys as the saints understood it--Reciprocal rights--The saint expected to curse the enemies of the secular tribe--Asceticism--A legal process carried into religion--Story of the three clerks--A higher idea of asceticism gained ground--S. Columba and the nettles--The saints and animals--And children--How they used their powers--What they did for womankind--The biographies, how far trustworthy--The interest in knowing something of the founders of the Churches.

THE story goes that the devil one day came to the Tamar from the Devon side and stood rubbing his chin and considering.

"No," said he, "I won't risk it. Yonder every person is made into a saint, and everything into squab pie. I do not feel qualified for either position."

And it is a fact that nowhere else in England are there so many villages bearing the names of saints, and these names strange, and such as may be sought out in vain in the calendars that are easily accessible. One is impressed with the idea that the vast majority of these saints are unknown and negligible quantities.

This, however, is an entirely false assumption, and it is based on the fact that their history has not been studied.

On close examination it will be found that the saintly names in Cornwall belong to certain well-defined groups, and when we have determined the localities occupied by these groups we have taken the first step towards the elucidation of some important problems in the early history of Cornwall.

Now let us look at these groups.

I. The first belongs to members of the royal Dumnonian family that ruled Devon and Cornwall.

The first-known prince was Constantine the Blessed (about 460), whose brother Aldor migrated to Brittany, and married the sister of Germanus of Auxerre, who came to Britain in 429 and 447 to oppose the spread of the Pelagian heresy.

Constantine's son Erbin, prince of the Dumnonii, died about 480. We know nothing of him save that he was the father of Geraint, the heroic king who fell at Langport, in Somersetshire, in 522, fighting against the Saxons.

His name is familiar to us as the husband of Enid, daughter of the lord of Caerleon, whose virtues and pathetic story have been revived with fresh interest in Tennyson's idyl. Geraint has left his name at Dingerrein, where was his palace, near the church he founded--S. Gerrans, in Roseland--and a tomb, supposed to be his, is still pointed out. Although his story is preserved in the Mabinogion, this story has no pretence to be regarded as history.

His first cousin was Gwen of the Three Breasts, married to Fragan, also a cousin, who migrated to Brittany. There is a curious monument of Gwen in Brittany, on which she is actually represented as having three breasts. But the expression three-or four-breasted was used of a woman who was married thrice or four times, and had a family by each husband. The mother of S. Domangard was called the four-breasted for no other reason than this.

Fragan and Gwen had three sons--Winwaloe, Wethenoc or Winock, and James--and although the great field of their labours was in Brittany, yet they certainly visited their cousins in Cornwall and obtained grants of land there, for they founded churches in two districts, where their names remain to this day somewhat disguised in Gunwalloe, Lewanick, and Jacobstow. Geraint and Enid had several children; the eldest was Solomon or Selyf, who died about 550.

He married Gwen, sister of Non, the mother of S. David, and it was due to this connection that Non and her son came to Cornwall and founded Altarnon, Pelynt, and Davidstowe.

Gwen herself we recognise as S. Wenn; she was the mother of S. Cuby, founder of Duloe and Tregony. Docwin or Cyngar, brother of Solomon, was an abbot in Somersetshire. In his old age his nephew Cuby took his uncle with him to Ireland, where he kept a cow for providing the old man with her milk. A chief carried off the cow, and Cuby left Ireland and brought the aged uncle back with him. Docwin or Cyngar was the founder of S. Kew.

Again, another uncle of S. Cuby was Cado, Duke of Cornwall, who makes a great figure in Geoffrey of Monmouth's fabulous history, and in the Arthurian romances. He was father of Constantine, whom Gildas attacked so venomously in his spiteful letter about 547, and who was converted by S. Petrock in his old age. We have in Cornwall two of his foundations and one in Devon.

After his conversion Constantine went to Ireland and entered a monastery without disclosing who he was. He was discovered by accident; for, having been set to grind corn with a hand-quern, he was overheard laughing and saying, "What would my Cornish subjects think were they to see me thus engaged?"

II. The second group of saints is of Irish-Welsh origin. The Welsh have a droll legend to account for the Irish conquest of Brecknock.

Meurig, king of Garth-Madrin (a part of Brecknockshire), had a daughter, Marchell, who said to her father in coaxing terms, "I *do* want a fur cloak; the winters here are abominably cold."

"You shall have one," answered the father.

On cool reflection Meurig considered that fur cloaks were expensive luxuries, far beyond the means of a petty Welsh prince.

So he said to Marchell, "My dear, I am going to marry you to a very agreeable young man, Aulac" (Amalgaidh), "an Irish prince, and he has ample means at his disposal to provide you with the desired fur cloak."

So Aulac was invited over, found Marchell charming, and carried her back with him to Ireland.

Now whilst he was in Wales he had allowed his eyes to wander, and he had seen that there was a good deal of rich and covetable land there. So he speedily returned at the head of a host of Irish kernes, and overran, not Brecknock alone, but all Cardigan, Carmarthen, and Pembroke, and established himself as prince there.

Whether Marchell ever got her fur cloak history does not say.

Aulac and Marchell had a son, Brychan (the Speckled or Tartan-clad), who has given his name to the county of Brecknockshire.

Brychan was a much-wived man, unless he be greatly misrepresented, and had a numerous family.

Not only do the Welsh genealogists give him forty-nine children, but the Irish, the Cornish, and the Bretons attribute to him several more.

The fact is that all Brychan's family, grandchildren as well as children, have been run together, for all such as exercised tribal rights formed the family clan.

In one of the S. Neot's windows may be seen good old Brychan seated on a throne, holding a lapful of progeny before him, dense as young rabbits.

In Ireland the tribes are called after the founder, as the Hy Conaill, Hy Fiachra, or sons of Conal, sons of Fiech, though grand, great-grand, and great-great-grandchildren.

Now the Irish who had invaded South Wales were not allowed a peaceful time in which to consolidate their power, for in the time of the grandchildren of Brychan, if not in that of his son Cledwyn, king of Carmarthen, there came down a Northern Briton, named Dyfnwal, into South Wales and drove them out, and pretty well exterminated the family of Cledwyn. This must have been about the year 500, and it was probably due to this that so many of Brychan's sons and daughters and grandchildren took to their heels and crossed the Severn Sea, and established themselves in North Devon and Cornwall.

It was not till about fifty years later that Caradoc Strong-i'-th'-Arm, the son of a granddaughter of Brychan and prince of Gallewig, the region about Callington, marched westward from the Severn, and expelled the invaders, and recovered Brecknockshire.

When the great migration took place it comprised not only the family of King Brychan, but also the Gwentian royal family, that was allied to it by blood.

Of course there has accumulated a certain amount of legend about Brychan, and we cannot really be sure that such a person ever existed; that, in fact, the name is not really that of a clan, for Breogan, which is the same as the Welsh Brychan, was the reputed ancestor of one of the branches of the Scots or Irish who migrated, according to legend, from Spain to the Emerald Isle.[1]

What is true is that a certain Irish clan did invade and occupy Brecknock and Carmarthen, as well as Pembrokeshire, and that about 530 they were driven out of the two first counties, and that they thereupon invaded and occupied North-East Cornwall from Padstow harbour, and the north of Devon as far as Exmoor. This was not by any means a first descent. The whole coast had been a prey to invasions from Ireland for two centuries. On this occasion among the Irish-Welsh from Gwent and Brecknock came a great number of saints, that is to say, princes and princesses devoted to the ecclesiastical profession. The significance of this I shall explain presently.

I will here only point out that almost all the foundations of churches in North-east Cornwall were made by members of the same Gwent-Brecknock family. Is there, it may be asked, any Irish record of this invasion? We have a good many records of earlier forays and occupations of Britain by the Irish, but of this particular one only a somewhat confused legend. There was a certain Princess Earca, married to a king named Saran, in Ireland, who was much engaged in raids in Britain. She was the daughter of Loarn, king of Alba or Scotland, from whom Lorn takes its name, the date of whose birth is given by the Irish annalists as taking place in 434. He was, in fact, one of the Irish Ulster adventurers who invaded Scotland.

Earca ran away from her husband to be with Murtogh, a distant cousin of Saran, and she bore him four sons. The most noted of all was Murtogh MacEarca, who in time became king of Ireland. Saran then married Earca's sister, and by her became the father of S. Cairnech and Lurig, king of the Scots (Irish) in Britain. Murtogh having committed several murders in Ireland, fled for protection to his grandfather, Loarn, in Alba, and murdered him. Thereupon he was banished from what we now call Scotland. He went to his cousin S. Cairnech to bless his arms, as it was his intention to offer his services to one of the kings of Britain, and do as much fighting as came in his way. Before leaving Cairnech he murdered in cold blood his cousin Luirig, and carried off his wife.

In Britain this ruffian, we are told, became the father of Constantine and Goidel Ficht, who became the reigning princes in Cornwall.

Murtogh was back in Ireland in 488, for we find him there fighting; and he remained there stirring up strife, and a cause of bloodshed till he was elected king of Ireland in 508.

Now, Murtogh most certainly when he went to Britain led a body of adventurers like himself. He is said to have been the father of Goidel Ficht, who remained there as sovereign. Now, Goidel Fichti signifies the Irish Picts, neither more nor less, a generic name, and his fatherhood of the Irish Picts means no more than that his clan or horde, which swooped down on Cornwall and Wales, regarded themselves as Hy Murtogh.

It is rather remarkable that his cousin, the whole brother of S. Cairnech, was named Broechan or Brychan.

Now, in this story, attached to a perfectly historical character, I cannot but suspect that we have a reference to a descent on Wales and Cornwall in or about 470-480.

Perhaps it may interest the reader to hear what was the end of this ruffian.

On his return to Ireland he brawled and fought till he became king in 508.

He was married to a good wife named Duiseach, and had by her a family, but he fell under the fascinations of a beautiful woman called Shin, whereupon he turned away his wife; and--by the witchcraft, so it was supposed, of the witch--one after another of his children was carried off by disease, possibly by poison. Duiseach fled for refuge to S. Cairnech, who blessed her and all who would take up her cause, and gathered together a body of men resolved on fighting to replace her. Cairnech gave a book and his staff to be carried to battle before the host.

Now it happened that in a battle fought in 524 Murtogh had killed Shin's father and brother, and though the beautiful woman continued to exercise her blandishments on the king, she had vowed revenge in her heart against him. She awaited her opportunity. It came on the eve of Samhain, All Hallows, when high revelry was kept in the hall at Cletty, where Murtogh was residing. She had the hall secretly surrounded by her men, and herself set fire to it. Murtogh was very drunk, the fire caught his clothes, and, unable to escape by the doors, which were guarded, he threw himself into a vat of wine to quench the flames, and so perished, partly by fire, partly by wine, in 527.

It is possible--I cannot say more--that as this incursion, mentioned by the Irish writers, took place precisely at the period of the Brychan descent, it may refer to it, and that Brychan may actually have been Murtogh's half-brother, who accompanied him to Britain to carve out for himself a kingdom.

III. The third group is likewise Irish, but unmixed with Welsh elements. This consists of a swarm, or succession of swarms, that descended about the year 500 upon the Land's End and Lizard district.

Concerning them we know something more than we do about the second group.

Happily Leland, who visited Cornwall in the reign of Henry VIII., made extracts from their legends then in existence, very scanty extracts, but nevertheless precious. Moreover, we have one complete legend, that of S. Fingar or Gwinear, written by a Saxon monk of the name of Anselm. And we have the lives of many of those who made a temporary stay in the Land's End and Lizard districts, preserved in

Irish MSS.

IV. A fourth group is that of saints, half Welsh and half Breton, who made a short stay in Cornwall on their way to and fro.

According to Celtic law, all sons equally divided the inheritance and principalities of their father. The consequence was that on the death of a king the most masterful of his sons cut the throats of such of his brothers as he could lay hold of. And as these little games were enacted periodically in Brittany, the breath was no sooner out of the body of a prince than such sons as felt that they had no chance of maintaining their rights made a bolt of it, crossed into Cornwall, and either halted there or passed through it on their way to Wales, where they very generally got married.

Then either they or their sons returned to Cornwall and lingered there, watching events in Brittany for the safe moment to go back and reassert their rights, and as they rarely could recover princely rights, they became ecclesiastics; a compromise was effected, and they were allowed to return and set up as founders of saintly tribes.

Whilst they tarried in Cornwall they occupied their leisure in founding churches.

Such was S. Samson, with his disciples S. Mewan, S. Austell, and S. Erme.

Such again was S. Padarn, who established a large settlement where are the Petherwins.

When Samson crossed from Wales to Cornwall on his way to Brittany, he sent word to Padarn that he was going to visit him. They were first cousins. Padarn heard the news just as he had left his bed, and had pulled on one shoe and stocking. So delighted was he to hear that Samson was approaching that he ran to meet him with one leg and foot shod and the other bare.

Samson founded churches at Southill and Golant.

V. A fifth group consists of importations. In the year 919 or 920, on account of the devastations of the Normans, Brittany was almost depopulated. The Count of Poher fled with a number of his Bretons to Athelstan, and he took with him Alan his son, afterwards called Barbe-torte, who was Athelstan's godson. At this date Athelstan could do little for them; he did not ascend the throne till 924, and it was not till 926 that he defeated Howel, king of the West Welsh, as the Cornish and Devon Britons were called, and forced him to submission. In 935 Athelstan passed through Cornwall to Land's End and Scilly, and possibly enough he may have then allowed some of these fugitive Bretons to settle in Cornwall; and this explains the existence there of churches bearing the names of merely local and uninteresting saints, as S. Meriadoc at Camborne, S. Moran, and S. Corentin of Cury. These foundations mean no more than that some of the Breton settlers had brought with them the relics of their patrons in Rennes, Nantes, and Quimper. But an early Celtic foundation had quite another meaning. Among the Celts churches were not generally called after *dead* saints, but after their founders. The process of consecration was this:--

A saint went to a spot where a bit of territory had been granted him, and fasted there for forty days and nights, and continued instant in prayer, partaking of a single meal in the day, that plain, and indulging in an egg only on Sundays. At the conclusion of this period the *llan* or *cell* was his for ever inalienably, and ever after it bore his name. Moreover, among Celtic saints there existed quite a rage after multiplication of foundations, *daltha* churches, as they were called. Unless a saint could point to his baker's dozen of churches founded by himself, he was nought. But not all churches bearing a saint's name, say that of Petrock, were founded by him in person. A saint was supposed never to die, never to let go his hold over his territory. And when in after-years a chief surrendered land to a monastery, he gave it, not to the community, but to the saint; and the church built on that land would bear the name of the saint whose property it was.

The reader may like to hear something about the organisation of the Church in Celtic lands. But to understand this I must first very shortly explain the political organisation.

This among all Celtic people was tribal. The tribe, cinnel, clan, was under a chief, who had his *dun* or fort. Every subdivision of the tribe had also its camp of refuge and its headman.

When the British became Christian, Christianity in no way altered their political organisation. This we may see from the conduct of S. Patrick, who converted the Irish. He left their organisation untouched, and accommodated his arrangements for the religious supervision of the people to that, as almost certainly it existed in Britain, except perhaps in the Roman colonial cities.

Now this was very peculiar, quite unlike anything that existed in the civilised Roman world.

This organisation consisted in the creation of an ecclesiastical tribe side by side with the tribe of the land. The saint was given by the king or chief a certain territory, and at once he set to work thereon to constitute an ecclesiastical tribe subject to his rule, precisely similar to the secular tribe subject to the rule of the chieftain. A rill of water usually divided the two settlements. The idea of the church and the priest in the midst of the tribe of the land, acting as chapel and chaplain did to the Saxon thane or the Norman baron, did not occur to the Celt. The two tribes coexisted as separate units, but tied together by reciprocal rights.

The saint having been given a bit of land, at once constituted his sanctuary. He put up stones or crosses marking his bounds, a thousand paces from his cell, in a circle.

Every noble, *arglwyd*, or *flath* exercised rights of sanctuary, and the extent of his sanctuary constituted his *llan*, or lawn. The lowest grade of noble had the limits of his lawn marked at the distance of three throws of a spear or a ploughshare from his door; the *rig* or king had his as far as sixty-four pitches.

Now all those who took refuge within the lawn had sanctuary for a limited period, and the noble or the saint employed this time of respite to come to terms with the prosecutor, and furnish the fine (*eric*) appointed by law for the offence committed by the refugee. If he could not pay the fine he surrendered the man who had come for sanctuary, but if he paid it, thenceforth that man became his client, and he provided him with a *bod* or *both*, a habitation, and land to cultivate; he became one of his men. This was an important means whereby the saint recruited his tribe.

Throughout Cornwall a number of sanctuaries, remain, under the name of "sentry fields." If we could find out how many and where they are, we should know what were the mother *llans* of the early saints.

But a saintly tribe was recruited in another way. Every firstling of the secular tribe was made over to the saint: the first son of a family, the first lamb and calf. The son did not necessarily become an ecclesiastic, but he passed into the ecclesiastical tribe, and became subject to the jurisdiction of the saint.

But it may be asked, What happened when the saint died?

Every chief had his *taanist*, or successor, appointed during his life, and enjoying certain privileges. So every saint had his *coarb* chosen to rule in his name, his steward, his representative on earth. Here came in an usage very strange to Latin minds. The *coarb* must be of the royal or chieftain's race, and the right to rule in the ecclesiastical tribe belonged to the founder's family, and was hereditary, whether he were in ecclesiastical orders or not, to a female as well as to a male. Thus, although in an ecclesiastical establishment there was always a bishop to confer orders, he did not exercise jurisdiction. The rule was in the hands of the head of the sacred tribe. Thus S. Bridget kept her tame bishop, Conlaeth, who was wholly under petticoat government. He did kick once, and was devoured of wolves as a judgment, having strayed, against Bridget's orders, among the mountains. S. Ninnocha had as many as four bishops under her command. Bishop Etchen was subject to the jurisdiction of S. Columba, who was in priest's orders.

The Celtic Church as we know it, till gradually brought under Roman discipline, was purely monastic. The monasteries were the centres whence the ministry of souls was exercised. Within the sanctuary a rampart was thrown up, generally of earth, and within this was the church, and about it the separate circular cells occupied by the monks. Outside the sanctuary and throughout the lands belonging to the saint lived those subject to the rule of the saint or his coarb.

There was a right exercised by the saint which had previously been accorded to the bard. It was that of *ill-wishing*. The right was a legal one, but hedged about with restrictions. A bard, and after him a saint, might not ill-wish unless he had been refused a just request. If he ill-wished unjustly, then it was held that the ill-wish returned on the head of him who had launched it.

And there can be no doubt that this legal power conferred on the saints inspired terror. If a chief's horse fell under him, or his cows refused their milk, if he got a bad cold or rheumatic pains, he immediately supposed that he had been ill-wished, and sent for the saint, and endeavoured to satisfy him.

That this supposed power may have been employed occasionally for ambitious purposes is likely enough, but in general it was exercised only for good, to release captives, to mitigate barbarities, to stay bloodshed, to protect the weak against the strong.

A cheap and easy way of explaining the exercise of this power by the saints is that of saying that they traded on the credulity of the people. But it is, I am sure, a false appreciation. They were of the people, steeped in their ideas, and did not rise above them. To trade on credulity implies a superiority they did not possess. Besides, it was the exercise of a formal legal right.

There is one rather significant feature in all the missionary work of the Celtic saints which contrasts sharply with that of our modern emissaries into "foreign parts."

What we do is to collect moneys and start a missioner, who, wherever he goes, draws for his supplies on the mother-country, and depends, and his entire mission depends, on the charity of those at home. The Celtic method was absolutely the reverse. The missioner went among strange people, and threw himself on their hospitality. That is just one of the great virtues of a savage race, and these Celtic saints caught at the one noble trait in the characters of the half-barbarians among whom they went, and worked upon that and from that point.

The chiefs and kings felt themselves bound in hospitality to maintain them, to protect them, and to give them settlements. How strongly this feeling operated may be judged by an instance in the life of S. Patrick, who went to Laogaire, the Irish king, without any backing up from behind and without presents. When Laogaire refused Patrick something he wanted, the apostle and his little band refused to eat. The king was so alarmed lest they should be starved to death, and it be imputed to him as due to his niggardliness, that he gave way, and let Patrick have what he desired.

But this system worked on the material interests of the chiefs. They argued in their calculating way, "Here are all these missionaries. We have been feeding them, giving them land and cattle; it is a drain on our resources. We must really get something out of them in return."

And so, out of that frugal mind which was not the exclusive prerogative of Mrs. Gilpin, they accepted the gospel--at least, the ministrations of the saints--as a return for what they had themselves granted them: acres and cows.

There is a story in the life of S. Bridget that illustrates this somewhat sordid view taken of their dealings with the saints.

Bridget's father had been lent a sword by King Illand, son of Dunlaing of Leinster. He asked his daughter to negotiate with the king that this sword should become his personal property. She agreed. At the same time one of Illand's men threw himself upon her, and begged her to put him into her tribe. So she asked the king for two things: the man and the sword.

"Humph!" said he. "What am I to have in return?"

"I will obtain for you eternal life, for one thing, and for the other the assurance that the crown shall remain to your sons."

"As to eternal life," replied the practical and sceptical king, "I have never seen it, and so do not know what it is worth; as to the boys, if they are worth their salt, they will maintain their own rights. Give me victory over those Ulster rascals, and you shall have my man and the sword."

So Bridget agreed to this.

These Celtic saints certainly appropriated to themselves the right of the keys, to give heaven to whom they would, and to exclude from it whoever offended them. Of course they could appeal to the Bible for their authority, and who were these half-wild men to dispute it with them and quibble the text away? That they were sincere in their belief that the power of the keys was given to them is certain.

I have mentioned reciprocal rights.

Now one of those demanded of the saint by the chief of the land was to march with him to battle and to curse his enemies.

This had been what was expected and exacted of the chief Druid; and in this, as in many another particular, the saint stepped into the shoes of the Druid. This is frankly enough admitted in one life, in which we are told that the king sent for S. Finnchu to curse his enemies, because the Druid was too old and feeble to do the job effectively.

When a saint passed out of this world he left a bell, a book, or a crosier, to be the *cathair* of the tribe, and his coarb marched with it in his name before the tribesmen.

When the tribe was successful in battle, then certain dues were paid to the saint for his assistance.

In the lives of some of the early Celtic saints we are told strange stories of their self-mortification, their rigorous fasts. This was due to a very curious cause.

According to the Celtic law of distress, the appellant took the matter into his own hands. There was no executive administration of law. Everyone who was aggrieved had to exact the penalty as best he might. If he were too weak to recover the penalty by force, then the legal proceeding for him was to fast against the debtor or aggressor. He sat down at his door and starved himself. The person fasted against almost always gave way, as the fact of the institution of the fast doubled the fine, and as he did not venture to allow the creditor to proceed to the last extremities lest he should entail on himself a blood feud.

When S. Patrick wanted to carry a point with King Lear (Laogaire) he adopted this method and succeeded, and the king gave way.

There is a very odd story--of course mere legend--of S. Germanus when he came to Britain to oppose the Pelagian heresy. He found one particular city mightily opposed to the orthodox doctrine, and as he could not convince the citizens by reasoning with them, he and his attendant clerks sat down at the gates and starved themselves to force the citizens into adopting the true faith.

The same law of distress is found in the code of Menu, and the British Government has had to forbid the *dharma--i.e.* the legal fasting against a creditor--from being put in practice in India.

Now, very naturally, and by an easy transition, the early Celtic saints carried their legal ideas into their religion, and just as when S. Patrick, wanting something from King Lear, fasted against him till he obtained it, so did the followers of Patrick, when they desired something of God for themselves or for others, proceed against Him by the legal method of levying a distress.

This is frankly admitted in an odd story in the *Book of Lismore*. Three clerks agreed together that they would each recite a certain number of psalms daily, and that should one die the other two would share his psalms between them. All went smoothly enough for a while. Then one died, whereupon the survivors divided his portion of the Psalter between them. But soon after a second died, whereat the third found himself saddled with the sets of psalms that appertained to both the others. He was very angry. He thought the Almighty had dealt unfairly by him in letting the other two off so lightly and overburdening him, and in a fit of spleen and resentment *he fasted against Him*.

But this view of asceticism was held only at the outset, and rapidly sounder ideas gained the mastery, and we find self-denial in the saints assume quite another complexion.

An instance in point is in the life of S. Columba. One day he saw a poor widow gathering stinging-nettles, and he asked her why she did it. "For the pot," said she; "I have no other food."

The good old man was troubled. He went back to the monastery and said to the cook, "I will eat nettles only now."

When this had gone on for some time, his disciple who cooked the nettles for him saw that he was falling away in flesh, so he took a hollow elder-stick, put butter into the tube, and by this means enriched the dish.

S. Columba said, "The nettles do not taste as before. They have a richer flavour. What have you done to them?"

"Master dear," answered his disciple, "I have put nothing into the pot but this stick, wherewith I stirred its contents."

Nor were they pedantic in observance of rule.

Travellers came to S. Cronan, and he had meat and ale set on the board, and he himself and his monks sat down to make merry with them.

"Humph!" said a formalist among them, "at this rate I do not see much prospect of matins being said."

"My friend," answered Cronan, "in receiving strangers we receive Christ; as to the matins, the angels will sing them in our room."

Finding that some travellers had wandered all night unable to find shelter, "This will never do," said he; "I shall move my quarters to the roadside."

Though rough in their treatment of themselves, they were tender-hearted and kind to bird and beast and man. It was through a frightened fawn flying for refuge to S. Petrock that Constantine was brought to repentance. S. Columba prayed with his arms extended till the birds perched on his hands. Another Columba, the founder, as I suspect, of Columb Major and Minor, was almost incommoded with their affection, fluttering about his face.

"How is it," asked one of his disciples, "that the birds avoid us and gather round you?"

"Is it not natural," answered the saint, "that birds should come to a bird?"

A play on his name, for Columba signifies a dove.

S. Cainnech saw a rich lady with a starved dog.

"Who feeds that poor brute?" he asked.

"I do," answered the lady.

"Feed it? Maltreat it. Go and eat what you cast to the poor hound, and in a week return and tell me how you relish such treatment."

One day an abbot saw a little bird with drooping wings.

"Why is the poor thing so wretched?" he asked.

"Do you not know," said a bystander, "that Molua is dead? He was full of pity to all animals. Never did he injure one. Do you marvel then that the little birds lament his decease?"

It was the same with regard to children.

One day King Eochaid sent his little son with a message to S. Maccarthen. The child's mother gave him an apple to eat on the way. The boy played with it, and it rolled from him and was lost. He hunted for his apple till the sun set, and then, tired, laid himself down in the middle of the road and fell asleep. Maccarthen was going along the road and found the sleeping child there. He at once wrapped his mantle round him, and sat by him all night. Many horsemen and cars passed before the child woke, but the old man made them get by as best they might, and he would neither suffer the child to be disturbed, nor let an accident befall him in the dark.

Great as were the powers conferred on the Celtic saints or arrogated to themselves, there can be no doubt but that they employed them mainly as a means of delivering the innocent, and in putting down barbarous customs.

S. Erc--in Cornwall Erth--made use of his influence to prevent the king of Connaught from baptising his new lance, after pagan custom, in the blood of an infant; S. Euny his in rescuing a boy from being tossed on the spears of some soldiers. Again, finding after a battle that it was the custom to cut off the heads of all who had fallen, and stack them at the king's door to be counted, he with difficulty induced the victors to take turves instead of the heads.

I do not think we at all adequately appreciate the service the saints rendered to the Celtic nations in raising the tone of appreciation of woman.

Next to founding their own monastic establishments, they were careful to induce their mothers or sisters to establish communities for the education of the daughters of the chiefs and of all such maidens as would be entrusted to them.

The estimation in which woman had been held was very low. In the gloss to the law of Adamnán is a description of her position in the house. A trench three feet deep was dug between the door and the hearth, and in this, in a condition almost of nudity, the women spent the day cooking, and making candles out of mutton suet. In the evening they were required to hold these candles whilst the men caroused and feasted, and then were sent to sleep in kennels, like dogs, outside the house as guardians, lest a hostile attack should be made during the darkness.

The current coin seems to have been, in Ireland, a serving-maid, for all fines were calculated by *cumals*--that is, maidservants--and the value of one woman was the same as that of three cows.

A brother of one of the saints came to him to say that he was bankrupt; he owed a debt of seven maidservants to his creditor, and could not rake so many together. The saint paid the fine in cows.

Bridget's mother was sold as a slave by the father of Bridget to a Druid, and the father afterwards tried to sell his daughter; but as the idea had got about that she was wasteful in the kitchen, he could not find a purchaser.

But this condition of affairs was rapidly altered, and it was so through the influence of the saints and the foundation of the great schools for girls by Bridget, Itha, Brig, and Buriana.

Till the times of Adamnán women were called out to fight as well as the men, and dared not refuse the summons. Their exemption was due to this abbot. He came on a field of battle and saw one woman who had driven a reaping-hook into the bosom of another, and was dragging her away thereby. Horror-struck, he went about among the kings of Ireland and insisted on the convocation of an assembly in which he carried a law that women were thenceforth exempted from this odious obligation.

I have but touched the fringe of a great subject, which is one that has been unduly neglected. The early history of Cornwall is inextricably mixed up with that of the saints who settled there, or who sprang from the native royal family. We have unhappily no annals, hardly a Cornish record, of those early times. Irish, Welsh, Bretons, have been wiser, and have preserved theirs; and it is to them we are forced to appeal to know anything of the early history of our peninsula. As to the saintly lives, it is true that they contain much fable; but we know that they were originally written by contemporaries, or by writers very near the time. S. Columba of Tir-da-Glas, whom I take to have been the founder of the two Columbs in Cornwall and Culbone in Somersetshire, caught one of his disciples acting as his Boswell, noting down what he said and did, and he was so angry that he took the MS. and threw it in the fire, and insisted on none of his pupils attempting to write his life.

S. Erc was wont to retire in Lent to jot down his reminiscences of S. Patrick. The writer of the *Life of S. Abban* says, "I who have composed this am the grandson of him whom S. Abban baptised." But about the eleventh century a fashion set in for rewriting these histories and elaborating the simple narratives into marvellous tales of miracle, just as in James I.'s reign the grand simple old ballads of the English nation were recomposed in stilted style that robbed them of all their poetry and most of their value.

Now it is almost always possible to disengage the plain threads of history from the flourish and frippery that was woven in at this late period. The eye of the superficial reader is at once caught by all the foolery of grotesque miracle, and turns in disgust from the narrative; but if these histories be critically examined, it will almost always be found that the substratum is historical.

Surely it affords an interest, and gives a zest to an excursion into Cornwall, when we know something of the founders of the churches, and they stand out before us as living, energetic characters, with some faults, but many virtues, and are to us no longer *nuda nomina.*

CHAPTER II.

THE HOLY WELLS

S. Patrick in Ireland--A pagan holy well--S. Samson--Celtic saints very particular about the water they drank--S. Piran and S. Germoe--S. Erth and the goose-eggs--S. Sithney and the polluted well--Dropping of pins into wells--Hanging rags about--Well-chapel of S. Clether--Venton Ia--Jordan wells--Gwennap ceremony--Fice's well--Modern stupidity about contaminated water.

THE system adopted by S. Patrick in Ireland was that of making as little alteration as he could in the customs of the people, except only when such customs were flatly opposed to the precepts of the gospel. He did not overthrow their lechs or pillar-stones; he simply cut crosses on them. When he found that the pagans had a holy well, he contented himself with converting the well into a baptistery. It is a question of judgment whether to wean people gently and by slow degrees from their old customs, or whether wholly to forbid these usages. S. Patrick must have known perfectly what the episcopal system was in Gaul, yet when he came into a land where the Roman territorial organisation had never prevailed, he accommodated Christian Church government to the conditions of Celtic tribal organisation.

He found that the Irish, like all other Celtic peoples, held wells in great veneration. He did not preach against this, denounce it as idolatrous, or pass canons condemning it. He quietly appropriated these wells to the service of the Church, and made of them baptisteries.

What Patrick did in Ireland was what had been done elsewhere.

When S. Samson was travelling in Cornwall between Padstow and Southill, and visited his cousin Padarn on the way; at a place called Tregear he found the people dancing round an upright stone, and offering it idolatrous worship. He did not smash it in pieces. He contented himself with cutting a cross on it.

Now the Celtic saints were mighty choice in their tipple. They insisted on having the purest of water for their drink; and not only did they require it for imbibing, but they did a great deal of tubbing.

One day S. Germoe paid S. Piran a visit; after they had prayed together, "It is my tubbing time," said Piran. "Will you have a bath too?" "With the greatest of pleasure," responded Germoe. So the two saints got into the tub together. But the water was so cold that Germoe's teeth began to chatter, and he put one leg over the edge, intending to scramble out. "Nonsense!" said Piran; "bide in a bit, and you will feel the cold less sharply."

Germoe did this. Presently Piran yelled out, "Heigh! a fish! a fish!" and, between them, the two nude saints succeeded in capturing a trout that was in the vat.

"I rejoice that we have the trout," said Piran, "for I am expecting home my old pupil Carthagh, and I was short of victuals. We will cook it for his supper."

Some of the saints had the fancy for saying their prayers standing up to their necks in water.

There is a story of S. Erc, the S. Erth of Land's End district, to the purpose, but I admit it is on late authority.

Domnhal, king of Ireland, sent his servants to collect goose-eggs. They found a woman carrying a black basket on her head piled up with the eggs of geese. The king's servants demanded them, but she answered that they were intended as a present to Erc, who spent the day immersed to the armpits in running water, with his Psalter on the bank, from which he recited the psalms. In the evening he emerged from his bath, shook himself, and ate an egg and a half together with three bunches of watercress.

However, regardless of the saint's necessities, the servants carried the eggs away.

When S. Erc came out of the river, dripping from every limb, and found there were no eggs for his supper, he waxed warm, and roundly cursed the rascals who had despoiled him, and those who had set them on, and all such as should eat them.

The story goes on to tell how these eggs became veritable apples of discord, breeding internecine strife.

But to return to the wells.

Whether taught by experience, or illumined by the light of nature, I cannot say, but most assuredly the saints of Ireland, Wales, and Cornwall were vastly particular as to their wells being of the purest and coldest water obtainable.

S. Senan had settled for a while by a well in Inis Caorach, and one day his disciple Setna--our Cornish Sithney--found a woman washing her child's dirty clothes in the fountain. He flew into a fury, and his companion Liberius was equally abusive in the language employed. Shortly after the boy tumbled over the rocks into the sea.

The distracted mother ran to S. Senan, and when he heard the circumstances, assuming that this was due to the imprecations called down on the woman and her child by his two pupils, he bade both of them depart and not see his face again, unless the child should be produced uninjured. Setna and Liberius sneaked away very disconsolate, but as they happily found the lad on the beach uninjured, they were once more received into favour.

It is unnecessary here to repeat all the hackneyed references to the cult of fountains among the Celts; they may be taken for granted. We know that such was the case, and that the same cult continues very little altered among the Irish and Breton peasantry to the present day. In Cornwall there is now little or none of it. "When I was a man I put away childish things," says S. Paul, and the same applies to peoples. When they are in their cultural childhood they have their superstitious beliefs and practices; but they grow out of them, and we pity those who stick in the observance of usages that are unreasonable.

In pagan times money was dropped into wells and springs, and divination was taken from the rising of bubbles. Now the only relic of such a proceeding is the dropping in of pins or rush crosses.

Wells were also sought for curative purposes, and unquestionably some springs have medicinal qualities, but these are entirely unconnected with the saints, and depend altogether on their chemical constituents.

It is said that rags may still be seen on the bushes about Madron well as they are about holy wells in Ireland and about the tombs of fakirs and Mussulman saints. I doubt if any Cornish people are so foolish as to do such a thing as suspend rags about a well with the idea of these rags serving as an oblation to the patron of the spring for the sake of obtaining benefits from him.

In Pembrokeshire till quite recently persons, even Dissenters, were wont to drink water from S. Teilo's well out of a portion of the reputed skull of S. Teilo, of which the Melchior family are the hereditary custodians.

The immersing of the bone of a saint in water, and the drinking of the water thus rendered salutary, is still practised in Brittany. This was done when Ireland was pagan; but the bones soaked were those of Druids.

There is a curious illustration, as I take it, of this practice in S. Clether's well chapel, recently restored. Here the stone altar remains *in situ*; it has never been disturbed.

WELL-CHAPEL OF S. CLETHER

S. Clether was the son of Clydwyn, prince of Carmarthen and grandson of Brychan. He came to Cornwall in consequence of the invasion of his territories by Dyfnwal, and here he spent a great part of his life, and died at an advanced age. He settled in the Inney valley in a most picturesque spot between great ruins of rock, where a perennial spring of the coolest, clearest water gushes forth. There can be very little doubt that S. Clether employed this spring as his baptistery, for the traditional usage of fetching water from it for baptisms in the parish church has lingered on there.

The holy well lies north-east of the chapel or oratory. When the chapel was reconstructed in the fifteenth century the water from the holy well was conveyed in a cut granite channel under the wall, and came sparkling forth in a sort of locker on the right side of the altar in the thickness of the wall.

To reach this there was a descent of a step in the floor. Thence the water flowed away underground, and gushed forth in a second holy well, constructed in the depth of the chapel wall outside on the south near the east end. Consequently there are two holy wells. The first, I take it, was the baptismal well; the second was used to drink from. A relic of the saint was placed in the channel where exposed; the water flowed over it, acquired miraculous virtues, and was drunk at the second well outside the chapel by those who desired healing.

That there was a further significance in the management of the course of the water I do not doubt.

An attempt was made to carry out the imagery of the vision of the holy waters in Ezekiel:--

"Afterward he brought me again unto the door of the house; and, behold, waters issued out from under the threshold of the house eastward: for the forefront of the house stood toward the east, and the waters came down from under from the right side of the house, at the south side of the altar." (xlvii. I.)

S. MELOR'S WELL, LINKINHORNE

Cornwall possesses a vast number of holy wells, many of them in very bad repair. That at S. Cleer has been restored admirably; Dupath is in perfect condition; that of S. Guron at Bodmin has been restored; S. Melor's well at Linkinhorn is very beautiful and in perfect condition; S. John's well, Morwenstow, S. Julian's, Mount Edgcumbe, S. Indract's in the parish of S. Dominic, the well of S. Sidwell and S. Wulvella at Laneast, S. Samson's, Southill, Menacuddle, S. Anne's, Whitstone, S. Neot's, S. Nin's, Pelynt, Roche, S. Ruan's, are in good condition, but many are ruinous, or have been so altered as to have lost their interest. That of S. Mawes has been built up, and two great cast-iron pipes carried up from it for the circulation of air over the water, which is drawn away to a tap which supplies the town or village.[2]

Here is a melancholy account of the condition to which a holy well has sunk:--

"Venton Eia (S. Ia's well), on the cliff overlooking Porthmeor.--This ancient well, associated with the memory of the patron saint of the town (S. Ives), was formerly held in the highest reverence. Entries occur in the borough records of sums paid for cleansing and repairing it, under 1668-9 and 1692-3. On the last of these occasions the well was covered, faced, and floored with hewn granite blocks in two compartments. It is still known as 'the Wishing Well,' from the old custom of divination by crooked pins dropped into the water. For some years past, however, this ancient source of purity has been shamefully outraged by contact with all that is foul. Close to it is a cluster of sties, known as 'Pig's Town,' and the well has become the receptacle for stinking fish and all kinds of offal. Just above it are the walls of the new cemetery. All veneration for this spot, so dear to countless generations of our forefathers, seems to have departed."[3]

The well of S. Bridget at Landue remains, but the saint's chapel is gone. Stables near the well are thought to have polluted the water, and the well is closed lest the incautious should drink of the reputedly contaminated waters.

There are a good many holy wells in Devon also, but none of mark. At Sticklepath above the well rises a very early inscribed stone. There is a holy well, ruinous, at Halwell, one, probably of S. Lo, at Broadwood, one at Ermington, from which water is still drawn for baptisms, one at Lifton, one at Ashburton, probably dedicated to S. Wulvela. S. Sidwell and S. Anne each has her well at Exeter, and the water of the latter has of late become of repute, and is in request under the form of beer. It supplies a brewery.

When S. Cadoc returned from the Holy Land he brought with him a bottle of water from the Jordan, and poured it into a well in Cornwall. None that I know of bears his name, but that at Laneast is called Jordan well.

There is a very singular custom still observed in connection with a stream in place of a holy well at Gwennap. There, on Good Friday, children seek two spots by a stream to baptise their *dolls*. This can be due only to a dim reminiscence of baptising in the open.

In addition to the holy wells, there are the pixy wells, where the ancient spirits have not been dispossessed by the saints.

Poughill parish takes its name from a puck or pisgie well.

Fice's well, near Prince Town, has on it "J. F. 1568." John Fitz, the astrologer, and his lady were once pixy-led whilst riding on Dartmoor. After long wanderings in the vain effort to find their way, they lighted on a pure spring, drank of it; and their eyes were opened to know where they were and which was their right direction. In gratitude for this deliverance, old John Fitz caused the stone memorial to be set over the spring for the advantage of all pixy-led wanderers. Alas! the convict establishment has enclosed the moor all round, and now this well, though intact, no longer stands, as I remember it, in wild moorland, but enclosed by a protecting wall in a field.

In a certain large village of which I know something water was introduced by means of earthenware pipes for a considerable distance, and then conveyed to taps at convenient spots by iron and lead.

Now there was one of these taps placed outside the Board school. The master said within himself, "If I go to the tap, I shall have to pay the water rate, which will be very heavy; if I never turn the tap, I surely cannot be required to pay. So I know what I will do. Go to! I will draw all my water from the well in the yard of the farm at the back of my premises."

He did so, and lost his wife and child by diphtheria. Verily even modern Board school masters might learn something from these wild old pure water-loving Celtic saints.

NOTE.--Book on Cornish Holy Wells:--

QUILLER-COUCH (M. and L.), *Ancient and Holy Wells of Cornwall.* London: Clark, 1894.

CHAPTER III.

CORNISH CROSSES

Abundance of crosses--The menhîr--Crosses marked the limits of a Llan--Crosses marked places for public prayer--Instance of a Cornish Dissenter--Churches anciently few and far between--The cross erected where was no church--Which therefore precedes the village church--Crosses as waymarks--The Abbot's Way--Interlaced work--The plait a subject for study.

THERE is no county in England where crosses abound as they do in Cornwall. Second to it comes Devonshire. Indeed, on Dartmoor and in the west of the latter county they are as numerous as in Cornwall.

Their origin is various.

In the first place, where the pagans worshipped a menhîr or standing stone, there it was Christianised by being turned into a cross. In the second place, crosses marked the bounds of a *minihi* or *llan*, the sanctuary of the saint.

CROSS, S. LEVAN

Then, again, the Celtic churches were very small, mere oratories, that

28

could not possibly contain a moderate congregation. The saints took their station at a cross, and preached thence. With the Saxons there was a rooted dread of entering an enclosed place for anything like worship, fearing, as they did, the exercise of magical rites; and they were accustomed to hold all their meetings in the open air. S. Walpurga, the sister of S. Willibald, who wrote in 750, and was a Wessex woman, says:--

"It is the custom of the Saxon race that on many estates of nobles and of good men they are wont to have not a church, but the standard of the holy cross dedicated to our Lord and reverenced with great honour, lifted up on high so as to be convenient for the frequency of daily prayer."

In connection with this, I may mention a fact. In the parish of Altarnon was an old pious Wesleyan, and when the weather was too bad for him to go to chapel he was wont to go to one of the crosses of granite that stood near his cottage, kneel there, and say his prayers. He died not long ago.

Bede, some twenty years before Walpurga, says that--

"The religious habit was then held in great veneration, so that wheresoever a clerk or a monk happened to come he was joyfully received, ... and if they chanced to meet him upon the way, they ran to him, and bowing, were glad to be signed with his hand and blessed with his mouth. On Sundays they flocked largely to the" (bishop's) "church or the monasteries to hear the word of God. And if any presbyter chanced to come into a village, the inhabitants flocked together to hear the word of life; for the presbyters and clerks went into the villages on no other account than to preach, baptise, visit the sick, and in short to take care of souls" (*H.E.*, iii. 16).

This shows that, in the first place, among the Anglo-Saxons there were no churches except the cathedral and the monastic church, and no parochial clergy. Bede does not actually say that there was a cross set up from which the itinerant clergy preached, and to which the faithful resorted for prayer, but this additional fact we have learned from Walpurga.

So we come to this very interesting conclusion, that the *village cross preceded the parish church*. The crosses were, in fact, the religious centres of church life, and we ought accordingly to value and preserve them with the tenderest care. A great many of those that we have now on our village greens are comparatively modern, and date from the fourteenth or fifteenth century, but there still remain a vast number, not in the midst of a village, but on moors and by highways of an extremely early description, and which most assuredly have been the scene of many a primitive "camp meeting" in the fifth and sixth centuries.

On Sourton Down beside the road stands a cross of very coarse granite. On it is inscribed PRINCIPI FIL AVDEI, and above it an early and rude cross of Constantine. Some time in the Middle Ages the rudeness of the stone gave dissatisfaction, and its head was trimmed into a cross.

A third occasion for the erection of crosses was as waymarks. Across Dartmoor such a succession of rude crosses exists where was what is called the Abbot's Way from Buckfast to Tavistock and to Plympton. But there are others not on these lines, and such may have served both as guiding marks and also as stations for prayer. That the monks of Buckland--and Buckland goes back to pre-Saxon times--did go out to the moor and there minister to the tin-streamers or squatters and shepherds, I cannot doubt, and accordingly look with much emotion at these grey monuments of early Christianity.

The interlaced work which is found on some of the crosses is of the same character as the ornamentation in the early Irish MSS., and it was adopted from the Celtic clergy by their Anglian and Saxon converts.

But whence came it?

We know that the Britons delighted in plaited work with osiers, and it was with wattle that they built their houses, their kings' palaces, and defended their camps. By constant use of wattle through long ages they became extraordinarily skilful in devising plaits; and when they began to work on stone they copied thereon the delicate interlaced work they loved to exhibit in their domestic buildings.

The various plaits have been worked out by Mr. A. G. Langdon in his admirable study of the Cornish crosses. At a meeting of the British Association he exhibited a hundred drawings of different crosses, etc., illustrative of a paper read by Mr. J. Romilly Allen on "The Early Christian Monuments of Cornwall." When some incredulity was expressed as to there being so many examples in that county, Mr. Langdon explained that not only did all these come from Cornwall, but that the examples brought before the Association represented only about one-third of the whole number known to exist. And since that date a good many more have been noticed. The variety in design of the crosses is very great indeed. Some affect the

Greek cross, some the Latin; some are with a figure on them, some plain, others richly ornamented. But what is remarkable about them is, in the first place, they are nearly all in granite, a material in which nothing was done from the seventh century down to the fifteenth, as though the capability of working such a hard intractable stone had been lost. And, in the second place, the ornamentation is in the lost art of plaiting, of the beauty and difficulty of which we can hardly conceive till we attempt it. There is first the four-string plait, then that with six, and lastly that with eight. Then three strings are combined together in each plait, then split, forming the so-called Stafford knot; the knot and the plait are worked together; now a loop is dropped, forming a bold and pleasing interruption in the pattern. Then a ring is introduced and plaited into the pattern; then chain-work is introduced; in fact, an endless variety is formed, exercising the ingenuity of the artist to the uttermost. It would be an excellent amusement and occupation for a rainy day in an hotel for the tourist to set to work upon and unravel the mysteries of these Celtic knots.

The old interlaced work, or the tradition of it, seems to have lingered on in the glazing of windows, and some very beautiful examples remain in England and in France. Mr. Romilly Allen points out:--

"In Egyptian, Greek, and Roman decorative art the only kind of interlaced work is the plait, without any modification whatever; and the man who discovered how to devise new patterns from a simple plait, by making what I term *breaks*, laid the foundation of all the wonderfully complicated and truly bewildering forms of interlaced ornament found on such a masterpiece of the art of illumination as the *Book of Kells*. Although we do not know *who* made the discovery of how to make breaks in a plait, we know pretty nearly *when* it was made."[4]

He goes on to show that the transition from plaitwork to knotwork took place *in Italy* between 563 and 774. But is that not a proof of introduction into Italy, and not of its discovery there? I am rather disposed to think that partly through the adoption of the osier wattle in domestic architecture, partly through the employment of the tartan, the plait in all its intricacy was a much earlier product of the genius of the Celtic race.

There is a pretty story in the life of an early Irish saint. He had been put at school, but could not learn. At last, sick of books, he ran away. He found a man at work with willow rods, weaving them to form the walls of a house he was building. He dipped them in water, and laced them in and out with wonderful neatness, patience, and dexterity. And the boy, looking on, marvelled at it all, took it to heart, and said to himself, "These osiers flip out; but when there are patience and skill combined, they can be made into the most exquisite patterns, and plaited together into a most solid screen. Why may not I be thus shaped, if I allow myself to be bent, and am docile in my master's hands?" So he went back to school.

CHAPTER IV.

CORNISH CASTLES

The ancient camps--Their kinds--1. Rectangular, Roman--2. The Saxon burh--3. The Celtic circular or oval camp--The *lis* and the *dun*--4. Stone fortresses--Heroic legends in Ireland--The Firbolgs--5. The stone castle with mortar, Norman--No good examples.

ANYONE with a very little experience can at once "spot" a camp or castle by the appearance from a distance of a hill or headland; and the traveller in Devon and Cornwall will pass scores of them, as he will see by his Ordnance Survey Map, without giving much attention to them, without supposing that they can be of great interest, unless his attention has been previously directed to the subject. It is a pity that anyone should go through a country which may really be said to make ancient camps and castles its speciality and not know something about them.

Of hill castles or camps there are several kinds:--

1. Those that are rectangular or approximately so, and which have been attributed to the Romans. Of these in Cornwall there are but few. Tregear, near Bodmin, and Bossens, in S. Erth, have yielded Roman coins and relics of pottery; but whether actually Roman or Romano-British remains undecided.

2. There are those which consist of a tump or mound, sometimes wholly artificial, usually natural, and adapted by art, and in connection with this is a bass-court, usually, but not universally, quadrilateral. This was the Saxon type of *burh*; it was also that of the Merovingian. The classic passage descriptive of these is in the *Life of S. John of Terouanne*, written in the eleventh century:--

"It was customary for the rich men and nobles of these parts, because their main occupation is the carrying on of feuds, to heap up a mound of earth as high as they are able to raise it, and to dig round it a broad, open, and deep ditch, and to girdle the whole upper edge of the bank with a barrier of wooden planks, stoutly fastened together, and set round with numerous turrets, and this in place of a wall.

"Within was constructed a house, or rather a citadel, commanding the whole area, so that the gate of it could alone be reached by means of a bridge that sprang from the counterside of the ditch, and was gradually raised as it advanced, supported by sets of piers, two, or even three, trussed on each side, over convenient spans, crossing the moat with a managed ascent, so as to attain the upper level of the mound, landing on its edge level with the threshold of the door."

A very good idea of such a camp may be derived from the representation of the fortifications of Dinan on the Bayeux tapestry.

LAUNCESTON

In France the *mottes* on which the wooden dongeons of the Merovingian chiefs were planted certainly abound; but in many cases the bank enclosing the bass-court has disappeared. Good examples may be seen at Plympton, at Lydford, and at Launceston. At the former and latter Norman walls took the place of the palisading; but at Lydford a keep was erected on the tump, but the line of earthworks was never walled.

In Ireland and in Scotland such camps abound; they are there due to Saxon and Danish invaders. In Ireland they are called *motes*, in England *burhs*. They afforded the type on which the Normans constructed their castles.

3. A much more common form of camp in Devon and Cornwall is one that is circular or oval, and consists of concentric rings of earth, or earth and stone mixed, with ditches between.

There is, however, a variant where a headland is fortified, either one standing above the sea into which it juts, or at the junction of two streams. There it sufficed to run defensive banks and ditches across the neck of the promontory.

This description of camp or castle is usually supposed to be Celtic.

In Ireland such a camp is a *rath*. The same word is employed for similar camps in a portion of Pembrokeshire.

Every noble had a right to have a *rath*, and every chief had his *lis* or *dun*.

A lis was an enclosed space, with an earth-mound surrounding it, and was the place in which justice was administered. *Lis* enters into many place-names in Cornwall, as Liskeard, Lesnewth, Listewdrig, the court of that king who killed S. Gwynear and bullied S. Ewny and the other Irish settlers; Lescaddock, Lescawn, Lestormel, now corrupted into Restormel.

In Ireland *les* had a wider meaning. S. Carthagh was throwing up a mound around a plot of land where he was going to plant a monastery.

"What are you about there?" asked an inquisitive woman.

"Only engaged in the construction of a little *lis*," was the reply.

"Lis beg!" (small lis), exclaimed the woman. "I call it a lis mor" (a big lis). And Lismore is its name to this day.

In Ireland every king had his *dun*. This was an enlarged rath with an outer court in which he held his hostages, for the law required this: "He is no king who has not hostages in lock-up."

Dun in Welsh is *din*, and *dinas* is but another form of the same word, and signifies a royal residence.

A gloss to an old Irish law tract says that a royal dun must have two walls and a moat for water.

Dun in Scotland is applied to any fort. According to the Gaelic dictionaries, it is "a heap or mound," and even a dung-hill is a dun.

In fact, the French *dune* and the Cornish *towan* derive from the same root. Dun so much resembles the Anglo-Saxon *tun* that we cannot always be sure of the derivation of a place-name that ends in tun.

Every tribe had its dun, to which the cattle were driven, and where the women and children were placed in security in times of danger. This would be in addition to the royal residence, that is the dun of the *rig*.

Within the dun were numerous structures of timber, roofed with oak shingles, some of a large description, such as a banqueting hall; but the habitations of the garrison were circular, of wicker-work, and thatched with rushes.

In Cornwall there is Dingerrein, the dinas of S. Geraint; Castel-an-Dinas; Damelioc (Din-Maeloc); Dunheved, the old name for Launceston; Dundagel.

4. I come now to the stone fortresses that are found in parts of Cornwall and Wales. They are also to be seen in Scotland and Ireland. These are called caerau in Wales. A cathair is the term applied to them in Ireland, and cathair signifies as well a city.

They are found in England only in Somersetshire, Devon, and Cornwall; and in Wales only in such parts as were invaded and occupied from Ireland.

In Kerry and the isles of Arran are those in best preservation, and from these we can see that the walls were regularly built up with double faces, rubble being between them. Very usually in Arran stones are placed with the end outwards, so that they serve as ties to hold the walls together.

The Welsh examples are very perfect, and precisely similar to those in Ireland.

We know that the Gauls built stone camps--Cæsar calls them their *oppida*--but they employed beams of timber along with the stone to tie the walls together. The wood has everywhere rotted away, and the enclosing walls of the Gaulish camps now present the same appearance precisely as do the similar stone camps in Devon, Somerset, and Cornwall. When the timber decayed the stones fell into heaps. In Arran and Anglesey there was no timber; consequently stones were employed as ties, and there the walls remain comparatively intact.

Within the *caer* were circular stone beehive huts; also chambers that were circular were contrived in the thickness of the walls. These "sentry boxes" have been noticed in Wales, and also in Cornwall and Devon.

The account of Castel-an-Dinas, before it was robbed for the erection of a tower, is precisely such as might be given of one of those in Ireland or Wales:--

"It consisted of two stone walls, one within the other, in a circular form, surrounding the area of the hill. The ruins are now fallen on each side of the walls, and show the work to have been of great height and thickness. There was also a third or outer wall built more than half-way round. Within these walls are many little enclosures of a circular form, about seven yards in diameter, with little walls round them of two or three feet high; they appear to have been so many huts for the shelter of the garrison."

In fact, this was a royal dinas. Not only had it the requisite double wall, but also the *drecht gialnai*, or dyke of the hostages. Every king retained about him pledges from the under-chiefs that they would be faithful.

There are several of these stone camps in Devon and Cornwall. In Somersetshire Whorlebury is very interesting; in Devon are Whit Tor and Cranbrook; in Cornwall the Cheesewring camp, Carn Brea, Chun Castle, the camp of Caer Conan on Tregonning Hill, Helborough, beside Castel-an-Dinas in Ludgvan.

The heroic legends of Ireland attribute these stone camps to the Firbolgs, the non-Aryan dusky race that was in possession previous to the arrival of the Celts. But that the Milesians learned from them the art of constructing such castles is very certain, for in Christian times the monks imitated them in some of their settlements.

Lord Dunraven, who has photographed these stone duns, says:--

"The legends of the early builders are preserved in the compilations of Irish scribes and bardic writers dating from the twelfth to the fifteenth centuries. The story, which is said by these writers to have been handed down orally during the earliest centuries of the Christian era, and committed to writing when that art first became known in Ireland, is the history of the wanderings and final destruction of a hunted and persecuted race, whose fate would seem to have been mournful and strange as the ruined fortresses of the lost tribe which now stand before us. Coming to Ireland through Britain, they seem to have been long beaten hither and thither, till, flying still westward, they were protected by Ailill and Maeve, who are said to have reigned in Connaught about the first century of the Christian era. From these monarchs they obtained a grant of lands along the western coast of Galway, as well as the islands of Arran, where they remained till their final expulsion. Thus their forms seem to pass across the deep abyss of time, like the white flakes of foam that are seen drifted by the hurrying wind over the wild and wasted ruins of their fortresses."

Excavations show that these stone caers are more ancient than the Christian era; they belong to the period of flint weapons and the introduction of bronze. But, as already stated, the conquerors of the rude stone monument builders adopted some of their arts, and some of their camps are much later.

5. The stone castle, the walls set in mortar, is not earlier in Devon and Cornwall than the Norman Conquest. There are no really stately castles in either county, with the exception of Launceston. Rougemont, Exeter, is eminently unpicturesque; Tiverton, Totnes,

Plympton, are almost complete ruins; Lydford--well, as Browne the poet wrote of it in the reign of James I.:--
"They have a castle on a hill;
I took it for an old windmill,
The vanes blown off by weather;
To lie therein one night, 'tis guessed
'Twere better to be stoned or pressed
Or hanged ere you come hither."
And ruin that has fallen on it has not improved its appearance.
Okehampton is but a mean relic; Restormel is circular; Trematon is like a pork-pie; Pendennis, S. Mawes, late and insignificant. Tintagel owes everything to its superb situation and to the legend that it was the place where King Arthur was born. The most picturesque of all is Pengersick, near Breage, but that is late. Its story shall be told in the chapter on Penzance.

CHAPTER V.

TIN MINING

The granite eruptions in Devon and Cornwall--*Elvans*--*Lodes*--Tin passing into copper--Stream-tin--Story of S. Piran and S. Chigwidden--Dartmoor stream-tin--Joseph of Arimathea--The Cassiterides--Jutes--Danish incursions--Tin in King John's time--Richard, Earl of Cornwall--Elizabeth introduces German engineers--Stannary towns--Carew on mining--Blowing-houses--Miners' terms--Stannary Courts--Dr. Borlase on tin mining--Present state.

I REMEMBER being at a ball many years ago at that epoch in the development of woman when her "body" was hooked along her dorsal ridge. Now I learn from competent authorities that it is held together in other fashion.

There was at the ball a very lusty stout lady in slate-grey satin.

By nature and age, assisted by victuals, she was unadapted to take violent exercise. Nevertheless dance she would. Dance she did, till there ensued an explosion. Hooks, eyes, buttons, yielded, and there ensued an eruption of subjacent material. In places the fastenings held so that the tumescent under-garments foamed out at intervals in large bulging masses.

This is precisely what took place with Mother Earth in one of her gambols. Her slate panoply gave way, parted from N.E. to S.W., and out burst the granite, which had been kept under and was not intended for show.

Her hooks and eyes gave way first of all in South Devon, and out swelled the great mass of Dartmoor. They held for a little space, and then out broke another mass that constitutes the Bodmin moors. It heaved to the surface again north of S. Austell, then was held back as far as Redruth and Camborne. A few more hooks remained firm, and then the garment gave way for the Land's End district, and, finally, out of the sea it shows again in Scilly.

Or take it in another way. Cornwall is something like a leg. Let it be a leg vested in a grey stocking. That stocking has so many "potatoes" in it, and each "potato" is eruptive granite.

Granite, however, likewise cracked, formed "faults," as they are called, in parallel lines with the great parent crack to which it owed its appearance, and cracks also formed across these; and through the earlier cracks up gushed later granite in a molten condition, and these are dykes.

Moreover, the satin body not only gave way down its great line of cleavage, but the satin itself in places yielded, revealing, not now the under-linen which boiled out at the great faults, but some material which, I believe, was the lining. So when the granite broke forth there were subsidiary rifts in the slate, and through these rifts a material was extruded, not exactly granite, but like it, called *elvan*. These elvan dykes vary from a few feet to as many as four hundred in breadth, and many can be traced for several miles. The younger granite intruded into the older granite is also called elvan.

But when the secondary fissures occurred, the intrusive matter was not only a bastard granite, but with it came also tin and copper. And these metallic lines, which run on Dartmoor from E. to W., and in Cornwall from E.N.E. to W.S.W., are called *lodes*.

The cross-cracks do not contain metal. They are called *cross-courses*.

In addition there are some capricious veins that do not run in the normal direction, and these are called *counter-lodes*. Their usual direction is N.E.

The cross-courses, although without metal, are of considerable value to the miner, because, as he knows well, the best lodes are those which are thus traversed.

There is, however, one description of cross-course that is called *floocan*, and which is packed with clay, and holds back water. These are accordingly not cut through if it can possibly be avoided.

A very curious feature in the lodes is, that after going down to a variable depth the tin is replaced by copper.

Percy was the first to establish this, towards the close of last century. He pointed out that many an old tin mine was in his time worked for copper. And it came to be supposed that this would be found to be an unchanging law: Go deep enough after tin, and you come to copper. But this opinion was shaken when it was found that Dolcoath, the profoundest mine in Cornwall, which had for some time been worked for copper, became next rich in tin. What seems to have been the case was this: when a vent offered, there was a scramble between the two minerals which should get through first and out of the confinement under earth's crust, and now a little tin got ahead; then came copper trampling on its heels, but was itself tripped up by more tin.

Now, when the granite came to the surface, it did not have everything its own way, and hold its nose on high, and lord it over

40

every other rock as being the most ancient of all, though not the earliest to put in an appearance. There was a considerable amount of water about. There is plenty and to spare in the west of England now, but we may feel grateful that we do not exist in such detestable weather, nor exposed to such sousing rains, nor have to stand against such deluges, as those which granite had to encounter. Hot, over-hot, it may have been below, but it was cold and horribly wet above.

The rains descended; the floods came, and beat on the granite, which, being perhaps at the time warm and soft, and being always very absorbent, began to dissolve.

As it dissolved, the water swept away all its component parts, and deposited the heaviest near at hand, and took the lightest far away. Now the heaviest of all were the ore from the veins or lodes, and the water swept this down into the valleys and left it there, but it carried off the dissolved feldspar and deposited it where it conveniently could and when it was tired of carrying it. The former is stream-tin; the latter is china clay.

Now to get at stream-tin very little trouble is needed. The rubble brought down and lodged in the valleys has to be turned over; and the ore is distinguishable by its weight and by a pink tinge, like the rouge ladies were wont (a hundred years ago) to put on their cheeks and lips. There is no tunnelling, no nasty shafts and adits to be made; and shafts and adits were beyond the capacity of primitive man, furnished with bone and oak picks only. Besides, why take the trouble to mine when the tin lay ready to be picked up?

The story told in Cornwall of the discovery of tin is this:--

S. Piran came over from Ireland in a coracle, and, like a prudent man, brought with him a bottle of whisky. On landing on the north coast he found that there was a hermit there named Chigwidden. The latter was quite agreeable to be friends with the new-comer, who was full of Irish tales, Irish blarney, and had, to boot, a bottle of Irish whisky. Who would not love a stranger under the circumstances? Brothers Chigwidden and Piran drank up the bottle.

"By dad," said Piran, "bothered if there be another dhrop to be squeezed out! Never mind, my spiritual brother; I'll show you how to distil the crayture. Pile me up some stones, and we'll get up the divil of a fire, and we shall manage to make enough to expel the deuce out of ould Cornwall."

So Chigwidden collected a number of black stones, and the two saints made a fine fire--when, lo! out of the black stones thus exposed to the heat ran a stream like liquid silver. Thus was tin discovered.

The story won't wash.

Tin was invented a thousand years at least before either Piran or Chigwidden were thought of. But that was most certainly the way in which it was revealed.

On Dartmoor the stream tin can thus be run out of the ore with a peat fire. And the Dartmoor stream tin has this merit: it is absolutely pure, whereas tin elsewhere is mingled with wolfram, that makes it brittle as glass; and to separate wolfram from tin requires a second roasting and is a delicate process.

Another Cornish story is to the effect that Joseph of Arimathea came in a boat to Cornwall, and brought the Child Jesus with him, and the latter taught him how to extract the tin and purge it of its wolfram. This story possibly grew out of the fact that the Jews under the Angevin kings farmed the tin of Cornwall. When tin is flashed, then the tinner shouts, "Joseph was in the tin trade," which is probably a corruption of "S. Joseph to the tinner's aid!"

We will now shortly take the history of tin mining in Devon and Cornwall.

Whether the west of Cornwall and Scilly were the Cassiterides of the ancients is doubtful. But one thing is sure: that they had their tin, or some of it, from Britain.

Diodorus Siculus, who flourished in the time of Augustus, says so:--

"The inhabitants of that extremity of Britain which is called Belerion both excel in hospitality"--they do so still--"and also, by reason of their intercourse with foreign merchants, are civilised in their mode of life"--very much so. "These prepare the tin, working very skilfully the earth which produces it. The ground is rocky, but it has in it earthy veins, the produce of which is brought down and melted and purified. Then, when they have cast it into the form of cubes, they carry it to a certain island adjoining Britain, called Ictis. During the recess of the tide the intervening space is left dry, and they carry over abundance of tin in carts.... From thence the traders who purchase the tin of the natives transport it to Gaul, and finally, travelling through Gaul on foot, in about thirty days bring their burdens on horses to the mouth of the Rhine."

Ictis has been variously supposed to be S. Michael's Mount, the Isle of Wight, and Romney in Kent.

Whether the Romans worked the tin in Devon and Cornwall is very questionable. No evidence has been produced that they did so. The Saxon invasion must have destroyed what little mining activity existed in the two counties, at least in Devon. It is noticeable that, although Athelstan penetrated to Land's End and crossed to Scilly, he is not said to have paid any attention to the tin workings, which he assuredly would have done had they then been valuable. To the incursions of the Saxons succeeded those of the Danish freebooters, who ran up the rivers and burnt Tavistock and Lydford in 997, and carried fire and sword through the stannary districts of Devon.

Under the Norman rule mining revived. The general use of bells in churches caused a considerable demand for tin, more particularly as those for cathedrals were of large calibre. The chief emporium of the tin trade was Bruges, whence the merchants of Italy obtained the west of England tin and distributed it through the Levant. There exists an interesting record of Florentine commercial industry by one Balducci, composed between 1332 and 1345, in which is described the trade in Cornish tin, and how it was remelted into bars at Venice and stamped with the lion of S. Mark.

In King John's time the tin mines were farmed by the Jews. The right to it was claimed by the king as Earl of Cornwall.

Old smelting-houses in the peninsula are still called "Jews' houses," and, judging by certain noses and lips that one comes across occasionally in the Duchy, they left their half-breeds behind them.

During the time of Richard, Earl of Cornwall and King of the Romans, the produce of the tin mines was considerable, and it was in fact largely due to his reputed wealth from this source that he was elected (1257).

The tin workings went on with varying prosperity till the reign of Elizabeth, when she introduced German engineers and workmen, with improved appliances. In her time the tinners of Cornwall were divided into four portions, named from the principal works of that period. Each of these divisions had its steward under the Lord Warden, who kept his court once in every three weeks. The four stannary towns of Cornwall were Helston, Truro, Lostwithiel, and Liskeard; and at Lostwithiel may be seen the remains of the ducal palace; and at Luxulyan the church, in the tower of which the stannary records and charters were formerly preserved.

In Devon the stannary towns were Tavistock, Ashburton, and Chagford, to which Plympton was added in the reign of Edward III., and Lydford was appointed as the stannary prison.

Ordinary justices of the peace had no jurisdiction over the miners in their disputes.

Carew, who was about the court of Queen Elizabeth, has furnished us with a valuable record of the state of the mines before the introduction of new German machinery and methods.

He notices both the stream-works and the lodes, and his opinion was that the deposits in the former were the result of the Deluge.

He then describes the process of *shoding*, that is of tracing the direction of a vein by fragments found near the surface. The shode pits, which are also called costeening pits, were holes sunk into the ground to no great depth till indications of the lode were reached. The miners next sank pits seven or eight feet deep till they reached the lode itself.

"If they misse the load in one place, they sincke a like shaft" (pit) "in another beyond that, commonly further up the hill, and so a third and a fourth, until they light at last upon it."

Over Dartmoor and the Bodmin moors "the old men's workings" may be seen; hardly a gully has not been streamed, every river-bed has been turned over. The face of the moor is in places welted to such an extent that it alters the character of the scene. These workings are now grass-grown; they are very ancient, and clearly were conducted open to the sky. As the miners worked up a river-bed they built a colander behind them of rude blocks of granite, through which the stream might flow away, and many a rivulet now runs underground through these artificial passages.

In dressing the ore the miners broke it with hammers, and then "vanned" it on their broad oak shovels. The wind bore away the valueless dust, leaving the metal behind. By the side of the "goyles," or deep workings, may be found "vanning-steads" where this process was conducted. But with the introduction of machinery the *crazing-mill* was employed, worked by a waterwheel, in which the ore was passed between two grinding-stones. The washing of the dust which took the place of the dry process was this:--

"The streame, after it hath forsaken the mill, is made to fall by certayne degrees" (steps) "one somewhat distant from another, upon each of which at every descent lyeth a green turfe, three or four foote square and one foote thick. On this the tinner layeth a certayne portion of the sandie tinne, and with his shovell softly tosseth the same to and fro, that through this stirring the water, which runneth over it, may wash away the light earth from the tinne, which, of a heavier substance, lyeth fast to the turfe."

After the black tin, or ore, had been thus treated it was conveyed to the blowing-house. The usage on Dartmoor was, when a miner was far from one of these, to tie the ore in a bag marked with his name or sign, and hang it about a dog's neck; the beast then conveyed it to the mill.

Of the "blowing-houses" a great many remain on Dartmoor. There are two on the Yealm, one, very perfect, on the Erme, one very early, before the introduction of the waterwheel, at Deep Swincombe, several on the Dart.

The blowing-house was a small structure of one chamber and a *cache*, or storeplace, underground. The doorway was rarely high enough to admit a man without stooping double. The walls were of stone without mortar, and, as far as can be judged from their remains, had no window. The furnace was heated with charcoal, and the fire blown by means of a great pair of bellows worked by a tiny waterwheel. The process was so roughly conducted that "divers light sparkles" of tin are said to have lodged in the thatched roof in sufficient quantities to render the burning of the roof once in seven years worth the undertaking. The melted metal ran out into a spoon-shaped hollow in a block of granite, or elvan, and was run into moulds also cut in slabs, many of which remain near the old blowing-houses.

A TIN MOULD

The white tin was then conveyed to a royal smelting-house, where it received a stamp; and no miner was suffered to dispose of his metal till it had thus been marked, and he had paid his due to the Crown for it.

Some of the terms used by tin miners may not prove uninteresting.
Stream-tin when found scattered beneath the surface on a small declivity is called *shode*, and runs to a depth that varies from one to ten feet. A right to work a certain portion is called a *sett*. The rubbish thrown out of a mine is called *stent*; sand or gravel, including tin, is termed *gard*; the walling on each side of a *tye* or adit is called *stilling*; the channels by which superfluous water is let run off are *cundards*, a corruption of "conduits." Oblong pits for a washing-floor are *gounces*; the frame of iron bars above is a *ruddle*.

Buckets are *kibbals*; breaking up ore is *bucking*.

A *whim* is said to have derived its name from this: A man named Coster, observing the labour that was expended on bringing up the refuse from the mines in buckets, fell a-thinking.

"Well, old man," said a mate, "what be up wi' you?"

"I have a whim in my head," he answered, "and I'm tryin' to reduce he to practice."

Coster's whim was much joked about, but when set up outside his head at the pit mouth, it proved to be no joke at all, but a real boon.

Superincumbent earth is *burden*.

A miner worked at Headland Warren mines, on the Webburn, and lived at Challacombe. Every day when leaving work he brought away with him a lump of ore in his pocket, and on reaching his lodging threw it away among the furze bushes. Years after the farmer at Challacombe removed three cartloads of these lumps; that was when tin was at £60 a ton.

From a speech of Sir Walter Raleigh in Parliament in 1601, when Lord Warden of the Stannaries, it would appear that the pay of a working tinner was then four shillings per week, finding himself. Of this he boasts as a great change for the better, inasmuch as previously the tinner had received but half that amount. By all accounts the tinners were in a worse condition than the agricultural labourers.

The Stannary Parliament for the tinners on Dartmoor sat on Crockern Tor till the court was removed to Truro.

The first Parliament held there of which records remain was on September 11th, 1494; the last I have heard of was held at the close of last century.

The Cornish tinners had their Stannary Court on Caradon.

Already in Carew's time mines had been driven into the bowels of the earth. It would appear that levels were at about five fathoms under each other, and the water was raised to the surface by means of "a winder and keeble, or leathern bags, pumps, or buckets."

Dr. Borlase describes the engines that were employed just after the middle of last century. He took a mine in Illogan as typical.

There were seven shafts upon the lode, upon one of which there was a fire-engine working the pumps, and raising the water of the mine to the adit level, twenty fathoms from the surface. Another shaft had a whim upon it, and the remaining six had common winzes at their heads. The walls of the lode were supported by timber, and planks were laid on them for the *deads*, or unprofitable rock. Captains superintended the work. The machines employed were the *water-whim*, the *rag and chain pump*, the *bobs*, and the *fire-engine*. The whim was much the same as the common horse-whim of the present day, employed to draw up the water in kibbles or buckets. The rag and chain pump consisted of an iron chain, furnished at intervals with knobs of cloth, stiffened with leather, which on being turned round a wheel was made to pass through a wooden pump cylinder, twelve or fifteen feet long, and to heave up the water that rose in this cylinder between the knobs of rag. These pumps were worked by hand. The water-wheels with bobs worked other pumps.

The machinery seems to us clumsy and imperfect in the extreme.

The atmospheric or steam-engine of Newcomen was costly, as it consumed an enormous amount of coal; but in 1778 it began to give place to Watt's engine.

Since then the machinery employed advanced with strides till reaching perfection, when the need for any ceased in Cornwall and Devon, where nearly all mines have been abandoned. Barca tin can be raised so much more cheaply, being surface tin, that lode tin cannot compete with it in the market.

Now the mining districts of Cornwall are desolate. Heaps of refuse, gaunt engine-houses, with their chimneys, stand against the sky, hideous objects, and as useless as they are ugly. The Cornish miner has gone abroad. There he remains till he has made his little pile, when he returns home, builds a house for his wife and children, remains idle till money gets low, when away he goes again.

A good deal of discussion has taken place relative to the causes of the decline and extinction of the mining industry in Cornwall. The primary cause is that already referred to, but there is another. Into that industry too much dishonesty was allowed to intrude. Speculators became shy of embarking capital in companies to work bogus mines. The promotion of such schemes was too frequent not in the end to discredit Cornish mining altogether.

The surface tin in the "Straits" mines must come to an end shortly, and then let us trust captains in Cornwall will have learned by experience that in the end honesty is the best policy.

Formerly the metals were taken out of Cornwall for distribution over Europe. Now the coined metal is being brought into Cornwall by trainloads of tourists, by coveys of bicyclists, come to visit one of the most interesting of English counties and inhale the most invigorating air, and everywhere they drop their coin. So life is full of compensations.

CHAPTER VI.

LAUNCESTON

Launceston a borrowed name--Celtic system of separation between town of the castle and town of the church--A saint's curse--Old name Dunheved--Castle--Church--Sir Henry Trecarrel--The river Tamar--Old houses--S. Clether's Chapel--Altarnon--The corn man--Cutting a neck--The Petherwins--Story of S. Padarn--Is visited by his cousin, Samson--Trewortha Marsh--Kilmar--An ancient village--Redmire--Cornish bogs--Dozmare Pool--Lewanick--Cresset-stone--Trecarrel--Old mansions--The Botathen ghost.

THE most singular thing about the former capital of Cornwall is that it does not bear its true name. Launceston is Llan Stephan, the church of S. Stephen. Now the church of S. Stephen is on the summit of a hill on the further side of the river, divided from the town by the ancient borough of Newport.

The true name of the town is Dunheved. It grew up about the Norman castle, instead of about the church, and as it grew, and the colony at S. Stephen's dwindled, it drew to itself the name of the church town.

LAUNCESTON CHURCH PORCH

Launceston is, in fact, one of those very interesting instances of the *caer* and the *llan*, separated the one from the other by a stream.

According to the Celtic system, a church must stand in its own lawn, surrounded by its own tribesmen, and the chief in his *caer* or *dun* must also be without competing authority surrounded by his own vassals. Consequently, in Cornwall, churches are, as a rule, away from the towns, which latter have grown up about the chieftain's residence, except in such instances as Padstow and Bodmin, where a religious, monastic settlement formed the nucleus. Camelford, an old borough town, is over two miles from its parish church, Lanteglos, without even a chapel-of-ease in it, an ecclesiastical scandal in the diocese. Callington, the old capital of the principality of Galewig, is three miles from its church of Southill.

The church of Launceston has grown up out of a small chapel erected for the convenience of those who lived about the castle walls, hangers-on upon the garrison.

The Norman baron, and perhaps the Saxon eorlderman, liked to have his chaplain forming part of his household, and much at his disposal to say mass and sing matins in a chapel to which he could go without inconvenience, forming part of his residence. But such an arrangement was alien to Celtic ideas. Among the Celts the saint stood on an entirely independent footing over against the secular chief, and was in no way subordinate to him. The chaplain of the Norman might hesitate about reprimanding too sharply the noble who supplied him with his bread-and-butter. But the Celtic saint had no scruples of that sort. If a chief had carried off a widow's cow, or had snatched a pretty wench from her parents, the saint seized his staff and went to the *dun* and demanded admittance. A saint's curse was esteemed a most formidable thing. If unjustly pronounced, it recoiled like a boomerang against him who had hurled it. Once pronounced, it must produce its effect, and the only means of averting its fall was to turn it aside against a tree or a rock, which it shivered to atoms. In this the Celtic saint merely stepped into the prerogatives of the Druid.

In Cormac's *Glossary of Old Irishisms*--and Cormac, king-bishop of Cashel, died in 903--is a curious instance of the force of a curse in pagan times.

The wife of Caier fell in love with Neidhe the bard, her husband's nephew. Now a bard had the privilege of hurling a curse if a request made by him should be refused, but not else. So the woman, desiring to be rid of her husband, bade the bard ask of the king a knife which had been given to him in Alba, on condition that he never parted with it. Neidhe demanded the knife.

"Woe and alas!" said Caier, "it is prohibited to me to give it away."

Neidhe was now able to pronounce a *glam dichinn*, or curse. Here it is:--

"Evil, death, and short life to Caier!

May spears of battle slay Caier;

The rejected of the land be Caier;

Buried under mounds and stones be Caier!"

Caier went out next morning to wash at the well, when he found that boils and blains had broken out over his face, disqualifying him for reigning, as a king must be unblemished. He accordingly fled the country, and concealed his disgrace in the dun on the Old Head of Kinsale, and Neidhe took to him the wife and throne of his uncle. Caier remained at Kinsale till he died, blasted by the curse pronounced by the bard.

The saints did just the same, only not for such scandalous reasons; they did it in the cause of humanity, and for the protection of the weak against the strong.

But it will be seen, from what has been said, that the Celtic saint was a very independent personage, and that he and the chief had their separate residences. It will be found that usually a stream divided the territory of the saint from that of the chieftain.

All this in illustration of Llan Stephan and Dunheved, the castle and the church facing and glowering at each other from opposite heights.

Launceston Castle is Norman. That there stood here a castle in Celtic times is certain; the name Dunheved indicates as much. The *heved* in composition is a difficulty. Some suppose it a Saxon addition: *haefod*, a head; but it is more probable that the whole name is Celtic, and signifies the summer *dun*. *Hafod* is a summer residence in contradistinction to a *hendre*, which is that for the winter--the old house, in principal use. The keep consists of concentric rings on a mound natural originally, but much adapted by art. That the castle was employed to dominate the West Welsh, first by the Saxons and then by the Normans, is indisputable. It formed one in a chain of fortresses employed by the Saxon kings, of which Warbstow and Helborough and Killibury were others. That the garrison of Warbstow was composed of Mercians is probable, as they dedicated their chapel to S. Werburga, a Mercian princess-saint. Another contingent was planted at Wembury, commanding Plymouth harbour, where also they introduced the same saint, who really had no "call" to come into these parts.

The parish church of Launceston, dedicated to S. Mary Magdalen, is a very interesting structure externally, of carved granite of extraordinary but somewhat barbaric richness.

The church was begun in 1511. Henry Trecarell, of Trecarell, in Lezant, was rebuilding his mansion there in great splendour. He had already constructed a chapel and a noble banqueting hall, and had got masses of carved granite ready for a gateway, when his only son, a child, was drowned in a basin of water whilst the nurse was bathing him, she having left him for a few moments. The mother survived the shock only a few hours. Henry Trecarell, the father, dropped for ever the intended mansion for himself, and devoted his wealth to a higher ambition--the glory of God. He rebuilt not only the church of Linkinhorne, but also that of Launceston. On the south porch of the latter on a shield appear the Trecarell arms, arg. two chevrons *sable*, which are those of Ashe of Devon, Trecarell being really an Ashe, but he bore the name of his Cornish residence. On a scroll is the date 1511. The niche over the door has lost its image, but on the left are S. George and the dragon, and on the right S. Martin dividing his cloak with a beggar. Above S. George is the Good Samaritan, and above S. Martin is Balaam striking his ass.

At the east end of the chancel, externally in the central gable, are the royal arms, the supporters of which are the lion and red dragon (the unicorn was substituted for the dragon by James I. in 1603). Under the sill of this window, in an arched recess, is a recumbent figure of the Magdalen. Four surpliced minstrels are on each side of the niche, and above the line of the niche similar figures ascend in pairs, but those in the two topmost storeys seem never to have been completed. The instruments which these musicians hold are the rebec, the lute, the bagpipe, shawm, and harps, and one plays the viol, turning a handle like a hurdy-gurdy. The leader of each set of minstrels carries a *bâton*, and wears a chain about his neck.

The devices carved round the church are repetitions of the plumes of the Prince of Wales, pomegranates, balm-plants dropping precious gums, the Tudor rose, and the arms of Trecarell, Kellaway (three pears), and the castle of Dunheved. Above the plinth encircling the building is a line of panelled tracery. In every alternate panel is a shield, bearing a letter, that make up the words: "Ave Maria, gracia plena! Dominus tecum! Sponsus amat sponsum. Maria optimam partem elegit. O quam terribilis ac metuendus est locus iste! Vere aliud non est hic nisi domus Dei et porta celi" ("Hail, Mary, full of grace! The Lord be with thee! The bridegroom loves the bride. Mary hath chosen the best part. Oh, how terrible and fearful is this place! Truly this is no other than the house of God and the gate of heaven").

The church was consecrated on June 18th, 1524. It was never completed, as may be seen by the condition of the west end. The tower belongs to the earlier church, and is twenty-six feet west of the church. Trecarell doubtless intended to rebuild that in a stately style according with the church, but the religious disturbances of the Reformation took all heart out of him, and he abandoned his task. The interior is very disappointing, but it must be remembered it was intended to have a screen of surpassing richness, which would have brought the whole into proportion. The pulpit alone was completed, and that is of singular richness. The modern carving in the church is thin and fanciful.

The neighbourhood of Launceston is rich in objects of interest and scenes of great beauty. The Inney valley will well repay a visit. There is an Inney also in South Wales. It is an excellent stream for fishing, and flows into the Tamar at Cartamartha (*Caer Tamar*), in a glen of wooded loveliness. The unfinished mansion of Trecarell deserves a visit. There are also old houses at Treguddic and Basil, both much spoiled by bad "restoration." On the heights commanding the river are Laneast, with old bench-ends, old glass, and a holy well, and S. Clether, with its well chapel, recently reconstructed. It was in a condition of complete ruin; almost every stone was prostrate, and the rebuilding was like the putting together of a child's puzzle. At the north-east of the chapel is a rather fine holy well, about three feet six inches from the north wall. A description has already been given in the chapter on holy wells, and the explanation of some very curious features in it.

But there is one further feature of interest in this structure that deserves to be noted. The old granite altar, rude, like a cromlech, had never been cast down. It remained intact, and has been left intact in the reconstructed chapel.

S. Clether was the son of Clydwyn, king of Carmarthen. Clydwyn's sister was married to an Irish priest, Brynach, who, on account of the ill-favour in which the Irish were regarded in South Wales, moved into Cornwall and Devon. After a long while he returned, but was again badly received. However, Clether welcomed him, and Brynach spoke to his nephew of the God-forsaken condition of North

Cornwall, and an overpowering impulse came over the king to surrender his principality to his sons, and to depart for Cornwall, there to labour for the evangelisation of his Welsh brethren in the peninsula. He had relatives there. His uncle Gwynys was at S. Genes, on the coast, and his aunt Morwenna at Morwenstow. How long he remained at S. Clether we do not know, but he probably moved on to S. Cleer, near Liskeard, where also he has a fine holy well, and there died. We do not know the precise date, but it was about A.D. 550.[5]

A very fine and interesting church, deserving a visit, is that of Altarnon (*Alt-ar-Nôn*, the cliff of S. Non). The village is called Penpont (the head of the bridge). The church is rich in carved oak, benches, and screen. On several of the benches may be seen carved the corn man, that is to say the little figure that was plaited out of the heads of wheat in the last sheaf at a harvest.

About this and the custom of "crying, 'A neck!'" at harvest I will say a few words.

Towards the end of last century the member for North Devon was extremely unpopular, especially with the lower classes, and there had been a disturbance on the occasion of his election, in which he had run some personal risk. The time was when Lord North was Prime Minister.

Not long after the election he went to Dunsland, the seat of George Bickford.

Whilst strolling near the house he came near a harvest field, whereon he saw a rush of men, and he heard a cry of "Us have'n! us have'n! A neck! a neck!"

Panic-stricken, he ran, nimble as a hare, to the house, and shouted to Mr. Bickford, "For God's sake, hide me, anywhere, in the cellar or the attics! There is a mob after me who want to string me up!"

What the M.P. for North Devon saw and heard was the "crying, 'A neck!'" a custom universal in Devon and Cornwall till reaping machines came in and abolished it. It is now most rarely practised, but I can remember it in full swing some forty or fifty years ago.

Mrs. Bray, in her *Borders of the Tamar and Tavy*, thus describes it in 1832:--

"One evening, about the end of harvest, I was riding out on my pony, attended by a servant who was born and bred a Devonian. We were passing near a field on the borders of Dartmoor, where the reapers were assembled. In a moment the pony started nearly from one side of the way to the other, so sudden came a shout from the field which gave him this alarm. On my stopping to ask my servant what all that noise was about, he seemed surprised by the question, and said, 'it was only the people making their games, as they always did, to the *spirit of the harvest*.' Such a reply was quite sufficient to induce me to stop immediately, as I felt certain here was to be observed some curious vestige of a most ancient superstition; and I soon gained all the information I could wish to obtain upon the subject. The offering to the 'spirit of the harvest' is thus made:--

"When the reaping is finished, towards evening the labourers select some of the best ears of corn from the sheaves; these they tie together, and it is called the *nack*. Sometimes, as it was when I witnessed the custom, the nack is decorated with flowers, twisted in with the seed, which gives it a gay and fantastic appearance. The reapers then proceed to a *high place* (such, in fact, was the field, on the side of a steep hill, where I saw them), and there they go, to use their own words, to 'holla the nack.' The man who bears the offering stands in the midst and elevates it, whilst all the other labourers form themselves into a circle about him; each holds aloft his hook, and in a moment they all shout as loud as they can these words, which I spell as I heard them pronounced, and I presume they are not to be found in any written record: 'Arnack, arnack, arnack, wehaven, wehaven, wehaven.' This is repeated several times; and the firkin is handed round between each shout, by way, I conclude, of libation. When the weather is fine, different parties of reapers, each stationed on some height, may be heard for miles round, shouting, as it were, in answer to each other.

"The evening I witnessed this ceremony many women and children, some carrying boughs, and others having flowers in their caps, or in their hands, or in their bonnets, were seen, some dancing, others singing, whilst the men (whose exclamations so startled my pony) practised the above rites in a ring."

Mrs. Bray goes on to add a good deal of antiquated archæological nonsense about Druids, Phœnicians, and fantastic derivations. She makes "wehaven" to be "a corruption of *wee ane*" "a little one," which is rubbish. "Wehaven" is "we have'n," or "us have'n," "we have got him." As I remember the crying of the neck at Lew Trenchard, there was a slight difference in the procedure from that described by Mrs. Bray. The field was reaped till a portion was left where was the best wheat, and then the circle was formed, the men shouted, "A neck! A neck! We have 'n!" and proceeded to reap it.

Then it was hastily bound in a bundle, the ears were plaited together with flowers at the top of the sheaf, and this was heaved up, with the sickles raised, and a great shout of "A neck! A neck!" etc., again, and the drink, of course.

The wheat of the last sheaf was preserved apart through the winter, and was either mixed with the seed-corn next year or given to the best bullock.

My old coachman, William Pengelly, who had been with my grandfather, father, and then with myself, and who died at an advanced age in 1894, was wont annually, till he became childish with age, to make the little corn man or neck, and bring it to be set up in the church for the harvest decorations. I kept a couple of these for some years, till the mice got at them and destroyed them.

In Essex a stranger passing a harvest field stands the chance of being run up to by the harvesters, caught in a loop of straw twisted, and held till he has paid a forfeit. To the present day in Devon, at haysel, the haymakers will make a twist of dry grass, and with this band catch a girl--or a girl will catch a boy--and hold her or him till the forfeit of a kiss has been paid, and this is called "making sweet hay." Hereby hangs a tale.

The Quakers in Cornwall have, as elsewhere, their Monthly Advices read to them in the meeting-house, wherein are admonitions against various sorts of evil. Among these is one against "vain sports." Now, just about haymaking-time a newly-joined member heard this injunction, and he timidly inquired whether "making sweet hay with the mïdens" came under the category. "Naw, sure!" was the answer; "that's a' i' the way o' Natur'."

Our Guy Fawkes is actually the straw man transferred from harvest to November.

These straw men take the place of human victims, and the redemption with silver or a kiss is also a last reminiscence of the capture of a victim to be sacrificed for the sake of a future harvest to the Earth Spirit. In Poland the man who gives the last stroke at thrashing is wrapped in corn and wheeled through the village. In Bavaria he is tied up in straw and cast on a dunghill.

Among the Pawnees, as late as 1838, the sacrifice was carried out in grim reality. A girl was burnt over a slow fire, and whilst her flesh was still warm it was cut to pieces, and bits were carried away to be buried in the cornfields. At Lagos, in Guinea, it was till quite recently the custom to impale a young girl alive to ensure good crops. A similar sacrifice was offered at Benin. The Marimos, a Bechuana tribe, sacrifice a human being for the crops. He is captured, then intoxicated, carried into the fields, and there slaughtered. His blood and ashes, after the body has been burned, are distributed over the tilled land to ensure a good harvest next year. The Gonds of India kidnapped Brahman boys for the same purpose. The British Government had to act with great resolution in putting down the similar sacrifices of the Khonds some half-century ago.

The mode of performing these sacrifices was as follows. Ten or twelve days before the sacrifice the victim's hair was cut. Crowds assembled to witness the sacrifice. On the day before, the victim was tied to a post and anointed with oil. Great struggles ensued to scrape off some of this oil or to obtain a drop of spittle from the victim. The crowd danced round the post, saying, "O god, we offer this sacrifice for good crops, seasons, and health." On the day of the sacrifice the legs and arms were first broken, and he was either squeezed to death or strangled. Then the crowd rushed on him with knives and hacked the flesh from the bones. Sometimes he was cut up alive. Another very common mode was to fasten the victim to the proboscis of a wooden elephant, which revolved on a stout post, and as it whirled round the crowd cut the flesh off while life remained. In some villages as many as fourteen of these wooden elephants were found, all of which had been used for this purpose. In one district the victim was put to death slowly by fire. A low stage was erected, sloping on each side like a roof; upon this the victim was placed, his limbs wound about with cords to prevent his escape. Fires were then lighted and hot brands applied to make him roll up and down the slopes of the stage as much as possible, for the more tears he shed the more abundant would be the supply of rain. The next day the body was cut to pieces. The flesh was at once taken home by delegates of the villages. To secure its rapid arrival it was sometimes forwarded by relays of men, and conveyed with postal fleetness fifty or sixty miles. In each village all who had remained at home fasted until the flesh arrived. When it came it was divided into two portions, one of which was offered to the Earth Goddess by burying it in a hole in the ground. The other portion was divided into as many shares as there were heads of houses present. Each head of a house rolled his share in leaves and buried it in his favourite field. In some places each man carried his portion of flesh to the stream that watered his fields.

Since the British Government has suppressed the human sacrifices inferior victims have been substituted, such as goats.

Here, then, we have almost before our eyes a change of the victim. A still further change takes place when an image is used as a substitute; and there is again modification when the person captured and destined for sacrifice is allowed to redeem himself with a handsel or a kiss. But the fact that in Europe, aye, and in England, we have these modified customs only now dying out, is an almost sure proof that at a remote period our ancestors practised the awful rites at harvest and in spring, of which a description has been given as still in use in Africa, and as only just put an end to in America and in India.

North and west of Launceston is the Petherwin district; the former of these is in Devon, although lying west of the Tamar, as is also Werrington.

These three churches, all dedicated to S. Padarn, form a large territory once under his government. It was his Gwynedd, but whether so called from its being open moorland or from its being exposed to the winds--windblown (*Gwynt*)--I cannot say. Padarn was son of Pedredin and Gwen Julitta, and was first cousin of S. Samson. He was born in Brittany, but owing to a family revolution his father and uncles fled to Wales, but Padarn remained as a babe with his mother. Finding her often in tears, he asked her the reason, and she told him that she mourned the loss of his father. So when Padarn had come to man's estate he went in quest of him, and finally found him in Ireland, where, old rascal, he had embraced the monastic life, entirely regardless of what was due to the wife of his bosom. As Pedredin absolutely refused to leave his newly-chosen mode of life, Padarn returned to his mother, and they went together to Wales, passing through Cornwall. In Wales he founded Llanbadarn Fawr in Cardiganshire, which became an episcopal see; but he got across with Maelgwn, king of North Wales, as also with King Arthur, who in the lives of the Welsh saints is always represented as a bully, showing that they were written before that king had been elevated into the position of a hero of romance by Geoffrey of Monmouth in the twelfth century. His position now became untenable, and he left Wales. It was then, I presume, that he made his great settlement in East Cornwall.

According to one account he crossed into Brittany with Caradoc Strong-i'-th'-Arm, but the expedition ended in no results, and he returned. Now after a while Cousin Samson arrived in Padstow harbour, and resolved on making a Cornish tour before he crossed into Brittany, whither he much desired to go and see what could be done towards the recovery of his paternal acres. At Padstow he visited S. Petrock. Then he went along the north-east, and as he approached Gwynedd, or Padarn's Venedotia, he sent word that he was coming. Now Padarn was getting out of bed when the tidings reached him, and he had pulled on one stocking and shoe; but so delighted was he to hear that his cousin was at hand, that he ran to meet him with one leg shod and the other bare.

The dates of his life are approximately these. He came to Wales in 525, remained there till 547, when he migrated to Devon and Cornwall, where he remained to his death in 560.[6] When the Saxons obtained the mastery, North Petherwin and Werrington were given to the abbey of Tavistock, and the old Celtic foundation of Padarn ceased--monastically.

TREWORTHA MARSH

A pleasant excursion may be made from Launceston to Trewartha Marsh. This occupies the site of a lake, but it has been filled by detritus from the granite tors around, and this rubble has been turned over and over by tin-streamers, who not only extracted the baser metal, but also gold.

On the way Trebartha is passed, one of the loveliest sites in England, second in my mind only to Bolton Abbey. It is the seat of F. R. Rodd, Esq. The parish church of Northill is a foundation of S. Tighernach or Torney, godchild of S. Bridget. There are two ways up to Trewortha: one is by Higher and Lower Castick, where a picturesque old farm is passed, by Trewartha Tor, on which is shown King Arthur's bed; the other is by the bridge at the back of Trebartha. The stream flowing from the marsh forms a really beautiful fall in the grounds.

The marsh itself and its surroundings are desolate, but Killmar (*Cêl-mawr*, the great place of shelter) rising above it is a noble tor, and the view from the north-west, by Grey Mare Rock looking over the flat marsh to Killmar, is as fine as anything on the Bodmin moors. On the west side of the marsh is an ancient British settlement, apparently unconnected with the stream-works for tin. The houses were long and quadrangular; one was apparently a council chamber, having a judge's seat in granite and benches of granite down the sides. Unfortunately these have been wantonly destroyed recently by a man who was building pigsties. The houses had separate bakeries, and two or three of these with their ovens remain in a tolerably perfect condition. The same long building was occupied by two or three families, divided off from each other by an upright slab of granite, making so many horseboxes, but each family had its own hearth. The pottery found there was all wheel-turned; and as many hones were found, no doubt could exist that the occupants belonged to the iron age. No other village of the kind has as yet been noticed on the moors except another somewhat higher up the stream that feeds Trewartha Marsh, and this has been much mutilated of late years. Independent of these singular quadrangular buildings are hut circles belonging to a far earlier age, before steel and iron were known.

PLAN OF HABITATION ON TREWORTHA MARSH
(*By kind permission of "The Daily Graphic"*)

The whole of the hillside is cut up into paddocks, and a conduit of water was brought from the little stream at Rushleford Gate to supply the settlers with pure drinking water. No traces of burnt slag were found, and consequently the ovens cannot be pronounced to have been made to smelt the ore, but it is strange that there should be several of these ovens. The whole settlement is so curious that I give a plan and a sketch of some of the hovels. The doorways are in several instances perfect. Against the wind and rain the hovels were protected by a high bank to the west. From the Cheesewring, about two and a half miles distant, a line of rails was carried to just above this singular village, and there abandoned. The visitor may well wonder *why* a railway was carried into the heart of this desolate region; it was apparently an excuse for wasting the money of investors. The bulk of their deposits have disappeared, and no profits have been realised. Trewartha Marsh occupies the bed of a lake that decants over a granite lip into the valley of the Lynher. At some remote period the miners cut down the lip and let off the water, and then turned over the lake bed. A former owner of Trebartha Hall gave to his daughters on their marriage heavy gold rings from the precious ore washed out of the gravel of Trewartha. A stroll among the refuse-heaps that occupy the lake-bed among lanes of water and stretches of morass will show the visitor how great was the industry of the ancient streamers. There are several cairns and barrows on the heights, but none that have been explored have given other results than small stone cists containing bone and wood ash.

On the north side of the marsh were some old cottages, that have been destroyed, and their materials employed for building purposes, in which coins of Elizabeth and Queen Mary were found. A vague tradition exists that a town existed at Tresillern, one of the reaches of the lake, which was submerged for the iniquity of the inhabitants.

A basin of bog--also once a lake--exists at Redmire, and near it is a small circle of upright stones. I was as near lost as might be in this bog in 1891. The Ordnance Survey Office had sent down an official to go over and correct the map of this district, and I was with him. When dusk set in we started for Five Lanes, and lost our way. We both got into Redmire, and had to trip along warily from one apparently firm spot to another. The winter and summer had been unusually wet, and the marsh was brimming with water. Six bullocks had already been lost in it that year.

All at once I sank above my waist, and was being sucked further down. I cried to my companion, but in the darkness he could not see me, and had he seen me he could have done nothing for me. The water finally reached my armpits. Happily I had a stout bamboo, some six feet long, and I placed this athwart the surface and held it with my arms as far expanded as possible. By jerks I gradually succeeded in lifting myself and throwing my body forward, till finally I was able to cast myself full length on the surface. The suction had been so great as to tear the leather gaiters I wore off my legs. I lay full length gasping for nearly a quarter of an hour before I had breath and strength to advance, and then wormed myself along on my breast till I reached dry land.

Some of the Cornish bogs are far worse than those on Dartmoor. Crowdy is particularly ugly and dangerous. In a dry summer they may, however, be traversed, as the surface becomes caked.

Dozmare Pool is, next to Loe Pool, the largest sheet of sweet water in

Cornwall. It abounds in fish, and was formerly a great resort of the worker in flint, as innumerable traces of the industry testify. Arrow- and spear-heads, scrapers, and an almost unlimited amount of chips and flakes may be found near it. In the lake is a cranogue, or subaqueous cairn, on which was formerly a palafite dwelling. The bottom of the pool is certain to richly repay exploration.

For those who desire to enjoy moor air at a high elevation, there is a pleasant little inn at Bolventor, called the "Jamaca Inn"; but the visitor must take with him his own supply of liquor, as it is a "temperance house."

The moors about well reward exploration; they abound in prehistoric antiquities, and in scenes of great but desolate beauty.

Lewanick (Llan-Winoc) was an interesting church with good bench-ends, but an unfortunate fire destroyed the interior, and almost everything of interest has disappeared. There is, however, in the church a cresset-stone. This is a structure like a font, but with the surface scooped out into five little bowls for containing oil and floating wicks. Formerly, in the days when there existed a difficulty in kindling a fire, it was important that a light should be kept perpetually burning in the church, to which the parishioners might have resort in the event of their fires going out. But such cresset-stones are now extremely rare. There is one at Calder Abbey with sixteen bowls, one at Furness with five. At Ballagawne, in the Isle of Man, is one with one large bowl and nine small ones. A cresset-stone exists in the court before San Ambrogio, Milan, and I saw one set up before a very early church at Civeaux, in Vienne, upon which the schoolboys amused themselves with jumping and dancing.

There are inscribed stones and oghams in the churchyard. The village carpenter, an unusually intelligent man, has been zealous in search after, and the discovery of, these stones. In the porch, under the stone bench, a hare-hunt is carved on polyphant stone. The quarry of this beautiful stone is near by. There are several crosses and holy wells in the parish, one of S. Blaunder, which is a corruption of Branwalader, who is identical with S. Brendan, the great navigator and explorer in the sixth century. He is even supposed to have reached America, but actually, it may be suspected, visited only the Canary Isles and Madeira.

In Northill Church is a curious monument to a chrisom child.

Trecarrel is the old house of Sir Henry, who erected Launceston Church. The hall is specially fine. He never completed the mansion.

The chapel remains, and when I saw it a goose was sitting on her eggs on the site of the altar. But it was never consecrated. About the yard lie the richly-carved stones intended for the gateway to the court, but the gatehouse was not set up. There are several old houses which may be visited from Launceston. Bradstone, on the Devon side of the Tamar, has a most picturesque gatehouse. The venerable mansion formerly belonged to the Cloberry family, whose cognisance was bats; it is quite intact. Bradstone takes its name from a broad stone, in fact, a cromlech that has been thrown down, but the cap remains, and is used as a stile.

Kelly Church has some fine old glass. Sydenham is an untouched seventeenth-century mansion; so is Wortham, in Lifton parish. A magnificent relic is Penheale, with its granite entrance and panelled rooms. It is in Egloskerry parish, and formerly belonged to the Earl of Huntingdon. It passed by sale from one hand to another, and is now the property of Mr. Simcoe.

In Egloskerry Church is a remarkably good helmet. The church contains an alabaster figure of an Italian flower-girl. Treguddick, once a seat of a family of that name, has been so mutilated in alteration that it presents little of interest. The same may be said of Basil.

Botathen, once the seat of the Bligh family, has not in it anything of interest, but is associated with one of the best ghost stories on record, written by the Rev. John Ruddle, vicar of Launceston, who laid a ghost in a field that appeared to and tormented a boy of the name of Bligh.

Ruddle was parson of Launceston between 1663 and 1698. Defoe got hold of Ruddle's MS. account of the transaction, and published it in 1720. It has been often surmised that Defoe had touched up the original, or had invented the whole story; but Mr. A. Robins has carefully entered into an examination of the circumstances, and has proved that the account was by Ruddle, and all those persons mentioned in it actually lived at the period.

In 1665 John Ruddle was schoolmaster in Launceston as well as vicar, and one of his pupils died. He preached a sermon at the funeral on June 20th, and after leaving church he was addressed by an old gentleman, who informed him that his own son was sadly troubled by having several times met a ghost, or, at all events, the boy pretended that he had. The gentleman, Mr. Bligh, of Botathen, invited Ruddle to his house to see the lad.

After conferences with the boy Ruddle gained his confidence, and, says he, "he told me with all naked freedom and a flood of tears that his friends were unjust and unkind to him, neither to believe nor pity him, and that if any man would go with him to the place he might be convinced that the thing was real." The rest of the story shall be told from a MS. now in the possession of a lady in Launceston, copied by William Ruddle, the son, from his father's original MS.:--

"By ys time he found me able to comisrate his condition and to be attentive to his relation of it, therefore he went on in ys manner. This woman wch appears to me (saith he) Lived a nighbour here to my father, and dyed about 8 years since. Her name Dorothy Dingle, of such a stature, such an age and complexion. She never speaks to me, but passeth by hastyly and always Leaves ye footpath to me, and she comonly meets me twice or thrice in ye breadth of ye field. It was abt 2 months before I took any notice of it, and tho' ye shape of ye face was in my memory yet I could not recal ye name of ye person, but without more thoughtfullnes I did suppose it was some woman who lived thereabout and had frequent occasion that way, nor did I imagine anything to ye contrary before she began to meet me constantly morning and evening, and always in ye same field, and sometimes twice or thrice in ye breadth of it. The first time I took notice of her was abt a year since and when I first began to suspect and beleive it to be a Ghost I had courage enough not to be affraid, but kept it to myself a good while and only pondered very much at it. I did often speak to it, but never had a word in answer. Then I changed my way and went to school ye Under Horse Road, and then she always met me in ye narrow Lane between ye Quarry Park and ye Nursery, which was worse. At Length I began to be terrifyd at it, and prayed continually that God would either free me from it, or Let me know ye meaning of it. Night and day, sleeping and wakeing ye shape was ever runing in my mind.

"Thus (said he) by degrees I grew very pensive, in so much that it was taken notice of by all our family, whereupon, being urg'd to it, I told my brother William of it, and he privately acquainted my father and mother wth it, and they kept it to themselves for sometime. Ye successe of this discovery was only that they sometimes Laugh at me, sometimes elude me, but still comanded me to keep my school and put such fageries out of my head.

I did accordingly go often to school, but always met ye woman in ye way.

"This and much more to ye same purpose (yea as much as held a Dialogue of near 2 hours) was our conference in ye orchard, which ended wth my profer to him that (without makeing any privy to our intent) I would next day walk wth him to ye place abt 6 o'clock. He was even transported wth joy at ye mention of it, and replyed, 'but will ye sure Sr, will ye sure Sr? Thank God! now I hope I shall be beleived!' Upon this conclusion we retired to ye hous. The gent, his wife, and Mr. S. were impatient to know ye event, insomuch that they came out of ye parlour into ye hall to meet us, and seeing ye Lad Look chearfully ye first complement from ye old man was 'Come, Mr. Ruddle! ye have talked with S. I hope now he will have more wit, an idle boy, an idle boy.' At these words ye Lad ran up ye stairs to his chamber without replying, and I soon stopt ye curiosity of ye 3 expectants by telling them that I had promised silence, and was resolved to be as good as my word; but when things were riper they might know all, at prsent I desired them to rest in my faithfull pmise that I would do my utmost in their service and for ye good of their son. With this they were silenced, I cannot say satisfyed.

"The next morning before 5 o'clock ye Lad was in my chamber and very brisk. I arose and went with him. Ye field he Led me to I guested to be abt 20 acres in an open country and abt 3 furlongs from any hous. We went into ye field, and had not gone above a third parte before the Spectrum in ye shape of a woman wth all ye circumstances he had described her to me in ye orchard ye day before (as much as ye suddennesse of itts appearance and evanition would prmit me to discover) met us and passed by. I was a Little surprised at it, yet I had not ye power, nor indeed durst I Look back, yet took care not to show any fear to my pupil and guide, and therefore, only telling him that I was satysfyed in ye truth of his complaint we walked to ye end of ye field and returned, nor did ye Ghost meet us at yt time above once. I perceved in ye young man a kind of boldnes mixt wth astonismt, ye first caused by my prsence, and ye proof he had given of his own relation, ye other by ye sight of his prsecutor.

"In short he went home; I somewhat puzled, he much animated. At our return ye gentlewoman (whose inquisitiveness had mist us) watched to speak with me, I gave her a convenience, and told her that my opinion was her son's complaint was not to be slighted, nor altogether discredited, yet that my judgment in his case was not setled. I gave her caution moreover that ye thing might not take wind Lest ye whole country should ring wth what we yet had no assurance of. In this juncture of time I had busines wch would admit no delay, wherefore I went for Launceston that evening, but prmised to see him again next week,--yet I was prevented by an occasion which pleaded a sufficient excuse, for my wife was that week brought home from a nighbours house very ill. However my mind was upon ye adventure. I studyed ye case, and abt 3 weeks after went again resolving by ye help of God to see ye utmost.

"The next Monday, being ye 27th day of July 1665, I went to ye haunted field by myself and walked ye baedth of it without any encounter. I returned and took ye other walk, and then ye Spectrum appeared to me, much about ye same place I saw it before when ye young gent was wth me. In my thoughts it moved swifter than ye time before, and abt 30 feet distant from me on my right hand in so much that I had not time to speak, as I determined with myself beforehand.

"The evening of that day ye parents, ye son, and myself being in ye chamber where I Lay, I propounded to them our going altogether to ye place next morning, and after some asseverration that there was no danger in it we all resolved upon it.

"The morning being come Lest we shd alarm ye family of servts, they went under pretence of seeing a field of wheat, and I took my horse and fetched a compas another way, and so met at ye stile we had appointed; thence we al four walked Leisurely into ye Quartils, and had not passed above half ye field before ye Ghost made appearance. It then came over ye stile just before us, and moved with such swiftness that by ye time we had gone 6 or 7 steps it passed by; I 'mediately turned head and ran after it wth ye young man by my side. We saw it passe over ye stile at wch we entred, but no further. I stept upon ye hedg at one place, he at another, but could discern nothing, whereas I dare averr that ye swiftest horse in England could not have conveyed himself out of sight in yt short space of time.

"Two things I observed in this day's appearance, viz.: 1. that a spaniel dog which followed ye company unregarded, did bark and run away as ye Spectrum passed by, whence 'tis easy to conclude yt it was not our fear or fancy wch made ye apparition. 2. that ye motion of ye Spectrum was not gradatim, or by steps and moveing ye feet, but a kind of glideing as children upon ye ice, or a boat down a swift river, which punctually answers ye descriptions ye antients gave of ye motion of their Lemures.

"But to prceed: this ocular evidence clearly convinced, but withall sharply affrighted ye old gent and his wife who knew ys D. D. in her Lifetime,--were at her buryal, and now plainly saw her features in this prsent apparition. I encouraged them as wel as I could, but after this they went no more. However I was resolved to prceed and use such Lawfull means as God hath discovered and Learned men have successfully practiced in these unvulgar cases.

"The next morning being Thursday I went out very early by myself and walked for abt an hour's space in meditation and prayer in ye field next adjoyning to ye Quartils. Soon after five I stept over ye stile into ye disturbed field, and had not gone above 30 or 40 paces before ye Ghost appeared at ye further stile. I spake to it with a Loud voice in some such sentences as ye way of these dealings directed me, whereupon it approached, but slowly. When I came near it, it mov'd not. I spake again and it answered in a voice neither very audible nor intelligable. I was not in ye Least terrifyed, and therefore persisted untill it spake again, and gave me satisfaction.

"But ye work could not be finished at this time; wherefore ye same evening, an hour after sun-set, it met me again near ye same place, and after a few words of each side it quietly vanished, and neither doth appear since, nor ever will more to any man's disturbance.

"N.B. The discourse in ye morning Lasted abt a quarter of an hour.

"These things are true. I know them to be so with as much certainty as eyes and ears can give me; and until I can be perswaded that my senses do deceve me abt their proper objects (and by that perswasion deprive myself of ye strongest inducement to beleive ye Christian Religion) I must and will assert that these things in this paper are true."

I omit the reflections made on this by the writer, who signs: "September 4th, 1665, John Ruddle."

Every person and every place can be and has been identified by Mr. Robins, to whose article I refer the reader, should he care to go over the ground.[7]

NOTE.--Books on Launceston:--

ROBINS (A. F.), *Launceston, Past and Present*. Launceston, 1884.

PETER (R.), *The Histories of Launceston and Dunheved*. Plymouth, 1885.

CHAPTER VII.

CALLINGTON

A town with a past--The principality of Gallewick--A royal residence--The Boy and the Mantle--Caradock and Tegau--Arthur and Guenever--Southill--S. Samson--Callington Church--The Borough--Dupath Well--Hingesdon Hill--S. Ive--Linkinhorne--Story of S. Melor--The Cheesewring--Camp--The Hurlers--Trethevy stone--S. Cleer--The Tamar--Arsenic manufacture--Poisoning--Production--Pentillie.

CALLINGTON is a town with a past; whether it has a future is problematical. Its past is remote; and if it has a future, that will be equally distant. Issachar was a strong ass couching between two burdens; and Callington lies low between the great bunches of Caradon and Hingesdon, two huge masses of moor said to be rich in minerals. In the times of Callington's prosperity it throve on these lodes of tin and copper. But now the mines are abandoned and the population has leaked away. Should the two mountains be again worked, then the profits will go to Liskeard, seated on a railway, on one side, and to Gunnislake, planted on the Tamar, on the other.

CALLINGTON

Callington occupies the site of the royal residence of the kings of Cornwall as princes of Gallewick. Here Selyf and his wife S. Wenn had their residence, and here S. Cuby was born. Here it is asserted that Arthur once had his court. And here also at one time was Caradoc Freichfras with his wife Tegau, the most honest woman in Arthur's court.

Who can say that it was not here that the boy appeared with the mantle, the ballad concerning which is in *Percy's Reliques*, though indeed in that it is said to have occurred in Carlisle?

"'Now have thou here, King Arthur,
Have this here of mee,
And give unto thy comely queen
All-shapen as you see.

"'No wife it shall become
That once hath been to blame.'
Then every knight in Arthur's court
Slye glaunced at his dame.

"And first came Lady Guenever,
The mantle she must trye.
This dame, she was new-fangled,
And of a roving eye.

"When she had tane the mantle,
And all was with it cladde,
From top to toe it shiver'd down,
As tho' with sheers beshradde.

"Down she threw the mantle,
She longer would not stay;
But, storming like a fury,
To her chamber flung away."

So one lady after another attempted to wear the mantle, and it curled and became contracted on each, and all were shamed in the sight of Arthur and the whole court.

"Sir Cradock call'd his lady,
And bade her to come neare:
'Come win this mantle, lady,
And do me credit here.'

"The lady gently blushing
With modest grace came on,
And now to trye the wondrous charm
Courageously is gone.

"When she had tane the mantle,
And put it on her backe,
About the hem it seemed
To wrinkle and to cracke.

"'Lye still,' she cryed, 'O mantle!
And shame me not for naught,

I'll freely own whate'er amiss
Or blameful I have wrought.
"'Once I kist Sir Cradocke
Beneathe the greenwood tree:
Once I kist Sir Cradocke's mouth
Before he married me.'
"When thus she had her shriven,
And her worst fault had told,
The mantle soon became her
Right comely as it shold.
"Most rich and fair of colour
Like gold it glittering shone;
And much the knights in Arthur's court
Admir'd her every one."

I do not hold that this story belongs to Carlisle, but to Caerleon or to Callington.

This last place was one of the three royal cities of Britain, of which Caerleon was the second, says a Welsh triad, and the third I cannot identify. At one of these three Arthur was wont to celebrate the high festivals of Christmas, Easter, and Whitsuntide. Caradoc Freichfras, the Sir Cradock of the ballad, was chieftain in Gelliwig, or the region of which Callington was capital, and Bedwin was the bishop there. But this Bedwin is only known through the mediæval romances. It was here that Gwenever held court when insulted by Modred, Arthur's nephew, during the king's absence in Brittany, when he dragged her with contumely from her throne and drove her from the palace. The fatal battle of Camalon was fought to avenge this insult. The region of Gelli, which gives its name to or derives its name from Brown Willy and Brown Gelli, two tors in the upland metalliferous district, was valuable because of the abundance of stream-tin and of gold that was found there. Callington is a corruption of Gellewick-ton.

Caradoc Freichfras, that is to say Strong-i'-th'-Arm was son of Llyr Merini, a Cornish prince, and his wife Gwen, who was a granddaughter of Brychan of Brecknock. According to a saying attributed to Arthur himself, he was styled "the pillar of the Cymry." His prowess in the great battle of Cattraeth against the Saxons is commemorated by the contemporary poet Aneurin, who is the same as the sour Gildas, historian of the Britons:--

"When Caradoc rushed into the battle

It was like the tearing onset of the woodland boar,
The bull of combat in the field of slaughter,
He attracted the wild dogs by the motion of his hand.
My witnesses are Owen ap Eulat
And Gwrien, and Gwynn and Gwriat.
From Cattraeth and its carnage,
From the battle encounter,
After the clear bright mead was served,
He saw no more the dwelling of his father."
Aneurin represents Caradoc as having fallen in this battle.

It is possible that Caradon may take its name from him, and that it may have been Dun Caradock.

Caradoc and his true wife Tegau were laid hold of by the Anglo-Norman romancers. They could not understand his nickname, and rendered it "Brise-Bras," and supposed that his arm was wasted away, whereas the Celtic title implies that it was brawny. To explain the wasted arm they invented a story. They told of an enchanter who made a serpent attach itself to the arm of Caradoc, from whose wasting tooth he could never be relieved until she whom he loved best should consent to undergo the torture in his stead. The faithful Tegau, on hearing this, was not to be deterred from giving him this proof of her devotion. As, however, the serpent was in the act of springing from the wasted arm of the knight to the lily-white neck of the lady, her brother Cado, Earl of Cornwall, struck off its head with his sword, and thus dispelled the enchantment.[8]

If Tegau was actually the sister of Cado, then we may flatter ourselves that Cornwall presented the two noblest and purest types of womanhood at the Arthurian period--Tegau and Enid, the wife of Geraint.

Three miles out of Callington is the parish church--Southill--one of the many instances of an ecclesiastical settlement at a respectable distance from the secular*caer* or tribal centre, that each might live its own life and have its own independent organisation.

Southill was founded by S. Samson. As we have already seen, he had landed on the north Cornish coast and made his way to Petherwin, where he had visited his first cousin Padarn. On his way, he passed through the district of Trecor, now Trigg, deriving its name from three notable caers or camps,--Helborough, Warbstow, and Launceston. As Samson was in this district, he found the people performing idolatrous rites about a tall upright stone, and this with the sanction of their chief, who was called Gwythian. Samson did not throw down the menhîr; he contented himself with cutting a cross upon it.

I wonder whether this is the stone that still stands at Southill, on which is cut the cross of Constantine. It is an inscribed stone to one Connetoc, and is of the period of S. Samson.

Whilst tarrying in Cornwall, Samson heard that his old master, Dubricius, was very infirm and failing, and he hastened to South Wales to revisit him. The old man, who was dying, committed to his charge a favourite disciple named Morinus. Samson did not particularly relish the charge, for he did not believe the young man was sincere. However, he took Morinus back with him, but soon after, the disciple became insane and died. The monks, regarding this as possession, removed his body and buried it outside their cemetery. Samson was, however, very uneasy, because the deacon had been entrusted to him with such solemnity by Dubricius, whom he loved and reverenced with all his heart, and he prayed incessantly for the poor fellow who had died mad, till one night he dreamed that Dubricius appeared to him and assured him that Morinus was admitted to the company of the blessed. With a glad heart Samson ordered the body to be at once exhumed and laid in consecrated ground.

One night in midwinter a thief got into the church, and stole thence a cross adorned with gems and gold and all the money he could lay his hands on, and ran away with the spoil wrapped in a bundle. He made for the moors and ventured over a bog, trusting that the frozen surface would bear him. But his weight broke through the thin ice, and he sank to his waist. Afraid of going under altogether, he threw away his burden, and did that which everyone who has wits will do in a bog--spread out his arms on the crust.

There the man remained till morning, when a hue and cry was set up after the stolen goods. He was found and the plunder recovered. He was dead of cold when discovered next day. At Southill is S. Samson's Well, and it was in clearing it out, having become choked, that the stone with the inscription on it was found.

The old tribeland or principality of Gallewick was reduced in the Middle Ages to a manor of Kelliland, which, however, remained of considerable importance, and is now held by Countess Compton. The church is Perpendicular, of no particular interest, but it possesses an Easter sepulchre, and an early font on which are carved grotesque animals and a representation of the Tree of Life. Callington has in it a fine church that is chapel-of-ease to Southill. It is good Perpendicular, and suffered a "restoration" under the hands of an incompetent architect. Happily, since then, genius has been invoked to supplement the defects of mediocrity, and the north aisle that was added by Mr. Edmund Sedding is one of the ablest works of that clever architect. Viewed internally or externally it is delightful.

CALLINGTON CROSS

There are a few quaint old cottages in Callington, and there is a late mediæval cross that is picturesque. In the church, moreover, is a very fine monument to Sir Robert Willoughby de Broke, who died in 1503; he was steward of the Duchy of Cornwall, and took part in the battle of Bosworth.

Callington was made a borough in 1584, and its earliest patrons were the Pauletts. From them the patronage passed to the Rolles, who divided it with the Corytons. Then it went to the Walpoles, next to Lord Clinton, and finally to the first Lord Ashburton. It never bore arms, nor had a corporation, but there is an early and interesting silver mace, now in the custody of the portreeve, who is elected with other officers annually at the manor court of Kelliland.

Perhaps the most quaint and beautiful of the chapel wells in Cornwall is Dupath, near Callington, though not in the parish, but in that of S. Dominick. Unhappily dirty farmyard surroundings disfigure the scene, and make one fear pollution of the sparkling water.

Hingesdon, on the N.E., rises to the height of 1091 feet, its highest point being called Kit Hill, where are remains of a camp; the moor, moreover, is strewn with barrows. It was on Hingesdon that the Britons, uniting their forces with some Danes who had come up the Tamar, met and fought Egbert in 833, and were defeated. The surface of Hingesdon and Kit Hill has been much interfered with by mines, and the summit is crowned with a ruined windmill erected to work the machinery in a mine hard by. The road to Tavistock passes over Hingesdon at a height of 900 feet, and thence after nightfall can be seen the Eddystone light.

On the Liskeard road, beside the Lynher, is a well-preserved oval camp called Cadsonbury. Other camps are at Tokenbury and Roundbury.

S. Ive (pronounced Eve) is probably a foundation of one of the Brychan family, and certainly not dedicated to S. Ive of Huntingdonshire, who is an impostor, nor to S. Ive of the Land's End district. The church is interesting, but has been unfeelingly "restored." The east window, with its niches, deserves special notice.

By far the finest church in the neighbourhood is Linkinhorne (Llan Tighern), the church of the king, that is, of S. Melor. It was erected by Sir Henry Trecarrel, who built Launceston Church, but Linkinhorne is in far superior style. The story of S. Melor is this. He was the son of Melyan, prince of Devon and Cornwall and of Brittany. Melyan's brother was Riwhal, or Hoel the Great, cousin of King Arthur. Hoel, being an ambitious man, murdered his brother Melyan, and cut off the hand and foot of his nephew Melor, so as to incapacitate him from reigning; as a cripple, according to Celtic law, might not succeed to the headship of a clan or of aprincipality. In the place of the hand and foot of flesh and blood the boy was supplied with metal substitutes, and the hand was formed of silver.

For precaution the child was sent to Quimper, and placed there in a monastery.

Now it fell out that Melor and other boys were nutting in a wood, and his comrades made their little pile of hazel nuts and brought them to Melor. To their great surprise they found that, notwithstanding that his hand was of metal, he was able therewith to twitch off the nuts from the trees.

As the misfortunes of the unhappy prince attracted much sympathy, Howel sent for a man named Cerialtan, Melor's foster-father, and promised him an extensive grant of lands if he would make away quietly with the young prince. Cerialtan consented, and confided his purpose to his wife. She was horrified, and resolved on saving the boy. During her husband's temporary absence, she fled with her nephew to the wife of Count Conmor at Carhaix in Brittany, who was Melor's aunt. When Howel heard of this he was incensed, and urged Cerialtan to get the boy back into his power. Accordingly this worthless fellow took his son Justan with him, a lad who had been Melor's playmate, and to whom the young prince was much attached. The treacherous foster-father persuaded Melor that no harm was intended, and he and Justan were given the same bed as Melor in which to sleep.

During the night Cerialtan rose and cut the young prince's throat, then roused his son, and they escaped together over the walls of Carhaix. But in so doing Justan missed his hold and fell, and was killed.

On reaching the residence of Howel, Cerialtan produced the head of Melor, which he had cut off, in token that he had accomplished his undertaking. Howel grimly promised to show the man the lands he had promised him, but first put out his eyes.

In Brittany it is held that Melor was buried at Lan Meur, near Morlaix, but no tomb exists there, nor does there seem to have ever been one.

The whole story is legendary, yet certainly is framed about some threads of historic truth. But whether the murder was committed in Brittany or in Cornwall is uncertain. That Melor's father was assassinated in Cornwall I shall show later on to be probable. Mylor Church as well as Linkinhorne are dedicated to this boy martyr; Thornecombe Church in Dorset is also named after him, and it was held that his body had been transferred to Amesbury, where, during the Middle Ages, his relics attracted pilgrims.

From Callington a pleasing excursion may be made to the Cheesewring; and there is a very comfortable little inn there, where one can tarry and be well fed and cared for.

The height is a thousand feet, and the view thence over the fertile rolling land of Devon and East Cornwall is magnificent, contrasting strikingly with the desolation of the moors to the north. Here is Craddock Moor, taking its name in all probability from that Caradoc who ruled for Arthur in Gallewick, or Gelliwig.

The whole of the neighbourhood has been searched for metal, and the Phœnix Mines employed many hundreds of hands till the blight fell on Cornish tin mining, and they were shut down.

THE CHEESEWRING

The head of the Cheesewring hill has been enclosed in a stone *caer*. The common opinion is that every stone composing it was brought up from the bed of the Lynher, but this is almost certainly a fiction. The circles of the Hurlers are near, with a couple of outstanding stones. The legend is that some men were hurling the ball on Sunday, whilst a couple of pipers played to them. As a judgment for desecration of the Lord's-day they were all turned into stone. There are three circles, eleven stones in one, of which all but three have fallen; fourteen in the second, of which nine are standing; twelve in the third, but only five have not fallen. A curious instance of the persistency of tradition may be mentioned in connection with the cairn near the Hurlers and the Cheesewring, in which a gold cup was found a few years ago.

The story long told is that a party were hunting the wild boar in Trewartha Marsh. Whenever a hunter came near the Cheesewring a prophet--by whom an Archdruid is meant--who lived there received him, seated in the stone chair, and offered him to drink out of his golden goblet, and if there were as many as fifty hunters approach, each drank, and the goblet was not emptied. Now on this day of the boar hunt one of those hunting vowed that he would drink the cup dry. So he rode up to the rocks, and there saw the grey Druid holding out his cup. The hunter took the goblet and drank till he could drink no more, and he was so incensed at his failure that he dashed what remained of the wine in the Druid's face, and spurred his horse to ride away with the cup. But the steed plunged over the rocks and fell with his rider, who broke his neck, and as he still clutched the cup he was buried with it.

Immediately outside the rampart of the stone fort above the Cheesewring is a large natural block of granite, hollowed out by the weather into a seat called the Druid's Chair.

Just below the Cheesewring is a rude hut cell or cromlech, formed of large slabs of granite, which is called "Daniel Gumb's House." It was inhabited in the last century by an eccentric individual, who lived there, and brought up a family in a state of primæval savagery. On one of the jambs is inscribed, "D. Gumb, 1735," and on the top of the roofing slab is an incised figure of the diagram of Euclid's 47th proposition in the First Book.

At some little distance is the very fine cromlech called the Trethevy Stone. It is well worth a digression to see, as being, if not the finest, at least the most picturesque in Cornwall.

S. Cleer has a holy well in very good condition, carefully restored. Near it is a cross.

In the parish is the inscribed stone of Doniert, the British king, who was drowned in 872.

From Callington, Calstock--the stock or stockade in the Gelli district on the Tamar--may be visited. The river scenery is of the finest description, rolling coppice and jutting crags, the most beautiful portion being at Morwell.

ARSENIC MANUFACTURE

There are several arsenic works in this district. The mundic (mispickel-arsenic), which was formerly cast aside from the copper mines as worthless, is calcined.

The works consist in the crushing of the rock, it being chewed up by machinery; then the broken stone is gone over by girls, who in an inclined position select that which is profitable, and cast aside the stone without mundic in it. This is then ground and washed, and finally the ground mundic is burnt in large revolving cylinders.

The fumes given off in calcining are condensed in chambers for the purpose, and deposited in a snow-white powder. The arsenic is a heavy substance with a sweetish taste, and is soluble in water. In the process of calcining a large amount of sulphurous acid is given off--a pungent, suffocating gas--and this, escaping through the stack, is so destructive to trees and grass, that it blights the region immediately surrounding. When, however, a stack is of sufficient height the amount of damage done to herbage is greatly reduced, as at Greenhill, where there is a healthy plantation within two hundred yards of the stack.

When the workmen have to scrape out the receivers or condensers, the utmost precaution has to be taken against inhaling the dust of arsenic. The men engaged wear a protection over the mouth and nostrils, which consists in first covering the nostrils with lint, and then tying a folded handkerchief outside this with a corner hanging over the chin. When the arsenic soot has been scraped out of the flues and chambers in which it has condensed, it is packed in barrels.

Every precaution possible is adopted to reduce danger, but with certain winds gases escape in puffs from the furnace doors, which the men designate "smeeches," and these contain arsenic in a vaporised form, which has an extremely irritating effect on the bronchial tubes.

One great protection against arsenical sores is soap and water. Arsenic dust has a tendency to produce sore places about the mouth, the ankles, and the wrists. Moreover, if it be allowed to settle in any of the folds of the flesh it produces a nasty raw. On leaving their work the men are required to bathe and completely cleanse themselves from every particle of the poison that may adhere to them.

ARSENIC WORKS

As touching inadvertent arsenical poisoning, I will mention a circumstance that may be of use to some of my readers.

When living in the East of England I found my children troubled with obstinate sores, chiefly about the joints. They would not heal. I sent for the local doctor, and he tinkered at them, but instead of mending, the wounds got worse. This went on for many weeks. Suddenly an idea struck me. I had papered some of my rooms with highly æsthetic wall coverings by a certain well-known artist-poet who had a business in wall-papers. I passed my hand over the wall, and found that the colouring matter came off on my hand. At once I drove into the nearest town and submitted the paper to an analyst. He told me that it was charged with sulphuret of arsenic, common orpiment, and that as the glue employed for holding the paint had lost all power, this arsenical dust floated freely in the air. I at once sent my children away, and they had not been from home a week before they began to recover. Of course, all the wall-papers were removed.

About a month later I was in Freiburg, in Baden, and immediately on my arrival called on an old friend, and asked how he and all his were. "Only fairly well," he replied. "We are all--the young people especially--suffering from sores. Whether it is the food--"

"Or," said I, interrupting him, "the paper."

Then I told him my experience.

"Why," said he, "a neighbour, a German baron, has his children ill in the same way."

At once he ran into the baron's house and told him what I had said. Both proceeded immediately to the public analyst with specimens of the papers from the rooms in which the children slept. The papers were found to be heavily laden with arsenic.

Unhappily, in spite of all precautions, the work at the arsenic mine and manufactory is prejudicial to health. The workers are disabled permanently at an average age of forty. Of deaths in the district, eighty-three per cent. are due to respiratory diseases, while sixty-six per cent. are due to bronchitis alone. For the last three years, out of every hundred deaths among persons of all ages in the parish of Calstock twenty-six have been due to diseases of the respiratory organs, but out of every hundred employés at the arsenic works who have died or become disabled eighty-three deaths have been due to respiratory diseases. It is evident that with such an unusual proportion of one particular disease in the most able-bodied portion of the community there must be a definite existing cause.

No doubt that a very minute amount of arsenic may pass through the nostrils and down the throat, but what is far more prejudicial than that is the sulphurous acid which cannot be excluded by the handkerchief and lint, but passes freely through both. This is extremely irritating to the mucous membrane. But the fact of working for hours with the breathing impeded by the wraps about mouth and nose is probably the leading cause of the mischief.

Suggestions of remedies have been made, but none practical. A mask has been proposed, but this does not answer, as it causes sores, and is difficult to keep clean.

Devon Consols produces about 150 tons of arsenic per month; Gawlor, 100 tons; Greenhill, 50; Coombe, 25; and Devon Friendship about the same. In all about 350 tons per month. This to the workers is worth £10 per ton, or a revenue to the neighbourhood of £42,000 per annum.

In S. Mellion parish, on the Tamar, finely situated, is Pentillie Castle. The original name of the place was Pillaton, but it was bought by a man of the name of Tillie in the reign of James II., who called it after his own name. He was a self-made man, who was knighted, and not having any right to arms of his own, assumed those of Count Tilly, of the Holy Roman empire. But this came to the ears of the Herald's College, and an inquisition into the matter was made, and Sir James was fined, and his assumed arms were defaced and torn down.

He died in 1712, and by will required his adopted heir, one Woolley, his sister's son, not only to assume his name, but also not to inter his body in the earth, but to set it up in the chair in which he died, in hat, wig, rings, gloves, and his best apparel, shoes and stockings, and surround him with his books and papers, with pen and ink ready; and for the reception of his body to erect a walled chamber on a height, with a room above it in which his portrait was to be hung; and the whole was to be surmounted by a tower and spire.

About two hours before he died Sir James said, "In a couple of years I shall be back again, and unless Woolley has done what I have required, I will resume all again."

Mr. Woolley accordingly erected the tower that still stands above Sir James' vault. But the knight did not return. He crumbled away; moth and worm attacked his feathers and velvets; and after some years nothing was left of him but a mass of bone and dust that had fallen out of the chair.

CHAPTER VIII.

CAMELFORD

A rotten borough--Without a church or chapel-of-ease--History of the borough--Contest between the Earl of Darlington and Lord Yarmouth--Brown Willy and Rough Tor--Helborough--S. Itha--Slaughter Bridge--King Arthur--The reason for the creation of the Arthur myth--Geoffrey of Monmouth--The truth about King Arthur--The story of his birth--Damelioc and Tintagel--How it is that he appears in so many places--King Arthur's Hall--The remains of Tintagel--The Cornish chough--Crowdy Marsh--Brown Willy and the beehive cottages on it--Fernworthy--Lord Camelford--His story--Penvose--S. Tudy--Slate monuments--Basil--S. Kew--The Carminows--Helland--A telegram--Battle.

THAT this little town of a single street should have been a borough and have returned two members to Parliament is a surprise. It is a further surprise to find that it is a town without a church, and that no rector of Lanteglos, two miles distant, should have deemed it a scandal to leave it without even a chapel-of-ease is the greatest surprise of all.

Camelford was invested with the dignity of a borough in 1547, when it was under the control of the Roscarrock family. From them it passed to the Manatons living at Kilworthy, near Tavistock. Then it fell into the hands of an attorney named Phillipps. He parted with his interest to the Duke of Bedford, and he in turn to the Earl of Darlington, afterwards Duke of Cleveland.

The electors were the free burgesses paying scot and lot. "Scot" signifies taxes or rates. But the mayor was the returning officer, and he controlled the election.

In George IV.'s reign there was a warm contest between the Earl of Darlington and Lord Yarmouth. The latter ran up a great building, into which he crowded a number of faggot voters. But the Earl of Darlington possessed rights of search for minerals; so he drove a mine under this structure, and blew it up with gunpowder. The voters hearing what was purposed, ran away in time, and consequently Lord Yarmouth lost the election.

In the election of 1812 each voter received a hundred pounds for his vote. In the election of 1818 the mayor, Matthew Pope, announced his intention of giving the majority to Lord Darlington's nominee, and of turning out of their freeholds all who opposed. The other party had a club called "The Bundle of Sticks," and engaged a chemist named William Hallett, of S. Mary Axe, to manage the election for them, and put £6000 into his hand to distribute among the electors, £400 apiece.

Hanmer and Stewart got ten votes apiece, Milbrook and Maitland thirteen. But there was an appeal, and a new election; but this again led to a petition, and a scandalous story was told of bribery and corruption of the most barefaced description. The election was declared void, and many persons, including Hallett, the chemist, were reported. It was proposed to disfranchise the borough, but George III. died in 1820, and new writs had to be at once issued.

Camelford has no public buildings of interest. It is situate on very high ground, on a wind-blown waste 700 feet above the sea, exposed to furious gales from the Atlantic; but it has this advantage, that it forms headquarters for an excursion to the Bodmin moors, to Brown Willy (1375 feet), and Rough Tor (1250 feet). These tors, though by no means so high as those on Dartmoor, are yet deserving of a visit, on account of their bold outlines, the desolation of the wilderness out of which they rise, and the numerous relics of antiquity strewn over the moors about them.

Of these presently.

The parish church of Camelford, two miles off, is Lanteglos. The dedication is to S. Julitta, but this would seem to have been a rededication, and the true patroness to have been either Jutwara or Jutwell, sister of St. Sidwell, or of Ilut, one of King Brythan's daughters.

There was a royal deer-park there, as the old castle of Helborough, though not occupied, was in the possession of the Duke of Cornwall.

This is really a prehistoric camp of Irish construction, and in the midst of it are the ruins of a chapel to S. Sith or Itha, the Bridget of Munster. Itha had a number of churches ranging from the Padstow estuary to Exeter, showing that this portion of Dumnonia received colonists from the south-west of Ireland. Her name is disguised as Issey and as Teath. She was a remarkable person, as it was she who sent her foster-son Brendan with three ships, manned by thirty in each, on an exploring excursion across the Atlantic to the west, which, possibly, led to the discovery of Madeira in the sixth century. But the truth is so disguised by fable that little certainty can be obtained as to the results of the voyage. Brendan made, in fact, two expeditions; in the first his ships were of wicker, with three coats of leather over the basket frame; the second time, by Itha's advice, he made his boats of timber.

Itha never was herself in Cornwall, her great foundation was Kill-eedy in Limerick, and she was taken as the tutelary saint or patroness of Hy-Conaill, but there were establishments, daughters of the parent house, what the Irish called daltha (*i.e.* pupil) churches, enjoying much the same rights as the mother house.

Camelford has by some been supposed to be the Gavulford where the last battle was fought between the West Welsh and Athelstan; but there was no reason for his advancing into Cornwall this way, where all was bleak, and by no old road.

There is, however, a Slaughter Bridge on the Camel, but this is taken to have acquired its name from having been the scene of the fight between King Arthur and his rebellious nephew Mordred, *circ.* 537.

King Arthur is a personage who has had hard measure dealt out to him. That there was such an individual one can hardly doubt. There is a good deal of evidence towards establishing his existence. He was chief king over all the Britons from Cornwall to Strathclyde (*i.e.* the region from the Firth of Clyde to Cumberland). He was constantly engaged, first in one part, then in another, against the Saxons; but his principal battles were fought in Scotland. He occurs in the Welsh accounts of the saints, but never as a hero, always as a despot and tyrant. His immediate predecessor, Geraint, in like manner is met with, mainly in Cornwall, but also in Wales, where he had a church, and in Herefordshire. He had to keep the frontier against the Saxons.

What played the mischief with Arthur was that Geoffrey of Monmouth, who became bishop of S. Asaph in 1152, published, about 1140, his fabulous *History of the Britons*, which elevated Arthur into a hero. Geoffrey had an object in view when he wrote this wonderful romance. The period was one in which the Welsh had been horribly maltreated, dispossessed of their lands, their churches taken from them and given to Normans, who neither understood their language nor regarded their traditions. The foreigners had castles planted over the country filled with Norman soldiery, tormenting, plundering, insulting the natives. Poor Wales wept tears of blood. Now Henry I. had received the beautiful Nest, daughter of Rhys, king of South Wales, as a hostage when her father had fallen in battle, and, instead of respecting his trust, he had wronged her in her defenceless condition in a cruel manner, and had by her a son, Robert,

84

who was raised by him to be Duke of Gloucester. To this Robert, half Welsh, Geoffrey dedicated his book, a glorification of the British kings, a book that surrounded the past history of the Welsh with a halo of glory. The book at once seized on the imagination of English and Normans, and a change took place in the way in which the Welsh were regarded. The triumph of the Saxon over the Briton came to be viewed in an entirely new light, as that of brutality over heroic virtue.

Geoffrey succeeded in his object, but he produced bewilderment among chroniclers and historians, and seriously influenced them when they began to write on the history of England.

KING ARTHUR

Now, although all the early portion of Geoffrey's work is a *tour de force* of pure imagination, yet he was cautious enough as he drew near to historic times, of which records were still extant, to use historic facts and work them into his narrative, so that in the latter portion all is not unadulterated fable; it is a hotch-potch of fact and fiction, with a preponderance of the latter, indeed, but not without some genuine history mixed up with it. The difficulty his book presents now is to discriminate between the false and the true.

As far as can be judged, it is true that Arthur was son of Uthr, who was Pendragon, or chief king of the Britons, and of Igerna, wife of the Duke of Cornwall, whom Geoffrey calls Gorlois, but who is otherwise unknown. Uthr saw Igerna at a court feast, and "continually served her with tit-bits, and sent her golden cups, and bestowed on her all his smiles, and to her addressed his whole discourse." Gorlois naturally objected, and removed his wife into Cornwall, and refused to attend the king when summoned to do so. Uthr now marched against him. The Duke placed Igerna in the cliff-castle of Tintagel, but himself retreated into Damelioc, a strong caer, that remains almost intact, in the parish of S. Kew. Uthr invested Damelioc, and whilst Gorlois was thus hemmed in he went to Tintagel and obtained admission by an artifice. Gorlois was killed in a sally, Damelioc was taken and plundered, and Uthr made Igerna his wife. It was the old story over again of David and the wife of Uriah the Hittite.

The result of this union was a son, Arthur, and a daughter, Ann, who eventually became the wife of Lot, king of Lothian, and mother of Modred.

We have no means of checking this story and saying how much of it is fact and how much false. But it is worth pointing out that in Geoffrey's account there is one significant thing mentioned that looks much like truth. He says that when Uthr was marching against him, Gorlois at once appealed for help from Ireland. Now, considering that all this district was colonised by Irish and half-Irish, this is just what a chieftain of the country would have done, but Geoffrey almost certainly knew nothing of this colonisation. Moreover, he had something to go upon with regard to Damelioc and Tintagel, unless, which is hardly likely, he had lived some time in North-eastern Cornwall, and had seen the earthworks of the former and the fortified headland of the latter, and so was able to use them up in his fabulous tale.

Damelioc is but five or six miles from Tintagel, and in Geoffrey's story they are represented as at no great distance apart. Had Geoffrey been in this part of Cornwall and invented the whole story, he would have been more likely to make Gorlois take refuge in the far stronger and more commanding Helbury, occupying a conical height 700 feet above the sea, than Damelioc, 500 feet, only, on an extensive plateau. King Arthur has been so laid hold of by the romancers, and his story has been so embellished with astounding flourishes of the imagination, that we are inclined to doubt whether he ever existed, and all the more so because we find legend attached to him and associated with localities alike in Cornwall, Wales, and Scotland. Mr. Skene has shown very good cause for identifying the sites of some of his battles with remains of fortifications in Scotland.[9] How, then, can we account for his presence in Cornwall and Wales? As a matter of fact, this is perfectly explicable. The Saxons held possession of the whole east of Britain as far as the ridge which runs between Yorkshire and Lancashire; as also the region about Leeds, which latter constituted the kingdom of Elmet. Needwood and Arden forests lay between the rival people. Strathclyde, Cumberland, Rheged, now Lancashire, all Wales, with Powis occupying Shropshire and Cheshire, Gloucester, Bath, and Dumnonia, extending through Cornwall, Devon, and Somerset, formed one great confederation of Britons under a head king. Geraint had previously been head of the confederacy, and we find traces of him accordingly in Cornwall, Somerset, Wales, and at Hereford. The Pendragon, or chief king, had to be at every post along the frontier that was menaced. So with Arthur; he was in Cornwall, indeed, but he was also in Wales, where he is spoken of in the lives of some of the saints, as we have seen, always as a bully. And he was in Scotland opposing the advance of the Bernicians. His father, Uthr, had been head king before him, but Geraint had been chosen as Pendragon on the death of Uthr; Geraint fell in 522, and it is held that Arthur perished in 537. There are several reminiscences of King Arthur in the district. At Slaughter Bridge he is thought to have fallen. Above Camelford rise Dinnevor (Dinnas-vawr), the Great Castle, and King Arthur's Downs, with a singular oblong rectangular structure on it called King Arthur's Hall, the purport of which has not been discovered. At Tintagel are his cups and saucers, hollows in the rock, and his spirit is said to haunt the height as a monstrous white gull wailing over the past glories of Britain. At Killmar is his bed. At Tintagel is Porthiern, which is either the Iron Port or that of Igerna, Arthur's mother; at Boscastle is Pentargon (Arthur's Head). The Christian name of Gwenivere, his faithless wife, is still by no means rare, as Genefer.

Tintagel is but a fragment. There was anciently a rift with a bridge over it between one court of the castle and the other; but the rift has expanded to a gaping mouth, and rock and wall have fallen to form a mound of *débris* that now connects the mainland with what, but for this heap, would be an islet.

TINTAGEL

Tintagel, properly Dun-diogl, the "Safe Castle," has been built of the black slate rock, with shells burnt for lime. A few fragments of wall remain on the mainland, and a few more on the island, where is also the ruin of a little chapel, with its stone altar still *in situ*. The situation is superb, and were the ruins less ruinous, the scene from the little bay that commands the headland would be hardly surpassed. On Barras Head, opposite, a company are erecting a fashionable modern hotel.

About the cliffs may still be seen the Cornish chough, with its scarlet legs, but the bird is becoming scarce. The south coast of Cornwall is now entirely deserted by the choughs, and the only remaining colonies are found at intervals on the side facing the Atlantic. Unhappily visitors are doing their utmost to get them exterminated by buying the young birds that are caught and offered for sale. But the jackdaws are also driving them, and probably in-and-in breeding is leading to their diminution. The choughs not being migratory birds, and sticking much to the same localities, those who desire to obtain their eggs or rob the nests of the young know exactly which are their haunts year by year.

"The free wild temperament of choughs," writes Mr. A. H. Malan, "will not brook any confinement, but must have absolute liberty and full exercise for their wings. If this is not the case, they generally get an attack of asthma, which usually proves fatal, in their first year.

"Everyone has seen a chough, if only in a museum; and therefore knows the beautiful glossy black of the adult plumage, the long wings crossed over the back and extending beyond the squared tail, the long, slender red legs, and the brilliant red curved bill. But only those who have kept them know their marvellous docility. You may train a falcon to sit on your wrist and come down to the lure, with infinite labour; but to a chough brought up from the nest it comes quite natural to be at one moment flying in high air--it may be hotly pursued by a party of rooks, and leading them a merry dance, since, being long-winged birds, choughs hold the rooks, crows, and jackdaws very cheap, inasmuch as these baser creatures can never come near enough to injure them--and the next to come in at the open window, alight on the table, or jump on one's knee and sit there any length of time, absolutely still, while the head and back are stroked with the hand or a pen, combining the complete confidence of a cat or a dog with the wild freedom of the swallow. No other bird with which I am acquainted thus unites the perfection of tameness with the limitless impetuosity of unreclaimed nature."[10]

Brown Willy and Rough Tor are fine hills rising out of really ghastly bogs, Crowdy and Stannon and Rough Tor marshes, worse than anything of the sort on Dartmoor, places to which you hardly desire to consign your worst enemies, always excepting promoters of certain companies. I really should enjoy seeing them flounder there.

Brown Willy (*bryn geled*=conspicuous hill) has five heads, and these are crowned with cairns.

Owing mainly to the remoteness of this mountain from the habitations of men, and from the mischievous activity of stone quarriers for buildings, there are scattered about this stately five-pointed tor some very interesting relics of antiquity, of an antiquity that goes back to prehistoric times. Among these most interesting of all are the beehive huts that cluster about the granite rocks like the mud nests of swallows.

The whole of the Cornish moors, like Dartmoor, are strewn with prehistoric villages and towns of circular houses, sometimes within rings of rude walling that served as a protection to the settlement, and connected with enclosures for the cattle against wolves. But though in many cases the doorways remain, of upright jambs with a rude lintel of granite thrown across, complete examples roofed in are rare, and those to which we direct attention now are known to very few persons indeed. The huts in question measure internally from six to eight feet in diameter; the walls are composed of moorstones rudely laid in courses, without having been touched by any tool or bedded in mortar. The walls are some two to three feet thick. Sometimes they are formed of two concentric rings of stones set upright in the ground, filled in between with smaller stones, but such huts were never stone-roofed. Beehive-roofed they were, but with their dome formed of oak boughs brought together in the centre, the ends resting on these walls, and the whole thatched with straw or heather or fern. But the stone-built and roofed huts have walls of granite blocks laid in courses, and after five feet they are brought to dome over by the overlapping of the coverers, in the primitive fashion that preceded the invention of the arch.

BEEHIVE HUT (Beehive Hut Fernaker, Logan Rock Lenden,

Section of the Fernaker Hut.)
(By kind permission of "The Daily Graphic")
The roof was thus gathered in about a smoke-hole, which was itself finally closed with a wide, thin granite slab, and thus the whole roof and sides were buried in turf, so that the structure resembled a huge ant-hill. Most of this encasing flesh and skin has gone, and the bone beneath is exposed. Nevertheless; it does remain in some cases, and has been the means of preserving these curious structures. One such, very perfect, is on the river Erme, above Piles Wood, on Dartmoor. Into this it is quite possible to crawl and take refuge from a shower. It is completely watertight, but it is not easy to find, as it is overgrown with dense masses of heather. Another is close to the farmhouse of Fernaker, between Brown Willy and Rough Tor, and it has been spared because the farmer thought it might serve his purpose as a pig-sty or a butter-house. This Fernaker hut is rudely quadrangular, and one side is formed by a great block of granite rising out of the ground five feet and nine feet long. On this basis the house has been built and roofed in the usual manner by five courses of overlapping stones. The highest peak of Brown Willy is occupied by a huge cairn that has never been explored, owing to the expense and labour of working into it. It probably covers some old Cornish king. Immediately below it, some forty feet, are two beehive huts, in very fair condition, one eight feet in diameter, with a second, much smaller, only four feet six inches in diameter, close to it, opposite the door, with an entrance so small that it probably served as a store-chamber. One huge slab of granite, some twelve feet long and six feet wide, forms half the roof of the larger hut; the remainder has fallen in.

On the other side of Brown Willy, the west side, at no great distance from the source of the river Fowey, is another beehive hut, not absolutely perfect, but nearly so; one course and the smoke-hole coverer have fallen in on one side. The doors to these hovels are so low that he who enters one must crawl on hands and knees. In the beehive hut last mentioned the height in the middle is but three feet six inches, so that those who tenanted it could not stand upright inside. On Rough Tor, divided from Brown Willy by a valley, are three or four more of these huts, and the flanks of the mountains are covered with others, hundreds of them, in a more or less dilapidated condition. Some of these were originally stone-roofed; others were not. In connection with these remains of habitations are numerous relics of interments at some distance from them, for our primeval population always buried their dead away from the living. These consist of cairns, covering stone coffins or kistvaens that have been for the most part rifled by treasure-seekers. One has a somewhat pathetic interest, for beside the large stone chest just outside the ring of upright stones that encloses it is a child's cist, formed of four blocks of granite two feet seven inches long, the covering-stone removed, and the contents scattered to the winds. Near at hand also is the largest circle of upright stones in Cornwall. The stones themselves are not tall, and are much sunk in the boggy soil, but it is very perfect, consisting of fifty-five stones, and 140 feet in diameter. On the neighbouring height of Leudon is a logan rock that still oscillates easily. The question naturally arises, Do these beehive huts actually date back to prehistoric times? That is not a question we can answer with certainty, for we know that the same methods of construction were observed to a comparatively late period, and that in the Isles of Lewis and Harris, in the Hebrides, precisely similar huts are even now inhabited, and are certainly in many cases of recent construction. But what is extremely interesting to find is the existence in Cornwall of these beehive habitations of man exactly like those found in Scotland; and in Cornwall, as in Scotland, associated with rude stone monuments of pre-Christian times. In the Hebrides the beehive huts still occupied are not stone-roofed. The roof is of straw, and is renewed every year because of the value as manure of the peat smoke that saturates it. But there remain earlier beehive huts in Lewis of exactly the same nature as those in Cornwall. It is therefore by no means unlikely that both belong to the primitive race that first colonised our isles.

Camelford has given a title, and that to a remarkable man, Lord Camelford, the duellist. He was the great-grandson of Governor Pitt, who acquired an ample fortune in India. He was born in 1775, and even when a boy was violent and unmanageable. He was put in the navy, but owing to his refractory conduct was treated with severity by his captain, Vancouver, and on his return home, meeting Vancouver in Bond Street, was only prevented from striking his captain by his brother throwing himself in the way.

In town he was incessantly embroiled. On the night of April 2nd, 1799, during a disturbance at Drury Lane Theatre, he savagely attacked and wounded a gentleman, and was fined for so doing the sum of £500 by the Court of Queen's Bench. He attacked watchmen, insulted anyone who crossed his humour in the least degree, committed all kinds of violence, till his name became a terror, and he was involved in first one quarrel and then in another. His irritable and ungovernable temper at length brought about fatal consequences to himself. He had been acquainted with a Mrs. Simmons. He was told that a Captain Best had reported to her a bit of scandal relative to himself. This so incensed his lordship, that on March 6th, 1804, meeting with Best at a coffee-house, he went up to him, and in the hearing of everyone called him "a scoundrel, a liar, and a ruffian." A challenge followed, and the meeting was fixed for the next morning. The seconds having ascertained the occasion of Lord Camelford's wrath, Best declared himself ready to apologise, and to retract any words that had given offence which he had used to Mrs. Simmons, but his lordship refused to accept such an apology. Agreeably to an appointment made by the seconds, Lord Camelford and the captain met early next morning at a coffee-house in Oxford Street, where Captain Best made another effort to prevail on Lord Camelford to make up the quarrel and to withdraw the expressions he had addressed to him in public. To all remonstrance he replied, "Let it go on."

Accordingly both mounted their horses and took the road to Kensington, followed by their seconds in a post-chaise. On their arrival at the "Horse and Groom" they dismounted, and entered the fields behind Holland House. The seconds measured the ground, and took their stations at the distance of thirty paces. Lord Camelford fired first, but without effect. An interval ensued, and those who looked on from a distance believed that Best was again urging his lordship to come to amicable terms. But Lord Camelford shook his head; then Best fired, and his lordship fell at full length. The seconds, together with the captain, at once ran to his assistance, when he seized his antagonist by the hand and said, "Best, I am a dead man; you have killed me, but I freely forgive you." The report of the pistols had attracted the attention of some of Lord Holland's gardeners and servants, who ran to the spot and endeavoured to arrest Captain Best and his second, who were making off. Lord Camelford asked "why they endeavoured to detain the gentlemen; he himself was the aggressor, and he frankly forgave the gentleman who had shot him, and he hoped that God would forgive him as well."

A chair was procured, and Lord Camelford was carried into Little Holland House, where he expired after three days of suffering.

On the morning after his decease an inquest was held on the body, and a verdict of wilful murder was returned against "some person or persons unknown." A bill of indictment was, however, preferred against Captain Best and his second, but was ignored by the grand jury, who were sensible that Lord Camelford had brought his death on himself.

In the neighbourhood of Camelford are several very charming old mansions of Cornish families, small but eminently picturesque, all now converted into farmhouses. In next generation they will not be considered good enough for labourers. One of these is Penvose in S. Tudy, another Trewane, hard by the station of Port Isaac Road. Both these belonged to the Nicholls family, to two brothers it is said, and the magnificent carved slate monuments of the family are to be seen in S. Tudy Church. The slate in this district was sculptured in a way really marvellous, and there are numerous examples in the churches round. In S. Endellion are Treshunger, the seat of the Matthews family, and Rosecarrock--a fragment only. Basil, previously mentioned, is in S. Clether. It belonged to the Trevillians. One day a party of Roundheads came to Basil to seize on the squire. Trevillian looked out of the window. "If you come on," said he, "I will send out my spearmen against you." As they *did* come on, he threw a beehive among them, and away they fled, every man. Near Slaughter Bridge is Worthyvale, the seat of a family of the same name.

The churches of this district are planted, some on the top of hills, and with high towers, to serve as waymarks over land that was all formerly waste, or else nestle into sweet dells surrounded by Cornish elms--warm, sunny nooks where the primrose comes out early and the grass is emerald-green all the winter. Of the former description are S. Tudy and S. Mabyn. Of the latter S. Kew, a church on no account to be passed over, as it is not only singularly beautiful and well restored, but alsocontains superb old glass, moved from Bodmin Priory at its dissolution. One window represents the Passion, and is perfect; another once contained a Jesse tree, but is much broken and defective.

S. Kew is really Docwin, otherwise called Cyngar, the founder of Congresbury, in Somersetshire. He was a son of Gildas the historian, that sour creature who threw all the dirt he could at the princes, people, and clergy of his own blood and tongue, and told us the least possible about their history, filling his pages with pious scurrility.

In S. Teath (S. Itha) is a very fine churchyard cross. Here may be noticed the arms of the Carminow family, once perhaps the most powerful in Cornwall, now gone—without a living representative remaining of the name. A junior branch was settled at Trehannick, in S. Teath, at which place William Carminow died in 1646, the last male heir of this ancient family, which was at home when the Conqueror came. Their arms are simplicity itself—azure, a bend or—the same as those of Scrope and of Grosvenor. In the reign of Richard II. there was a great heraldic dispute over these arms, and it was carried before the Earl of Northampton, who was king of arms, and was then in France. As the Carminows could show that they had borne this coat from time immemorial, certainly as long as any Scropes and Grosvenors, it was allowed.

If there be churches dedicated to odd and out-of-the-way saints in this region, there be also parishes with odd and out-of-this-world names, as Helland and Blisland. Of the former a tale circulates.

The vicar was going to town, and hoped that the Archdeacon of Cornwall could be induced to take his service on the Sunday following, and he left it to his neighbour at Blisland to negotiate this little arrangement for him. All went well, and the latter gave in a telegram at the nearest office:--

"The Archdeacon of Cornwall is going to Helland; you need not return."

But when it was delivered in London it was thus divided:--

"The Archdeacon of Cornwall is going to Hell; and you need not return."

Slaughter Bridge, the scene as reputed of the fatal battle between Arthur and his nephew Modred, should be seen, a bleak spot hard by Camelford Road Station. Under a rock, prostrate by the river-bank, lies an early inscribed stone to Latinus, son of Macari, an Irish form of name. Here--

"All day long the noise of battle roll'd
Among the mountains by the winter sea;
Until King Arthur's Table, man by man,
Had fall'n in Lyonness about their Lord."

CHAPTER IX.

BUDE

An ugly place--Its charm in the air--Stratton--The battle of Stamford Hill--Churches--Norman remains--Frescoes at Poughill--Pancras Week--Bench-ends--Tonnacombe--Marhayes--Old Stowe--Church towers--Landmarks--The candle-end in Bridgerule Church--Bridget churches--The clover-field--Ogbeare Hall--Whitstone--Camps--Thomasine Bonaventura--Week S. Mary--The coast about Bude--Morwenstow--Robert S. Hawker--One of his ballads.

AN unpicturesque, uninteresting place, windblown, treeless, but with sands--not always obtainable on the north coast--and with noble cliff scenery within easy reach.

There is nothing commendable in the place itself; the houses are as ugly as tasteless builders could contrive to erect; the church is of the meanest cheap Gothic of seventy years ago; but the air is exhilarating, the temperature is even, there are golf-links, and a shore for bathers.

BUDE

Nestling in a valley by a little stream newly designated the "Strat," as though Stratton were called from the stream and not the street--the Roman road that runs through it--is the parent town, crouching with its hair ruffled, and casting a sidelong, dissatisfied eye at its pert and pushing offspring, Bude. But Stratton has no reason to be discontented. It is sheltered from the furious gales, which Bude is not; it has trees and flowers about it, which Bude has not; it has a fine parish church, which Bude has not; and it has a history, deficient to Bude, which is a parvenu, and self-assertive accordingly.

And Stratton further has got its battlefield. The height above the town was the scene of one of those encounters in which the Royalist forces for Charles I. were successful. The following description of the battle is from Professor Gardiner's *History of the Great Civil War*:--[11]

"The Earl of Stamford placed himself at the head of the army under his command, and resolved on carrying the war into Cornwall. As he could dispose of 6800 men, whilst Hopton and the Cornish leaders at Launceston had with them less than half the number, he determined to despatch the greater part of his horse to Bodmin in order to suppress any attempt to muster the trained bands there. With his infantry and a few remaining horse he established himself near Stratton, in the extreme north-west of the county, in a position apparently strong enough to secure him from attack, at least till his cavalry returned.

"The ground occupied by Stamford was well chosen. A ridge of high ground running from the north to south parallel with the coast dips sharply down, and rises as sharply again to a grassy hill, from the southern end of which there is a still deeper cleft through which the road descends steeply to the left into the valley in which lies the little town of Stratton. On the top of this hill, the sides of which slope in all directions from the highest point to the edge of the plateau, the Parliamentary army lay. Beyond this plateau the ground falls away in all directions, more especially on the eastern side, where the position was almost impregnable if seriously defended. The ascent from the west was decidedly the easiest, but an earthwork had been thrown up on this side, the guns from which commanded the whole approach from this quarter.[12]

"Undismayed by the odds against them, Hopton and his comrades resolved to break up from Launceston in order to seek the enemy. As they approached Stratton on the morning of the 16th (May, 1643) they had the advantage of having amongst them one to whom every inch of ground must have been perfectly familiar. But a few miles to the north, on the bleak hillside above the waves of the Atlantic, lay that house of Stowe from which Sir Richard Grenville had gone forth to die in the *Revenge*, and where doubtless the Lady Grenville of a younger generation was watching anxiously for the return of him who had ventured his life in the king's quarrel. It would have been strange if on this day of peril the ordering of the fight had not fallen into Sir Bevil Grenville's hands.

"The little army of Royalists consisted of but 2400, whilst their adversaries could number 5400, well provided with cannon and ammunition. The attacking force was divided into four bands, prepared to storm, or at least to threaten, the hill from every side. For some hours every effort was in vain against superiority of numbers and superiority of position. At three in the afternoon word was brought to the commanders that their scanty stock of powder was almost exhausted. A retreat under such circumstances would have been fatal, and the word was given that a supreme effort must be made. Trusting to pike and sword alone, the lithe Cornishmen pressed onwards and upwards. Their silent march seems to have struck their opponents with a sense of power. The defence grew feeble, and on the easier western slope, where Grenville fought, and on the northern, on which Sir John Berkeley led the attack, the outer edge of the plateau was first gained. Immediately the handful of horse which had remained with Stamford turned and fled, the commander-in-chief, it is said, setting the example. In vain Chudleigh, now second in command, rallied the force for a desperate charge. For a moment he seemed to make an impression on the approaching foe, but he incautiously pressed too far in advance, and was surrounded and captured. His men, left without a commander, at once gave way, and retreated to the further part of the plateau. By this time the other two Royalist detachments, finding resistance slackening, had made their way up, and the victorious commanders embraced one another on the hard-won hill-top, thanking God for a success for which at one time they had hardly ventured to hope. It was no time to prolong their rejoicings, as the enemy, demoralised as he was, still clung to the heights. Seizing the cannons which had been abandoned in the earthwork, the Royalist commanders turned them upon Stamford's cowed followers. The frightened men had no one to encourage them to deeds of hardihood, and, following the example of the cavalry, they too dashed down the slope in headlong flight. Of the Parliamentary soldiers, 300 had been killed and 1700 were taken prisoners, besides Chudleigh and thirty of his officers. All the cannon, with a large store of ammunition and provisions, fell into the hands of the victors. From that day the spot on which the wealthy earl demonstrated his signal incompetence as a leader of men has been known as Stamford Hill."

The scene of the battle deserves a visit, as it has remained almost unaltered since that day. Whether the earthworks belong to the period or were earlier, utilised by Stamford, remains open to question. They hardly seem disposed with skill and intelligence for the use of cannon.

The Royalists were not merely about half in number to the Roundheads, but they were short of ammunition, and without cannon. They were also "so destitute of provisions, that the best officers had but a biscuit a man."

A monument erected on the hill in commemoration of the battle was destroyed a few years ago, and the plate with an inscription on it recording the victory moved to the front of a house in Stratton.

There is a good deal to be seen in the way of old houses and churches near Bude. Stratton Church itself is fine, and contains a good tomb of an Arundell. It has suffered less than most of the sacred edifices in the neighbourhood from the wrecker. Week S. Mary under his hands has become a shell out of which life and beauty have fled. Morwenstow has been reduced to nakedness, but its grand Norman pillars and arches and doorway remain. Kilkhampton has been lovingly treated and the wrecker held at bay. It also has a Norman doorway, and very fine bench-ends; Poughill has these latter, also two frescoes of S. Christopher that have been restored--one, through a blunder, as King Olaf. The idea grew up in the fifteenth century that he who looked on a figure of S. Christopher would not that day die a sudden death. Consequently representations of the saint were multiplied. On the river Wulf in Devon at a ford it was held that at night anyone who came to the side of the water and cried out was caught up and carried over by a gigantic spirit, and there are those alive who protest that they have been so transported across the Wulf. Recently the County Council has built a bridge, and so this spectral Christopher's occupation is gone.

Pancras Week has a very fine waggon roof of richly-carved wood. Holsworthy is a good church well restored. Here during the restoration a skeleton was found in the wall, evidently hastily covered up with mortar and stone.

At Poundstock and Launcells are good bench-ends. The most interesting old house in the district, because best preserved, is Tonnacombe in Morwenstow, very small, with hall and minstrel gallery and panelled parlours, but perfect and untouched by the restorer, except in the most conservative manner.

Penfound in Poundstock, the seat of the ancient family of Penfound, is in a condition verging on ruin. The family has its representatives in Bude as plain labourers. The last squire died in the poor-house in 1847.

What is so delightful about these old Cornish houses is the way that, in a wind-swept region, they nestle into leafy combes.

Elford, now the parsonage of Bude, was the seat of the Arundells, but it has been so altered as to have lost most of its character. Marhamchurch has a good Jacobean pulpit, and in the parish is Marhayes, an interesting house, the basement Tudor, on top of which a Charles II. house was reared. In one room is a superb ceiling of plaster-work. At Dunsland is another, richer, but not so good in design. Sutcombe Church has the remains of a remarkably good screen and some bench-ends. The church has been judiciously restored and not wrecked.

In Poughill, close to Bude, old Broom Hill, now turned into cottages, has a good Elizabethan ceiling. It was here that Sir Bevil Grenville slept the night before the battle of Stamford Hill.

In the deep glen that leads from Kilkhampton to the sea is the site of Stowe House, built by John, Earl of Bath, in 1680. The title became extinct in 1711, and Stowe became the property of the widow of Lord Carteret, who was created Countess Grenville. The house was pulled down in 1720, so that the same persons saw it built and saw its destruction. The Earl of Bath had the best artists brought there to decorate the mansion, and it is due to this that so much splendid plaster-work is to be seen in North-east Cornwall and near Holsworthy. An exquisite plaster ceiling of delicate refinement and beauty existed at Whitstone, but was destroyed by the owner of the house, who had not any idea of its artistic beauty.

Marsland in Morwenstow, without any architectural features, is a charming example of a small country squire's house of the seventeenth century. Stowe Barton, though much altered and spoiled, is the ancient seat of the Grenvilles; that has stood, whilst the splendid mansion has disappeared, leaving only its terraces to show where it once was.

Bridgerule Church stands high; its tower, that of Pancras Week, and that of Week S. Mary were landmarks when all the land except the combes was a great furzy and rushy waste. The soil is cold, clayey, and unproductive. It serves for the breeding of horses and for rough stock, and grew grain when grain-growing paid; now it is reverting to moor, but anciently it was entirely uncultivated and open, saving in the valleys. Bridgerule has a fine tower, and in the church is a respectable modern screen, though not of local character. About the rood-loft door hangs a tale.

There was a widow who had a beautiful daughter, and one evening a gentleman in a carriage drawn by four black horses and with a black-liveried driver on the box drove to the cottage door. The gentleman descended. He was a swarthy but handsome man. He entered the cottage on some excuse, sat by the fire and talked, and eyed the damsel. Then he called, and his liveried servant brought in wines from the sword-case of his carriage, and they drank, till the fire was in their veins, and the gentleman asked the girl if she would accompany him home if he came for her on the following night. She consented. He would arrive at midnight, so he said.

Now next morning the mother's mind misgave her, and she went to Bridgerule and consulted the parson. Said he, "That was the devil. Did you see his feet?"

"No--that is, I saw one," said the widow. "One that was stretched out by the fire, but the other he kept under the chair, and he had let fall his cloak over it. But I did notice that he limped as he walked."

"Now," said the parson, "here is a consecrated candle; it has burned on the altar. Take it home, and when the visitor asks your wench to go with him, let her say she will do so as soon as the candle is burnt out. He will consent. At once take the candle and run to Bridgerule Church and give it to me, and see what happens."

Next night the woman lit the candle and set it on the table, and it burnt cheerily. But just before midnight the tramp of horses was heard and the roll of wheels, and the black coach drew up at her door and the gentleman descended. He entered the cottage and asked if Genefer were ready to attend him.

"She is upstairs dressing in her Sunday gown," replied the mother.

"I am impatient; let her come as she is," said the stranger.

"Suffer her to have time till this candle burns into the socket," asked the mother.

"I consent, but not for a moment longer," was his reply.

Then the widow took the candle, and saying she went in quest of her daughter, she left the room, went out at the back door, extinguished the candle, and ran till she reached the church, where the parson awaited her with his clerk, who was a mason. He took the candle, gave it to his clerk, who placed it in a recess in the wall, and at once proceeded to build up the recess.

The mother hastened home. But as she came to a moor called Affaland she saw the coach drawn by four black horses arrive on it, and proceed to a pool that was there, but is now dried up or drained away, and in went horses, driver, coach, and all, and a great spout of blue flame came up where they descended, and after that, they were seen no more. When she came home, she found her daughter in a dead faint.

Now that candle remains behind the wall that closes up the rood-stair door. And the devil cannot claim the girl, because the candle is not burnt out. But if ever that wall be pulled down and the candle be removed, and anyone be wicked enough to burn it, then he will ascend from the place of outer darkness and the gnashing of teeth, and snatch the soul of Genefer away, even though it be in Abraham's bosom.

Bridgerule is Llan-Bridget, that was granted at the Conquest to a certain Raoul. It is one of the cluster of Bridget churches that are found near the Tamar, of which the others are Virginstow and Bridestow, and Landue--now only a house with a holy well of S. Bridget and the foundations of a chapel. Clearly there was in this district a colony from Leinster, from Magh Brea, the great plain in which Bridget had her foundations. S. Bridget was a real person, and one of great force of character; but what gave her such an enormous popularity in Ireland was that she inherited the name of one of the old pagan goddesses, she of the fire, also the earth mother, and the great helper of women in their trouble.

When the real Bridget saw the vast plain in Leinster covered with white clover, from which the wind that wafted over it was sweet as if it had breathed from paradise, "Oh!" said she, "if this lovely plain were mine I would give it to God."

S. Columba heard this story. He smiled, and said, "God accepts the will for the deed. It is the same to Him as if Bridget had freely given Him the wide white clover field."

The centre of the cult of S. Bridget in ancient Dumnonia must have been Bridestow, for there is a sanctuary which marks the main monastic establishment.

One day a party of bishops and clergy arrived at Bridget's house of Kildare very hungry and clamorous for food, and particularly desirous to know what they were going to have for dinner.

"Now," said Bridget, "I and my spiritual daughters also suffer from hunger. We have not the Word of God ministered to us but exceptionally when a stray priest comes this way. Let us go to church first, and do ye feed us with spiritual nourishment whilst dinner is getting ready, and then do you eat your fill."

It is a long way to North Tamerton, but worth a visit, for the church is well situated above the Tamar, and contains some good bench-ends; and in the parish is Ogbeare with a very fine old hall, but a very modern villa residence attached to it--new cloth on the old garment.

Whitstone is so called from the church being founded on a piece of white sparry rock. When the late Archbishop Benson was bishop of Truro he came to open the church after restoration. As the rector was taking him in he pointed out the white stone. Bishop Benson at once seized on the idea suggested, and preached to the people on the text, "To him that overcometh will I give ... a white stone." (Rev. ii. 17.) In the churchyard is a holy well of S. Anne, not of the reputed mother of the Virgin, for her cult is comparatively modern, not much earlier than the fifteenth century, but dedicated to the mother of S. Sampson, sister of S. Padarn's mother. There must have been much fighting at some time in this neighbourhood. There is a fine camp in Swannacot Wood over against Whitstone. Week S. Mary occupies an old camp site, and another is in West Wood, and another, again, in Key Wood, all within a rifle-shot of each other.

Week S. Mary occupies a wind-blasted elevation, over 500 feet above the sea, and with no intervening hills to break the force of the gales from the Atlantic. The place has interest as the birthsite of Thomasine Bonaventura. She was the daughter of a labourer, and was one day keeping sheep on the moor, when she engaged the attention of a London merchant who was travelling that way, and stayed to ask of her his direction.

Pleased with her Cornish grace of manner, with her fresh face and honest eyes, he took her to London as servant to his wife, and when the latter died he made her the mistress of his house. Dying himself shortly afterwards, he bequeathed to her a large fortune. She then married a person of the name of Gale, whom also she survived. Then Sir John Percival, Lord Mayor of London, succumbed to her charms of face, and above all of manner, and he became her third husband. But he also died, and she was once more a widow. The lady was by this time content with her experience as a wife, and returning from London to Week S. Mary--think of that! to Week S. Mary, the wind-blown and desolate--she devoted her days and fortune to good works. She founded there a college and chantry, and doubtless largely contributed towards the building of the parish church. She repaired the roads, built bridges, gave dowries to maidens, and relieved the poor. She contributed also to the building of the tower of S. Stephen's by Launceston.

Her college for the education of the youth of the neighbourhood continued to flourish till the Reformation, and the best gentlemen's sons of Devon and Cornwall went there for their education. But as there was a chantry attached to the school, this served as an excuse for the rapacity of those who desired to increase their goods at the cost of Church and poor, and school and chantry were suppressed together. Week S. Mary till lately had its mayor, and was esteemed a borough, though it never returned members.

Externally it is fine, the tower remarkably so. In the tower may be observed curious results of a lightning flash.

The coast of North Cornwall right and left of Bude is very fine; the carboniferous rocks stand up with their strata almost perpendicular, but there are bays and coves that allow of descent to the sea. Widmouth promises to become some day a great watering-place.

To see this coast it is in vain to take the coach road to Bideford or to Boscastle. The road runs on the ridge of high land from which the streams descend and spill into the sea. The only way in which to appreciate its wildness and beauty is to take the coast road that climbs and descends a succession of rocky waves. By that means scenes of the greatest picturesqueness and of the utmost variety are revealed. One excursion must on no account be omitted, that to Morwenstow, for many years the home of a fine poet, an eccentric man, the Rev. Robert S. Hawker.

He was born at Stoke Damerel on December 3rd, 1804, and was the son of Mr. Jacob Stephen Hawker, at one time a medical man, but afterwards ordained and vicar of Stratton. Mr. J. S. Hawker was the son of the famous Dr. Hawker, incumbent of Charles Church, Plymouth, author of *Morning and Evening Portions*, a book of devotional reading at one time in great request.

Young Robert was committed to his grandfather to be educated. He was sent to Oxford, but his father, then a poor curate, was unable to maintain him there, and told him so. The difficulty was, however, happily surmounted. He proposed to a lady rather older than his mother, but who had about £200 per annum. She accepted him; he was then aged twenty and she was forty-one, and had taught him his letters. By this means he was enabled to continue his studies at Oxford. He was given the living of Morwenstow in 1834, and remained there till his death in 1875.

A writer in the *Standard* of this latter year thus describes his first acquaintance with the vicar of Morwenstow:--

"It was on a solemn occasion that we first saw Morwenstow. The sea was still surly and troubled, with wild lights breaking over it and torn clouds driving through the sky. Up from the shore, along a narrow path between jagged rocks and steep banks tufted with thrift, came the vicar, wearing cassock and surplice, and conducting a sad procession, which bore along with it the bodies of two seamen flung up the same morning on the sands. The office used by Mr. Hawker at such times had been arranged by himself, not without reference to certain peculiarities which, as he conceived, were features of the primitive Cornish Church, the same which had had its bishops and its traditions long before the conference of Augustine with its leaders under the great oak by the Severn. Indeed, at one time he carried his adhesion to these Cornish traditions to some unusual lengths. There was, we remember, a peculiar yellow vestment, in which he appeared much like a Lama of Thibet, which he wore in his house and about his parish, and which he insisted was an exact copy of a priestly robe worn by S. Padarn and S. Teilo. We have seen him in this attire proceeding through the lanes on the back of a well-groomed mule-- the only fitting beast, as he remarked, for a churchman."

We have here an instance out of many of the manner in which he delighted in hoaxing visitors. The yellow vestment was a poncho. It came into use in the following manner:--

Mr. Martyn, of Tonnacombe, was in conversation one day with Mr. Hawker, when the latter complained that he could not get a greatcoat to his fancy, and one that would keep him dry against the rainstorms.

"Why not have a poncho?" asked his neighbour.

"Poncho! what is that?"

"Nothing but a blanket with a hole in the middle."

"Do you put your legs through the hole and tie the four corners over your head?"

"No," answered Mr. Martyn. "I will fetch you mine, and you shall try it on."

The poncho was produced; it was dark blue, and the vicar was delighted with it. Next time he went to Bideford he bought a

106

yellowish brown rug, and had a hole cut in the middle through which to thrust his head.

"I wouldn't wear your livery, Martyn," said he, "nor your political colours, so I have got a yellow poncho."

Those who knew him can picture to themselves the sly twinkle in his eye as he informed his credulous visitor that he was invested in the habit of S. Padarn and S. Teilo.

But his dress was extraordinary enough without the poncho. He was wont to wear a knitted blue sailor's jersey, sea-boots above his knees, and a claret-coloured coat and a clerical wide-awake of the same colour. He had a great aversion to black. "Why should we parsons be like crows--birds of ill-luck?" he would say. "Black--black--are we children of darkness? Black is the colour of devils only."

A real poet he was, but desultory, rarely able to remain fixed at work and carry out a project to the end. He was an excellent ballad-writer, but he could do better than write ballads. He began a great poem on the "Quest of the Sangreal," but it remains a fragment.

Here is one short specimen of a ballad, the lament of a Cornish mother over her dead child:--

"They say 'tis a sin to sorrow--
That what God doth is best,
But 'tis only a month to-morrow
I buried it from my breast.
"I know it should be a pleasure
Your child to God to send;
But mine was a precious treasure,
To me and my poor friend.
"I thought it would call me mother,
The very first words it said;
Oh! I never can love another
Like the blessed babe that's dead.
"Well, God is its own dear Father,
It was carried to church and bless'd;
And our Saviour's arms will gather
Such children to their rest.
"I will check this foolish sorrow,
For what God doth is best;
But oh! 'tis a month to-morrow
I buried it from my breast."

NOTE.--For further information see my *Vicar of Morwenstow*. New and revised edition. Methuen. 1899.

CHAPTER X.

SALTASH

"**JUST** three weeks too late."

That was the answer I received on reaching Saltash and inquiring after the old Town Hall. It had been pulled down and carted away, and now a hole in a range of buildings, like that in the jaw produced by the extraction of a tooth, shows where the old Town Hall had been.

It is a pity it is gone.

MACES AND SEAL OF SALTASH

Beside it stood an ancient house that had been occupied during the Commonwealth and the reign of Charles II. by Nicholas Tyack, the mayor. Nicholas Tyack was a turncoat, but somehow, whichever way he turned his coat he always turned it to his advantage.

Under the Commonwealth he was not only mayor, but a great Presbyterian luminary. He harangued and expounded Revelation always in favour of the Commonwealth and Presbyterianism, and against the Crown and the Mitre. But no sooner did Charles II. land than he swung completely round. All his political and religious views changed, and he declared that the great horn was Old Noll and the little horn was Dickon. By this means Nicholas Tyack secured his position, and remained mayor of Saltash. He had been high-handed in his proceedings before; he became more high-handed under the Restoration. He wanted to apprentice his son in London; so he took the youth to town, lived well whilst there, and on his return charged the expenses to the town.

Nicholas had a great advantage in living next door to the Town Hall, for he was able to break a way into it through the intervening wall. According to custom and rule, when a meeting of the Town Council was convened, the Town Hall bell had to be rung; but there was no specification as to the *hour* at which a meeting was to be held, nor was it laid down in black and white that the Hall door was to be unlocked for the occasion. Now when Nicholas Tyack desired to pass his accounts, or to transfer some bit of Corporation land to himself, or legitimatise any other little game to his advantage and the detriment of the public, he rang the bell at night, kept the Hall door locked, and admitted his adherents through his private door, held the meeting in the council-chamber, and passed his accounts and resolutions *nem. con.*

But now both the Town Hall and Tyack's house have been swept away. The latter had a fine mullioned and many-light window. The house went first; then the Guildhall.

IN SALTASH

The story of the borough of Esh, Esc, or Saltash is specially interesting, as it affords us a precious glimpse into the history of the origin and growth of our municipal towns.

Esh, that is to say, *water*, was so-called because situated on the tidal estuary of the united Tamar and Tavy, which junction bears the name of the Hamoaze (Hem-uisg), the border water between Devon and Cornwall, between the English and the British tongues.

Here by the water-side settled some serfs, or "natives in stock," of the Baron de Valletort.

"Natives of stock were the purest and most absolute bondmen. They were entirely subject to the will of their lord, and were subject to being placed in any tenement in which he might think fit to place them; and were compelled to do for him any work he might call upon them to do; and to pay a sort of capitation tax if they were allowed to be employed elsewhere."[13]

Living beside the water, these serfs ferried across to Devonport, managed the fishery, raised oysters, had a mill, and tilled the land for their lord. But a charter of 1381 exists which is a confirmation by Reginald de Valletort of earlier charters, wherein his ancestors had emancipated these serfs, and had conferred on them considerable liberties. They had been granted certain holdings of land as customary tenants. They were given a certain tract of land for common use, for pasturage, etc.; they were accorded the "ferébote," the mill, and the right to organise themselves into a corporation with an elected "prepositur." For all this and other liberties they were required to pay a small acknowledgment to the feudal lord.

This charter was confirmed by royal grant in 1385.

Now the number of conventional tenancies was always the same, but some of the old habitations on them were pulled down and the sites converted into gardens, and others were divided up and numerous houses erected on them. The holders of the tenancies were free burgesses, and formed the sole body which elected the aldermen and mayor.

In course of time a very curious condition of affairs arose. The ancient burgage holdings were 160; but many had fallen and were not rebuilt, and the population of Saltash had vastly extended beyond the bounds of the ancient borough.

The corporators, or holders of the old free burgages, engrossed to themselves all power and profit, and excluded from participation the inhabitants who were not living in the old tenements or on the land where these had stood. This led to a series of angry disputes. The privileges were worth fighting for. The corporators grew fat on them, and their faces shone. The harbour dues--one shilling from every English vessel and two from every foreign keel that anchored in the Hamoaze, and seven from each Spanish ship, charged after the Armada[14]--this brought in much money; so did the common land now built over, so did the oyster fishery, so did the ferry.

Almost every election of mayor and aldermen led to riots, and the place simmered perpetually with discontent. This angry feeling was greatly aggravated when Saltash became a borough, returning two members, and political controversy was added to the local and borough grievance. By this time, moreover, the number of free burgages had sunk to about sixty. Contest succeeded contest, the inhabitants claiming a right to vote.

In 1784 the corporation, won over by Government promises and appointments, voted as one man for their nominees. But forty-five freeholders tendered their votes for the opposition candidates put forward by their overlords. The House of Commons decided against these latter, and the Government candidates and the rights of the corporators were confirmed. Two years later, this decision against the freeholders was reversed. During four years (1786-1790) the question in whom the right of voting rested was four times decided-- now in one way, then in another. Finally a compromise was arrived at--one representative of each set of electors sat for Saltash and "tied" on every important vote in the House. In 1806 the corporation was again successful.

By the Reform Bill of 1832 it was curtailed in its representation--it returned one member. Croker tried to prove borough and parish to be conterminous, but when it was discovered that this was not the case Saltash was put on Schedule A, and its representative history came to an end. More fortunate than some other Cornish boroughs, it has retained its municipal privileges, and boasts of a mayor and corporation to the present day.

Saltash was enfranchised in 1553 by Edward VI. "A little town," as described by Captain Courtney, "screening itself under the patronage of the Earls of Cornwall, and then of the Dukes, it paid tribute to the Black Prince, and received charters and royalties from Elizabeth."

In her time great sailors and ships of merchandise sailed from Saltash. The Castle of Trematon, which had belonged to the Valletorts, became a royal castle, and it was hoped by the advisers of Edward VI. that the newly-enfranchised borough would be completely subservient to the Crown.

But, like most of the other creations of this period, it passed almost at once into other hands, and the history of the borough shows the rise and supremacy of the Buller interest, unbroken during the Protectorate and unimpaired under the Stuarts. In spite of occasional lapses, the electors of this little borough continued faithful to the Bullers till within a few years before the Reform Bill, the connection broken now and then with flashes of independence.

In 1722 the electors gave thirty-two votes to Swanton and Hughes against twenty-five for the Buller candidates. The borough, however, soon learned to repent its independence, and returned to subservience. For fifty years there was no contested election, but in 1772 the Buller candidate was defeated. Nevertheless, on petition he secured the seat.

In 1780 ensued another struggle with the patrons, and the Bullers were defeated, much to the joy of George III.

Again there was a contest in 1784, rendered, like the former struggles, doubtful because of the ambiguity in the right of voting, as already described.

As early as 1393 the county assizes were held in Saltash. The first charter of incorporation--that already alluded to--was granted in the reign of Henry III., and received confirmation under Richard II. Charles II. renewed it, with additional privileges, in 1662. Thus, like Camelford, Saltash has had six centuries of corporate existence, and, grey and antique, seems to gaze with scorn upon the odious Albert Bridge flung across the Hamoaze by Brunel in 1857-9, at a cost of £230,000, for the Cornwall line, and which, from whatever point it be looked at, is an eyesore.

Saltash occupies the steep slope of the hill that descends to the water's edge. The main street is as steep as the side of a roof. In it on each side are the remains of very ancient houses that were once those of merchants of substance and corporators exercising almost despotic power in the little town. Old windows, carved doorways, and even, when these have disappeared, panelled rooms and handsome plaster ceilings, proclaim at once antiquity and wealth.

There is much of interest remaining in Saltash. Not only are there in it still many ancient houses, but several of the ancient families that were burgage tenants hundreds of years ago are still represented there. As an instance we may notice the Porters. These were the janitors of Trematon Castle. The first of this family in a deed of the thirteenth century, noticed as gatekeeper of Trematon, was granted a plot of land outside the castle walls, which has remained in the hands of the Porters to the present day. The arms of the family--sable, three bells argent, a canton ermine--have undoubted reference to the duties of the porter to answer the bell and to ring the alarum. The motto "Vigilantibus" is no less significant.

The Bonds of Earth were landholders under the Valletorts; they remained for centuries on the soil, and in their name recalled their origin; and the name Tyack has much the same significance in Cornish.

Saltash has long been famous for its boatwomen. Mr. Justice Boucaut, a Saltash man, and late Premier of South Australia, at a recent banquet at Adelaide, spoke with affection of his native Ashe, and in the course of his speech said:--

"I won't even dilate on the pluck and endurance of the Saltash women rowers. It was a pretty sight to see half a dozen boats start in a regatta with all the women in snow-white frilled caps and frilled jackets. One crew, of which Ann Glanville was stroke, and which I have seen row, would beat a crew of men of the same number, and would not, I believe, have thought it anything very wonderful to beat a crew of men with a couple of men extra. I read in the *Times* that Ann Glanville, then an old woman, upwards of eighty, was introduced to the Duke of Cornwall when he was down West, and I have often heard that she used to row round the captain's man-of-war gigs in the Hamoaze and chaff the bluejackets."

ANNE GLANVILLE

This Ann Glanville (stroke), Jane House, Emilia Lee, and Hyatt Hocking formed the crew of the celebrated Saltash rowing women who won against crews of men at Plymouth, Portsmouth, Liverpool, and Hull. In 1850 a match was arranged between the Saltash women and a crew of Frenchmen, and Ann Glanville with the rest went to Havre in the *Brunswick* (Captain Russell). They were escorted into the town by bands and the military, and received by the mayor and corporation.

The Saltash crew, steered by Captain Russell, won easily in the match. The women were dressed in black skirts, long white bedgowns, and nightcaps. Mrs. House was so elated at the victory, that on reaching the committee-boat she plunged into the water, dived under the vessel, and came up with dripping and drooping nightcap on the opposite side.

Ann was well known to H.R.H. the Duke of Edinburgh, R.N., and Lord Charles Beresford, R.N. She died in 1880 at the age of eighty-four.

A boat of Saltash women still appears at regattas, but it is now difficult to--can we say *man* it? The present generation of women do not take to the water as did their mothers.

Saltash has for long been an unrivalled nursery for the navy, and a place to which old salts love to retire.

In 1643 the Cornish forces, about 7000 strong, lay at Saltash under Slanning, at Liskeard under Lord Mohun, at Launceston under Trevanion, and at Stratton under Sir Bevil Grenville. At the outbreak of war, King Charles fortified Saltash, but in the following year, 1644, it was taken by the Parliamentary forces under Lord Essex, who at once strengthened the works, and also added a 400-ton ship, and sixteen pieces of cannon at the bottom of the hill. After the Royalist victory at Braddock Down, near Liskeard, the vanquished, under General Ruthven, retreated to their stronghold at Saltash, and here made an obstinate resistance; but the Royalists, led by Grenville and Mohun, attacked the place, took it, and made havoc among the rebels, many of whom were drowned. Their leader, Ruthven, succeeded in effecting his escape to Plymouth, which was held for the Parliament by a member of my own family, Colonel William Gould.

This resulted in the Royalists recovering the whole of Cornwall. Saltash, however, was again occupied by the Parliamentary forces in 1645.

CHALICE, SALTASH

Among the rights and privileges exercised by the borough of Saltash was that the mayor or recorder held a court of quarter sessions till 1886. In 1772 a woman was sentenced to be stripped to her waist and whipped in public for stealing a hat. But this sentence, if repugnant to our sense of decency, was light compared to one passed in 1844 on two women for stealing some shirting wherewith to make garments for their husbands. They were transported for seven years. The natural result was that they married again and settled in Botany Bay, and the husbands found for themselves fresh mates at Saltash. In this century the mayor sentenced a man to transportation for stealing a watch at a regatta. The only church at Saltash is the chapel of the Guildhall, and the chaplain formerly had a bad time of it as the creature of the mayor. Happily the advowson was sold in 1836 for £405, and fell to the bishop. The church possesses a splendid piece of plate, a silver cup over a foot high. This was given to the church in 1624 by Ambrose and Abraham Jennens and William Pawley, but it is far older.

It is said in the place that it is of Spanish workmanship, and was part of the spoil of a vessel of the great Armada. This, however, is not the case; it is a fine example of English silversmith's work of the reign of Henry VII.

The Castle of Trematon, to which the original serfs of Saltash owed service, still exists. It is not remarkable for picturesqueness. It occupies the top of a wooded hill on the banks of the Lynher, overlooking the Hamoaze and Plymouth harbour, and consists of a keep, the base-court, and the gate-house. The keep, placed at the north-east angle of the court, is oval in form, and dates from the thirteenth century. The walls are ten feet thick and thirty feet high. It was wrecked by the Cornish peasants, who rose against the Reformation, stormed the castle, and took the governor prisoner.

Among the many broils that took place in Saltash between the corporation and the great body of townsmen the most serious was in 1806, when the Rev. John Buller was mayor. On this occasion the mob broke into the Guildhall, where the mayor stood to his post on the stairs, and for some time held back the crowd, dealing mighty blows with the silver-gilt mace, and cracking therewith many crowns. Finally the rioters succeeded in getting hold of the chest, and they destroyed or purloined all the documents it contained, with the object of getting rid of the evidence in favour of the corporation. At the same time they carried off the silver oar, the symbol of jurisdiction over the Hamoaze, and this was not recovered for fifty years.

The corporation maces are singularly handsome and weighty, and are of silver-gilt.

The present Guildhall is erected over the market-house, and was built in 1770. It is ugly, and has this alone to recommend it, that it is unpretentious.

On the daïs within are three handsome carved oak chairs, that for the mayor having the arms of the borough on the panel--a lion rampant within a bordure bezanted. On each side of the shield is a Prince of Wales' ostrich plume.

A late mayor was the brother of the famous astronomer, Professor Adams.

The official costume of the mayor includes a robe of scarlet cloth trimmed with sable and a cocked hat; the justice or ex-mayor has a black mantle; and the mace-bearers have scarlet, silver-laced gowns and three-cornered hats. The maces date from 1696, and were presented by Francis Buller, Esq., and are three feet seven inches high.

Near the water, almost crushed under the mighty arch of Brunel's viaduct, is a little old shop with the date on it of 1584, and it is one of the very few specimens of a shop of that period that remain to us absolutely untouched.

It is precisely the sort of shop "in our alley" from which Sally must have issued to meet her lover.

And verily, as I stood drawing the quaint old place, there peeped out at me an absolutely ideal Sally.
"Her father he makes cabbage nets,
And through the streets does cry 'em;
Her mother she sells laces long,
To such as please to buy 'em.
But sure such folks could ne'er beget
So sweet a girl as Sally!
She is the darling of my heart,
And she lives in our alley."

CHAPTER XI.

BODMIN

Grown up about a monastery--S. Petrock--Theft of his relics--Ivory reliquary--"Lord's measures"--The Allan rivers--Pencarrow--S. Breock--Padstow--The Hobby-horse--The neighbourhood--The Towans--Pentyre--Porth Isaac--A cemetery.

A TOWN that has grown up about a monastery. The name is a contraction of Bod-minachau, "the habitation of monks"; and it owes its origin to S. Petrock. Petrock is Peter or Pedr, with the diminutive *oc* added to the name. He was a son of Glwys, king of Gwent or Monmouthshire, according to one account, but according to another his father's name was Clement. Anyhow, he formed one of the great migration from Gwent to North-east Cornwall. He found a hermit occupying a cell at Bodmin whose name was Guron, and this man surrendered to him his humble habitation. S. Guron's Well is in the churchyard near the west end of the church.

PADSTOW HARBOUR

For his education he went to Ireland, where for twenty years he studied profane and sacred literature. He was probably a disciple of S. Eugenius, for Kevin, when aged seven, was entrusted to him by his parents to be reared for the monastic life, and Kevin, we know, learned his psalms from Eugenius.

So soon as Petrock considered that he knew as much as could be taught him by his master, he resolved on returning to Cornwall, and embarked on the same boat which had borne him to Ireland twenty years before--a great vessel of wicker-work, covered with three coatings of hide, and with a leathern sail.

Petrock and his companions came ashore in the Hayle, or saltflats, by Padstow. He was ill received on his arrival by a party of harvesters, who refused him water. In fact, the north of Cornwall had suffered so severely from the Irish, that the natives looked with suspicion on anyone coming from the Green Isle.

Petrock landed, and inquired whether any religious man lived in the neighbourhood, and was told that Samson was there. This was Samson who afterwards became Bishop of Dol. His chapel was demolished when Place House, above Padstow, was built. At Padstow, Petrock remained for thirty years with his disciples, one of whom was Dagan, who disputed with Laurence, Archbishop of Canterbury (597-604) and other Roman missionaries. He refused not only to eat with them, Bede tells us, but even to be under the same roof with them. The story of Petrock's pilgrimage to the East is full of myth, but the account of the reason why he undertook it is probably true.

There had been a rainy season. One day Petrock assured his disciples that next day the rain would cease, and it would be fine. But on the morrow the rain came down in streams. Petrock was so disgusted at his prophecy having failed, that he left the place, and resolved on visiting the East.

The rest is mere romance.

He went to India. There he saw a silver bowl floating on the sea. He stepped into it, whereupon the silver bowl carried him far away to a certain island in which he spent seven years, living on a single fish that he caught daily, and which, however often eaten, always returned sound to be eaten again next day.

At the end of the seven years the shining bowl reappeared. He stepped into it again, and was conveyed back to the coast whence he had started. There he found a wolf that had kept guard over his sheepskin and staff which he had left on the shore seven years before. Clearly we have here ingrafted into the history a Cornish myth relative to the man in the moon; for the silver bowl cannot be mistaken--it is the latter--and for the dog of the modern version, we here have a wolf.

Through the rest of his journeyings the wolf attended Petrock. On his return to Cornwall he had some unpleasantness with Tewdrig, the king, who had opposed the landing of the Irish at St. Ives, and had killed some of them. He remonstrated with him for some of his barbarities, and Tewdrig had sufficient grace to make him grants of land.

Petrock now moved to Bodmin, and thence he made many excursions through Devon, founding churches and monasteries. The date of his death was about A.D.575.

A curious circumstance occurred relative to his relics. In 1177 a canon of Bodmin, named Martin, made a clean bolt with the shrine of the saint, an ivory box that contained his bones, and carried them to S. Maen, in Brittany. There were "ructions." The Prior of Bodmin appealed to Henry II., who sent orders to the Justiciary of Brittany to insist on their surrender. Accordingly the prior and this officer went to S. Maen, but when required to give up the holy bones the abbot demurred. However, the justiciary would stand no nonsense, and threatened to use such severe measures that the abbot was forced to give way, and Prior Roger, of Bodmin, marched away with the recovered ivory box and its contents.

Curiously enough this identical box, quaintly ornamented with paintings, still exists, and belongs to the municipality: the contents have, of course, disappeared.

In the market-house is a very interesting granite corn measure.

It will not be out of place to notice here the "lord's measures" found in great numbers about Cornwall. They are small basins cut in granite or in some volcanic free stone, usually with lobes or ears outside. At S. Enodoc, near the "Rock Inn" on the Padstow estuary, a quantity of them have been collected, and are ranged beside the churchyard path. There is another large collection in the parsonage garden at Veryan.

They were probably standard measures for grain, and were preserved in the churches.

In Bodmin Church, which is fine, is the rich monument of Prior Vivian, 1533.

The bench-ends were carved by one Matthew More in 1491.

Castle Canyck is a fine circular camp, probably Celtic, and west of the town is a quadrangular entrenchment where Roman remains have been found. The Allan and the Camallan, or Crooked Allan, unite to form the Hayle or Saltings. Allan is the name of the river at S. David's, Pembrokeshire. The name is found also in Scotland, as the Ilen in Ireland, and as the Aulne in Finistère. The derivation is doubtful.

On the right hand are the woods of Pencarrow (Pencaerau), the headland of camps, with, in fact, remains of two; one must have been important. Here, perhaps, dwelt a chieftain Conan.

S. Breock was on his way from Cardigan to Brittany when his hide-covered boat was nearly upset by a whale, and so great was the alarm of those sailing with him that the vessel put into Hayle estuary and ran up to the head.

Breock was now an old man, and could not walk, so his companions made for him a sort of cart in which he could sit, and in which they drew him about. One day they left him to sing psalms in his cart whilst they were engaged at a distance over some pressing business. When they returned they found a pack of wolves round the old man, but whether his sanctity, or toughness, kept them from eating him is left undecided. They drove the wolves off, and were careful in future not to leave him unattended. Conan, the chief, who lived at Pencarrow, came to know him, and, if we may believe the *Life*, was baptised by him, and made him a grant of land; this is S. Breock on the opposite side of the river to Pencarrow, where there is an interesting church in a lovely situation. It is only a coincidence that at the foot of Pencarrow is a chapel bearing Conan's name. It is dedicated to a tenth-century bishop.

From Cornwall Breock departed for Brittany, about the year 500, and died there at an advanced age--over ninety--about 510.

Padstow should be visited on May Day. It is one of the few places where the hobby-horse still prances; but the glory of the old May Feast is much curtailed.

During the days that precede the festival no garden is safe. Walls, railings, even barbed wire, are surmounted by boys and men in quest of flowers. Conservatories have to be fast locked, or they will be invaded. The house that has a show of flowers in the windows is besieged by pretty children with roguish eyes begging for blossoms which they cannot steal.

During the evening before May Day in years gone by, before shipbuilding had ceased to be an industry of Padstow, when the shipwrights left work they brought with them from the yard two poles, and carried them up the street, fastened one above the other, decorated at the top with branches of willow, furze, sycamore, and all kinds of spring flowers made into garlands, and from it were suspended strings of gulls' eggs. There hung from it also long streamers of coloured ribbon.

A pit was dug, and the Maypole secured by ropes fastened to stakes. In the pavement was a cross laid in with paving stones differently coloured from the rest in the street; these were taken up every time the Maypole was planted, to be again relaid when the merry-making was over. But a doctor who lived in the house facing the pole objected, and so opposed the planting of the Maypole and the dancing before his door, that the merry-makers moved to an open space somewhat higher up the street, which was much less convenient. Opposition followed them even there, and a few years ago the Maypole was finally abandoned.

The "Hobby-horse Pairs," as it was called, *i.e.* a party of eight men, then repaired to the "Golden Lion," at that time the first inn in Padstow, and sat down to a hearty supper of leg of mutton and plum-pudding, given them by the landlord. After supper a great many young men joined the "Pairs," *i.e.* the *peers*, the lords of the merriment, and all started for the country, and went round from one farmhouse to another, singing at the doors of each, and soliciting contributions to the festivities of the morrow.

They returned into Padstow about three o'clock in the morning, and promenaded the streets singing the "Night Song." After that they retired to rest for a few hours. At ten o'clock in the morning the "Pairs" assembled at the "Golden Lion" again, and now was brought forth the hobby-horse. The drum and fife band was marshalled to precede, and then came the young girls of Padstow dressed in white, with garlands of flowers in their hair, and their white gowns pinned up with flowers. The men followed armed with pistols, loaded with a little powder, which they fired into the air or at the spectators. Lastly came the hobby-horse, ambling, curvetting, and snapping its jaws. It may be remarked that the Padstow hobby-horse is wonderfully like the Celtic horse decoration found on old pillars and crosses with interlaced work. The procession went first to Prideaux Place, where the late squire, Mr. Prideaux Brune, always emptied a purse of money into the hands of the "Pairs." Then the procession visited the vicarage, and was welcomed by the parson. After that it went forth from the town to Treator Pool "for the horse to drink."

124

The Mayers finally arrived at the Maypole, and danced round it singing the "Day Song."

Refrain. "Awake, S. George, our English knight, O!

For summer is a-come, and winter is a-go.

1. "Where is S. George? and where is he, O?

He's down in his long boat, upon the salt sea, O!

2. "Where are the French dogs that made such a boast, O?

They shall eat the goose feathers, and we'll eat the roast, O!

3. "Thou might'st ha' shown thy knavish face and tarried at home, O!

But thou shalt be a rascal, and shalt wear the horns, O!

4. "Up flies the kite, down falls the lark, O!

Aunt Ursula Birdwood she had an old ewe.

5. "Aunt Ursula Birdwood she had an old ewe,

And she died in her own park long ago."

It is obvious that the song is very corrupt, but the air to this and to the "Morning Song" are very bold and ancient.[15]

Although the Maypole has been given up, the hobby-horse still prances on May Day.

Padstow Harbour is spoiled by the Doom Bar, a shifting bank of sand at the mouth. But this might be placed under control and rectified by the expenditure of money, and the mouth of the Hayle be made into what is sorely needed, a harbour of refuge on the north coast.

The neighbourhood of Padstow abounds in interest; the cliffs are superb, towering above a sea blue as a peacock's neck, here and there crowned with cliff castles. In the sand-dunes or Towans is the buried church of S. Constantine, a convert of S. Petrock, Duke or King of Cornwall, who was so ballyragged by Gildas. There are old Cornish mansions, such as Treshunger, lying in dips among trees; and churches on wind-blown heights, their towers intended as landmarks. But this is not a guide-book, and such details must be passed over.

On no account should Pentyre Point be missed. It is a grand and glorious cliff, and a projection called the Rumps is occupied by a well-preserved cliff-castle. Porth Gaverne, Porth Isaac, Porthquin, Polzeath are all delightful little bays. The pilchard cellars cut in the rocks should be noticed. Porthquin was once a flourishing little place, but in a terrible storm nearly every man connected with the place, being out fishing, was lost, and it has never recovered.

Porth Isaac--let not those amiable faddists who hold that we are Anglo-Israelites fasten on the name--means the Corn Port, Porthquin the White Port, from the spar in the rock, and Porth Gaverne the Goat

Port. A curious fact, to be noted, is that there exists an extensive ancient cemetery close to where is now rising a cluster of new houses at Trevose. Bones are continually turned up by the sea as it encroaches, but all record of a church with burial-ground there is lost. There is a ruined chapel of S. Cadoc, but that is half a mile distant. Cadoc was an elder brother or cousin--it is not certain which--of S. Petrock of Padstow. He must have come here to visit his kinsman.

The story goes that he had made a pilgrimage to the Holy Land, and he brought back with him some of the water of Jordan, and this he poured into a well at this place, which thenceforth possessed marvellous powers. The well is not now easily traced, but bits of carved stone of the chapel lie strewn around. Cadoc was for a while in an island of the lagoon d'Elet, near Belz, in the Morbihan, where he constructed a causeway to the mainland, of which traces remain. He was one of the most restless beings conceivable, and no sooner had he established a monastic centre in one place than he tired of it, and started off to found another somewhere else. He played a scurvy trick once on a South Welsh chief, who with a large party came down on him and imperiously demanded meat and drink. They took all they could get, and got drunk and incapable on the spot. Cadoc shaved half of their heads and beards as they thus lay, but, worse than this, cut off the lips of their horses. He was a violent-tempered man, of tremendous energy in all he did. According to one account he fell a victim to his rashness or enthusiasm; he tried to carry the Gospel to the Saxons, but was cut down by their axes at the foot of the altar.

CHAPTER XII.

THE TWO LOOES

East Looe--Church--Narrow and picturesque streets--A fair--A strolling company--West Looe--Looe Island--The Fyns--Smuggling--The East Looe river--Duloe--S. Keyne's Well--Liskeard--Menheniot--The West Looe river--Trelawne--The Trelawny ballad--Polperro--Privateers--Robert Jeffrey--Tom Potter--Lanreath.

EAST and West Looe, separated by a tidal stream, the Looe (the same as Liffey from Welsh *llifo* to flow, *llif* a flood[16]), and united by a long bridge, at one time returned four members to Parliament.

East Looe is the more considerable place of the two, and possesses a new and respectable Guildhall, and some quaint old houses and an ancient picturesque market-house. The church is modern and poor of its kind--one of those structures that do not convey an idea to the mind of either beauty or of ugliness, but are mediocre in conception and execution. It occupies the site of an earlier church dedicated to S. Keyne, but it is now dedicated to S. Anne, who formerly had a chapel on the bridge.

The streets are narrow and full of quaint bits. As I first saw Looe it struck me as one of the oddest old-world places in England. A man had been there selling paper flags and coloured streamers also of paper, and the children in the narrow alleys were fluttering these, and had hung them from the windows, and were dancing with coloured paper caps on their heads or harlequin sashes about their bodies, whilst an Italian organ-grinder played to them. From the narrow casements leaned their mothers, watching, laughing, and encouraging the dancers. A little way back was a booth theatre, hardly up to the level of that of Mr. Vincent Crummel's, enclosed in dingy green canvas. Reserved seats, 6*d.*; back seats, 3*d.* and 1*d.* The *répertoire* comprised blood-curdling tragedies. I went in and saw "The Midnight Assassin; or, The Dumb Witness."

Next evening was to be given "The Vampire's Feast; or, The Rifled Tomb." The tragedy was followed by Allingham's play, "Fortune's Frolick" (1799), adapted to the narrow capacities of the company. It was performed in broad Cornish, and interspersed with some rather good and, I fancy, original songs. But surely nowhere else but at Looe could such a reminiscence of the old strolling company-show of fifty or sixty years ago be seen.

But this is not all. A stranger having seen something I wrote about puppet-shows in a paper, wherein I said that the last I had sat through was sixty years ago, wrote to me:--

"At West Looe, far more recently, at the annual fair, which commences on the 6th May, I saw a show in which the figures were all moved by strings manipulated from above. I regret that I am unable to remember the subject of the play, but the droll antics of the puppets, the rapidity of their movements, and the cleverness of the whole thing, remains distinctly impressed on my mind."

I believe that venerable amusements we old folks saw in our childhood are "resurrected" at West Looe at that 6th May fair. Therefore, if you want to see funny things, go there. The place is still out of the world, but will not long be so, as a London company has bought the cliffs, and is blasting a road in them to make promenade, hotel, and bring the world and the twentieth century to Looe and rumple up the old place.

East Looe is properly in S. Martin's parish, and the church was a chapel-of-ease to it. At S. Martin's are a Norman doorway and an early font.

West Looe has a little church, dedicated to S. Nicholas, that long served as town hall and as a theatre for strolling players. Here also are some quaint old slated houses; the "valleys" are not leaded, but the slates are so worked as to fold over the angles very ingeniously and picturesquely, and admirably answering the object in view of carrying off the water.

Off the coast lies Looe Island. This was for many years the dwelling-place of a man named Fyn and his sister, "Black Joan." They were son and daughter of an outlaw, who had spent his life since his outlawry on the Mewstone off Gara Point, at the entrance of Plymouth Sound. Here he and his wife lived a wild life like sea-mews, and there reared their young, who grew up without any religious, moral, or intellectual training. The outlaw died on the Mewstone, and Fyn and his sister, accustomed from infancy to an island life, could not endure the thought of going to the mainland for the rest of their days, and so they settled on Looe Island. Here they were joined by a negro, and by their united efforts honeycombed the ground under their hovel and the large barn adjoining for the accommodation of smuggled goods. Their only associates were the free-traders.

One day the black man vanished, and it was never known what had become of him, whether he had left or been murdered by Fyn and his sister. There were naturally no witnesses; nothing could be proved against them. Recently a skull has been dug up near the house, and is kept in a box in the dwelling, but it is not that of a negro. Actually there is a layer of human remains about two feet below the surface of the turf, exposed on the east side of the island, where wind and spray are gnawing away the cliff, and any number of teeth and bones may be picked out. Whether these are the remains of an early Christian monastic cemetery, or of shipwrecked sailors buried on the cliffs, cannot be told, as no investigation has been made to discover the approximate period to which this layer of dead men's bones belongs.

Formerly there was a chapel on the summit of the island, but only its foundations remain. The island belonged to the monastery of Lamana (*lan-manachau*, the church of the monks) on the mainland.

But to return to the Fyns.

On that island they spent many years, hand in glove with the smugglers.

There was an old fellow, a farmer on the mainland, who rode a white horse into Looe. He acted as spy, and was intimate with the preventive men, who trusted him, and perhaps some of them had their palms greased to give him information. If the white horse were seen returning along the coast road to the west, that was a signal to Fyn that all was safe. But sometimes the horse was too lame or tired to return home, and the farmer went his way on foot; that always coincided with activity among the officers of the revenue.

From Looe Island, Fyn or his sister signalled by lights to the smugglers lying in the offing.

At length their daring and their success induced the Government to establish one of their guard on the island itself--the station is still there--and the man was bidden keep a watchful eye on Black Joan and her brother.

Now the Fyns had their secret stores full of a cargo they desired to run ashore, but were afraid of being seen by this man.

One day Black Joan hastened to the preventive officer with, "Oh, my dear! Now ther's that terr'ble put out I be. What du'y think now? My boat hev a broke her moorings, and is driftin' wi' the tide out to say. Oh, my dear man, du'y now bring her in for me." The officer ran to the cliff, and sure enough there was the boat slowly floating away on the ebb of the tide.

Being a good-natured man, and suspecting no ill, he at once got into his own boat and rowed hard after that which was adrift. The moment he was gone, a swarm of boats and men appeared on the shore on the further side of the island, and before the fellow was back, every keg had been carried across to the mainland.

But the officer in command had great difficulties with the station on Looe Isle. Partly through Black Joan's fascinations, mainly through the liberal flow of drink at the hut of the Fyns, and the tedium of the long evenings in solitude, he could never rely on a man who was sent to Looe Island. In some way or other he was bamboozled, so that goods were landed there and transferred to the mainland almost as freely as formerly.

What was the end of this family I have not learned.

A few years ago, when a picnic party went to the island and were allowed the barn to feed in, as a drizzle had come on, suddenly the floor collapsed, and it was thus discovered that beneath was a cellar for the accommodation of spirits that were not intended to pay duty.

The East and the West Looe rivers unite above the bridge, where also formerly stood a most picturesque tidal mill. Each stream runs through a narrow, well-wooded valley, and passes points of some interest. Ascending the East Looe, we have on the right the creek of Morval with the ancient house of the Bullers. Further up on the left is Duloe, with S. Cuby's holy well, and a so-called Druidical circle. The place takes its name from being between the two Looes. Higher up again on the same side is S. Keyne, with an interesting church and a well, the story of which is sufficiently known, made the subject of a ballad by Southey.

Liskeard is a town that was surmounted by a castle that has now disappeared. Its name implies that it was a *lis* or court on a rock. A copious spring, once a holy well, pours forth from the rock and supplies the town. But no ancient masonry remains about it.

Liskeard Church has an interesting lych-gate, a fine tower, and a good pulpit of 1627. At Menheniot (*Maen-hên-Niot*, the old stone of S. Neot) are some fine camps, Padesbury and Blackaton Rings. Clicker Tor, under which runs the line, is an outcrop of serpentine, which stone does not reappear till the Lizard is reached. A visit to S. Neot, with its superb old windows, should on no account be omitted. No collection of ancient stained glass comparable to it exists elsewhere in Devon or Cornwall.

The West Looe flows past several camps, two of which are in Pelynt parish. The church here is dedicated to S. Nun, mother of S. David, and her gabled holy well remains in tolerable condition. In this parish also is Trelawne, the seat of the Trelawny family, an ancient house, but much modernised. It contains some fine portraits, and in the church is a model of the pastoral staff of Bishop Jonathan Trelawny, Bishop of Bristol, and afterwards successively of Exeter and Winchester. He was one of the seven bishops who had been committed to the Tower by James II. Of him the song was sung:--

"A good sword and trusty sword!
A merry heart and true!
King James's men shall understand
What Cornish lads can do!
"And have they fixed the where and when?
And shall Trelawny die?
There's twenty thousand Cornish men
Will know the reason why.
"Out spake their captain brave and bold,
A merry wight was he;
If London Tower were Michael's hold,
We'll set Trelawny free!
"We'll cross the Tamar, land to land,
The Severn is no stay--
With One and All and hand in hand,
And who shall bid us nay?
"And when we come to London Wall,
A pleasant sight to view,
Come forth! come forth! ye cowards all,
Here's men as good as you.
"Trelawny he's in keep and hold,
Trelawny he may die--
But twenty thousand Cornish bold
Will know the reason why!"

With the exception of the choral lines--

"And shall Trelawny die?
Here's twenty thousand Cornishmen
Will know the reason why!"

the rest is mainly, if not wholly, the composition of the late Rev. R. S. Hawker, of Morwenstow. It was written by him in 1825, and was printed first in a Plymouth paper, and then by Mr. Davies Gilbert, the antiquary and historian. It appeared in the *Gentleman's Magazine* of November, 1827. Sir Walter Scott, and later, Lord Macaulay, quite thought it was a genuine ancient ballad.

That it is not an antique is almost certain, as it has no local and original air to which it is set; it is sung to "Le Petit Tambour," and no old miners or labourers know it.

There is a novel by Mrs. Bray, *Trelawny of Trelawne*, written in 1834, that relates to this house, and by no means deserves to be forgotten. Mrs. Bray's novels, though old-fashioned, are guides to the neighbourhood of Tavistock, and that just mentioned interests the reader in the district about Trelawne.[17]

"Looe," says she, "beautiful as it is, is not to be compared to Polperro, two miles distant from Trelawne. The descent to it is so steep, that I, who was not accustomed to the path, could only get down by clinging to Mr. Bray's arm for support; it was slippery, and so rocky that in some places there were steps cut in the road for the convenience of the passenger. The view of the little port, the old town in the bottom (if town it can be called), the cliffs, and the spiked rocks, that start up in the wildest and most abrupt manner, breaking the direct sweep of the waves towards the harbour, altogether produced such a combination of magnificent coast scenery as may truly be called sublime."

Access to Polperro is very much easier than it was in 1833, when visited by Mrs. Bray. A good many of the quaint old houses have been pulled down, but the place is still eminently picturesque, and is a haunt of artists.

In 1807, the year of the treacherous peace of Tilsit, privateering was carried on briskly at Polperro. Among other vessels, the *Lord Nelson* sailed from this port, manned by a crew of hardy and experienced sailors. After cruising in the Channel for a week without success, she put into Falmouth for provisions. Here she was boarded by the *Recruit*, and several of the men were impressed. Amongst these was one Robert Jeffrey, who had been brought up as a blacksmith by his stepfather. The *Recruit* was a sloop-of-war commanded by Captain Lake, which at once sailed for the West Indies. Whilst cruising in the Caribbean Sea, Jeffrey got at a barrel of spruce beer. The captain, very angry, ordered the boat to be lowered, and Jeffrey to be taken to a barren rock and left there.

The order was obeyed with some reluctance, and the poor young fellow was deserted on the rock, without food, and with nothing save a kerchief, a knife, and a piece of wood, which had been given him by his comrades for the purpose of signalling any passing ship.

The place on which he had been left was the islet of Sombrero, one of the Leeward group, desolate and treeless, a naked lump of rock, with no springs. Jeffrey suffered frightfully from hunger, and worse from thirst.

The *Recruit*, on leaving the island, steered for Barbadoes to join the squadron under the command of Admiral Sir Alexander Cochrane. The story of Jeffrey's punishment got wind, and the admiral, hearing of it, severely reprimanded Captain Lake for his brutality, and ordered him to return to Sombrero and rescue Jeffrey if he were still alive. Captain Lake accordingly went back to the islet, but found no one on it. A pair of trousers (not Jeffrey's) and a tomahawk handle were the only vestiges of humanity discoverable. The admiral was satisfied that the poor fellow had been rescued by some passing ship, and let the matter rest.

The story was, however, so widely circulated, that on his return to England Captain Lake was court-martialled and cashiered.

Whilst this was passing, the greatest uncertainty existed as to the man's fate. His wrongs were commented on in the House by Sir Francis Burdett, and the case was kept so perseveringly before the public, that the Government issued orders for a strict inquiry to be made as to whether he were still alive or dead.

Presently an account was received, purporting to be by Jeffrey, giving an account of his rescue and his condition in America; but as to this was appended a cross for his signature, whereas Jeffrey was known to have been able to write, the public were led to suspect that this was a fabrication contrived by Lake's relatives and friends.

To settle the matter finally, a ship was despatched to bring Jeffrey home, and he arrived at Portsmouth in October, 1810, three years after his adventure on the island of Sombrero.

His escape had been due to his signals of distress having been seen and responded to by the captain of an American schooner, but when taken on board he was too exhausted to speak. He was conveyed to Marblehead, in Massachusetts, where he had remained working at a forge, and had culpably neglected to send home word of his escape. The reason he gave for not having signed the paper relative to his being taken off Sombrero was that it was presented to him by gentlemen, and he was too nervous in their presence to append his proper signature.

There was vast rejoicing at Polperro on his return. Almost the whole village turned out to welcome him, with a band playing and flags flying.

He was then persuaded to let himself be made a public show, and hired himself out at some of the minor London theatres to be exhibited as "Jeffrey the Sailor." After a few months he returned to Polperro with money in his pocket enough to purchase a small schooner intended for the coasting trade.

The speculation was unsuccessful. Jeffrey fell into consumption, and died leaving a wife and daughter in great poverty.

Polperro was also a notorious hole for smugglers. The last affair with them in which life was lost was in 1810, or thereabouts.

One morning a lugger was descried by the crew of the revenue boat, then stationed on shore. She was lying becalmed in Whitsand Bay. The glass informed them that it was the *Lottery*, of Polperro, well known for her fast sailing qualities, as well as for the hardihood of her crew. There was little doubt that with the springing up of the breeze she would put to sea. Accordingly the officer in command, with all despatch, manned two or three boats and put off, making sure of a rare capture, for there seemed little chance of an escape.

Their movements were, however, observed by the smugglers, who made preparations for resistance. The boats, on seeing their intentions, commenced firing when at a considerable distance; but it was not until they had approached her pretty near that the shots were returned from the lugger, which now assumed an unmistakable attitude of defiance. When within a few yards of the expected prize, Ambrose Bowden, who pulled the bow-oar of one of the attacking boats, fell mortally wounded.

It was plain that the Polperro men had come to a determination not to give up their fine craft and valuable cargo without a struggle, so the boats withdrew, and allowed the *Lottery* to proceed to sea. This affray was reported to the authorities, and orders were issued at all hazards to arrest the vessel and her crew. The smugglers were alarmed at what had been done, and at the dogged manner in which the officers of justice pursued them. They were kept continually concealed in pilchard cellars, in barns, in closets, and were liable at dead of night to have their houses surrounded and searched by a troop of dragoons, who made stealthy descents on the town.

At length a certain Toms, who had formed one of the crew of the *Lottery*, gave himself up, and declared that a man named Tom Potter had fired the fatal shot.

The Polperro people made common cause of this, and resolved at once to preserve Potter and to punish Toms. The revenue men knew the danger in which the latter stood, and they took him on board a cutter cruising off the coast.

On a certain occasion the cutter was off Polruan, when some of the Polperro men persuaded Toms' wife to decoy him on land, solemnly assuring her that they would not touch his life, and that all they desired was to remove the only evidence that existed against Potter.

She fell in with their wishes, and by her means Toms was seized and at once carried off, kept in hiding-places till an opportunity occurred, when he was shipped to Guernsey, preparatory to conveying him to America. But he was traced, and was pounced on by the Government officers in the hold of an outward-bound vessel.

Meanwhile the dragoons, who had been engaged in the search at home, discovered that their movements were observed, and that intelligence of their approach from Plymouth was sure to precede them to Polperro. A detachment was therefore sent to Truro, with orders to march from the west, in which way they were enabled to come on Polperro unobserved. On one of these visits Potter was captured. He was taken to London, tried at the Old Bailey, convicted on the evidence of Toms, and hanged. The evidence, however, was strongly believed to be false. The shot had entered the breast of Bowden in a direction opposite to the fire of the smugglers; and one of the coastguardsmen who were engaged in the affair averred that the unfortunate man Bowden was accidentally shot by one of his own crew.

Toms was never able to show his face again in Polperro, and a place was found for him in a menial capacity in Newgate, where he ended his days.

Lanreath stands between the Fowey and the Looe rivers, about midway. It has a fine church with a beautiful screen. Usually the paintings on these screens are mere daubs, but such as remain at Lanreath, though sadly defaced, show that there was at the end of the fifteenth or beginning of the sixteenth century a school of real artists in the West. Unhappily, only scanty remains of the paintings can be seen. A late rector is said to have proposed to scrape one half the screen if the parish would do the other half. Accordingly he effaced all the beautiful painted work of the portion between nave and chancel. The parish, however, did not like this sort of "restoration," and happily refused to complete the defacing of this work of art.

Court, near the church, is the old nest of the Grylls family, a picturesque mansion containing much of interest. It is in such a ruinous condition that it will have to be largely rebuilt, but the owner, Mr. T. H. Spry, purposes doing this in a thoroughly conservative spirit. The house contains one very handsome room with rich carved oak panelling.

NOTE.--Books to be consulted on Looe and Polperro:--

BOND (T.), *Topographical and Historical Sketches of East and West Looe*. London, 1823.

COUCH (T. Q.), *The History of Polperro*. Truro, 1871.

CHAPTER XIII.

FOWEY

Derivation of the name Fowey--The Fowey river--Lostwithiel--A rotten borough--Old Stannary Court--S. Winnow--His Settlement in Brittany--Beating the bounds--Golant--S. Samson--Dol--Tower of Fowey--Place--S. Finbar--The "Lugger Inn"--Polruan--The Mohun family--Death of Lord Mohun--The Rashleigh family--Sale of the borough.

ALTHOUGH pronounced Foye, the name of the place is spelled Fowey; it takes its appellation from the river. Mr. Ferguson, in his *River Names of Europe*, derives this from the Gaelic *fuair*, sound, *faoi*, a rising stream, and instances the Foyers in Inverness, and the Gaur in Perthshire, for *fuair* takes also the form *gaoir*, signifying din, and the Foyers is noted as forming one of the finest falls in Britain. But this won't do. The Foye is the meekest, quietest, and most unbrawling of rivers. The name is identical with that of the Fal, but the *l* has been dropped, and both derive from *falbh*, running, waving, flowing.

FOWEY HARBOUR

The river takes its rise on High Moor under Buttern Hill on the Bodmin moors, a mile north-west of Fowey Well that is under Brown Willy, which probably takes its name from being supposed to

137

ebb and flow with the tide, which, however, it does not. The river has a fall of nine hundred feet before it reaches the sea. It does not present anything remarkable till it comes in sight of the highway from Liskeard to Bodmin, as also of the railway, when at once it turns sharply to the west, at right angles to its previous course, and runs through a well-wooded and picturesque valley under the camp of Largin. Then, after flowing side by side with road and rail till it reaches Bodmin Road Station, it turns abruptly south, attending the railway to Lostwithiel, slipping under Restormel Castle.

LOSTWITHIEL BRIDGE

Lostwithiel is not Lost-wi'in-a-hill as is the popular derivation, but Les-Gwythiel, the palace in the wood, as Liskeard is that on the rock. It is charmingly situated.

It is an old rotten borough, once in the hands of the Earls of Mount Edgcumbe. But before that it was a seat of the Stannary Court for Cornwall, and here the Dukes of Cornwall had their palace. Of this considerable remains exist, but it has been meddled with, and vulgarised by the insertion of quite unsuitable windows.

The church is interesting; it possesses a fine lantern of a character nowhere else met with in the West. Anciently the tide came up as far as the town, and the portreeve had rights over the river, for which reason the town arms are represented with an oar.

Below the town the river to Fowey is full of beauty. It passes S. Winnow, with fine fifteenth-century glass; the church is beautifully situated. Here is a chapel of S. Nectan, of Hartland, to which latter was attached a college of secular priests endowed by Gytha, wife of Godwin, Earl of Kent. The priests of this college were married and allowed to marry, as all Celtic clergy were.

S. Winnow was son of Gildas the historian. Gildas and Finian were together for some time at S. David's monastery, and became close friends. Then Gildas entrusted his son Winnoc, or Winnow, to Finian to be educated, and Finian took the boy with him to Clonard and educated him. When Winnoc thought that it was time for him to leave, he returned to Britain and settled in Cornwall. As he was allied to the royal family, he received large grants of land, and certainly chose a lovely spot for his establishment. S. Veep, or Wennapa, was his aunt, and he served as her spiritual adviser. After a while, for some reason unknown, but probably on account of a breeze with his kinsman King Constantine, whom Winnow's father, Gildas, has abused in the most uncompromising terms, and Constantine's mother as well, Winnow left Cornwall and settled in Brittany. He was accompanied by his brother Madoc and his sister, whom the Welsh call Dolgar and the Bretons Tugdonia. He landed in the neighbourhood of Brest, where he was found by Conmor, Count of Pouhir, the usurper, who was killed in 555. Conmor granted him as much land as he could enclose in a day. The story goes that Madoc, or Madan, as the Bretons call him,[18] took a pitchfork and drew it behind him, and it formed a ditch and a bank that enclosed a bit of land. The fosse and embankment exist to the present day, and the story means no more than that under Madoc's supervision the*lis* or *rath* was thrown up to enclose the monastic settlement.

Within this defensive work Winnow constituted his establishment, built a church, and erected a number of beehive cells. Outside he set up stones to mark the bounds of his *minihi*, or sanctuary, and all who took refuge in this were allowed to pass under his protection and become members of his tribe.

One day Winnow went to Quimperlé, where some building was in progress. He incautiously stood under the scaffolding, and a mason who was above let fall his hammer on his head. This killed him.

The Welsh call him Gwynnog, and the Bretons Gouzenou. A very funny story is told of his establishment. It became a custom to beat the bounds every Ascension Day. The clergy with banners, and preceded by a cross, led the procession. One day the rain came down in torrents, and the clergy did not relish being wet to the skin, so they decided not to beat the bounds. However, cross and banners would not be done out of their little flirt, and to the astonishment of all, away they trotted, none bearing them, and made the rounds by themselves. Popular tradition is prudently silent as to when this took place.

That Winnow should have been forced to leave Cornwall after his father had addressed the king in such forcible but inelegant terms as "Tyrannical whelp of the unclean lioness of Dumnonia," is not surprising. You could not well stay in the house of a man in whose face your venerable father has spat--not if you have any self-respect.

A little further down the river is Golant, or S. Samson. This is a foundation of a man better known than S. Winnow. His story deserves telling, at least so much of it as pertains to Cornwall.

Samson was son of Amwn the Black, Prince of Bro-Weroc in Brittany, that is to say, the country about Vannes which had been colonised by British settlers. There ensued a little family brawl, which obliged Amwn to fly for his life. He escaped into Wales, where he married Anne, daughter of the Prince of Glamorgan. Samson was educated by S. Iltyd in Caldey Isle, and was taught "all the Old and New Testament, and all sorts of philosophy, to wit, geometry and rhetoric, grammar and arithmetic, and all the arts known in Britain."

He devoted himself to the ecclesiastical state, and spent many years in Wales. He paid a visit to Ireland, inspected the monasteries there, and then returned to Wales, where he was ordained bishop. After a while he considered that he might just as well try to get back to Brittany, and see whether he could recover some of the authority and the lands and position of which his father had been deprived. Accordingly he crossed to Cornwall and landed at Padstow, where he dedicated a little chapel, where now stands Prideaux Place. Here he was visited by S. Petrock on his arrival, as also by S. Winnow, not the Winnow of the Fowey river, but another, a brother of S. Winwaloe, who had settled at Lewanick. He was related to Samson through his mother.

The arrival of Petrock determined Samson to depart. He went on to Petherwin, where his first cousin, S. Padarn, was settled. He had brought with him all the sacred vessels and books he could collect, and had laden with them a waggon, drawn by two horses that he had brought from Ireland.

He sent forward a messenger to tell Padarn that he was on his way, and drawing near. The story has been already told how the news reached Padarn at the time he was dressing. Whilst in the district of Trigg Samson made the acquaintance of the chieftain, named Gwythian, and rendered him some service with his son, who was stunned by a fall from his horse. Gwythian seems to have followed him. Later on he became a disciple of S. Winwaloe, and founded a church in West Cornwall. Samson went on to Northill, where he remained for some time, and then proceeded to Golant. His main object in remaining in Cornwall was to watch affairs in Brittany. He had with him several companions--disciples from Wales, Austell, and Mewan and Erme. At Golant Samson continued till the arrival of his cousin, Maglorius, with tidings from Brittany, whereupon he entrusted his church to a disciple, crossed over, and settled at Dol. Conmor, usurper of Domnonia, had murdered Jonas, the reigning prince, in 540, and had usurped the throne. Judual, the son of the murdered king, had fled to the court of Childebert, King of the Franks. Samson visited Paris, and used persuasion to induce the Frank king to interfere and reinstate Judual. Childebert would not do this, but finally gave Samson leave to do what he could off his own bat. Samson then retired to the Channel Islands, where he enlisted soldiers and drilled them, and then landed on the Brittany coast, and proclaimed Judual. In the meantime Mewan had acted as his agent, travelling through the country preparing for a general revolt. Three bloody battles were fought, and in the third Conmor was killed by the hand of Prince Judual, A.D. 555, whereupon Judual ascended the throne, and rewarded Samson as liberally as he could have desired, but the bishop died five years later. Samson must have spent a good many years in Cornwall if he left Wales in 548 to escape the yellow plague which was then ravaging the land.

At Golant the saying is that there is to be seen "a tree above the tower, a well in the porch, and a chimney in the roof." The tree was probably once growing out of the stones on the top of the tower; the well is there still, close to the entrance to the church, under a rude arch. It is a holy well, and is said to have been a spring elicited by Samson with his staff.

The church is late Perpendicular.[19] The pulpit and reading-desk are made up of old bench-ends, representing S. Samson, the M of Mary, and the lily of the Annunciation, and instruments of the Passion.

On the tower of S. Austell under niches are representations of S. Samson habited as an archbishop--which he was not--and his disciple S. Austell. The reason of his being represented as an archbishop is curious. In 848 Nominoe, King of Brittany, determined to free his country from being Frenchified, and he not only made it independent of the Frank crown, but he also dismissed the Frank bishops from the

Breton sees, and filled their places with native prelates. He also elevated the see of Dol into an archbishopric over all the British-speaking races in Armorica. Now it so happened that there had been a Samson of York, but he was never more than a priest, and he was quite a different man from Samson, son of Amwn the Black, who settled at Dol. However, because York was an archiepiscopal see, and a Samson had once been there, it was supposed that he had been archbishop. Next he was confounded with Samson of Dol, and it was pretended that he had resigned York and come to Dol to set up his archiepiscopal see there. This served quite well enough as an excuse for withdrawing Dol and all the Breton bishoprics from allegiance to the Metropolitan of Tours; and Dol was able to maintain itself as a Breton archbishopric till 1199, that is to say, for over three hundred years.

Near S. Samson, or Golant, is Castle Dor, a very early fortification, that was, in historic times, held by the Crown, and a castle erected on the spot to keep the Cornish in order.

Fowey itself lies near the river-mouth; it much resembles a miniature Dartmouth. Opposite the town opens the creek that runs to Lanteglos. There were and are two castles, as at Dartmouth, commanding the entrance to the harbour, but they are insignificant, and form no feature of the scenery. Fowey is a curious, rambling place--one long street twisting in and out among houses, commanded by Place, the beautiful mansion of the Treffry family, that would have been entirely beautiful but for absurd and tasteless additions. This stands on a rock above the town, which is crowded below it.

The very fine church, with noble tower, is dedicated to, because founded by, S. Finbar, afterwards Bishop of Cork. In 1336 Bishop Grandisson rededicated the church to S. Nicholas. He sought persistently to drive out the local and Celtic saints and substitute for them such as were in the Roman calendar. But he has failed; the Irish patron maintains his place. Finbar was a disciple of S. David. His origin was not very creditable. He was the son of a noble lady by a vulgar intrigue with a smith, for which both were sentenced to be burnt alive, but the sentence was commuted to expulsion from the kingdom of Connaught. Finbar's real name was Lochan, but he received the other in allusion to his fair hair.

In a gloss by the O'Clerys on the martyrology of Oengus is a funny legend of S. Finbar. One day, as he was walking on the sea, on his way home to Ireland from Cornwall, he met S. Scuthin similarly walking, starting on his pilgrimage to Rome. "Arrah, now!" said Finbar, "how come you to be walkin' on the salt say?" "Why not?" answered Scuthin; "ain't I now walking over an illegant meadow?" Then he stooped, plucked a purple flower, and threw it at Finbar. The latter at once bowed, put down his hand, caught a salmon, and threw it flop into S. Scuthin's face. The O'Clerys got this from popular legend. Finbar died in 623.

The only really picturesque old house in Fowey is the "Lugger Inn," where Mr. Varco, the kindly host, has, more than once, made me very comfortable. A beam in the house bears the date 1633. The "Ship" is older; it was built in 1570, as the date over the chimney-piece records, but the house has been modernised externally. Near the club, on the south side, stands the house of Peter Pindar.

Immediately opposite Fowey is Polruan, the Pool of S. Ruan, who was an Irishman like Finbar. His bones were translated by Ordgar, Earl of Devon, to Tavistock in 960. Thence an excursion can be made to Lanteglos, dedicated to S. Wyllow, a local saint, murdered by a kinsman, Melyn. The church is chiefly interesting as containing monuments of the Mohun family. Indeed, it would seem to have been their principal place after Dunster.

Reginald, a younger son of Baron John Mohun of Dunster (died 1330), married a daughter of John Fitz-William, and settled at Hall, in Lanteglos. From Hall the Mohun family removed to Boconnoc, and a baronetcy was obtained in 1612 for the head of the house. John, son of the first baronet, was a venal adherent of Charles I., and owed his elevation to the peerage mainly to the clamorous importunities of a still more venal placeman, Sir James Bagg. Writing to the Duke of Buckingham, the latter urged, "Mr. Mohun is so your servant, as in life and fortune will be my second. Enable him by honour to be fit for you; so in the Upper House or in the country will he be the more advantageous to your grace."

Mohun was created Baron of Okehampton in 1628. His great-grandson was Charles, the fifth and last Lord Mohun. This man, possessed of a passionate and vindictive temper, lost his father early; his mother married again, and his education was neglected. When he had scarcely attained the age of twenty he was mixed up in the murder of Mountford, the actor. He was tried before his peers in 1692, and was acquitted; but there can be no doubt that he was associated in the murder. Seven years afterwards, in 1699, he was again tried for his life, along with the Earl of Warwick, for the murder of Captain Coote. He was again acquitted. This second escape sobered him for a while. For long he and the Duke of Hamilton entertained ill-feeling towards each other, occasioned by some money disagreement. This came to a head in 1712, when it ended in a challenge. Which it was, however, who challenged the other was never certainly decided. Colonel Macartney was Lord Mohun's second, and Colonel Hamilton exercised the same office for the duke. They met in Hyde Park on Saturday morning, the 15th November, and swords were the weapons employed. A furious encounter ensued, the combatants fighting to the death with the savagery of demons, so that when the keepers of the park, hearing the clash of swords, hurried to the spot, they found both the Duke of Hamilton and Lord Mohun weltering in their blood and dying, and the two seconds also engaged in mortal combat. The keepers separated the latter. Then Colonel Hamilton and one keeper lifted the duke; Macartney and the other endeavoured to do the same by Lord Mohun, who, however, expired, and his body was sent home in the coach that had brought him. Swift, writing to Stella at the time, says that, "while the duke was over him, Mohun shortened his sword, and stabbed him in the shoulder to the heart." According to the evidence of the surgeons who examined the bodies, each had received four frightful wounds, and both appeared to have given each other the mortal thrust at the same instant.

Fowey has for long been a nursery of Treffrys and Rashleighs, though the latter really issue from a place called by the same name near Eggesford, in Devon, where is an interesting old house, their mansion, with beautiful Elizabethan plaster-work, and their very peculiar arms--a cross or between, in the dexter chief quarter a Cornish chough arg., beaked and legged gu., in the sinister chief quarter a text T, and in base two crescents, all arg. A coat, this, that suggests that some story must be connected with its origin, but what that story was is now forgotten. The history of Fowey is interwoven with that of the Rashleighs and the Treffrys.

Fowey was one of the rotten boroughs that were disfranchised. It was created by Elizabeth in 1571. In 1813 the borough manor of Fowey, formerly the property of the Duchy, passed from the control of the Rashleighs to Lucy of Charlescot, in Warwickshire; it was sold for £20,000 and an expenditure of £60,000 to acquire whole influence over voters. The Lucys opposed Lord Valletort, who had represented the borough since 1790--a long time for a Cornish borough--and desperate contests ensued, with varying success. When disfranchisement came they found they had laid out vast sums, and had nothing to show for it.

CHAPTER XIV.

THE FAL

THE cathedral city of Cornwall is planted at the head of a long creek that unites with the Tresillian river, and together they join the Fal. The name is thought to signify Three Roads, that united at this point. The town lies in a hollow, and the descent into it from the railway station is considerable. It has been a place of more consequence in the past than Bodmin, and several of the Cornish county families had their town residences in Truro, going there for the winter, to enjoy assembly balls and card parties.

The cathedral soars up above the houses, and is a fine structure, doing vast credit to the county, which has strained every nerve to erect it at a time of depression and the death of the chief industry. When completed the effect will be very noble. One may regret that the architect chose as his style a foreign type--French Early Pointed--instead of adhering to the Perpendicular, which is that of the churches of the county. Now, instead of looking like the mother of these, which are her chicks, she holds herself up as of a distinct and alien breed. The poorest features are its over-enriched porch, which is elaborate without being pleasing, and the reredos, which looks as if shorn away at the head, and cries out for rich pinnacle-work to take off its ugly baldness. But perhaps the most pleasing portion of the cathedral is S. Mary's aisle, that belonged to the old parish church. An enduring debt of gratitude is due to the first Bishop of Truro, afterwards Archbishop of Canterbury, in making a bold stand against the designing of the building being left to local incapacity.

A visit to Probus should on no account be omitted. The magnificent tower is interesting as having been erected so late as the reign of Elizabeth. The church is dedicated to S. Probus, to whom also Sherborne Abbey was dedicated by Cenwalch. His history is not known.

Just below Malpas, the point of juncture of the Truro river and that of

Tresillian, are the remains of Old Kea Church.

Kea is a contraction for Kenan. He was one of the hostages held by Laogaire when S. Patrick came before him. Every high king in Ireland retained about him hostages delivered over by the under kings who acknowledged his sway. In fact, as an Irish law tract says, "No hostages, no king," and a king's *dun* was always provided with a court for the hostages. When S. Patrick preached before Laogaire Kenan believed, and he obtained his release through the intervention of the apostle, and was consecrated bishop by him.

For some unknown reason he left Ireland and visited Wales, where he tarried for a while. Then he went further through Britain till he reached the Fal estuary, then called Hir-drech, or the long tidal creek. As he lay there on the grass where is now Tregothnan, he heard men talking on the further side of the creek. Said one to another, "Have you seen my cows anywhere?" The other replied, "Aye, I have; I saw them yesterday in Rosinis." Then Kea remembered having heard a voice come to him in a dream, which said, "Settle where you hear the name Rosinis called."

So he crossed the water along with his comrades, and they set to work to build huts where now stands Old Kea.

Now the king, or prince, lived at Goodern, where are still mounds of a *lis*, and he was by no means pleased to hear that foreign monks had settled on the river-bank without his permission.

He sent and had seven of the oxen and a cow belonging to Kea taken from him. The legend says that seven stags came from the forest, and allowed Kea to yoke them and make them draw the plough. But this is a fabulous addition to the history. What is really true is that he went to Goodern and remonstrated with the prince, who was none other than Tewdrig, who behaved so roughly to the colony of Irish saints in the Land's End district. Tewdrig flew into a passion and struck Kea in the mouth, so as to break one of his front teeth.

However, shortly after this Tewdrig fell ill--caught a heavy head-cold perhaps--and, thinking that he had been "ill-wished" by Kea, hastily reconciled himself with the saint, and restored his oxen. The Rosinis in the narrative is Roseland, but the Kestell Carveth, or Stag's Castle, where Kea made his first settlement, cannot be identified by name, though it was probably what is now called Woodbury.

But the relations with Tewdrig continued strained, and the condition of affairs was worse when the king fell from his horse and broke his neck. Kea, fearing lest this should be imputed to him, as occasioned by his "ill-wishing," resolved on flight to Brittany. He went to Landegu, *i.e.* Landege, the old name of the place, as we learn from Bishop Stapleton's Register (1310). Here was a merchant about to send a cargo of corn to Brittany, and Kea, with his companions, were permitted by the merchant to depart in the grain ship.

He reached the Brittany coast at Cleder, and there he remained till the discord broke out between Arthur and Mordred, when Kea returned to Britain, and endeavoured, but in vain, to reconcile them. After the death of Arthur, it was Kea who told Queen Gwenever some unpleasant home-truths, and induced her to retire into a convent. Then, in 542, he returned to Cleder, where he died shortly after at an advanced age. But this story of his connection with Arthur and Gwenever is very problematical, indeed impossible to reconcile with his history, if he was converted in 433. In Brittany he is called S. Kay, or Kea, as in Cornwall.

A little lower down the river is the wooded slope of Polgerran, and an ancient chapel stands above it. Gerran, or Geraint, was King of Cornwall, and married Enid, daughter of the Count-in-Chief of Caerleon. Tennyson has revivified her charming story. After the death of Arthur, he seems to have been elected Pendragon, or high king, over the Britons, and his life was spent in fighting the Saxons along the frontier from the Roman wall down to the Severn. S. Senan, of the Land's End, was on good terms with him, and there is a story told in the life of that saint concerning Geraint. The king had a fleet of six score vessels in the Severn, and the fatal battle in which he fell was at Langport on the Parret, whither at that time vessels could ascend. His palace was at Dingerrein, in the parish of S. Gerrans in Roseland. His tomb is shown at Carn Point, where he was said to lie in a golden boat with silver oars, an interesting instance of persistence of tradition in associating him with ships. When the tumulus was broken into, in 1855, by treasure-seekers, a kistvaen was discovered and bones, but no precious metal. As Geraint fell at Langport he would hardly have been brought to Cornwall for interment. But there were two other princes of Cornwall of the same name, who reigned later.

The long Restronguet Creek enters the estuary of the Fal where that estuary becomes wide and a fine sheet of water. The peninsula is Roseland, the old Rosinis--Moorland Isle.

Restronguet Creek has been choked with the wash coming down

from the ancient tin mines. At one time it was a fine long arm of water. Immediately opposite each other are Mylor and S. Just, the latter hidden in a lovely creek and buried in trees. The interesting little church stands by the water-side. It was founded by Just, or Justin, one of the sons of Geraint. By an odd mistake, over the north porch is inscribed, "I was glad when they said unto me, Let us *go up* unto the house of the Lord," whereas the congregation have to descend to it some two hundred feet, and the churchyard gate is level with the ridge of the roof.

Mylor Church is interesting as possessing old crosses with Celtic interlaced work. There were formerly curious frescoes in the church. It is dedicated to a prince of the blood royal. His father, Melyan, was brother of the ruffian Tewdrig, who carried off S. Kea's cows and killed some of the Irish colonists. His uncles were S. Oudoc, Bishop of Llandaff, and Ismael, a favourite pupil of S. David. But he had another, an ambitious uncle named Howel, who asked Melyan to meet him, and suddenly and treacherously stabbed him, in 537. This probably took place not far from Par, where are a Lan-melyan and a Merthan close together, indicative of a place of martyrdom, and a chapel to the martyred prince. Howel at once assumed the crown over Cornwall and Devon. In order to incapacitate his nephew Melor, son of the murdered Melyan, from menacing his throne, he had his right hand and one foot cut off, as by Celtic law no cripple or disfigured person is qualified to become a chief or a prince. Melor was sent into Brittany. But there he became such an object of interest and sympathy, that Howel was afraid, and had him also secretly assassinated.

The wonderful harbour of Falmouth now bursts on the view, almost closed between the jaws of Pendennis Point and S. Anthony's Head.

A creek runs up to the right to Penryn, and on the left, another penetrates deep into Roseland.

Falmouth is a modern place with a modern name. Anciently it was but a fishing hamlet--Penycomequick, *i.e.* Pen-y-cwm-wick, the village at the head of the valley--with another, Smithick, hard by about a forge. But the Killigrews had a fine place and deer-park at Arwenack.

Leland (about 1520), who mentions every place worth notice, including every "praty" and every "pore fisching town," says nothing of Falmouth beyond it being "a havyn very notable and famox."

Arwenack and the fortifications of Pendennis are noticed by Carew, but nothing is said of Falmouth.

Camden (in 1607) mentions Penryn, Pendennis Castle, S. Mawes Castle, and Arwenack, but says nothing of Falmouth.

When, however, Sir Walter Raleigh put into Falmouth Harbour on his way homewards from Guiana, he was entertained at the great house, but his men could hardly find any accommodation, and he represented the matter to Government, urging the importance of this splendid harbour.

Sir John Killigrew went repeatedly to town on the matter, but was opposed by the Penryn interest. However, he obtained a licence to build four houses on the spot. As the place rapidly increased beyond the licence, in 1613 Sir John was disposed to further extend it, and build a town, but was interrupted in his attempt by Truro, Penryn, and Helston, which exerted all their influence to prevent it. Truro was jealous of the prosperity of Penryn, and was deadly opposed to the growth of a new town so near the entrance of the harbour, one which would have many advantages over itself in point of situation.

In a petition to James I. it was said that the erection of a town at Smithick would tend to the impoverishment of the ancient coinage towns and market towns aforenamed, and therefore humbly prayed that Killigrew might be restrained in his undertaking. The king thereupon stopped the builders, and ordered his privy councillors to get information from the Governor of Pendennis Castle relative to the projected town. The latter replied that the project was excellent, as such a place, being at the mouth of the Fal Harbour, could at once and readily supply such ships as put in there, instead of forcing them to go up two miles to Penryn or nine to Truro. The king then resolved on erecting a town at Smithick, and Sir John Killigrew was encouraged to proceed.

During the protectorship of Cromwell, although the Killigrews had been staunch Royalists, yet Sir Peter succeeded in having the custom-house removed from Penryn to Smithick, and in 1652 in getting the place elevated to the position of market town. Smithick continued to be the name until August 20th, 1660, when, in consequence of an application from Sir Peter Killigrew, a proclamation was issued by Charles II. ordering "that Smithike, *alias* Penny-come-quick, should for ever after that day be called, named, and known by the name of Falmouth." In the following year a charter of incorporation was granted, and thenceforth the story of Falmouth is one of incessant quarrels between the corporation and the

Killigrews, the former intent on jobbing for their private advantage, whereas the Killigrews were ambitious in every way to benefit and enlarge the town.

The old mansion of Arwenack has almost disappeared--it has given its name to a street--and the Killigrews have also vanished. The last was killed in a tavern brawl at Penryn in 1687, and through females the property has passed to Erisey, to West, to Berkeley, and to Wodehouse, and is now owned by Lord Kimberley.

What made Falmouth at one time a place of importance was that from it sailed the packets. At first they were a matter of contract between the General Post Office and the captains of the several boats; and this system continued till 1823, when the packets were placed under the orders of the Board of Admiralty. The transfer of the packets from the Post Office to the Admiralty at first excited much alarm among the inhabitants, and doubtless many of them suffered, owing to the decreased demand for ships' stores of all descriptions, as the sloops-of-war were provided by the Government; but the change did not prove so disastrous as was expected, for many persons were drawn to live at the place, persons who belonged to the families of the commanders, and also because a greater number of men were employed on the new system. Packets were first stationed at Falmouth in or about the year 1688, when some were employed to sail to Corunna; and in 1705 they ran to the West Indies; in 1709 five sailed to Lisbon; and the number gradually increased. In 1827 there were thirty-nine packets employed. But all this came to an end in 1850, when the mails were sent from Southampton in place of Falmouth.

The church was dedicated in 1663 to Charles the Martyr. It is a mean building, without architectural merit, and with a stumpy tower, vastly inferior to the other church dedicated to the royal martyr at Plymouth. Pendennis Castle (Pen-Dinas, the Castle on the Head) is not a very striking feature. It was erected in the reign of Henry VIII., but it has been since somewhat extended. In 1644 Pendennis sheltered the unfortunate Henrietta Maria, when embarking for France. It was from hence that Arwenack House, esteemed the finest mansion in Cornwall, was fired, during the siege by the Parliamentary troops, lest it should furnish them with shelter. John Arundell, of Trerice, commonly called Jack-for-the-King, defended it for six months, he being in his eighty-seventh year, and only surrendered when starved out.

From the ramparts a fine view is obtained of the Lizard promontory, and of the terrible Manacles, on which the *Mohegan* was lost in October, 1898. Perhaps even more terrible was the wreck of the *Despatch*, in January, 1809, when, two days before Sir John Moore's death, three officers and seventy-two non-commissioned officers and privates were lost on Lowland Point; and almost simultaneously the *Primrose*, with 120 officers and men and six passengers, was wrecked on the Manacles.

About half-way across the mouth of the harbour is the Black Rock, exposed at low water, but covered when the tide rises. An eccentric Mr. Trefusis, of Trefusis, opposite Falmouth, one day invited his wife to boat with him to the Black Rock and picnic there. She incautiously accepted, and when he had landed her, he made his bow, and rowed away with, "Madam, we are mutually tired of each other, and you will agree with me that it were best to part."

Fortunately a fishing-smack picked her off just as the tide was flowing over it, and brought her back to Trefusis. "Be hanged to you rogues," said the husband. "I'd have given you a guinea each to let her drown; now you shan't have a shilling from me."

S. MAWES' CASTLE

S. Mawes Castle commands the harbour entrance from the other side, as also that to S. Mawes Creek. The long promontory, over four miles in length, that intervenes between the creek and the sea is Roseland. The neck of land dividing them is in two places very contracted. Roseland was a great harbour for smugglers, whose headquarters were at Porthscatho. When employed in conveying their goods ashore in Gerrans Bay, they always had their scouts on the hills, and as the customs station was at S. Mawes, no sooner did the preventive boat put forth, than notice was given, and the boats dispersed; so that by the time she came into the bay all was quiet. Finding this to be the case, the officer in command one day took his boat up the river, and had her carried by the crew across the neck of land, and he dropped into Gerrans Bay before the scouts were aware that he had left the harbour. He secured a good prize, and struck a severe blow at the contraband trade. Porthscatho, perhaps, takes its name from Cado, or Cathaw, the son of Geraint, and Duke of Cornwall. The whole of the district from Roseland to Grampound teems with reminiscences of the Cornish royal family. Lansallos is a foundation of Salomon, or Selyf, son of Geraint; and in S. Gerrans parish is a holy well of S. Non, mother of S. David, and sister to Selyf's wife, S. Wenn. Tregony Church is a foundation of S. Cuby, son of Selyf, and grandson of Geraint. Filleigh was founded by a son of Gildas, who was grandson of Geraint. Dingerrein, the royal palace, is now represented by a mound, but hence hailed one of the early bishops of Cornwall, Kenstig, who submitted to Canterbury in or about 850.

S. Mawes was formerly a borough returning two members. It consists of a row of houses looking upon the creek. It takes its name from an Irish settler, who perhaps came with S. Ruan. He arrived with two disciples. Tudy was one, or, as the Welsh call him, Tegwyn, so that in all likelihood he had halted for some time on his way in Wales, doubtless at S. David's. There was formerly a stone chair near the beach, but it has been built into the sea-wall. From this he taught the many pupils who came to him.

But whilst they listened to or pondered over his instructions, they were much distracted by the frolics of a great seal that came near, stared at them, and made grunting noises. This was so vexing that one day Mawes jumped out of his chair and, taking a big stone in his hand, ran into the shallow water to try conclusions with the seal. He got near enough to throw the stone at it, and to hit it on the head, after which he was no more troubled with the interruption.

The reason why Mawes settled where he did was probably this. His disciple, Tudy, was a cousin of S. Wenn, who was queen, the wife of Selyf, or Salomon, and Tudy doubtless advised his master to go to Cornwall, and see whether his kinsfolk would do something for them. However, Mawes does not seem to have been long satisfied with his entertainment, for he crossed into Brittany, where he died.

The holy well of S. Mawes is immediately opposite the post office, and supplies the place with drinking water. The pointed arched door is walled up, and two ugly ventilating shafts have been inserted to keep the air sweet above the spring.

From the land side, the castle of S. Mawes is a picturesque object.

One of the main charms of Falmouth and its neighbourhood is the climate. Sharp frosts are almost unknown, the mild and balmy air is wonderfully even in temperature, and the marvellous gardens of Enys show delicate kinds of rhododendron--elsewhere growing in greenhouses--luxuriating in the open air.

The climate is that of the lotus-eaters, pleasant but enervating.

"Propt on beds of amaranth and moly,
How sweet (while warm airs lull us, blowing lowly)
With half-dropt eyelids still,
Beneath a heaven dark and holy,
To watch the long bright river drawing slowly
His waters from the purple hill--
Only to hear and see the far-off sparkling brine,
Only to hear were sweet, stretch'd out beneath the pine.
    *   *   *   *   *
"Let us swear an oath, and keep it with equal mind,
In the hollow lotus-land to live, and lie reclined
On the hills like gods together, careless of mankind."

And there are good hotels at Falmouth where the lotus-eaters may do this.

Finally, a story of S. Just. He left Cornwall and settled in North Brittany, at Plestin, but left it for a pilgrimage. On his return he found his cell occupied by an Irish chief, S. Efflam, who had settled into it to follow a religious life. Whose should the cell be? "Let us sit down," said Just, "and he on whom the sun first falls, his the cell shall be." So they sat down. The golden streak through the little window travelled on, as the sun declined, and lighted up the face of Efflam. Just rose and departed, but surely bore away on his face the radiance of Charity, not on face only, but also in his heart.

CHAPTER XV.

NEWQUAY

Mr. Austin Treffry--The sands--Cliff-castles--Castel-an-Dinas--The Gannel--S. Carantock--Newlyn--Perranzabuloe--Church of S. Piran--History--Roche--S. Denis--Columb Major and Minor--S. Agnes--The Cornish rotten boroughs--How they passed away from the Crown--Mitchell--The town hall--Kit Hawkins--Trerice--Lanherne--Church--William Noye--S. Mawgan--The educator--The early missionaries.

NEWQUAY is a very new place; it was projected by Mr. J. T. (Austin) Treffry, of Place House, Fowey, a very remarkable man, far in advance of his time, to whom not Fowey only, but Cornwall generally owes a debt of gratitude. His projects have been worked out since his death with complete success.

In itself uninteresting to the last degree, it is the key to very fine coast scenery, and the air is bracing without being cold. It possesses excellent sands, both at Newquay and Fistral Bays. There is further a long tract of sand, two and a quarter miles long, to the north of S. Columb Porth, the Tregurian Beach. The rocks will interest the geologist as well as form a subject for the artist.

The coast presents examples of several cliff-castles, as at Kelsey, Trevelgue and Griffith's Heads, and Redcliff above Bedruthan; but the finest example of a castle is Castel-an-Dinas, near S. Columb Major.

This fortress comprises about six acres of land, enclosed within three concentric rings of bank and moat, built up of earth and stone together, about a pyramidal hill. The innermost enclosure contains about an acre and a half, and there were at one time indications of habitations therein, but these have now disappeared. There are, however, traces of a pit that was a well or tank for rain-water, as there is no spring on the hill. There are two entrances to this interesting camp or dinas.

According to legend, King Arthur lived here and hunted the wild deer on Tregoss Moors.

Near Perranzabuloe are Caer Kieff (*eyf*, perfect) and Caer Dane (dinas).

To the south of Newquay is the curious creek called the Gannel (*ganhael*, the mouth of saltings). A very slight thread of sweet water descends from the land into a creek of three miles of salt marsh and sand, filled at high water with the tide. Here it was that S. Patrick's companion, adviser, and friend, Carantock, on leaving Ireland, set up his residence. He was a remarkable man, for he was one of the three bishops chosen by Laogaire at Tara to revise the laws of Ireland. When the Irish accepted Christianity it was obvious that the laws needed modification. King Laogaire was not and never did become a Christian, but he accepted the situation, and appointed a commission for the revision of the laws, and on this sat Carantock. The result was the Senchus Mor, the great code by which the Irish were ruled till 1600. Carantock was an acquaintance of King Arthur, but he met him, not at Castel-an-Dinas, but on the Severn at Dinedor, and did not get on well with him.

An odd story is told of his fixing the site for his church at Crantock. After he had landed in the Gannel he went up on the land, and began to till a scrap of land granted him; and when not at work on the soil, he whittled his staff, to make the handle smooth. Then, when he resumed his mattock, he saw a wood-pigeon fly down, pick up the shavings, and carry them off. He was curious to know what she did with them, so he followed, and saw that she dropped them in one spot in a little heap. "There must be some meaning in this," said Carantock, and he resolved to build his church there. Those Celtic saints looked out for some omen to direct them in all their doings.

Crantock Church was collegiate; it fell into a condition of decay, and was shockingly mutilated, but is about to be restored carefully and conservatively.

Another interesting church, one with a fine screen and in good condition, is Newlyn. This is probably situated on the patrimony of S. Newlyna--"the white cloud," as her name signifies. She was of noble birth, but, like the rest of the Celtic saints, thought she must travel, so she took ship at Newlyn West, where she has also left her name, and arrived in Brittany with her foster-mother as chaperon. There she had an unpleasant experience. She caught the fancy of a local magnate, who pursued her when she fled from him, and as she stubbornly repelled his advances, in a fit of fury, struck her with his sword and killed her. She is commemorated at Noualen, or Noyal-Poutivy, where the screen was formerly painted with a series of subjects relative to her story. This was destroyed in 1684 by order of the vicar-general, because it concealed the new reredos in the debased style of the period. This tasteless construction has been in turn demolished, and the paintings that formerly decorated the jubé have been reproduced in coloured glass in the windows.

The great towans, or sand dunes, of Penhale extend three miles in length, and almost two in parts inland. They are held in check to the north and north-east by the little stream that finds its way into Holywell Bay. In these sands was found S. Piran's Chapel, of the eighth or ninth century, in 1835, exactly resembling similar structures of the same date in Ireland. It was cleared out by Mr. William Mitchell, of Comprigney, near Truro, and he thus describes it:--

"The church, which is built nearly east and west, inclining only 4° north of west, is of but small dimensions, the length without the walls being 30 feet and within the walls 25 feet; the width within 13 feet in the chancel and 12 feet in the nave, and the height about 13 feet. There is a very neat arched doorway in a good state of preservation at the date of the work, viz. the day when I removed the sand from it, 7 ft. 4 in. by 2 ft. 4 in., ornamented with Saxon tracery [this is inaccurate, no Saxon about it], the arch itself having on its keystone the head of a tiger, and the points of its curve (*i.e.* label-terminations) the head of a man and that of a woman, rudely sculptured in stone, in the centre of the nave on the south wall; and another doorway in the north-east corner, near the altar, of similar dimensions and style, if we may judge from the remains of its arch lying near it, and which may be assumed to be that intended for the priest himself, leading into the chancel. The chancel is exactly 9-1/2 feet long, and shows in the north and south walls the precise spots where the railing (screen) separating it from the nave was fixed. Attached to the eastern wall of the church is an altar nearly equidistant between the north and south walls, 5 ft. 3 in. long by 2 ft. 3 in. wide, and 4 feet high, built of stone and neatly plastered with lime. Eight inches above this altar is a recess or niche about 12 inches high by 8 inches wide, in which, undoubtedly, was once S. Piran's shrine.... There is only one small aperture or window, 12 inches high by 10 inches wide, about 10 feet above the floor, in the south wall of the chancel.... A stone seat, raised 14 inches above the level of the floor, and 12 inches wide, covered with lime-plaster, runs all round the walls except the east and south walls of the chancel. The nave is exactly 15-1/2 feet long, its floor, together with the floor of the chancel, being composed of lime and sand, apparently as perfect as when first laid down. Each door has two low steps to descend into the church. The church itself is plastered with beautiful white lime. The masonry of the entire building is of the rudest kind, and evidently of very remote antiquity. There is not the slightest attempt at regular courses, but the stones, consisting of granite, quartz, sandstone, porphyry, etc., appear to have been thrown together almost at random--horizontally, perpendicularly, and at every angle of inclination--just as the hand, not the eye, of the workman happened to direct him. To render the church as perfect as when it was originally erected, nothing seemed wanting but its doors and roof. Not an atom of wood, except a piece of about 8 inches long by 2 inches wide, and an inch thick, was found within the walls. That there were many bodies interred both in the chancel and nave of the church is an unquestionable fact. Several skeletons have been found deposited about 2 feet below the floor. Three were discovered with their feet lying under the altar, one of them of gigantic dimensions, measuring about 7 ft. 6 in.... Their heads, which appeared to be almost cemented together, lay between the knees of the skeleton deposited nearest to the south wall.

"On the southern and western sides of this venerable ruin is the ancient burying-ground, strewed over tens of thousands of human bones and teeth as white as snow; and, strange as it may seem, the showers of sand which fall all around hardly ever remain on these melancholy relics of mortality."[20]

Unhappily nothing was done to preserve this little church after it had been excavated from the sand. The three heads from the doorway were carried off for Truro Museum; visitors pulled out stones, boys tore down the walls, and now little more than a gable remains. But to this was added the mischievous meddlesomeness of the curate-in-charge, the Rev. William Haslam, who turned the altar-stones about, as he had got a theory into his head that they had formed a tomb, and rebuilt them in this fashion, pointing east and west, and cut upon the altar-slab the words "S. Piranus." It is purposed to undo Mr. Haslam's work, and replace the altar as originally found. More should be done. Cement should be run along the top of such wall as remains to save it from falling.

The Rev. C. Collins Trelawny, soon after the discovery, wrote an account in a book entitled *Perranzabulo, the Lost Church Found*, which went through seven editions (1837-72).

In 1844 Mr. Haslam published another book on the subject, and again another in 1888, *From Death unto Life*, in which he assumed to himself the credit of Mr. Mitchell's discovery. The church has not the extreme antiquity attributed to it. The fact of there being a chancel is sufficient evidence that it does not belong to the sixth century, as none of the earliest Irish churches possess this feature.[21] It is about two centuries later, though doubtless a reconstruction of the old materials, and perhaps on the old lines. Judging from Irish examples, in one point only is Mr. Haslam more correct than Mr. Mitchell. He considered the niche over the altar to have been a walled-up window, and in this was right.

The story of S. Piran, or Kieran, as he is called in Ireland, is of sufficient interest to be given.

He was born in Clear Island, in the county of Cork, the extreme south point of Ireland. He established a monastery at Saighir, in the extreme north of Munster. The legend is that his first disciples were a boar, a fox, a badger, a wolf, and a doe. And in this we have an instance of the manner in which simple facts assume a fabulous character in the hands of late writers. The district was that of the clan of Hy Sinnach, *i.e.* the foxes; an adjoining tribe was that of the Hy Broc, or the badgers; an Ossorian disciple was regarded as *Os*, *i.e.* a doe; and his wolf was no other than one of the Hy Faeladh, which has a double meaning of "hospitable" or "wolfish;" another disciple was S. Tore, and the name means "boar."

Kieran, as his name is in Irish, invoked the assistance of his mother, Liadhain, and induced her to start a school for girls at Kellyon, not far from Saighir. The arrangement was not happy, as at least one of his disciples carried on a lively flirtation with Liadhain's damsels.

How Kieran placed Buriena the Slender with Liadhain, and how a chief ran away with her, and how Kieran got her back, shall be told when we come to Land's End. It was possibly on account of this unpleasantness that he withdrew to Cornwall, and brought with him both his nurse, Cocca, and Buriena. But there were other reasons. Kieran belonged to the royal race of Ossory, and in his time Ossory was overrun by Cucraidh, who massacred all he could lay hands on of the royal race of the O'Bairrche, to which Kieran belonged. Most of Kieran's clan migrated to the north of Ossory, where they maintained their independence till 642. It was not likely that Kieran cared to remain in the country under an usurper whose hands were steeped in the blood of his brethren. Cucraidh tried to make terms with the saint, and his granddaughter was either put under his rule, or else voluntarily entrusted herself to him. But even if Cucraidh invited Kieran to remain, he was but under-king to Aengus, King of Munster, and Kieran quarrelled with the latter and denounced him to death. In fact, Aengus was killed in battle in 489. There was consequently very good reason why the saint should leave Ireland.

Kieran's monastery at Saighir was on a princely scale. "Numerous were his cattle; there were ten doors to the shed of his kine, and ten stalls at every door, and ten calves for every stall, and ten cows with every calf.... Moreover, there were fifty tame horses with Kieran for tilling and ploughing the ground. And this was his dinner every night: a little bit of barley bread and two roots, and water of a spring. Skins of fawns were his raiment, and a haircloth over these. He always slept on a pillow of stone." Carantock was his scribe, and some of the books written by Carantock were long preserved at Saighir. One of Kieran's disciples was Carthag, who, although a saint, was a somewhat loose fish, and gave the abbot not a little trouble. S. Itha put one of his escapades in as delicate a way as might be when she said--

"A son will be born to Carthag,
And Carthag will not be thought better of accordingly."

On account of his disreputable conduct, Kieran kicked him out, and bade him go to Rome, hoping that he might sow his wild oats in that chaste and holy place.

One day Kieran of Clonmacneis and the two Brendans came to visit him. The steward approached him in dismay. "There is nothing to offer these distinguished guests except some scraps of rusty bacon and water."

"Then serve up the bacon and the water."

Now there was at table a lay brother, and when the bacon was set before him he thrust his platter contemptuously from him, for he was tired of bacon, and when out visiting, by dad! he expected to be fed like a gintleman.

"Hah!" said Kieran turning angry, "you are dainty, son of Comgal; it is just such as you who would not scruple to eat ass's flesh in Lent."

Across the backbone of Cornwall is Ladock, and if I am not mistaken, Kieran planted there his old nurse, Cocca, who also became head of a religious house for women.

It is said that every Christmas night, after divine service at his own monastery, Kieran started off walking, and arrived at early morning to perform divine worship for his old nurse, and give her the compliments of the season. The date of his death is not known, but it is thought to have been about 550.

A friend writes to me:--

"It may be foolishness, but to me such a place as the ruined church of Peranzabulo appeals most powerfully. I determined to find it unaided, and when found I spent hours there, sometimes at dark, trying as best I might to recall the place as it once was, and to revivify the bones which were lying in several little heaps where the workmen, who had been railing about the ruin, had collected them.

"It seems to me that one loses a great deal in stifling and choking the imagination.

"In the dusk of evening, with the swallows in vast quantities gathered for their flight to the south, and the white bones lying before me, the wind sighing and piping in the grass, and the sea moaning in the distance, the scene was one that deeply impressed me, and will never be forgotten."

There is now some talk of a very careful and conservative restoration, so as to preserve what yet remains.

The rock and hermitage of Roche, standing up in a district that has been turned over and undermined for tin, and is strewn with ruined engine-houses, deserve to be seen. The rock is a prong shooting up boldly, and a chapel and the cell of an ancient hermit have been constructed on it.

S. Denis is a conical hill with an earthwork round it; in fact, it was an old *Dinas*, or palace of a chief. The church within was called Lan-dinas. The bishops of Exeter, not understanding the real meaning, concluded that it was the church of S. Denis, and dedicated it to the Bishop-martyr of Paris, a somewhat apocryphal personage. So two fortified headlands were each Lan-an-dinas,[22] and they were converted into churches of S. Anthony.

S. Columb Major has a fine church, which unhappily suffered from an explosion of gunpowder in 1676, when three boys carelessly set fire to a barrel of this explosive, which had been placed in the rood-loft staircase. The windows and roof were blown away, and the pillars thrown out of the perpendicular. Happily the fine carved benches were unhurt; they are curious. Apparently a travelling show of wild beasts passed through the town when they were being carved, and the workmen reproduced on them the strange beasts they saw.

There is an interesting and picturesque old slated house at the entrance to the churchyard.

The old custom of hurling is still observed at S. Columb on the feast, which is in November, and the silver ball is thrown in the market-place.

S. Columb Minor bench-ends, according to Hals, were of black oak, and bore the date 1525, and it had a fine rood-screen with loft, "a most curious and costly piece of workmanship, carved, and painted with gold, silver, vermillion, and bice, and is the masterpiece of art in those parts of that kind." This has all disappeared now.

S. Agnes' Head, pronounced S. Anne's, presumedly takes its name from Ann, the mother of the gods among the Irish Celts, and probably also among the Cymri. She gives her name to the Two Paps of Ana, in the county of Kerry. The parish was constituted late. There was no such parish at the time of the Conquest, and the present church was built and consecrated in 1484.

A story is told of a house in S. Agnes. When Wesley visited this part of Cornwall preaching, he was refused shelter elsewhere than in an ancient mansion that was unoccupied because haunted by ghosts.

Wesley went to the house, and sat up reading by candlelight. At midnight he heard a noise in the hall, and on issuing from his room saw that a banquet was spread, and that richly-apparelled ladies and gentlemen were about the board.

Then one cavalier, with dark, piercing eyes and a pointed black beard, wearing a red feather in his cap, said: "We invite you to eat and to drink with us," and pointed to an empty chair.

Wesley at once took the place indicated, but before he put in his mouth a bite of food or drank a drop, said: "It is my custom to ask a blessing; stand all!" Then the spectres rose.

Wesley began his accustomed grace, "The name of God, high over all----" when suddenly the room darkened, and all the apparitions vanished.

The story of the creation, subsequent history, and extinction of those English boroughs which were swept away by the Reform Bill of 1832, and which were commonly designated as pocket or rotten boroughs, is too curious an episode in Parliamentary history to be allowed to remain in the limbo of Parliamentary reports--a charnel-house of the bones of facts--unclothed with the personal reminiscences and local details which invest these dry bones with flesh, and give to them a living interest.

In a very few years there will not be a man alive who can recall the last election for them. Their story is this: They were creations of the Crown when its tenure of power was insecure, and the object aimed at was to pack the House of Commons with members who were mere creatures of the Crown. The shock of the Reformation had upset men's minds. What had been held sacred for ages was sacred no longer, and the men who had been encouraged to profane the altar were ready enough to turn their hands against the throne. The revolt of the Parliament under Charles I. was long in brewing; its possibility was seen, and the creation of pocket boroughs was devised as an expedient to prevent it.

In order that the Crown might have a strong body of obedient henchmen in the House, a number of villages or mere insignificant hamlets were accorded the franchise, villages and hamlets on land belonging to the Duchy of Cornwall that went with the royal family as an appanage of the Prince of Wales, or were under the control of pliant courtiers. As the country was in a ferment of religious passion, many, if not most, of these new boroughs were specially chosen because far removed from ecclesiastical influence, either because they lay at the junction of several parishes, or because they were places remote from churches.

In Cornwall in the reign of Edward VI. eight petty places were given the privilege of returning two members apiece. These were Bossiney, a mound in a field, with a farmhouse adjoining, West Looe, Grampound, Penryn, Newport, Camelford, and Mitchell.

Queen Mary followed by raising S. Ives to the position of a borough; Elizabeth proceeded to confer the same privileges on S. Germans, S. Mawes, Tregony, East Looe, Fowey, and Callington. Those called into existence by Edward were all under Duchy influence with the exception of Mitchell, "the meanest hamlet within or without Cornwall," which was under the control of the Arundels of Lanherne.

Four of the new boroughs had been places belonging to monastic establishments, but since the suppression of the religious houses they had passed under the domination of the Crown. S. Ives, which had been constituted a borough by Philip and Mary, was in the hands of Paulet, Marquis of Winchester who could be relied upon. For the same reason Callington was given two members in 1584, as this also was held by the Paulets. The fear of ecclesiastical influence is conspicuous in numerous instances. Camelford is two miles distant from a church, and the only chapel in it was confiscated and demolished. Saltash was another churchless place; it belonged to the parish of S. Stephen's, two miles distant, and had in it no other place of worship than a municipal chapel. Grampound was at a like distance from its parish church, S. Creed; Tregony was planted at the junction of several parishes; Mitchell divided between two equidistant churches two miles away. Another remarkable feature in these boroughs is that they rapidly slipped away from the influence of the Crown, and fell under the control of great landlords. Founded for the servile support of the Throne, they became a prey, not even to Duchy tenants, but to private owners, and resolved into saleable commodities, that passed rapidly from hand to hand. In 1783 it was noticed that seven peers directed or influenced the return of twenty members; eleven commoners controlled the election of twenty-one; and the people one only, that of S. Ives. It was a recognised thing that the man who held six boroughs in his hand, that is to say, who could return twelve members to support the Ministry, could demand and obtain a peerage. Even a foreign Jew who, at a pinch, could assist the Ministry by means of three boroughs which he had bought, could exact a baronetage in part payment.

Cornwall returned forty members, as many, excepting one, as the entire kingdom of Scotland; more by two than Durham, Northumberland, and Yorkshire together; and along with Wiltshire, where was another nest of pocket boroughs, more than Yorkshire, Lancashire, Middlesex, Warwick, Worcester, and Somersetshire.

Another interesting feature in the pocket boroughs was the various methods of voting. In some it was close and secret; in others open and democratic. In some the electors were nominated by the patron; in others they maintained a measure of independence, and disposed of their votes to the highest bidder.

One of the most notorious of the rotten boroughs was Mitchell, Modishole, or, as it was sometimes called in error, S. Michael. It is a wretched hamlet on a bleak portion of the great backbone of Cornwall, exposed to every blast from the Atlantic, without trade, without manufacture, almost without agriculture, so poor and unremunerative is the soil. It owed its origin solely to the fact that it was a convenient centre for the distribution of contraband goods that had been run ashore in the bays between Crantock and Newquay. When raised into a borough it existed, without thriving, on the two demoralising businesses of smuggling and elections. In

Parliamentary lists it figures as S. Michael's, but the archangel has never had anything to do with it, never had even a chapel there. The place belongs in part to the parish of S. Enoder, in part to that of S. Newlyn.

The name of Mitchell given it was surely given in satire, for in Cornish this word signifies greatness.

The place consists at present of nineteen houses. At the time of its disfranchisement it had 180 inhabitants, but only three of these were qualified to vote, whose names were Retallack, Vincent, and Parker, and these three returned the two last members who sat for Mitchell.

A few sycamore and ash and thorn trees brave the gales that sweep the desolate slope on which the old borough stands. It has a handsome old inn with granite porch, some quaint old houses, one with the date 1683 on the parvise, and a diminutive town hall.

Whether the borough ever had a seal is uncertain: no impressions are known to exist. The town hall has gone through a series of uses since the place ceased to be a borough. For a while after 1832 it was a dame's school, then was converted into a Wesleyan chapel, then into one of the Church of England, next into a manure store, then into a carpenter's shop, and now it is a beer brewery, in a hamlet made up almost wholly of total abstainers.

The place, as already said, consists of nineteen houses. There is not a shop there. The dame's school has been transferred from the town hall to a one-roomed cottage, that crouches under a bank, and is overshadowed by sycamores.

The privileges it possessed proved to it a curse, for if there were voters in it sufficiently independent to think differently from the patron, he tore down their dwellings. After the last election but one Sir Christopher Hawkins swept away numerous cottages from his land, so as to reduce the number of voters, not because they were recalcitrant, but because all demanded payment for their votes; and to diminish the voters, as he did, from eighty to three meant a corresponding reduction in election expenses. At the election of 1831 there was no voting at all. The steward invited some two dozen individuals to dine with him in the inn; of these three only were nominated to vote. A worm-eaten chair was thrust on the balcony of the inn, and the nominee of the patron was declared chosen and chaired.

Immediately after this election the same patron, Sir Christopher Hawkins, pulled down twelve more houses; amongst these a handsome mansion opposite the town hall, that had been erected by Lord Falmouth in 1780, when he was dominant in the borough, and all the stonework was carried away for the construction of Lord Falmouth's new house at Tregothnan.

In the penultimate election there were but thirteen electors, who were nominated by the patron. But even these were not altogether submissive. A stranger came amongst them, and by large promises induced most of them to agree to vote for him as second representative. Dread of their patron, however, in the end proved too strong, and they returned both his nominees. The stranger, however, assured them that he would send them presents all round, and on a certain day the carrier arrived with a large chest addressed to the free and independent electors of Mitchell. On opening it, the chest was found to be full of stones, and to have thirteen halters on the top properly addressed to the several electors, among whom, by the way, were three parsons.

The unfortunate borough during the later years of its existence was a battleground of many combatants. It was never certain who had the right to vote. This question was left in ambiguity till 1700, and every successive election gave rise to a petition and Parliamentary inquiry.

In 1639, when Courtenay and Chadwell were elected, a petition was sent up to the House appealing against it, and the plea set up was that the members had got in by the aid of voters who were not qualified.

Between this date and 1705 the borough came before the Election Committee no less than fifteen times, and the right of voting was altered from time to time.

In 1660 the question arose whether the right of voting lay in the commonalty at large or in two functionaries called Eligers, nominated by the lord of the manor, and in twenty-two free men of their appointment. The Committee of the House considered that it rested with these nominees, and that the householders of Mitchell had no electoral rights whatever. But in 1689 the Committee decided that "the right of election lay with the lords of the borough, who were liable to be chosen portreeves, and in the householders of the same not receiving alms." Here was a fundamental change. All at once universal suffrage was introduced. Next year (1690) Rowe, for the second place, got in by thirty-one votes against twenty given for Courtenay. Upon investigation, it was proved that Rowe had bribed a dozen voters with £5 or £6 apiece.

In 1695 another election took place, when four members were

returned, two by a deputy-portreeve, and two by the actual portreeve, a certain Timothy Gully, who was an outlaw, and lived in White Friars.

The struggles of Anthony Rowe and Humphrey Courtenay occupy and almost proverbialise this epoch. About 1698 it was noted that "the cost of these struggles had been enormous, and William Courtenay, son and heir of Humphrey, was forced to petition the House to be allowed to sell his entailed estates to defray them."

Rowe was pronounced elected in 1696, but was unseated as speedily on appeal from the defeated side.

In 1707 "the traditional contest takes place at Mitchell between Rowe and two others. Rowe, who was elected, was soon confronted with the inevitable petition."

The right of voting for this distracted borough had already been changed from one of nominees of the patron to one purely democratic, and now, in 1701, it was again changed. This time it was invested in the portreeve, and in the inhabitants paying scot and lot.

For nearly half a century no election petition came up from Mitchell, but in 1754 the scandals became more flagrant than before, and the interest of the political world was drawn to this obscure and ragged hamlet. Lord Sandwich had squared the returning officer, and his candidate was elected by thirty against twenty-five. The Duke of Newcastle now disputed this election. There were, at that period, two taverns at Mitchell, each with its picturesque projecting porch on granite pillars. Each of these became the centre of party cabal and caucus, and this continued for ten months, during which ale and wine flowed and money circulated, and the electors ate and drank at the expense of the Earl of Sandwich and the Duke of Newcastle, and devoted all their energies to swell their several factions at the expense of the other. At last the duke's candidates, Luttrell and Hussey, were returned *vice* Clive (a cousin of the Indian Clive) and Stephenson, who were sustained by the earl.

After this "stranger succeeded stranger in the representation of Mitchell." In 1784 the two patrons were Lord Falmouth and Francis Basset, Esq. No sooner was the election declared than a petition against the return was sent up to the House, and the Committee found that the evidence of bribery and corruption by one of the returned members was so gross that he was forthwith unseated.

Sir Christopher Hawkins of Trewithen, Bart., was sole owner of the borough between 1784 and 1796, and he held it with an iron grasp.

By means of pulling down houses, this crafty baronet thinned down the electors to sixteen, and finally further reduced the number to three. Sir Christopher held Grampound and Tregony as well in his fist, and had runners at his several boroughs to keep him informed how election proceedings went on in each place. His high-handed proceedings and his closeness in everything not connected with elections made him vastly unpopular. One morning a paper was found affixed to the gates of Trewithen.

"A large house, and no cheer,
A large park, and no deer,
A large cellar, and no beer.
Sir Christopher Hawkins lives here."

Sir Kit died in 1829, unmarried, when the title became extinct, but his memory continues green, if not sweet, in the minds of Cornishmen of the parts where he ruled.

In 1806 one of the representatives of the borough was Arthur Wellesley, the subsequent Duke of Wellington.

During eleven years, 1807-1818, there were *nine* elections at Mitchell. No event of importance occurred after 1818, except the extraordinary and significant revelation made at the contested election of 1831, when Hawkins, the nephew of Sir Christopher, got two votes; Kenyon, a Tory, five; and Bent three. In the following year the five electors of Mitchell found their borough disfranchised.

There were, when I visited Mitchell in 1893, two old men, brothers, of the name of Manhire, one aged ninety-four, who could recollect the last election, and could tell some good stories about it.

Trerice, the ancient seat of the Arundells, is near Mitchell, which, it may be remembered, was made into a borough because completely under their control. But their influence rapidly declined, and they lost all power over the voters. The old house is converted into a farm, and is no longer in the possession of the Arundells. Its fine carved oak furniture was scattered.

More charmingly idyllic than Trerice is Lanherne, another seat of the Arundells. Roger de Arundell was at home when the Conqueror came to England. William Arundell had his lands forfeited for rebellion in the reign of King John, but they passed to his nephew, Humphrey Arundell, in 1216. His son, Sir Renfrey Arundell of Treffry, married the daughter and heiress of Sir John de Lanherne in the reign of Henry III., and since then Lanherne became one of the favourite family seats of a house that acquired the baronies of

Wardour and Trerice.

Lanherne lies in the loveliest vale in Cornwall, shut in and screened from the blasts that sweep from the Atlantic. The old house was abandoned in 1794 to the nuns of Mount Carmel, who fled to England for refuge from the storms of the French Revolution. The front of the mansion is of the date 1580, and is eminently picturesque. A modern range of buildings has been added for the accommodation of the nuns, but it is not unsightly. The lovely pinnacled tower of the church of S. Mawgan rises beside the ancient mansion, at a considerably lower level, and the interior is rich with sculptured oak, and with monuments of the Arundells.

Alas! the mighty family that once dominated in Cornwall, second in power only to the Princes of Wales, royal dukes of that duchy, is now represented in Cornwall by empty mansions, alienated to other holders, and by tombs.

The motto of the family is "Deo data--Given by God." It might be properly supplemented, If the Lord gave, the Lord hath also taken away.

Lanherne is in the parish of S. Mawgan. The church has been coldly and unsympathetically renovated by Mr. Butterfield. It contains very fine carved bench-ends and a screen that deserve inspection. The tower of the church is peculiarly beautiful, and the church rises above a grove of the true Cornish elm, growing like poplars, small-leaved.

Carnanton was formerly the dwelling of William Noye, a farmer of Buryan, who was bred as student-at-law in Lincoln's Inn, and afterwards became M. P. for S. Ives in Cornwall, in which capacity he stood for several Parliaments in the beginning of the reign of Charles I., and was one of the boldest and stoutest champions of the rights of Parliament against absolute monarchy. Charles I. then made him his attorney-general, 1631, whereupon his views underwent a complete change, "so that," as Halls says, "like the image of Janus at Rome, he looked forward and backward, and by means thereof greatly enriched himself." He it was who contrived the ship-money tax, which was so obnoxious, and was a principal occasion of the Rebellion.

The attorney-general one day was entertaining King Charles I. and the nobility of the court at dinner in his house in London. Ben Jonson and other choice spirits were at the same time in a tavern on the opposite side of the street, very much out of pocket, and with their stomachs equally empty.

Ben, knowing what was going on opposite, wrote this little metrical epistle and sent it to the attorney-general on a white wood trencher:--

"When the World was drown'd
No deer was found,
Because there was noe Park;
And here I sitt
Without een a bitt,
'Cause Noyah hath all in his Arke."

The presentation of this billet caused great amusement, and Noyes sent back a dish of venison with the rhymes recast, at the dictation of the king, in this fashion:--

"When the World was drown'd
There deer was found,
Althoe there was noe Park;
I send thee a bitt
To quicken thy witt,
Which comes from Noya's Arke."

Halls says:--

"William Noye was blow-coal, incendiary, and stirrer up of the Civil Wars by assisting and setting up the King's prerogative to the highest pitch, as King James I. had done before, beyond the laws of the land. As counsell for the King he prosecuted for King Charles I. the imprisoned members of the House of Commons, 1628; viz., Sir John Elyot, Mr. Coryton, and others; whom after much cost and trouble he got to be fined two thousand pounds each, the others five hundred pounds."

A portrait of William Noye, by Cornelius Jansen, is at Enys, the property of D. G. Enys, Esq.

S. Mawgan, the founder of the church, as also of that in Kerrier, was a man of extraordinary importance to the early Celtic Church in Ireland, Wales, Scotland, and Cornwall. He was the great educator of the saints, and perhaps the first head of a college in Britain. He had under him S. David, Paulinus, and the ill-conditioned Gildas; and he is probably the same as Maucan, "the master," entrusted by S. Patrick with the education of the clergy for the Irish mission. S. Euny and S. Torney were disciples of his, and it was he who gave to Brig, or Breaca, the rules by which a religious community of women should be governed.

His great educational establishment was at Ty Gwyn, or the White

House. This was planted on the slope of Carn Llidy, a purple, heather-clothed crag close to S. David's Head in Pembrokeshire, whence in the evening the sun can be seen setting behind the mountains of Wexford.

Here remains of a rude old chapel can be traced, and around it are countless very early interments in unhewn stone graves, pointing east and west. In fact, this is the necropolis of the great missionary home whence streamed the first Christian teachers into Ireland, and whence Scotland, Cornwall, and Wales were supplied with evangelists.[23]

His establishment was a double one, of female disciples as well as of males, and the consequences were not always satisfactory.

A British king named Drust (523-28) sent his daughter to Ty Gwyn to be educated. In the college were at the time Finnian, afterwards of Clonard, and two other Irishmen, Rioc and Talmage. Rioc fell in love with the girl, and bribed Finnian to be his go-between and get her for him as wife by the promise of a copy of all Mawgan's books that he undertook to make. Finnian agreed, but by treachery, or as a joke, did the courting for Talmage in place of Rioc. When the circumstances came to the ears of Mawgan he was very angry, and he gave his boy a hatchet, and told him to hide behind the chapel, and when Finnian came to matins to hew at him from behind. But instead of Finnian, the first to arrive was Mawgan himself, and he received the blow destined for Finnian. Happily, either because the boy missed his aim in the dark, or more probably because the order had been given to beat Finnian and not kill him, Mawgan was not mortally wounded.

Non, the mother of S. David, was brought up in the same house, and was there when it was visited by Gildas the historian, whose works we have.

It does not at all appear that the rule of celibacy was required of clergy, even of abbots, in the early Celtic Church, for this same Gildas was father of two founders of churches in Cornwall--S. Eval and S. Filius, of Philleigh; and S. Kenneth, the crippled Abbot of Gower, was the father of S. Enoder.

S. Patrick in Ireland did not require his bishops to be unmarried; all he demanded of them was that they should follow the apostolic rule, and that each should be the husband of one wife. The same regulation continued in force in Wales till the Norman invasion in the twelfth century.

S. Patrick was no doubt mainly guided in making his rule by what was ordered in Scripture, but he was also doubtless satisfied that on practical grounds it was the best course, for he had a difficult team of missionaries to drive. This comes out clearly enough in the "Lives" extant.

CHAPTER XVI.

THE LIZARD

Meneage--The meaning of Lizard--The character of the district--
Helston--The Furry Day--Pixy pots--Loe Pool--Tennyson--
Serpentine--The Cornish heath--The Strapwort--Other plants--Woad-
-S. Piran and the woad--Windmill--Peter Odger--Mullion--
Tregonning Hill--S. Ruan--S. Winwaloe--One and All--Gunwalloe
Church--Cury--The colonisation of Brittany--Wrecks.

"**THE** learned Scotus," says Addison in the 174th number of the
Tatler, "to distinguish the race of mankind, gives to every individual
of that species what he calls a seity, something peculiar to himself,
which makes him different from all other persons in the world."

What the learned Scotus said of individuals may as truly be said of
localities; and indisputably the seity of the Lizard is most
pronounced.

THE LIZARD

In itself the district is not beautiful. It consists of a tableland elevated
a few hundred feet above the sea, very bald and treeless, and without
hills to break its uniformity.

Properly it is not the Lizard at all, but Meneage, *i.e.* the land of the

Minachau, the monks. Lizard--Lis-arth, the high-placed or lofty Lis(court)--applies merely to the head and point where stands now Lizard Town, and where was formerly the enclosed court of a prince of the district, or perhaps that of the Irish monks, who occupied the region and appropriated it.

It is almost an island, for the Helford river runs up to Gweek, five miles from the Helston river, that opens into Loe Pool.

Helston is not a particularly interesting place in itself. It consists of a long street leading to the old bowling-green, which is preserved, and stands above the ravine of the Cober (Gael. *cobhair*, foam), where is an archway to William Millett Grylls, designed for execution in sugar-candy, and carried out in granite.

What makes Helston interesting is the annual observance of the Furry Day, on May 8th. It has been often described. The morning is ushered in by a peal of bells from the church tower, and at about nine o'clock the people assemble and demand their prescriptive holiday. They then collect donations, and repair to the fields "to bring home the May."

About noon they return, carrying flowers and branches, and a procession of dancing couples is formed at the Town Hall; and this proceeds down the town, dancing in at the front door of every house and out at the back, and so along their way, with a band preceding them, performing the traditional Furry Dance tune, which is not of any remarkable age, being a hornpipe. The dancers first trip in couples, hand in hand, during the first part of the tune, forming a string of from thirty to forty couples, or perhaps more; at the second part of the tune the first gentleman turns, with both hands, the lady behind him, and her partner turns in like manner as the first lady; then each gentleman turns his own partner, and they trip on as before. The other couples pair and turn in the same way and at the same time. It is considered a slight to pass a house and not to dance through it. Finally the train enters the Assembly Room, and there resolves itself into an ordinary waltz.

As soon as the first party has finished another goes through the same evolutions, and then another, and so on; and it is not till late at night that the town returns to its peaceful propriety.

The dancers on the first day are the gentlemen and ladies. The servants go through the same proceedings on the morrow.

I have given both the song and tune in my *Songs of the West*.

A few years ago the celebration was discontinued; but this provoked such dissatisfaction that it was revived with fresh zest.

The visitor to Helston may see an occasional pixy pot on a roof-ridge of an old house. This is a bulbous ornament, on which the pixies are supposed to dance, and in dancing drop luck on the house below.

Loe Pool is the largest lake in Cornwall; the only other is Dozmare. It is a beautiful sheet of fresh water cut off from the sea by a pebble ridge, which it was wont to overflow, but a culvert has been bored through the rocks to enable the Cober to discharge without, as formerly rising and inundating the land below Helston.

It is really marvellous to see how the mesembryanthemum flourishes here, throwing up masses of pink and white blossom.

In the neighbourhood it is fondly dreamed that this was the tarn into which Arthur had Excalibur cast.

"On one side lay the ocean, and on one
Lay a great water----"

After the sword had been cast in, hither Arthur was carried by Sir Bedivere.

"To left and right
The bare black cliff clang'd round him, as he based
His feet on juts of slippery crag, that rang
Sharp smitten with the dint of armed heels--
And on a sudden, lo! the level lake,
And the long glories of the winter moon."

Hither came the "dusky barge" that was to bear Arthur away to the isles of the blessed. This is very pretty; the lake, the black serpentine rocks agree well enough, but how was the fairy barge to get over the pebble ridge? Mr. Rogers had not then cut the culvert. No doubt it was brimming, but it must have been risky over the bar. I do not believe a word of it. Arthur never was down there. The reputed site of the battle is at Slaughter Bridge, near Camelford. But before we settle where the battle was fought, we must fix Arthur himself, and he is slippery (historically) as an eel.

What makes the Lizard district interesting is in the first place the serpentine rock that forms it, and then the plants which luxuriate on the serpentine.

The serpentine lies to the west, reared up in the magnificent cliffs of Mullion and Kynance coves, but the main body of the upheaved plateau consists of another volcanic rock called gabbro. The serpentine is so called because it has something of the glaze and greenness of a snake's skin.

The Lizard rocks have long been an object of interest and dispute among geologists. For a study of them I must refer to the papers of Mr. T. Clark in the *Transactions of the Polytechnic Institution of Cornwall*.

The most casual visitor must be struck, if in Meneage at the season of flowering, with the abundance of the beautiful Cornish heath (*Erica vagans*), which in growth and general appearance cannot for a moment be mistaken for the common heath. The Rev. C. A. Johns says of it in his *Week at the Lizard*:--

"The stems are much branched, and in the upper parts very leafy, from two to four feet high. The flowers are light purple, rose-coloured, or pure white. In the purple variety the anthers are dark purple; in the white, bright red; and in all cases they form a ring outside the corolla until they have shed their pollen, when they droop to the sides. On the Goonhilley Downs in Cornwall these varieties of heath grow together in the greatest profusion, covering many hundreds of acres, and almost excluding the two species so common elsewhere."

It flowers from July to September.

Another heath found there and near Truro is the *Erica ciliaris*, with bright purple flowers of oblong form; it is by far the most beautiful of our English heaths. The flowers are half an inch in length, growing down the upper part of the stem, and the leaves are delicately fringed with hairs. It has a somewhat glutinous feel. It is rare except in Cornwall.

A rare plant, and pretty withal, is the strapwort (*Corrigiola littoralis*), trailing among the shingle on the bar of Loe Pool. It has minute white flowers and glaucous leaves. The plant has a curious habit of shifting its quarters almost every year from one part of the shore to another.

"Sometimes, for instance, it abounds on the slaty beach at Penrose, but scarcely a single specimen is to be found on the opposite side of the lake. Next year, perhaps, it grows in profusion on the eastern beaches, but has disappeared from its former station." (JOHNS.)

The strapwort grows nowhere else in Britain but here and in two places in Devonshire.

On the cliffs may be seen the sky-blue vernal squill in May and June, but by midsummer it has disappeared to make room for the autumnal squill, a much less beautiful species.

In marshy spots may be found the pale pinguicula and the buckbean.

Four kinds of genistas are to be seen in flower, bright and yellow.

The purple allium, or chive garlic, may be found where water has stood during the winter.

The common asparagus grows in great abundance in the clefts of the rocks. In ravines flourishes the blood-red crane's-bill, and the common harebell, so desiderated on the granite formation, but not found there, may here be met with.

Mr. Johns says:--

"A sloping bank on the right hand of Caerthillian valley, about a hundred yards from the sea, produces, I think, more botanical rarities than any other spot of equal dimensions in Great Britain. Here are crowded together in so small a space that I actually covered with my hat growing specimens all together of *Lotus hispidus*, *Trifolium Bocconi*, *T. Molinerii*, and *T. Strictum*. The first of these is far from common, the others grow nowhere else in Great Britain."

The cross-leaved heath, found elsewhere pretty generally, with its little cluster of pale waxlike bells at the head of the stalk, does not affect the Lizard.

The woad, wherewith our British ancestors dyed themselves, flourishes abundantly in the Meneage peninsula. It has bright yellow flowers in panicles growing on an upright stem, some two or three feet high, and appears in June and July.

The woad (*Isatis tinctoria*) yields true indigo, but it contains only about one-thirtieth of the quantity found on the indigo tinctoria cultivated in India. The leaves are ground to a paste in a mill, and then allowed to ferment during eight or twelve days. After that they are formed into balls and dried.

In ancient times this pasty mess was directly used in dyeing by those who carried on all kinds of domestic works at home. During the putrefactive fermentation of the woad ammonia is formed and hydrogen evolved. The latter, while in the nascent state, reduces the blue indigo to the state of white indigo, which, being soluble, can penetrate the wool to be dyed, where it is deposited in the insoluble state as blue indigo, on exposure to the oxygen of the air.

There is an incident in the life of S. Piran, or Kieran, who founded a church, S. Keverne, in the Lizard district, which is connected with dyeing with woad.

His mother was one day engaged in preparing the dye, called by the Irish *glasin*. Kieran, then a child, was present; and as it was deemed unlucky for a male person to witness the preparation of the dye, she bundled him out of the cabin, whereon he uttered a curse, "May there be a dark stripe in the wool," and the cloth in dyeing actually did exhibit a dark grey stripe in it. The *glasin* was again prepared, and again Kieran was turned out of the house, whereon he again cursed the process that the material to be dyed might be whiter than bone, and again it was as he had said. The woad was prepared a third time, and Kieran's mother asked him not to spoil it, but, on the contrary, to bless it. This he did with such effect that there was not made before or after a *glasin* that was its equal, for what remained in the vat served not only to colour all the cloth of the tribe, but made the cats and dogs that touched it blue as well. The explanation of the miracle is very simple. The two failures were due to imperfect fermentation in one case and over-fermentation in the other, accidents to which woad was always liable, especially when prepared, as it was in ancient times, from the fresh leaves, in different stages of growth, and at one period of the year, when the weather was warm and changeable.[24]

We can see in this story how a fable of a miracle grew up. The circumstance certainly may have happened, and it was afterwards attributed to the saintly boy being turned out of doors, and ill-wishing the dye-vat.

Before the introduction of indigo, woad was specially cultivated in Europe, but after the former was brought in, the woad was no longer raised. At first, indeed, indigo and woad were employed together in dyeing; then came the plan of using certain chemicals in place of woad, which injured the wool and destroyed the quality of cloths; so that in Thuringia orders were issued by the Government prohibiting the employment of indigo.

There is plenty of material for dyeing to be found in Meneage. The moss *Hypnum cupressiformum* is still employed in the county of Mayo for the purpose of giving wool for stockings a reddish brown colour mottled with white. The white woollen yarn to be dyed is made into skeins; these are tied at intervals by very tight ligatures of linen thread, and then put into the dye vat. The binds prevent the dye from penetrating into that portion of the wool compressed by them, and these portions remain pure white, whereas the rest comes out a rich orange-brown colour. When this thread is knitted into stockings it produces a pretty mottled pattern--the heather, as it is now called. And in all probability the speckled garments to which old King Brychan owed his name were thus produced.

Bed-straw and madder again yield yellow and red, and alder and bogbean a fine black. So the Lizard, when other trades fail, can go in for dyeing.

There is a single windmill in the district.

The story goes that at one time it was rumoured that a second was about to be constructed. The miller was concerned. He went to see the man who entertained the scheme.

"I say, mate, be you goin' to set up another windmill?"

"I reckon I be; you don't object? There's room for more nor one."

"Oh, room, room enough! But there mayn't be wind enough to sarve us both."

An old chap named Peter Odger lived near Mullion. He was somewhat given to the bottle. One day he went with a cart and horse along the road, and took a keg of cider with him. The day was hot, the cider got into his head, and he fell asleep. Some boys found the horse standing in the road feeding. They took the brute out and drove it away.

An hour later Peter awoke, rubbed his eyes, and sat up. "Well, if iver!" said he. "Be I Peter Odger or be I not? 'Tes contrary any way. If I be Peter Odger, I've lost an 'orse; if I bain't, why I've gained a cart."

Peter and his wife did not get on very "suant" together. At last Peter could endure domestic broils no longer; so one day he took every penny he had, and started for the United States. He shipped from Liverpool.

As the vessel neared the Newfoundland coast it got into the cold current setting down from the north, and an iceberg hove in sight. This was too much for Peter. "I likes warmth," said he, "and the only warmth I don't like is when my wife gives it me. I reckon I'll go home." So he covenanted to work his passage back, and by some means or other he did not surrender his ticket for the passage across.

Without landing in America, Peter returned in the vessel in which he had gone out, and with his ticket in his pocket. He walked quietly into his cottage, and put the ticket up on the mantel-shelf.

"Thear, old woman," said he, "I've been and got your ticket for the other world. It cost a sight o' money, but I don't grudge it."

Mrs. Odger in the meanwhile had been hard put to it, with no money in the house, and had led a hand-to-mouth existence, mainly on charity. She did not like it. She was glad to see Peter back.

"You've been a long time away," she said.

"Ees, I reckon. I just tripped over to see that all were ready for you in the other world. They'm expectin' of you, and here's your ticket."

It is said that Mrs. Odger was amiable after that. The ticket was ever held in terror over her head.

At Mullion, once a quiet, lost corner of the world, are now three monster hotels with electric light; their windows look out seaward across the great bay towards Penzance and the granitic headlands of Penwith. From the Lizard the only prominent hill visible is Tregonning, which was held by the Irish colony in the beginning of the sixth century against the Cornish King Tewdrig, and is still crowned with their stone camp.

One of the Irish who settled in Meneage was S. Ruan, or Rumon. How long he remained there we do not know, but he not only founded two churches in the Lizard district and blessed there a holy well, but he also planted an establishment at Ruan Lanihorne, near Tregony, and a chapel at the mouth of the Fal; his bones were translated to Tavistock Abbey in 960. He was a convert of S. Patrick, but left his native island early for Britain, where he was ordained. On leaving Cornwall he visited Brittany, and got into trouble there, for the people took it into their heads that he was a magician, who every night went about in the form of a wolf and devoured their sheep and carried off their children. One woman even denounced him to the prince, Gradlo, for having eaten her daughter. The prince, or duke, could not directly oppose the superstition of his people, so he announced that he would expose Ruan to his wolf-dogs, and if they smelt anything of the wild beast about him they would tear him to pieces. This was a satisfactory decision; it promised sport. But, in the meantime, Gradlo suffered his hounds to be with Ruan, and to be fed from his hand. Accordingly, when the old Irish monk was produced before his accusers and the hounds let in on him, they licked his hands. The people were quite satisfied, and Ruan doubtless then had a hint to make tracks for Cornwall once more, where there were no wolves--at least, in the Lizard district.

Mullion Church is perhaps dedicated to S. Melyan, a prince of Cornwall, who was treacherously murdered by his brother-in-law, Riwhal, at a conference. I have already told the story. But it is also possible that the patron saint may be a Brittany bishop.

Landewednack and Gunwalloe are foundations of S. Winwaloe, related to the Cornish royal family, but chiefly known as a founder in Brittany.

His great foundation there was Landewennec; but that he visited Britain to see what was the rule observed in British monasteries is what we are expressly told in his *Life*. However, he clearly came to Britain to make foundations as well, and he not only established the Cornish Landewednack and Gunwalloe in the Lizard district, but churches near Launceston, and Portlemouth on the estuary of the Kingsbridge creek in Devon.

His mother is called Gwen the Three-breasted, and she is actually represented with three breasts on a monument in Brittany. She was niece of Constantine I. of Cornwall and Devon, and cousin of Geraint. Gwen had been married before, and had become the mother of S. Cadfan. She and her husband had a rough time of it when they landed in Brittany, at Brehat, at the mouth of the Gouet, as the region was almost void of population, and given up to wilderness and wood. Winwaloe was sent into the little islet of Brehat to S. Budoc, who lived there and received and taught disciples. It is interesting to know that the circular huts, or foundations of the huts, of his monastery still exist there as well as the cemetery, and the abbot's beehive habitation is kept in repair as a landmark for fishermen.

When Winwaloe came to man's estate he resolved on founding a monastery of his own. He gathered together a certain number of disciples, thirteen in all, and they settled on a bleak island off the western coast, and remained there for three years.

On this islet was a rocky hill, whereon S. Winwaloe sat and taught; and far away to the east, as he taught, he saw the green forests and the smiling pastures of the mainland golden with buttercups, and there rose the smoke from the hearths of the inhabitants.

Now when the three years were ended, one day there came an extraordinary ebb-tide. And when the saint saw that there was a way dry, or almost dry, to the land, "Arise," said he; "in God's name let us go over;" and he bade his disciples follow him. "But," said he, "let none go alone; let one hold my hand, and with his other hand hold his brother's, and so let us advance in chain, and we shall peradventure be able to reach the land before the tide turns and overwhelms all. Let us hold together, that the strong may support the weak, and that if one falls the others may lift him up."

Now when Winwaloe said this, he spoke like a true Cornishman, and it shows that the great Cornish principle of One and All was seated in his heart all those centuries ago; in fact, in the sixth century.

An old miner from Australia said to me the other day, "Never saw such fellows as those Cornishmen; they hold together like bees. When I was out in Australia there was a Cornishman with me, my pal. One day someone said to us, 'There is a Cornishman from Penzance just landed at Melbourne.' 'Where's his diggings?' asked my pal. 'Oh, he is gone up country to ----' I forget the name of the mine. Will you believe it, off went my pal walking, I can't tell you how far, and was away several days from his work--gone off, to see that newly-arrived chap; didn't know his name even, but *he was a Cornishman*, and that was enough to draw him."

Sir Redvers Buller told me a story. He was on his way with a regiment of soldiers to Canada. Off the entrance to the S. Lawrence the vessel was enveloped in fogs and delayed, so that provisions ran short. Now there was a station on an islet there for shipwrecked mariners, where were supplies. So Sir Redvers went ashore in a boat to visit the store and ask for assistance.

When he applied, he found a woman only in charge.

"No," said she; "the supplies are for those who be shipwrecked, not for such as you."

"But this is a Government depôt, and we are servants of the Crown."

"Can't help it; you'm not shipwrecked."

Now there was a very recognisable intonation in the woman's voice. Sir Redvers at once assumed the Cornish accent, and said, "What! not for dear old One and All, and I a Buller?"

"What! from Cornwall, and a Buller! Take everything there is in the place; you'm heartily welcome."

GUNWALLOC CHURCH

Gunwalloe is a chapelry in the parish of Cury. It has a singular tower standing by itself against the sandhill at the back. There is a holy well on the beach, but the tide has filled it with stones. It was formerly cleared out on S. Gunwalloe's Day, but this, unfortunately, is one of the good old customs that have fallen into neglect.

About Cury a word must be said. It is dedicated to S. Corentine, a saint of Quimper, in Brittany, and this is probably a place where Athelstan placed one of the batches of Bretons who fled to him for protection in 920, but whom he could not have planted in Cornwall till 936. That Cornwall should have received refugees from Brittany was but just, for Brittany had been colonised from Devon and Cornwall to a very considerable extent. As the facts are little known, I will narrate them here.

The advance of the Saxons and the rolling back of the Britons had heaped up crowds of refugees in Wales and in Devon and Cornwall, more in fact than the country could maintain. Accordingly an outlet had to be sought.

The Armorican peninsula was thinly populated.

In consequence of the exactions of the decaying empire, and the ravages of northern pirates, the Armorican seaboard was all but uninhabited, and the centre of the peninsula was occupied by a vast untrodden forest, or by barren stone-strewn moors. Armorica, therefore, was a promising field for colonisation.

Procopius says that in the sixth century swarms of immigrants arrived from Britain, men bringing with them their wives and children. These migrations assumed large dimensions in 450, 512-14, and between 561 and 566.

So early as 461 we hear of a "Bishop of the Britons" attending the Council of Tours. In 469 the British settlers were in sufficient force at the mouth of the Loire to become valuable auxiliaries against the invading Visigoths.

The author of the *Life of S. Winwalloe* says:--

"The sons of the Britons, leaving the British sea, landed on these shores at the period when the barbarian Saxon conquered the isle. These children of a beloved race established themselves in this country, glad to find repose after so many griefs. In the meantime the unfortunate Britons who had not quitted this country were decimated by plague. Their corpses lay without sepulchre. The major portion of the isle was depopulated. Then a small number of men, who had escaped the sword of the invaders, abandoned their native land to seek refuge, some among the Scots (Irish), the rest in Belgic Gaul."

The plague to which reference is made is the Yellow Death, that carried off Maelgwn Gwynedd, King of Wales, 547.

The invasion was not a military occupation; the settlers encountered no resistance. Every account we have represents them as landing in a country that was denuded of its population, except in the district of Vannes and on the Loire.

In or about 514 Riwhal, son of a Damnonian king, arrived with a large fleet on the north-east coast, and founded the colony and principality of Domnonia on the mainland.

One swarm came from Gwent, that is to say, Monmouthshire and Glamorganshire, where the Britons were hard pressed by the Saxons; and this Gwentian colony planted itself in the north-west of the Armorican peninsula, and called it Leon, or Lyonesse, after the Caerleon that had been abandoned.

This Leon was afterwards annexed to Domnonia in Brittany, so as to form a single kingdom.

Again another swarm took possession of the western seaboard, and called that Cornu, either after their Cornwall at home, or because Finisterre is, like that, a horn thrust forward into the Atlantic.

By degrees Vannes, itself a Gallo-Roman city, was enveloped by the new-comers, so that in 590 the Bishop Regalis complained that he was as it were imprisoned by them within the walls of his city. The Gallo-Roman prelate disliked these British invaders and their independent ways. S. Melanius of Rennes and S. Felix of Nantes shared his dislike. The prelates exercised much of the magisterial authority of the imperial governors, and to this the newly-arrived Britons refused to submit. The Britons brought with them their own laws, customs, and organisation, both civil and ecclesiastical, as well as their own language.

They were at first few in numbers, and did not desire to emancipate themselves wholly from Britain. Consequently, although establishing themselves in clans, they held themselves to be under the sovereignty of their native princes at home.

This appears from the coincidence of the names of the kings in Armorica and in insular Domnonia.[25]

About the downs may be seen numerous cairns and barrows. Some of these have been explored, and some fine urns of the Bronze Age, that were found near Gunwalloe, are now in the Truro Museum.

Alas! there is one thing for which Lizard is notorious, and that is wrecks. The last great tragedy of that nature was the loss of the *Mohegan*, in 1898. A mysterious loss, for the two lights of Lizard shone clear to the left, and she was steered straight on the deadly Manacles, where she went to pieces. The churchyards of S. Keverne, Landewednack, and Mullion contain the graves of many and many a drowned man and woman thrown up by the sea. But, be it remembered, formerly those thus cast up, unless known, were not buried in churchyards, but on the cliffs, as there was no guarantee that the bodies were those of Christians. For this reason it is by no means uncommon on these cliffs to come on bones protruding from the ground on the edge of the sea--the remains of drowned mariners, without name, and of an unknown date. Indeed, it was not till 1808 that an Act was passed requiring the bodies of those cast up by the sea to be buried in the parish churchyard. "What is the usual proceeding?" said a curate to some natives, as a drowned man from a wreck was washed ashore. "In such a case as this what should be done?"

"Sarch 'is pockets," was the prompt reply.

NOTE.--Books on the Lizard:--

JOHNS (C. P.), *A Week at the Lizard*. S.P.C.K., 1848. Though an old book, quite unsurpassed.

HARVEY (T. G.), *Mullyon*. Truro, 1875.

CUMMINS (A. H.), *Cury and Gunwalloe*. Truro, 1875. Good, but all these books are wild in their derivation of place-names, and not too much to be trusted in their history, as, for instance, when they mistake the Breton Cornouaille for Cornwall, and relate as occurring in the latter what actually belongs to the Breton Cornouaille.

CHAPTER XVII.

SMUGGLING

A *cache*--Smugglers' paths--Donkeys--Hiding-places--Connivance with smugglers--A baronet's carriage--Wrecking--"Fatal curiosity"--A ballad--Excuses made for smuggling--Story by Hawker--Desperate affrays--Sub-division of labour--"Creeping"--Fogous--One at Porthcothan.

THE other day I saw an old farmhouse in process of demolition in the parish of Altarnon, on the edge of the Bodmin moors. The great hall chimney was of unusual bulk, bulky as such chimneys usually are; and when it was thrown down it revealed the explanation of this unwonted size. Behind the back of the hearth was a chamber fashioned in the thickness of the wall, to which access might have been had at some time through a low walled-up doorway that was concealed behind the kitchen dresser and plastered over. This door was so low that it could be passed through only on all-fours.

Now the concealed chamber had also another way by which it could be entered, and this was through a hole in the floor of a bedroom above. A plank of the floor could be lifted, when an opening was disclosed by which anyone might pass under the wall through a sort of door, and down steps into this apartment, which was entirely without light. Of what use was this singular concealed chamber? There could be little question. It was a place in which formerly kegs of smuggled spirits and tobacco were hidden. The place lies some fourteen or fifteen miles from Boscastle, a dangerous little harbour on the North Cornish coast, and about a mile off the main road from London, by Exeter and Launceston, to Falmouth. The coach travellers in old days consumed a good deal of spirits, and here in a tangle of lanes lay a little emporium always kept well supplied with a stock of spirits which had not paid duty, and whence the taverners along the road could derive the contraband liquor, with which they supplied the travellers. Between this emporium and the sea the roads--parish roads--lie over wild moors or creep between high hedges of earth, on which the traveller can step along when the lane below is converted into the bed of a stream, also on which the wary smuggler could stride whilst his laden mules and asses stumbled forward in the concealment of the deep-set lane.

A very curious feature of the coasts of the West of England, where rocky or wild, is the trenched and banked-up paths from the coves along the coast. These are noticeable in Devon and Cornwall and along the Bristol Channel. That terrible sea-front consists of precipitous walls of rock, with only here and there a dip, where a brawling stream has sawn its course down to the sea; and here there is, perhaps, a sandy shore of diminutive proportions, and the rocks around are pierced in all directions with caverns. The smugglers formerly ran their goods into these coves when the weather permitted, or the preventive men were not on the look-out. They stowed away their goods in the caves, and gave notice to the farmers and gentry of the neighbourhood, all of whom were provided with numerous donkeys, which were forthwith sent down to the *caches*, and the kegs and bales were removed under cover of night or of storm.

As an excuse for keeping droves of donkeys, it was pretended that the sea-sand and the kelp served as admirable dressing for the land, and no doubt so they did. The trains of asses sometimes came up laden with sacks of sand, but not infrequently with kegs of brandy.

Now a wary preventive man might watch too narrowly the proceedings of these trains of asses. Accordingly squires, yeomen, farmers, alike set to work to cut deep ways in the face of the downs, along the slopes of the hills, and bank them up, so that whole caravans of laden beasts might travel up and down absolutely unseen from the sea, and greatly screened from the land side.

Undoubtedly the sunken ways and high banks are some protection against the weather. So they were represented to be, and no doubt greatly were the good folks commended for their consideration for the beasts and their drivers in thus, at great cost, shutting them off from the violence of the gale. Nevertheless, it can hardly be doubted that concealment from the eye of the coastguard was sought by this means quite as much as, if not more than, the sheltering the beasts of burden from the weather.

A few years ago an old church house was demolished. When it was pulled down it was found that the floor of large slate slabs in the lower room was undermined with hollows like graves, only of much larger dimensions, and these had served for the concealment of smuggled spirits. The clerk had, in fact, dug them out, and did a little trade on Sundays with selling contraband liquor from these stores.

The story is told of a certain baronet, who had a handsome house and park near the coast. By the way, he died at an advanced age only a couple of years ago. The preventive men had long suspected that Sir

Thomas had done more than wink at the proceedings of the receivers of smuggled goods. His park dipped in graceful undulations to the sea, and to a lovely creek, in which was his boathouse. But they never had been able to establish the fact that he favoured the smugglers, and allowed them to use his grounds and outbuildings.

However, at last, one night, a party of men with kegs on their shoulders was seen stealing through the park towards the mansion. They were observed also leaving without the kegs. Accordingly, next morning the officer in command called, together with several underlings. He apologised to the baronet for any inconvenience his visit might occasion--he was quite sure that Sir Thomas was ignorant of the use made of his park, his landing-place, even of his house--but there was evidence that "run" goods had been brought to the mansion the preceding night, and it was but the duty of the officer to point this out to Sir Thomas, and ask him to permit a search--which would be conducted with all the delicacy possible. The baronet, an exceedingly urbane man, promptly expressed his readiness to allow house, cellar, attic--every part of his house and every outbuilding--unreservedly to be searched. He produced his keys. The cellar was, of course, the place where wine and spirits were most likely to be found--let that be explored first. He had a cellar-book, which he produced, and he would be glad if the officer would compare what he found below with his entries in the book. The search was entered into with some zest, for the Government officers had long looked on Sir Thomas with mistrust, and yet were somewhat disarmed by the frankness with which he met them. But they ransacked the mansion from garret to cellar, and every part of the outbuildings, and found nothing. They had omitted to look into the family coach, which was full of rum kegs, so full that to prevent the springs being broken, or showing that the carriage was laden, the axle-trees had been "trigged up" below with blocks of wood.

Wrecking was another form of sea-poaching. Terrible stories of ships lured to destruction by the exhibition of false lights are told, but all belong to the past. I remember an old fellow--the last of the Cornish wreckers--who ended his days as keeper of a toll-gate. But he never would allow that he had wilfully drawn a vessel upon the breakers. When a ship was cast up by the gale it was another matter. The dwellers on the coast could not believe that they had not a perfect right to whatever was washed ashore. Nowadays the coastguards keep so sharp a look-out after a storm that very little can be picked up. The usual course at present is for those who are early on the beach, and have not time to secure--or fear the risk of securing--something they covet, to heave the article up the cliff and lodge it there where not easily accessible. If it be observed--when the auction takes place--it is knocked down for a trifle, and the man who put it where it is discerned obtains it by a lawful claim. If it be not observed, then he fetches it at his convenience. But it is now considered too risky after a wreck to carry off anything of size found, and as the number of bidders at a sale of wreckage is not large, and they do not compete with each other keenly, things of value are got for very slender payments.

The terrible story of the murder of a son by his father and mother, to secure his gold, they not knowing him, and believing him to be a cast-up from a wreck--the story on which the popular drama of *Fatal Curiosity*, by Lillo, was founded--actually took place at Boheland, near Penryn.

To return to the smugglers.

When a train of asses or mules conveyed contraband goods along a road, it was often customary to put stockings over the hoofs to deaden the sound of their steps.

One night, many years ago, a friend of the writer--a parson on the north coast of Cornwall--was walking along a lane in his parish at night. It was near midnight. He had been to see, or had been sitting up with, a dying person.

As he came to a branch in the lane he saw a man there, and he called out "Good-night." He then stood still a moment, to consider which lane he should take. Both led to his rectory, but one was somewhat shorter than the other. The shorter was, however, stony and very wet. He chose the longer way, and turned to the right. Thirty years after he was speaking with a parishioner who was ill, when the man said to him suddenly, "Do you remember such and such a night, when you came to the Y? You had been with Nankevill, who was dying."

"Yes, I do recall something about it."

"Do you remember you said 'Good-night' to me?"

"I remember that someone was there; I did not know it was you."

"And you turned right, instead of left?"

"I dare say."

"If you had taken the left-hand road you would never have seen next morning."

"Why so?"

"There was a large cargo of 'run' goods being transported that night, and you would have met it."

"What of that?"

"What of that? You would have been chucked over the cliffs."

"But how could they suppose I would peach?"

"Sir! They'd ha' took good care you shouldn't a' had the chance!"

I was sitting in a little seaport tavern in Cornwall one winter's evening, over a great fire, with a company of very old "salts," gossiping, yarning, singing, when up got a tough old fellow with a face the colour of mahogany, and dark, piercing eyes, and the nose of a hawk. Planting his feet wide apart, as though on deck in a rolling sea, he began to sing in stentorian tones a folk-song relative to a highwayman in the old times, when Sir John Fielding, the blind magistrate at Westminster, put down highway robbery.

The ballad told of the evil deeds of this mounted robber of the highways, and of how he was captured by "Fielding's crew" and condemned to die. It concluded:--

"When I am dead, borne to my grave,

A gallant funeral may I have;

Six highwaymen to carry me,

With good broad swords and sweet liberty.

"Six blooming maidens shall bear my pall,

Give them white gloves and pink ribbons all;

And when I'm dead they'll tell the truth,

I was a wild and a wicked youth."

At the conclusion of each verse the whole assembly repeated the two final lines. It was a striking scene; their eyes flashed, their colour mounted, they hammered with their fists on the table and with their heels on the floor. Some, in the wildness of their excitement, sprang up, thrust their hands through their white or grey hair, and flourished them, roaring like bulls.

When the song was done, and composure had settled over the faces of the excited men, one of them said apologetically to me, "You see, sir, we be all old smugglers, and have gone agin the law in our best days."

There is something to be said in extenuation of the wrongfulness of English smuggling.

The customs duties were imposed first in England for the purpose of protecting the coasts against pirates, who made descents on the undefended villages, and kidnapped and carried off children and men to sell as slaves in Africa, or who waylaid merchant vessels and plundered them. But when all danger from pirates ceased, the duties were not only maintained, but made more onerous.

It was consequently felt that there had been a violation of compact on the side of the Crown, and bold spirits entertained no scruple of conscience in carrying on contraband trade. The officers of the Crown no longer proceeded to capture, bring to justice, and hang notorious foreign pirates, but to capture, bring to justice, and hang native seamen and traders. The preventive service became a means of oppression, and not of relief.

That is the light in which the bold men of Cornwall regarded it; that is the way in which it was regarded, not by the ignorant seamen only, but by magistrates, country gentlemen, and parsons alike. As an illustration of this, we may quote the story told by the late Rev. R. S. Hawker, for many years vicar of Morwenstow, on the North Cornish coast:--

"It was full six o'clock in the afternoon of an autumn day when a traveller arrived where the road ran along by a sandy beach just above high-water mark.

"The stranger, a native of some inland town, and entirely unacquainted with Cornwall and its ways, had reached the brink of the tide just as a landing was coming off. It was a scene not only to instruct a townsman, but to dazzle and surprise.

"At sea, just beyond the billows, lay a vessel, well moored with anchors at stem and stern. Between the ship and the shore boats laden to the gunwale passed to and fro. Crowds assembled on the beach to help the cargo ashore.

"On the one hand a boisterous group surrounding a keg with the head knocked in, into which they dipped whatsoever vessel came first to hand; one man had filled his shoe. On the other side they fought and wrestled, cursed and swore.

"Horrified at what he saw, the stranger lost all self-command and, oblivious of personal danger, he began to shout: 'What a horrible sight! Have you no shame? Is there no magistrate at hand? Cannot any justice of the peace be found in this fearful country?'

"'No, thanks be,' answered a hoarse, gruff voice; 'none within eight miles.'

"'Well, then,' screamed the stranger, 'is there no clergyman hereabouts? Does no minister of the parish live among you on this coast?'

"'Aye, to be sure there is,' said the same deep voice.

"'Well, how far off does he live? Where is he?'

"'That's he, sir, yonder with the lantern.' And sure enough, there he stood on a rock, and poured, with pastoral diligence, 'the light of other days' on a busy congregation."

It may almost be said that the Government did its best to encourage smuggling by the harsh and vexatious restrictions it put on trade. A prohibitory list of goods which might under no conditions whatever be imported into Great Britain included gold and silver brocade, cocoanut shells, foreign embroidery, manufactures of gold and silver plate, ribbons and laces, chocolate and cocoa, calicoes printed or dyed abroad, gloves and mittens.

Beside these a vast number of goods were charged with heavy duties, as spirits, tea, tobacco. The duties on these were so exorbitant, that it was worth while for men to attempt to run a cargo without paying duty.

To quote a writer in the *Edinburgh Review*, at the time when smuggling was fairly rife:--

"To create by means of high duties an overwhelming temptation to indulge in crime, and then to punish men for indulging in it, is a proceeding wholly and completely subversive of every principle of justice. It revolts the natural feelings of the people, and teaches them to feel an interest in the worst characters, to espouse their cause and to avenge their wrongs."

Desperate affrays took place between smugglers and the preventive men, who were aware that the magistracy took a lenient view of the case when one of them fell, and brought in "murder" when an officer of the Crown shot a "free-trader."

One of the most terrible men on the Cornish coast, remembered by his evil repute, was "Cruel Coppinger." He had a house at Welcombe on the north coast, where lived his wife, an heiress. The bed is still shown to the post of which he tied her and thrashed her with a rope till she consented to make over her little fortune to his exclusive use.

Coppinger had a small estate at Roscoff, in Brittany, which was the headquarters of the smuggling trade during the European war. He was paid by the British Government to carry despatches to and from the French coast, but he took advantage of his credentials as a Government agent to do much contraband business himself.

I remember, as a boy, an evil-faced old man, his complexion flaming red and his hair very white, who kept a small tavern not in the best repute. A story of this innkeeper was told, and it is possible that it may be true--naturally the subject was not one on which it was possible to question him. He had been a smuggler in his day, and a wild one too.

On one occasion, as he and his men were rowing a cargo ashore they were pursued by a revenue boat. Tristram Davey, as I will call this man, knew this bit of coast perfectly. There was a reef of sharp slate rock that ran across the little bay, like a very keen saw with the teeth set outward, and there was but one point at which this saw could be crossed. Tristram knew the point to a nicety, even in the gloaming, and he made for it, the revenue boat following.

He, however, did not make direct for it, but steered a little on one side and then suddenly swerved and shot through the break. The revenue boat came straight on, went upon the jaws of the reef, was torn, and began to fill. Now the mate of this boat was one against whom Tristram entertained a deadly enmity, because he had been the means of a capture in which his property had been concerned. So he turned the boat, and running back, he stood up, levelled a gun and shot the mate through the heart; then away went the smuggling boat to shore, leaving the rest of the revenue men to shift as best they could with their injured boat.

The most noted smuggling centre between Penzance and Porthleven was Prussia Cove, and there to this day, stands the house of John Carter, "The King of Prussia," as he was called, the most successful and notorious smuggler of the district. His reign extended from 1777 to 1807, and he was succeeded by his son-in-law, Captain William Richards, under whom Prussia Cove maintained its old celebrity.

The story goes that John Carter, as a boy, playing at soldiers with other boys, received the nickname of "The King of Prussia." Formerly the cove was called Porthleah, but in recollection of his exploits it is now known as Prussia Cove.

On one occasion, during his absence from home, the excise officers carried off a cargo that had lately arrived for Carter from France. They conveyed it to the custom-house store. On his return, Carter summoned his men, and at night he and they broke into the stores and carried off all that he held to be his own, without touching a single article to which he considered he had no claim. On another occasion, when Carter was pursued by a revenue cutter, and sore pressed, he ran through a narrow passage in the reefs, and fired on the cutter's boat sent after him. The fire was continued till night fell, and Carter was then able to effect his escape.

Three classes of men were engaged in the smuggling business. First came the "freighter"--the man who entered on the business as a commercial speculation. He engaged a vessel and purchased the cargo, and made all the requisite arrangements for the landing. Then came the "runners," who transported the goods on shore from the vessels. And lastly the "tub-carriers," who conveyed the kegs on their backs, slung across their shoulders, up the cliff to their destination.

The tub-carriers were usually agricultural labourers in the employment of farmers near the coast.

These farmers were in understanding with the smugglers, and on a hint given, supplied them with their workmen, and were repaid with a keg of spirits.

The entire English coast was subjected to blockade by the Government to prevent the introduction into the country of goods that had not paid duty, and the utmost ingenuity and skill had to be exercised to run the blockade. But after that was done the smuggler still ran great risk, for the coast was patrolled.

Smuggling methods were infinitely varied, depending on a great variety of circumstances. Much daring, skill, and cleverness were required. The smuggler and the preventive man were engaged in a game in which each used all his faculties to overreach the other.

One means employed where the coast was well watched was for the kegs to be sunk. A whole "crop," as it was called, was attached to a rope, that was weighted with stones and fastened at both ends by an anchor. When a smuggling vessel saw no chance of landing its cargo, it sank it and fixed it with the anchors, and the bearings of the sunken "crop" were taken and communicated to the aiders and abettors on land, who waited their opportunity to fish it up.

But the revenue officers were well aware of this dodge, and one of their duties was to grope along the coast with hooks--"creeping" was the technical term--for such deposits. A crop that had been sunk in a hurry, and not in very deep water, was likely to suffer. The ropes chafed and broke, or a floating keg, or one washed ashore, was a certain betrayal of the presence of a crop not far off.

As a rule the contents of the sunken kegs suffered no deterioration from being under water for some time; but if submerged too long the spirits turned bad. Such deteriorated spirits were known amongst coastguardsmen as "stinkibus."

Every barrel of liquor as provided by the merchants at Roscoff and elsewhere was furnished with a pair of sling ropes ready for attachment to the cord in the event of sinking, and for carrying by the tub-men when safely worked on shore.

Very often when a rowboat, towing a line of kegs after it, was pursued, the smugglers were forced to let go the casks. Then the coastguard secured them, but found the magistrates loath to convict, because they could not swear that the kegs picked up were identical with those let go by the smugglers. Accordingly they were ordered, whenever such an event happened, to mark the line of kegs by casting to them a peculiarly painted buoy.

In order to have information relative to the smugglers, so as to be on the alert to "nab" them, the Government had paid spies in the foreign ports, and also in the English ports.

Woe betide a spy if he were caught! No mercy was shown him. There is here and there on the coast a pit, surrounded on all sides but one by the sea, that goes by the name of "Dead Man's Pool," in which tradition says that spies have been dropped.

Mr. Hawker, who has already been quoted, had as his man-of-all-work an ex-smuggler named Pentire, from whom he got many stories. One day Pentire asked Mr. Hawker:--

"Can you tell me the reason, sir, that no grass will ever grow on the grave of a man that's hanged unjustly?"

"Indeed! How came that about?"

"Why, you see, they got poor Will down to Bodmin, all among strangers; and there was bribery and false swearing, and so they agreed together and hanged poor Will. But his friends begged the body and brought the corpse home here to his own parish, and they turfed the grave, and they sowed the grass twenty times over, but 'twas all of no use, nothing would grow; he was hanged unjustly."

"Well, but, Pentire, what was he accused of? What had Will Pooly done?"

"Done, your honour? Oh, nothing at all--only killed an exciseman."

There are around the coast a great number of what are locally called Vougghas, or Fogous (*Welsh* Ogofau), caves that were artificially constructed for the stowing away of "run" goods.

There is one at Stoke Fleming, near Dartmouth. All along both south and north coasts they are fairly common. On Dartmoor there are also some, but these were for the preparation of spirits, most likely, and the stowing away of what was locally "burnt." They are now employed for turnip cellars.

At one of the wildest and most rugged points of a singularly wild and rugged coast, that of the north of Cornwall, are two tiny bays, Porth Cothan and Porth Mear, in the parishes of S. Merryn and S. Eval, at no great distance from Bedruthan, which has the credit of being the finest piece of cliff scenery on this coast. Here the cliffs tower up a hundred to a hundred and fifty feet above the sea; the raging surf foams over chains of islets formed by the waves, which burrow among the slaty, quartzose rocks, form caves, work further, insulate crags, and finally convert into islands these nodes of more durable rock. At Porth Cothan the cliffs fall away and form a lap of shore, into which flows a little stream, that loses itself in the shifting sands. A manor-house, a mill, a farmhouse or two are all the dwellings near Porth Cothan, and of highways there is none for many miles, the nearest being that from Wadebridge to S. Columb. About a mile up the glen that forms the channel through which the stream flows into Porth Cothan, is a tiny lateral combe, the steep sides covered with heather and dense clumps and patches of furze.

Rather more than half-way down the steep slope of the hill is a hole just large enough to admit of a man entering in a stooping posture. To be strictly accurate, the height is 3 ft. 6 in. and the width 3 ft. But once within, the cave is found to be loftier, and runs for 50 feet due west, the height varying from 7 ft. 6 in. to 8 ft. 6 in., and the width expanding to 8 ft. 3 in. Immediately within the entrance may be observed notches cut in the rock, into which a beam might be thrust to close the mouth of the cave, which was then filled in with earth and bramble bushes drawn over it, when it would require a very experienced eye to discover it. As it was, though the mouth was open, my guide was in fault and unable to find it, and it was by accident only that I lit upon it.

At 7 feet from the entrance a lateral gallery branches off to the right, extending at present but 17 feet, and of that a portion of the roof has fallen in. This gallery was much lower than the main one, not being higher than 3 feet, but probably in a portion now choked it rose, at all events in places, to a greater height. This side gallery never served for the storage of smuggled goods. It was a passage that originally was carried as far as the little cluster of cottages at Trevethan, whence, so it is said, another passage communicated with the sands of Porth Mear. The opening of the underground way is said to have been in a well at Trevethan. But the whole is now choked up. The tunnel was not carried in a straight line. It branched out of the trunk at an acute angle, and was carried in a sweep through the rocks with holes at intervals for the admission of light and air. The total length must have been nearly 3500 feet. The passage can in places be just traced by the falling in of the ground above, but it cannot be pursued within. At the beginning of this century this smugglers' cave was in use.

There is still living an old woman who can give information relative to the use of this cave.

"Well, Genefer, did you ever see smugglers who employed the Vouggha?"

Vouggha, as already stated, is the old Cornish word for cave.

"Well, no, sir. I can't say that; but my father did. He minded well the time when the Vouggha was filled wi' casks of spirits right chuck-full."

"But how were they got there?"

"That was easy enough. The boats ran their loads into Porth Cothan, or, if the preventive men were on the watch, into Porth Mear, which is hidden by the Island of Trescore, drawn like a screen in front. They then rolled the kegs, or carried 'em, to the mouth of the Vouggha or to Trevemedar, it did not matter which, and they rolled 'em into the big cave, and then stopped the mouth up. They could go and get a keg whenever they liked by the little passage that has its mouth in the garden."

"Did the preventive men never find out this place?"

"Never, sir, never. How could they? Who'd be that wicked as to tell them? and they wasn't clever enough to find it themselves. Besides, it would take a deal of cleverness to find the mouth of the Vouggha when closed with clats of turf and drawn over with brambles; and that in the garden could be covered in five minutes--easy." After a pause the old woman said, "Ah! it's a pity I be so old and feeble, or I could show you another as I knows of, and, I reckon, no one else. But my father he had the secret. Oh, dear! oh, dear! what is the world coming to--for education and all kinds o' wickedness? Sure, there's no smuggling now, and poor folks ha'n't got the means o' bettering themselves like proper Christians."

There are other of these smugglers' resorts extant in Cornwall, usually built up underground--one such at Marsland, in Morwenstow; another at Helliger, near Penzance. The Penrose cave is, however, cut out of the solid rock, and the pickmarks are distinctly traceable throughout. At the end, someone has cut his initials in the rock, with the date 1747.

CHAPTER XVIII.

PENZANCE

Penzance, the Holy Headland--Madron--A disciple of S. Piran--
Madron Well--The Feast--Climate--The Irish Colonisation--Penwith-
-S. Breage--Tregonning Hill--Pencaer--Movements of S. Breage--
Cross of coagulated blood--Frescoes--Former extent of Breage--
Sithney--Germoe Church and Chair--Germoe's story--Pengersick
Castle--The Millatons--The Giant's throw--Godolphin Hall--Skewis
and Henry Rogers--Clowance--The Irish invaders--Gwinear--
Ludgvan--The flower farms--S. Hilary--S. Michael's Mount--
Submerged forest--Castel-an-Dinas--Chysauster huts--The
"Rounds"--Newlyn--The Breton Newlyna.

PENZANCE, the most western market town in Cornwall, is of
comparatively modern growth. Formerly it was but a fishing village,
occupying a promontory now distinguished as the quay, where stood
a chapel dedicated to S. Anthony. The name signifies the Holy Head,
or Headland, and there was probably a chapel on the projecting
finger of land long before the time of S. Anthony of Padua (1231),
whose cult was fostered by the Franciscan Order. It is not improbable
that on this headland there may have been a camp, in which case the
dedication is merely a misconception of An-Dinas. The town arms
are S. John the Baptist's head on a charger, also through
misconception, the Holy Head being supposed to be his.

On the east side of the town near the shore was Lis-Cadock, or the
Court of Cadock. At one time the entrenchments were very distinct,
but they have now disappeared. This Cadock is probably Cado, Duke
of Cornwall, cousin of King Arthur, and famous as a warrior in
Geoffrey of Monmouth's lying history. The termination *oc* is a
diminutive.

Penzance is in the parish of Madron, the founder of which, S.
Maternus, as he is called in Latin, is the Irish Medrhan, a disciple of
S. Kieran, or Piran. His brother Odran was closely attached to S.
Senan. Madron and Odran were but lads of from ten to fourteen
when they first visited S. Piran to ask his advice about going a
pilgrimage. He very sensibly recommended them to go to school first,
and he retained them with himself, instructing them in letters. The
Irish have no tradition that he was buried in the Emerald Isle, so that
in all probability he laid his bones in Cornwall.

There was a famous well at Madron, but it has lost its repute of late years, and has fallen into ruin.

Children were formerly taken to the well on the first three Sunday mornings in May to be dipped in the water, that they might be cured of the rickets, or any other disorder with which they were troubled. They were plunged thrice into the water by the parent or nurse, who stood facing the east, and then they were clothed and laid on S. Madron's bed; should they go to sleep after the immersion, or should the water in the well bubble, it was considered a good omen. Strict silence was observed during the performance. At the present time the people go in crowds to the well on the first Sunday in May, when the Wesleyans hold a service there and a sermon is preached; after which the people throw two pins or pebbles in, or lay small crosses made of pieces of rush-pith united by a pin in the middle, in the water and draw auguries therefrom.

Miss Couch in her book on the Cornish holy wells says:--

"About thirty years ago I visited it, and it was then in a ruined state. There was nothing of the shapely and sculptured form of many of our eastern wells about it. It was merely an oblong space enclosed by rough old walling, in which were, in the south-west corner, a dilapidated well, with an inlet and outlet for water, a raised row of stones in front of this, and the remains of stone benches."

A plan exists drawn by Mr. Blight before the well was as ruined as at present. It is a crying scandal that it should be allowed to remain unrestored. The altar-stone remains with a square depression in the middle to receive the portable altar placed there on such occasions as the chapel was used for mass.

MOUNT'S BAY

Penzance, on the glorious Mount's Bay, enjoys a warm and balmy climate, and scarlet geraniums scramble up the house-fronts,

200

camellias bloom in the open air, and greenhouse rhododendrons flourish unprotected from frosts that never fall.

It is a relaxing place, and the visitor, till he is acclimatised, feels limp and lifeless. For this reason many now resort to St. Ives, on the north coast, which is open to the Atlantic breezes straight from Labrador, and Penzance is declining in favour.

But it is a pleasant, it is a most pleasant town, well furnished with all that can make a winter sojourn delightful; it has in addition to libraries and concert-halls and clubs, that may be found in any seaside place, an unrivalled neighbourhood, and with the warm climate it enjoys a winter may be spent delightfully in making excursions to the many surrounding objects of interest.

In my next chapter I shall treat of the Land's End district, and in this I shall attempt to give some idea of what is to be seen to the east.

As already intimated, the whole of this part of Cornwall was occupied at the end of the fifth and the first years of the sixth century by the Irish from the south, mainly from Ossory. An invasion from Munster into that kingdom had led to the cutting of the throats of most of the royal family and its subjugation under the invaders, who maintained their sovereignty there from 470, when the invasion took place, to the death of Scanlan, the descendant of the invader, in 642. It was probably in consequence of this invasion that a large number of Ossorians crossed over to Cornwall and established themselves in Penwith--the Welsh spell it Pengwaeth, the bloody headland; the name tells a story of resistance and butchery. Unhappily we have the most scanty references to this occupation; records we have none.

But a single legend remains that treats of it at some length; and with regard to the legends of the other settlers we have the meagre extracts made by Leland, the antiquary of Henry VIII., whose heart, so it is said, broke at the dispersion of the monastic libraries, and the destruction of historical records of supreme value. As far as we know, the great body of settlers all landed at Hayle. One large contingent, with S. Breaca at its head, made at the outstart a rush for Tregonning Hill, and established itself in the strong stone fort of Pencaer, or Caer Conan, on the summit.

Tregonning Hill is not very high, it rises not six hundred feet above the sea; but from the sea and from the country round it looks bold and lofty, because standing alone, or almost so, having but the inferior Godolphin Hill near it.

The fortress consists of at least two concentric rings of stone and earth. The interior has been disturbed by miners searching for tin, and the wall has also been ruined by them, but especially by roadmakers, who have quite recently destroyed nearly all one side.

Here the Irish remained till they were able to move further. S. Breaca went on to Talmeneth (the end of the mountain), where she established herself and erected a chapel.

Another of her chapels was further down the hill at Chynoweth, and a tradition of its existence remains there. Finally she went to Penbro. The church was, however, at a later period moved from that place to where it now stands. The local legend is that she saw the good people building this church, and she promised to throw all her bracelets and rings into the bell-metal if they would call it after her name.

She was a favourite disciple of S. Bridget, and this latter saint commissioned her to visit the great institution of the White House, near S. David's Head in Wales--to obtain thence rules by which her community might be directed. She was, it appears, the sister of S. Brendan the navigator, and it was in his sister's arms that the saint died. Brendan was a disciple of S. Erc, or Erth, on the Hayle river, and as Erc was one of the party, it is probable that Brendan made one as well.

Erc had been much trusted by S. Patrick, who appointed him as judge in all cases brought to him for decision, regarding him as a man of inviolable integrity and great calmness of judgment.

The church of Breage is large and fine. In the churchyard is an early cross of reddish conglomerate. The local story goes that there was a great fight, between Godolphin Hill and Tregonning Hill, fought by the natives with the Danes, and so much blood was shed that it compacted the granitic sand there into hard rock, and out of this rock Breaca's cross was cut. The fight was, of course, not with Danes, but was between the Cornish and the Irish. The cross is rude, with the Celtic interlaced work on it. The pedestal was also thus ornamented, but this is so worn that it can only be distinguished in certain lights.

In the church have been discovered several frescoes--S. Christopher, gigantic, of course; an equally gigantic figure of Christ covered with bleeding wounds; full-length representations of SS. Samson, Germoe, Giles, Corentine, etc. The church has been much decorated rather than restored. The modern woodwork screen and bench-ends are indifferent in design and mechanical in execution. Some Belgian carved work of the Adoration of the Magi blocks the east window, which was filled with peculiarly vulgar glass, and this is a possible excuse for completely obscuring it.

The sacred tribe under S. Breaca must have occupied a very extensive tract, for four parish churches are affiliated to it--S. Germoe, Godolphin, Cury, and Gunwalloe. This leads one to suspect that her territory stretched originally along the coast a good way past Loe Pool. She had as neighbours S. Crewena, another Irishwoman, and Sithney, or Setna, a disciple and companion of S. Senan, of Land's End. His mother was an aunt of S. David.

Sithney was asked:--

"Tell me, O Setna,
Tidings of the World's end.
How will the folk fare
That follow not the Truth?"

He answered in a poem that has been preserved. Prophecy is a dangerous game to play at, even for a saint, and Sithney made a very bad shot. He foretold that the Saxons would hold dominion in Ireland till 1350, after which the Irish natives would expel them.

Sithney almost certainly accompanied Kieran or Piran, and he succeeded him as abbot in his great monastery at Saighir.

The little church of Germoe is curious. It has a very early font, and a later Norman font lying broken outside the church. There is a curious structure, called Germoe's Chair, in the churchyard, that looks much like a summer-house manufactured out of old pillars turned upside-down. But it was in existence in the time of Henry VIII., for Leland mentions it. A new east window, quite out of character with the church, has been inserted, but the modern glass is good. A bust of S. Germoe is over the porch. He is represented as crowned, as he is supposed to have been an Irish king.

This is not quite correct. He was a bard, and perhaps of royal race, but we do not know his pedigree. He was a disciple of S. Kieran, and was the father of the first writer of the lives of the saints in Ireland. He composed a poem in honour of S. Finnan of Moville, and he had the honour of having under him, for a short while, the great Columba of Iona. He had several brothers, who passed into France, and are mentioned by Flodoard, the historian of the Franks. The date of his death was about 530. I have elsewhere told a story about him tubbing with S. Kieran, and catching a fish in the tub.

Near Germoe, but nearer the sea, is the very fine remnant of a castle, Pengersick. It was erected in the reign of Henry VIII. by a certain man of the name of Millaton, probably of Millaton in Bridestowe, Devon. He had committed a murder, and to escape justice he fled his native county and concealed himself in the dip of the land facing the sea at Pengersick, where he constructed a tower amply provided with means of defence. The basement is furnished with loopholes for firing upon anyone approaching, and above the door is a shoot for melted lead. The whole building is beautifully constructed.

Here Millaton remained in concealment till he died, never leaving his tower for more than a brief stroll. The land had not been purchased in his own name, but in that of his son Job, who, after his death, was made Governor of S. Michael's Mount. Job had a son, William, who was made Sheriff of Cornwall in 1565, and he married Honor, daughter of Sir William Godolphin of Godolphin.

According to a local legend, William Millaton and his wife Honor lived a cat-and-dog life. They hated each other with a deadly hate, and at length each severally resolved that this incompatible union must come to an end.

William Millaton said to his wife, "Honor, we have lived in wretchedness too long. Let us resolve on a reconciliation, forget the past, and begin a new life."

"Most certainly do I agree thereto," said she.

"And," continued William, "as a pledge of our reunion, let us have a feast together to-night"

So a banquet was spread in Pengersick Castle for them twain and none others.

And when they had well eaten, then William Millaton said, "Let us drink to our reunion."

"I will drink if you will drink," said she.

Then he drained his glass, and after that, she drained hers.

With a bitter laugh she said, "William, you have but three minutes to live. Your cup was poisoned."

"And you," retorted he, "have but five, for yours is poisoned."

"It is well," said Honor; "I am content. I shall have two minutes in which to triumph over your dead carcass, and to spurn it with my foot."

On the death of this William, the estate passed to his six sisters, who married into the families of Erisy, Lanyon, Trefusis, Arundell, Bonython, and Abbot of Hartland.

On the road from Breage, before the turn to Pengersick is reached, a stone lies by the roadside. It is one of those cast by the Giant of Godolphin Hill after his wife, of whom he was jealous, and who was wont to visit the Giant of Pengersick. The stone has often been removed, but such disaster has ensued to the man who has removed it, that it has always been brought back again. Godolphin Hill has been esteemed since the days of Elizabeth as one of the richest of ore deposits, and it was due to the urgency of Sir Francis Godolphin that miners were induced to come to Cornwall from the Erz Gebirge, in Saxony, to introduce new methods and machinery in the tin mines.

Godolphin Hall is an interesting old mansion, partly dating from the time of Henry VII. and partly belonging to the period of the Restoration. Some remains from a ruined church or chapel have been worked into one of the gateways. The old house has its stewponds and a few fine trees about it.

On the Marazion road, west of Millpool, in the hedge, are the impress of the devil's knees. One day, feeling the discomfort and forlornness of his position, his majesty resolved on praying to have it changed; so he knelt on a slab of granite, but his knees burned their way into the stone. Then he jumped up, saying that praying superinduced rheumatics, and he would have no more of it. The holes are not tin-moulds, for the latter are angular and oblong, but are very similar to the cup-markings found in many places in connection with prehistoric monuments. Some precisely similar are at Dumnakilty in Fermanagh.[26]

A strange circumstance occurred in 1734 at Skewis, close to the line from Gwinear Road Station to Helston.

Skewis had been for many generations the freehold patrimony of a yeoman family of the name of Rogers. There were two brothers. The elder married and lived on the farm, but without a family. The younger brother, Henry Rogers, was married and had several children. He carried on for several years in Helston the trade of a pewterer, then of considerable importance in Cornwall, although it is now at an end. A large portion of the tin raised was mixed with lead and exported in the form of pewter made into dishes, plates, etc., now superseded by earthenware. At the first introduction of earthenware, called cloam, in the West of England, a strong prejudice existed against it as liable to damage the tin trade, and it was a popular cry to destroy all cloam, so as to bring back the use of pewter. The elder Rogers died, and bequeathed the house of Skewis and the farm and everything thereon to his wife Anne. Henry was indignant. He believed in the inalienability of "heir land." He was suspicious that Anne Rogers would make over Skewis to her own relatives, of the name of Millett. Henry waited his opportunity, when his sister-in-law was out of the house, to enter it and bring in his wife and children and servants. He turned out the domestics of Anne, and occupied the whole house.

The widow appealed to law, but the voice of the whole county was against her, and the general opinion was that the will had been extorted from her husband. Even Sir John S. Aubyn, living at Clowance, hard by, favoured him, and had Henry Rogers acted in a reasonable manner would have backed him up. But Rogers took the law into his own hands, and when a judgment was given against him, he still refused to surrender.

The Sheriff of Cornwall accordingly was directed to eject him by force. Rogers, however, barricaded the house, and prepared to defend it. He supplied himself with gunpowder and slugs, and cut loopholes in his doors and shutters from which to fire at the assailants.

On June 18th, 1734, the Under-Sheriff and a *posse* went to Skewis and demanded the surrender of the house. From two to three hundred people attended, for the most part sympathisers with Rogers, but not willing to render him effectual assistance.

As the Under-Sheriff, Stephen Tillie, persisted in his demands, and threatened to break into the house, Rogers fired. The bullet passed through Tillie's wig, singed it, and greatly frightened him, especially as with the next discharge one of his officers fell at his side, shot through the head.

Several guns were fired, and then the Under-Sheriff deemed it advisable to withdraw and send for soldiers.

On the arrival of a captain with some regulars, Tillie again approached, when Rogers continued firing, and killed a bailiff and shot a soldier in the groin. Two more men were wounded, and then the military fired at the windows, but did no harm. Mrs. Rogers stood by her husband, loading and handing him his gun.

The whole attacking party now considering that discretion constituted the best part of valour, withdrew, and Rogers was allowed to remain in possession till March in the following year, that is to say, for nine months. Then he was again blockaded by soldiers, and the siege continued for several days, with the loss of two more men, when at last cannon were brought from Pendennis Castle.

Many years after, one of Rogers' sons gave the following account of his reminiscences of the siege:--"He recollected that his father was fired at, and had a snuff-box and powder-horn broken in his pocket by a ball. He recollected that whilst he himself (then a child) was in the bed several balls came in through the window of the room, and after striking against the wall rolled about on the floor. One brother and sister who were in the house went out to inquire what was wanted of their father, and they were not permitted to return. On the last night no one remained in the house but his father, himself, and the servant-maid. In the middle of the night they all went out, and got some distance from the house. In crossing a field, however, they were met by two soldiers, who asked them their business. The maid answered that they were looking for a cow, when they were permitted to proceed. The soldiers had their arms, and his father had his gun. The maid and himself were left at a farmhouse in the neighbourhood."

Henry Rogers, whom the soldiers had not recognised in the darkness, managed to escape, and pushed on in the direction of London, resolving to lay his grievances before the king. He was dressed in a whitish fustian frock, with imitation pearl buttons, and a blue riding-coat over it.

As soon as it was discovered that he had decamped, a reward of £350 was offered for his apprehension. He had already shot and killed five men, and had wounded seven. He was not, however, taken till he reached Salisbury Plain, where he hailed a postboy, who was returning with an empty chaise, and asked for a lift. He was still carrying his gun. The boy drove him to the inn, where he procured a bed; but the circumstances, and the description, had excited suspicion; he was secured in his sleep, and was removed to Cornwall, to be tried for murder at Launceston along with his serving-man, John Street.

His trial took place on August 1st, 1735, before Lord Chief Justice Hardwicke. Rogers was arraigned upon five indictments, and Street upon two. Both received sentence of death, and were executed on August 6th.

The house at Skewis has been recently in part rebuilt, when a bag of the slugs used by poor Rogers was found.

It is in Crowan parish.

The church of S. Crewenna stands on a hill, and has a good tower. It contains numerous monuments of the S. Aubyn family, and some brasses only recently restored to the church, after having lain for many years lost or forgotten in a cupboard at Clowance.

It is hard to say whether the fulsome memorial of Sir John S. Aubyn, who died in 1839, is more painful or amusing reading to such as know his story.

The church has been "restored" in a cold and unsympathetic fashion.

Clowance, the seat of the Molesworth S. Aubyn family, has noble trees, and is an oasis in the midst of the refuse-heaps of mines. There are some early crosses in the grounds.

But to return to the Irish invasion.

A second party of the colonists was under Fingar or Gwinear, son of Olilt, or Ailill, probably one of the Hy Bairrche family, which was expelled their country about 480. He brought over with him his sister Kiara, whose name has become Piala or Phillack in Cornish, according to a phonetic and constant rule. According to the legend he had over seven hundred emigrants with him. He and his party made their way from Hayle to Connerton, where they spent the night, and then pushed south to where now stands Gwinear. Here Fingar left his party to go ahead and explore. He reached Tregotha, where is a fine spring of water, and there paused to refresh himself, when, hearing cries from behind, he hurried back, and found that Tewdrig, the Cornish king or prince, who lived at Riviere, on a creek of the Hayle river, had hastened after the party of colonists, and had fallen on them and massacred them. When Fingar came up Tewdrig killed him also. Piala, the sister, does not seem to have been harmed; and as in the long-run the Irish succeeded in establishing themselves firmly in the district, she settled near Riviere and founded the church of Phillack.

Ludgvan has a fine tower and some old crosses, the font also is early, of polyphant stone; but the church has been badly churchwardenised and meanly restored. It was founded by Lithgean, or Lidgean, an Irish saint, son of Bronfinn or Gwendron. There is a representation of the mother in the rectory garden wall, where she is figured holding what is apparently a tree in one hand and in the other a fleur-de-lis.

Hereabouts the whole country is devoted to early potatoes and spring flowers. In March the fields are white with narcissus or golden with daffodil, or rich brown with the Harbinger wallflower. It is a curious fact that yellow wallflowers meet with no sale; consequently one kind only, and that dark, is grown.

The kinds of narcissus mostly grown are the Scilly White; of daffodils the Soleil d'Or, Grand Monarch, Emperor and Empress, Sir Watkin, and Princeps. These flowers are packed in baskets or boxes in bunches, a dozen blossoms in each bunch, and four dozen bunches in each basket. Women are employed to pick in the morning and to tie in bunches in the afternoon.

A special train takes up the flowers daily to London. The rate charged is £4 10s. per ton, but for fish £2 10s., as they take less room. The flower harvest lasts from February to June, and is followed by one of tomatoes.

Between Ludgvan and Perran-uthnoe intervenes the parish of S. Hilary. The church is devoid of interest, but there are inscribed stones in the churchyard. On the village inn may be read the invitation:--

"THE JOLLY TINNERS."

"Come, all true Cornish boys, walk in,
Here's Brandy, Beer, Rum, Shrub, and Gin.
You cannot do less than drink success
To Copper, Fish, and Tin."

A local riddle asked is:--

"As I went down by Hilary's steeple
I met three people.
They were not men, nor women, nor children.
Who were they then?"

The answer, of course, is one man, one woman, and a single child.

S. Michael's Mount is a grand upshoot of granite from the sea. As a rock it is far finer than its corelative in Brittany, but the buildings crowning the Cornish mount are vastly inferior to the magnificent pile on Mont Saint Michel. Nevertheless, those that now form the residence of Lord S. Levan are by no means insignificant or unworthy of their position. The masses of granite crag, especially to the west, are singularly bold, and if some of the modern work be poor in design, it might have been much worse.

Within there is not much to be seen--a chapel of no great interest, and a dining-hall with good plaster-work representation of a hare hunt running round it. The drawing-room is new and spacious, and contains some really noble portraits.

At the foot of the rock is a draw-well, and a little way up is a tank called the Giant's Well. S. Michael's Mount was the habitation of the famous giant with whom Tom Thumb tried conclusions.

In or about 710, according to William of Worcester, an apparition of S. Michael the archangel was seen on the *Tumba* in Cornwall. This Tumba was also called Hore-rock in the Wood, "and there was formerly grove and field and tilled land between the Mount and the Scilly Isles, and there were a hundred and forty churches of parishes between the said Mount and Scilly that were submerged.... The district was enclosed by a most vast forest stretching for six miles in from the sea,affording a most suitable refuge for wild beasts, and in this were formerly found monks serving the Lord."

It is quite true that there is a submerged forest in Mount's Bay, and that the marshy snipe-ground near Marazion Road Station covers large timber, a portion of this great forest, but the submergence cannot have taken place in historic times. That there was, however, an encroachment of the sea in the middle of the sixth century, we learn from the *Life of S. Paul*, Bishop of Leon. He came to the bay to visit his sister, Wulvella, of Gulval, when she complained to him that she was losing much of her best land by the advance of the sea; and he, who had been brought up in the Wentloog levels, and taught by his master, S. Iltyd, how to keep up the dykes against the tides in the Severn, banked out the sea for her.

This was precisely the time when the district of Gwaelod was submerged in the Bay of Cardigan. The king of the district was Gwyddno Longshanks. It was the duty of the warden of the dykes to ride along the embankments, that had probably been thrown up by the Roman legionaries, and see that they were in order. Seithenyn was the Dyke-grave at the time.

One night Gwyddno and his court were keeping high revel, and the dyke-master was very drunk. There was a concurrence of a spring-tide and a strong westerly wind, and the waves overwhelmed the banks. The king escaped with difficulty before the inrolling stormy sea. A poem by the king, who thus lost his kingdom, has been preserved.

In Brittany about the same time there was a similar catastrophe.

In Mount's Bay, however, an extraordinary tide may have done damage, but certainly did not cause such a submergence as was supposed by William of Worcester.

It has been supposed that the Mount is the Ictis of the ancients, which was the site of the great mart for tin, but this is more than unlikely. What would have been the advantage of making a market on this conical rock? It is much more likely that the great tin mart was in one of the low-lying islands of Kent.

Castel-an-Dinas commands an extensive view; it stands 763 feet above the sea, and is within sight and signalling distance of the two other similar castles on Trencrom and Tregonning. It is more perfect than either, and is very interesting, as it has got its wall with the face showing through the greater portion of the circuit. There were at least two concentric rings of fortifications and numerous hut circles within the area, but these have been much pulled about when an absurd imitation ruinous tower was erected on the summit. Within the camp is a well, and outside it on the west side is one cut in the rock, to which a descent is made by about twenty steps.

On the side of the hill is the very interesting and indeed wonderful group of clustered huts called Chysauster. Of these there remain four distinct groups, two of which have been dug out. They consist of an open space in the midst, with numerous beehive huts and galleries running out of it.

The period to which they pertain is very uncertain. They ought to be investigated by such as are experienced and trained in excavation of such objects, and not be meddled with by amateurs. The tenant has begun (1899) to destroy one of the groups. In the centre of one of the huts may be seen neatly cut the socket-hole of the pole which sustained the roof, and in another the lower stone of the quern in which grain was pounded. There are other collections of a similar character, but none so perfect.

In the neighbourhood of Penzance are some of the "Rounds," formerly employed for the representation of sacred dramas. They are, in fact, open-air amphitheatres. The well-known Gwennap Pit, in which John Wesley preached, has been mistaken for one of these, but was actually a disused mine-hole.

In these pits the miracle-plays in the old Cornish tongue were performed. Of these plays we have a few preserved, that have been printed by Professor Whitley Stokes. But the Cornish language ceased to be spoken, and after the Reformation religious plays ceased to be required. The people were learning the art of reading, and the press gave them the Bible, then these miracle-plays were replaced by low comedies, often very coarse in their humour, and spiced with many local allusionsand personal jokes. This continued till Wesleyanism denounced stage-plays, and then these pits were devoted to revival-meetings and displays of hysterical religion. There were two Rounds near Penzance, Tolcarre, and one at Castle Horneck.

Adjoining Penzance to the south is Newlyn, a fishing village formerly, now both a fishing village and a settlement of artists; for the advantage of the latter a good place of exhibition for their pictures has been provided by that generous-hearted son of Cornwall, who has done so much for his native county, Mr. Passmore Edwards.

Newlyn takes its name probably from S. Newlyna, whose church, founded on her own land, is near Crantock and Newquay. The name means the White Cloud. She migrated to Brittany, embarking, it may be supposed, at this port in Guavas Bay. She is a Breton replica of S. Winefred, for she had her head cut off by an admiring chieftain, whose affection was changed into anger at her resistance. In Brittany she has a fine church at Pontivy Noyala.

A cantique is sung there by the children, the first verse of which runs thus:--

"Deit, Créchénion, de gleuet

Buhé caër Santes Noaluen,

Ha disguet guet-he miret

Hag hou fé hag non lézen,"

which means, "Come, ye Christians, hearken all, and hear the tale of S. Noewlyn. From her example learn to keep your faith and your innocence."

S. Paul's takes its name from a founder who was born in Glamorganshire, and was educated by S. Iltyd. He was schoolfellow with S. David, S. Samson, and Gildas. He is said to have gone to a King Mark, but whether this were the Mark, King of Cornwall of the romancers, the husband of the fair and frail Ysseult, we cannot be sure. He quarrelled with the king, and left him, because he was refused a bell in Mark's possession, which he admired and asked for. He settled in Brittany, in Leon.

CHAPTER XIX.

THE LAND'S END

The Irish settlers in Penwith--Difference between Irish and Cornish languages--The Irish saints of Penwith--Other saints--Penzance--S. Ives--Restored brass--Wreck of Algerine pirates in 1760--Description of Penwith--The pilchard fishery--Song--Churches of the Land's End--S. Burian--S. Paul's and Dolly Pentreath--The Cornish language--Cornish dialect--Old churches and chapels--Madron--Prehistoric antiquities.

THE Land's End is properly Penwith, either Pen-gwaed, the Bloody Headland, or Pen-gwaedd, the Headland of Shouting. Probably it is the former, for it was the last place of refuge of the Ibernian population, and in the first years of the sixth century, even perhaps earlier, it was occupied by Irish settlers, and that there was fighting is clearly shown us in the legend of SS. Fingar and Piala. It must have been to the original people of the peninsula what Mona was to the Welsh.

LAND'S END

All we *know* about this invasion is what is told us in the legend just mentioned, and that states that Fingar, son of an Irish king, came to Hayle, landed there with his party, and was fallen upon by Tewdrig, the Cornish duke or king, who massacred some of the party. But the

213

names of the parishes tell us more than that. They show us that the Irish were not defeated, that they made good their landing, and that they spread and occupied the whole of Penwith and Carnmarth, that is to say, the entire district of West Cornwall up to Camborne and the Lizard district.

The colonists cannot have been few, and they must have purposed settling, for they brought women along with them; and that they were successful is assured by the fact that those killed by Tewdrig are recognised as martyrs. Had the Irish been driven away they would have been regarded as pirates who had met their deserts.

Now this inroad of saints was but one out of a succession of incursions, and the resistance of Tewdrig marks the revolt against Irish domination which took place after the death of Dathi in 428, the last Irish monarch who was able to exact tribute from Britain; though Oiliol Molt may have attempted it, he was too much hampered by internal wars to make Irish authority felt in Britain. Oiliol fell in 483.

The Irish saints came across in detachments. Senan, Erc (Erth), Setna (Sithney), Brig (Breage), Just were some of the earliest. There was trouble when Brig arrived, and she and her party fled from Tewdrig and fortified themselves on Tregonning Hill, where their camp still remains. But Kieran and his pupils, Medran (Madron) and Bruinech (Buriena), were unmolested; so also was S. Ruan.

One thing they could not do, and that was impress on the people the Scottish or Irish pronunciation. They were few among many, and they not only could not make the natives pronounce a hard *c*, but they were themselves obliged to suffer their own names to be softened, and the *c* in them to be turned into *p*, and the *f* into *gw*. Thus Kieran became Piran, and Fingar became Gwinear. The Irish *c* is always sounded like *k*, and the Cornish disliked this sound. When S. Kiera settled in Cornwall she had to accustom herself to be called Piala; and Eoghain was melted down into Euny, and Erc softened into Erth.

Just one advantage to Cornwall did this invasion afford; by it we know the histories of the founders of churches in West Cornwall; because the Irish had the wit to preserve their records and biographies, whereas of the home-grown saints, princes of blood royal, the Cornish have not kept a single history. Consequently, if we desire to know about the early kings and saints of the peninsula, we have to ask the Irish, the Welsh, and even go hat in hand to the Bretons. It is a sorry truth, but truth it is.

How thoroughly occupied by the Irish this district was may be judged when we come to look at who the saints were.

Let us take them in order from Newquay.

First we have Carantock, the fellow-worker with S. Patrick, who assisted him on the commission to draw up the laws of Ireland. Then we have Perranzabuloe, the settlement of Kieran of Saighir. Across the ridge, four miles off, is Ladock, where he planted his nurse as head of a community of women. Some of Kieran's young pupils found it not too far to trip across and flirt with the girls at Ladock, and there was a pretty to-do when this was discovered. He was wont, when he had ploughed his own lands, to send over his oxen to plough the fields of his nurse. At Redruth was S. Euny, whom the Irish called Eoghain, and who later was Bishop of Ardstraw. He was brother of S. Erc of Erth, as it was said in later times, but earlier writers frankly call Erc his father.

Illogan was son of Cormac, King of Leinster. Piety ran in the family. Cormac abdicated and assumed the monk's cowl in 535. The sisters of Illogan were Derwe and Ethnea, who accompanied him to Cornwall, and are numbered with its saints. He was father of S. Credan of Sancreed. Phillack is S. Piala, the sister of Gwynear (Fingar). S. Elwyn is but another form of the name Illogan. Erth, as already said, was father of S. Euny; he was a disciple of S. Brendan, the voyager, and was nursed by S. Itha, who was a woman almost as famous in Ireland as S. Bridget, and who has churches in Cornwall and Devon. S. Ives is really S. Hia, an Irishwoman. Zennor is, perhaps, dedicated to a disciple of S. Sennen of Land's End, the very woman about whom Tom Moore wrote his song of "The Saint and the Lady." S. Just was the deacon of S. Patrick, and he was S. Kieran's tutor. Sennen is Senan of Inscathy, in the Shannon. S. Levan was metal-worker for S. Patrick, but in holy orders also. S. Burian was the female disciple of S. Kieran. Germoe was a bard, and an intimate friend of Kieran, and so we see him planted near his friend, who was at Perran-uthnoe. Breage was a disciple of S. Bridget and a friend of S. Kieran. Crewenna was another Irishwoman. Sithney is Setna, a disciple of S. Senan. S. Ruan, in the Lizard district, and S. Kea, on the Fal--Irishmen as well--I have spoken of them elsewhere.

But along the south coast are some settlements of a different kind. Paul is Paul of Leon, a Briton, who came there to visit his sister, Wulvella, at Gulval before he crossed into Brittany; and Towednack is not an Irish foundation.

Senan and Kieran, or Piran, were such allies that the former was wont to call the latter "his inseparable friend and comrade." It is therefore no wonder that we find settlements of the two in West Cornwall together.

Senan and Kieran probably came to Cornwall some years later than Hia and Breaca, Fingar and Piala. Senan was very much attached to S. David, and both are said to have died on the same day in the same year.

As Sithney's mother was a sister of Non, the mother of S. David, it is possible that David may have induced his cousin to study with his friend Senan, and that when Senan came to Cornwall he hoped that Sithney would be able to smooth his way, as an aunt of his was queen there. This I have already pointed out.

It is noteworthy that Sithney parish is close to that of his first cousin Constantine.

The key to the Land's End district is Penzance. This is a comparatively modern town, and it was but a village in the parish of S. Madron, with a little chapel of S. Anthony on a spit of land running into the bay, till incorporated by James I.

That bay is singularly fine, and, facing the south, the climate is warm. Out of it stands up S. Michael's Mount crowned with a castle, formerly a monastery, now the residence of Lord S. Levan, and connected by a causeway with Marazion, or Market Jew. The name has nothing to do with "Bitter Waters of Zion," or with Israelites. Marazion is the Cornish for Thursday Market, and Market Jew is a corruption for *Jeudi* (Thursday) Market.

From Penzance a visit should be paid to S. Ives and to Hayle. The Hayle river flows in a natural furrow from near Germoe, and the whole of the district west is, as it were, cut off from the rest of the peninsula. It needed to have been but a little more depressed, and it would have been converted almost into an island, linked to the mainland only by the ridge between S. Hilary and Godolphin.

The great S. Ives Bay is conspicuous through its white hills of blown sand that form what are locally called Towans.

The church of S. Ives is interesting, and is, like most others in Cornwall, Perpendicular. It is of granite, and contains some fine oak carving in bench-ends and waggon-roof, and a portion of the screen presented, it is supposed, by Ralph Clies, a master smith; also a brass to Otho Trenwith and his wife. The latter is represented kneeling to and invoking the archangel Michael. The head of S. Michael has a comical effect. "Some perplexity may be felt at the appearance of Saint Michael's head, which looks like nothing so much as a Dutch cheese. The fact is, that when this brass lay on the floor, the feet of passers-by had gradually erased the features of the archangel, leaving only the circular nimbus or glory round his head. Some well-meaning but misguided restorer of later days has evidently taken the nimbus to be the outline of the head, and has roughly filled in eyes, nose, and mouth to correspond."[27]

An event occurred at Penzance in 1760 that was curious.

A large vessel was driven ashore on the beach. Numbers of persons crowded to the wreck to get from it what they could, when they were startled to see it manned by swarthy mariners with scimitars and turbans. At once a panic seized on those who had come out of interested motives to the wreck, and they scuttled off as hard as their legs would take them. Presently a company of volunteers was called out to roll of drum, and marched down to surround the 172 men who had disembarked from the wreck. These were gallantly captured and driven like sheep into a spacious barn, and left there under guard through the night.

Next morning it was ascertained from the men who had come ashore (some of whom could speak broken French), by means of some English officers who could understand a little French, especially when broken, that the vessel was an Algerine corsair, carrying twenty-four guns, and that the captain, finding his ship making water rapidly, had run her ashore in Mount's Bay, fully believing he was about the latitude of Cadiz. The instant it was known that the sailors were Algerines, a deadly panic fell on the neighbourhood, for now the plague was feared. The volunteers could hardly be kept at their posts, where they quaked, and felt internal qualms. Intelligence was conveyed to the Government, and orders were issued for troops to march from Plymouth. Happily, however, the panic rapidly abated; the local authorities convinced themselves that there was no plague among the strangers, and, slowly and cautiously, people approached to look and gape at the dark-moustached and bearded men with dusky skin, bare legs, and turbans. The pirates were on the whole kindly treated, and after some delay were sent back to Algiers.

The whole country is wind-blown, and everything looks small: the trees are stunted; the hills rise to no great heights, the very highest point reached is 827 feet; and Tregonning, which does not mount above 600 feet, assumes the airs of a mountain. The coast is fine, but by no means as fine as that of the Lizard. The rocks are of granite, and not of serpentine. But, on the other hand, the surface is less level than that of Meneage. It is crowded with prehistoric antiquities, cromlechs, camps, and stone circles. And the Land's End district has this great advantage, that if you are overdone with the soft and relaxing air on the south coast, you have but to ascend a hill and inhale the invigorating breath that comes from the Atlantic on the north.

Newlyn and Hayle are great fishing stations, and in the Land's End district as in the Lizard chances arise for watching the pilchard fishery.

So many seans, or nets, about 220 fathoms long and about 15 fathoms deep, belong to each fishing station, and three boats go to each sean. The first boat, which is also the largest, is called the sean-boat, as it carries the net and seven men; the next is termed the vollier, probably a corruption for "follower," and carries another sean, called the tuck-sean, which is about 100 fathoms long and 18 deep, this boat also carries seven men; the third boat is called the lurker, and contains but three or four men, and in this boat is the master, or commander.

Pilchards are migratory and gregarious fish, rather smaller than herrings, which they much resemble, but are cased in larger scales. They begin to appear at the end of June, but they are then at a great distance from the coast, and the boats have to go out far to sea before they encounter the shoals. It is a pretty sight to see a flight of fishing-smacks, with their white wings spread, issuing from one of the harbours, and all making for the spot where the fish are ascertained or supposed to be.

At nightfall the nets are set either across or parallel to the drift of the tide, and are suffered to be carried along by the current. About midnight the nets are hauled, and the fish having become entangled by their gills, are taken into the boats, and the nets are again set. It is only by night that fish can be caught in this way, as they are keen-sighted. This is drift-net fishing.

In the morning the boats return with the spoil, and the port, or harbour, is alive with women and children; these latter on such occasions can by no persuasion be induced to attend school. A string of carts is drawn up on the beach, each containing several "maunds," or panniers, to receive the silver load.

As the season advances the shool, or shoal, comes nearer the shore.

A saying is that
"When the corn is in the shock,
Then the fish are at the rock."
And now the time for drift-net fishing is over, and that of sean, or seine, fishing begins.

Pilchards swim in dense hosts, so that the sea seems to be in a state of effervescence.

On the cliffs men and boys are to be seen all day long lying about smoking, apparently doing nothing. But their keen eyes are on the sea. They are watching for the coming of the pilchards. It is not possible to see from the boat so as to surround a shoal; that is why a watch is maintained from the cliffs by "huers" (French *huer*, to shout). The moment their experienced eyes see by a change in the colour of the water that the shoal is approaching, by preconcerted signals the crew are informed as to the place where it is, and the direction it is taking.

The fish playing on the surface are called skimmers. The colour of the water, as seen from above where the fish are dense, is almost red; it is always darker than the water around.

Another token of the presence of a shoal is the sea birds hovering about, expecting their prey.

The boats are all in readiness.

The shoal is also known by the *stoiting*, or jumping, of the fish. When fish are observed stoiting a signal is given, whereupon the sean-boat and vollier get on the spot, and the crew of the foremost boat pass a warp, that is, throw a rope, which is fixed to the end of the sean on board the vollier, and then shoot the net overboard, which, having leaden weights at bottom, sinks, and the top is buoyed up with corks. The sean-boat is rowed in a circular course round where the fish are stoiting, and when they have reached the vollier the fish are enclosed. They then hem the two ends of the sean together with a cord to prevent the fish from breaking out, and whilst this is being done a man is engaged in frightening the fish away from the still open end by means of a stone fastened to a rope. This is termed throwing the minnies (*maen* stone, pl. *meini*). When the two ends of the net are laced together, grapes, *i.e.* grapnels, are let down to keep the net expanded and steady till the fish have been taken up. This latter process is called tucking the sean. The boat with the tuck-sean on board passes the warp of that sean to one of the other boats and then shoots this tuck-sean within the stop-sean, and next draws up the same to the edge of the water, when it is seen to be one quivering mass of silver. The fish are now taken or dipped out with baskets into the boats. When the boats are filled, if more fish remain in the large sean, it is left in the water, till by successive tuckings all the fish have been removed.

The fish that have been caught and brought on shore are taken to the cellars. Fish cellars are usually dug out of the rock, and in them the pilchards are deposited in heaps, to be cured by the women, who work at this night and day. The cellar floor is covered with a layer of salt for the distance of five or six feet from the walls, and on this is laid a row of fish with their tails touching the wall; then next to these is laid another row, and so on in concentric rings, till a sufficient space is paved with fish. On this foundation is laid more salt, and then more fish, and this process is continued till the pile is complete and the cellar is stacked with fish. They are now said to be "in bulk," and so are suffered to remain for some weeks, during which time boards are placed on them with stones, so as to squeeze out of them all superfluous water and oil. The process of salting completed, the fish are packed in barrels, and are sent away to market.

After July or August the pilchards leave the coast, and do not reappear until the end of October or the beginning of November. They now appear in the Bristol Channel, and come down towards Land's End, which they turn and follow the south coast of Cornwall, and then disappear.

Formerly pilchards were smoked, and went by the name of *fumadoes*. The name clung to them after the smoking was abandoned, and *fumadoes* is now corrupted into "fair maids."

There is a song of the pilchard fishery which is sung by the boatmen. I know of it but three verses, and I doubt if there be more.

"The cry is, 'All up! Let us all haste away!
And like hearty good fellows we'll row through the bay.
Haul away, my young men!
Pull away, my old blades!
For the county gives bounty
For the pilchard trades.'

"'Tis the silver 'fair maids' that cause such a strife
'Twixt the master-seiner and his drunken wife.
Haul away, etc.

"She throwed away her fiddles (?) and burnt all her thread,
And she turn'd him out o' doors for the good of the trade.

Haul away," etc.

The churches of the Land's End district are not remarkably fine. They are not, however, without interest.

The finest is that of S. Burian, about whom first of all a word or two. Buriena was an Irish damsel, noted for being both slender and beautiful. In fact, her willowy form obtained for her the nickname of Caol, or "the Slim." She was a daughter of one Crimthan, "the Fox," a Munster chieftain, a granddaughter of Aengus, King of Munster, who was baptised by S. Patrick, on which occasion the apostle ran the spike at the end of the pastoral staff into the foot of the king. Afterwards, when S. Patrick saw the wound and the blood, he was shocked, and said, "Why the dickens did you not tell me of it?" "I thought it was part of the ceremony," replied Aengus.

However, to return to Buriena, his granddaughter. She was so pretty and so graceful, that although she was at school with Liadhain, the mother of S. Piran, as her spiritual child, a chieftain named Dimma carried her off to his own castle. Liadhain came in a fume to S. Piran and told him of the outrage. At once the old man seized his staff and went after Dimma, who was head of the clan Hy Fiachta. It was midwinter, and the snow was on the ground. When Piran arrived at the gates of the cashel he was refused admittance. He would not return, but maintained his place, and next morning there he was still. He had stood there all night in the snow, waiting to insist on the restoration of the girl. Dimma now was alarmed. He saw that the saint was determined to "fast against him," a legal process, as has been described already, and he returned the damsel.

However, some days afterwards, feeling his passion still strong, he went at the head of a body of men to reclaim her. Buriena fainted when she saw his approach; but Piran had time to call out all his ecclesiastical tribe, and they surrounded the place where Liadhain and Buriena were, and he had sent a detachment to make a circuit and set fire to Dimma's cashel, so that the chief was compelled to beat a precipitate retreat. It was probably in consequence of this that Piran left Ireland and came to Cornwall.

S. Burian Church does not stand on the site of the old settlement of Buriena; that is about a mile south-east, at Bosliven, where the "sanctuary" remains about some mounds and ruins. It was destroyed by Shrubsall, one of Cromwell's miserable instruments of sacrilege. When Athelstan traversed Cornwall from east to west he made a vow that if he reached the Scilly Isles and returned in safety he would endow a collegiate church where was the oratory in which he made the vow. This he did, and the date of the foundation is supposed to have been 936.

The church had a superb screen, probably the finest in Cornwall, but it was taken down and destroyed in 1814. Some fragments have been preserved sufficient to admit of its complete reconstruction at some future day. Many of the bench-ends remain, and are fine. The church has been illtreated in that fashion which is in bitter mockery called "restoration." The new woodwork is a fair example of what woodwork never should be. It is treated like cheese.

S. Levan has fine old bench-ends and exquisitely bad modern woodwork, and in the neighbourhood is the Logan Rock and some of the finest coast scenery of the Land's End. S. Levan was priest and metal-worker in S. Patrick's company, and some of his bells and book-covers remained long preserved as treasures in Ireland.

S. Senan has been gutted by the restorer, and has in it no longer anything of interest except a mutilated statue of the Virgin and Child.

Madron has not much of interest, except the oft-quoted epitaph on George Daniel:--

"Belgia me Birth, Britain me Breeding gave,
Cornwall a Wife, ten children and a grave."

Paul's, dedicated to S. Paul of Leon, brother of S. Wulvella of Gulval, has a good tower, and several points of interest. Here was buried, 1778, Dolly Pentreath, the last person able to converse in the old Cornish language. Pentreath was her maiden name. She was married to a man of the name of Jeffery. It is still the custom in the villages of Mousehole and Newlyn for women to be called by their maiden names after marriage; indeed, there are some instances in which the husband goes by the maiden name of his wife, when his individuality disappears under her more pronounced personality. Such would doubtless be the case in the following instance I quote from the *Cornish Magazine*:--

Girl (selling papers): "If you please, sir, do you want a *'Ome Companion?*"

Householder (at door): "No, thank'ee, my dear. I got wan."

Girl: "*'Ome Chat*, sir?"

Householder: "*'Ome Chat!*" (throws open the door). "Here, just come fore and listen for yourself. Hark to her a bellerin' in the back kitchen."

Or in such a case as this.

Pasco Polglaze was henpecked. He opened his heart to Uncle Zackie at the "Dog and Pheasant."

"Now, look here," said Uncle Zackie, "you be a man and show yourself maister in your own 'ouse. You go 'ome and snap your vingers in the missus' vaice, and sit down on the table. I'll come in two minutes after and see your triumph--you maister and all."

"Right," said Pasco, and went home.

But when he had snapped his fingers under the nose of his wife she took the poker at him, and he took refuge under the table.

Tap! tap! at the door.

"Come out from under there," said Susan, his wife.

Then Pasco lifted up his voice and sang out as loud as thunder, "No, Sue! no, I want come out from under the table. I'll stick where I be; for all you say, I'll show Uncle Zackie as I'll be maister in my own house."

In 1768 the Hon. Daines Barrington visited Cornwall to ascertain whether the Cornish language had entirely died out or not, and in a letter written to John Lloyd a few years after he gives the result of his journey, and in it refers to Dolly Pentreath:--

"I set out from Penzance with the landlord of the principal inn for my guide towards Sennen, and when I approached the village I said there must probably be some remains of the language in those parts, if anywhere. My guide, however, told me that I should be disappointed; but that if I would ride about ten miles about in my return to Penzance, he would conduct me to a village called Mousehole, where was an old woman who could speak Cornish fluently. While we were travelling together I enquired how he knew that this woman spoke Cornish, when he informed me that he frequently went to Mousehole to buy fish which were sold by her, and that when he did not offer her a price that was satisfactory she grumbled to some other old woman in an unknown tongue, which he concluded to be Cornish.

"When we reached Mousehole I desired to be introduced as a person who had laid a wager that there was not one who could converse in Cornish, upon which Dolly Pentreath spoke in an angry tone for two or three minutes in a language which sounded very much like Welsh. The hut in which she lived was in a very narrow lane, opposite to two rather better houses, at the doors of which two other women stood, who were advanced in years, and who, I observed, were laughing at what Dolly said to me.

"Upon this I asked them whether she had not been abusing me, to which they answered, 'Very heartily,' and because I had supposed she could not speak Cornish.

"I then said that they must be able to talk the language, to which they answered that they could not speak it readily, but that they understood it, being only ten or twelve years younger than Dolly Pentreath.

"I had scarcely said or thought anything more about this matter till last summer (1772), having mentioned it to some Cornish people, I found that they could not credit that any person had existed within these few years who could speak their native language; and therefore, though I imagined there was but a small chance of Dolly Pentreath continuing to live, yet I wrote to the President (of the Society of Antiquaries), then in Devonshire, to desire that he would make some inquiry with regard to her, and he was so obliging as to procure me information from a gentleman whose house was within three miles of Mousehole, a considerable part of whose letter I shall subjoin:--

"'Dolly Pentreath is short of figure and bends very much with old age, being in her eighty-seventh year; so lusty, however, as to walk hither to Castle Horneck, about three miles, in bad weather in the morning and back again. She is somewhat deaf, but her intellect seemingly not impaired.... She does indeed talk Cornish as readily as others do English, being bred up from a child to know no other language, nor could she talk a word of English before she was past twenty years of age, as, her father being a fisherman, she was sent with fish to Penzance at twelve years old, and sold them in the Cornish language, which the inhabitants in general, even the gentry, did then well understand. She is positive, however, that there is neither in Mousehole, nor in any other part of the county, any other person who knows anything of it, or at least can converse in it. She is poor, and maintained partly by the parish, and partly by fortune-telling and gabbling Cornish.'"

A monument has been erected to her memory by Prince Lucien Bonaparte. She died on December 26th, 1777, and was buried in January, 1778. The following epitaph was written for her:--

Cornish.

"Coth Doll Pentreath caus ha deau;

Marow ha kledyz ed Paul plêa:--
Na ed an egloz, gan pobel brâs,
Bes ed egloz-hay coth Dolly es."

English.

"Old Doll Pentreath, one hundred aged and two,
Deceased, and buried in Paul parish too:--
Not in the church, with people great and high,
But in the church-yard doth old Dolly lie."

A word may here be added relative to the Cornish tongue. The Celtic language is divided into two branches, one represented by the Irish and Gaelic of North Scotland, and this is called the Goidhelic, or Gaelic; the other by the Welsh, old Cornish, and Breton, and this is called the Brythonic.

The main distinction between them consists in the Gaelic employing *k* or the hard *c* where the Welsh and Cornish would use *p.* Thus *pen* is used in the latter, and*ken* in the former. When the Irish adopted the word *purpur*, purple, they changed it into *corcair*; and when they took the low Latin *premter* for presbyter into their language they twisted it into *crumthir.* The Cornish was identical with old Welsh, and the Breton was originally identical with the Cornish; but in course of time some changes grew up differentiating the tongues, and forming dialects derived from the same mother tongue, that is all.

In or about 1540 Dr. Moreman, vicar of Menheniot, in the east of the county, was the first to teach the people the Creed, the Lord's Prayer, and the Commandments in English.

Carew, however, in his *Survey of Cornwall* in 1602 says, "Most of the inhabitants can speak no word of Cornish, but few are ignorant of English, and yet some so affect their own as to a stranger they will not speak it, for if meeting them by chance you inquire the way, your answer will be, '*Meeg nauidna cowzasawzneck*'--I can speak no Saxonage."

Carew's *Survey* was soon followed by that of Norden, who says that the tongue was chiefly confined to Penwith and Kirrier, and yet "though the husband and wife, parents and children, master and servants, do naturally communicate in their native language, yet there is none of them in a manner but is able to converse with a stranger in the English tongue, unless it be some obscure people who seldom confer with the better sort."

The Cornish was so well spoken in the parish of Feock till about the year 1640 "that Mr. William Jackman, the then vicar, ... was forced for divers years to administer the Sacrament to the communicants in the Cornish tongue, because the aged people did not well understand the English, as he himself often told me" (Hals).

So late as 1650 the Cornish language was currently spoken in the parishes of Paul and S. Just; and in 1678 the rector of Landewednack "preached a sermon to his parishioners in the Cornish language only."

It may seem paradoxical, but I contend that for intellectual culture it is a great loss to the Cornish to have abandoned their native tongue. To be bi-lingual is educative to the intellect in a very marked degree. In their determination not to abandon their tongue, the Welsh show great prudence. I have no hesitation in saying that a Welsh peasant is much ahead, intellectually, of the English peasant of the same social position, and I attribute this mainly to the fact of the greater agility given to his brain in having to think and speak in two languages. When he gives up one of these tongues he abandons mental gymnastics as well as the exercise of the vocal organs in two different modes of speech.

What we do with infinite labour in the upper and middle classes is to teach our children to acquire French and German as well as English, and this is not only because these tongues open to them literary treasures, but for educative purpose to the mind, teaching to acquire other words, forms of grammar, and modulation of sounds than those the children have at home.

By God's mercy the Welsh child is so situated that from infancy it has to acquire simultaneously two tongues, and that in the lowest class of life; and this I contend is an advantage of a very high order, which is not enjoyed by children of even a class above it in England.

The West Cornish dialect is a growth of comparatively recent times. It is on the outside not more than four hundred years old. Whence was it derived? That is a problem that has yet to be studied.

Mr. Jago says:--

"We have in the provincial dialect a singular mixture of old Cornish and old English words, which gives so strong an individuality to the Cornish speech. As, in speaking English, a Frenchman or a German uses more or less of the accent peculiar to each, so it is very probable that the accent with which the Cornish speak is one transferred from their ancient Cornish language. The *sing-song*, as strangers call it, in the Cornish speech is not so evident to Cornishmen when they listen to their own dialect."[28]

Sancreed screen, which must have been almost as fine as that of Burian, has disappeared all but a magnificent fragment. The church is dedicated to S. Credan, disciple of S. Petrock, an Irishman, who returned to the Emerald Isle. He was the son of S. Illogan, and he had two aunts in Cornwall--one at Camborne and the other at Stythians.

CHUN QUOIT

S. Just Church is late; it has rather handsomely carved capitals of the piers, with angels bearing shields, on which are figured the arms of the principal families connected with the parish. S. Just, as I have said, was deacon to S. Patrick, and was the tutor to S. Piran.

In Gwythian parish may be seen the early eighth-century chapel of the saint, which was for long buried under the sands, but was revealed by a drift in 1808.

At Porth Curnew, near S. Levan's, are the ruins of another of these early oratories.

Madron was founded by S. Medran, brother of Odran; they went as boys under fourteen to S. Piran, to consult him about making a pilgrimage. But Medran wished to stay with the old abbot, whereas Odran was for travelling. Odran said to S. Piran, "Do not part my brother from me. We agreed to stick together." "The Lord judge between you both," said the abbot. "Let Medran hold this lantern and blow on the smouldering wick. If it flames, then he stays. If not, he goes." Medran succeeded in producing a flame, and thenceforth he became an attached follower of S. Piran. Odran went his way.

It is chiefly for prehistoric antiquities that the Land's End district is remarkable. It possesses cliff-castles, and also some fine examples of the stone cashel. Such is Chûn; also beehive huts, as at Bosprennis, and a curious cluster of habitations at Chysauster already referred to. There are cromlechs, sacred circles, and menhîrs. These are so numerous and so interesting, that a visitor should take Mr. Lach-Szyrma's guide and examine them in detail.

NOTE.--Books to be consulted:--

BLIGHT (J. T.), *A Week at the Land's End.* 1861. *List of Antiquities in Kirrier and Penwith.* Truro, 1862. *Churches of West Cornwall.* Oxford: Parker, 1885 (second edition).

LACH-SZYRMA (W. S.), *Two Hundred and Twenty-two Antiquities in and about Penzance.* Plymouth: Luke. *n.d.*

MATTHEWS (J. H.), *A History of the Parishes of St. Ives, Lelant, etc.* London: Stock, 1892.

CHAPTER XX.

THE SCILLY ISLES

Armorel of Lyoness--A refuge for the Celtic saints--Lighthouses--The name of Scilly--Olaf Trygvason at Scilly--Mr. Augustus Smith--The flower trade--Flowers not allowed to blossom in the fields--Traces of tin-streaming--Contrast between the east coast and the west of England--Variety in Scilly--Sir Cloudesley Shovel.

FOR a guide to what is to be seen in this cluster there is no better book than Sir W. Besant's *Armorel of Lyoness*, to my mind one of the most delightful works of fiction I have ever read; I refer, of course, to the first part, that concerns Scilly. Let a visitor take that book, and go over the ground and be happy. Nothing can be added, but one word in caution. The whole is a *little* over-coloured. Scilly presents scenes of great interest, but the cliffs are by no means so fine as those of Land's End, and far inferior to those of the Lizard. Nevertheless, island clusters have a charm of their own distinct from the scenery of the fringe of the mainland, and a cluster Scilly is, intricate, and presenting great variety. There are one hundred and forty-five islets, large and small, forty miles due west from Lizard Point, and twenty-eight west-by-south from Land's End.

THE PULPIT ROCK, SCILLY

229

The views of the islands change remarkably, according to the state of the tide. At high-water the islands are separated by wide stretches of sea, while at the ebb extensive flats are uncovered, and some of the islands are apparently joined. The Crow Channel between S. Mary's and S. Martin's Isles has been forded on horseback, and a man is reported to have ridden from S. Mary's to Tresco, fording the arms of the sea at low spring-tide.

S. Martin's Island is difficult of approach at low tide from S. Mary's by boat on account of the distance to which the sands run out.

Such an archipelago was exactly suited to the requirements of the Celtic saints, who, if they spent most of their time in superintendence of their monasteries, retired for Lent to solitary places, and as they grew old resigned their pastoral staves to their coarbs (successors), and retreated to islets, there to prepare for the great change. The west coast of Ireland is studded with islets that still retain the cells of these solitaries. Wales had its Bardsey and Anglesea, and Caldey and Ramsey. And what these were to Irish and Welsh the Scilly group was to the saints of Cornwall. Thus we find there S. Elid, the Welsh S. Illog, S. Teon, who is the Euny of Lelant, S. Samson, and S. Warna.

I do not know that any of the remains of their venerable oratories have been found, but then they have not been looked for.

There are now churches on four of the isles.

There are three lighthouses--that of S. Agnes, a revolving light; that on an outlying rock, the Bishop, fixed; and that on Round Island, with a red light.

The heights in Scilly are not great; the highest point attained is one hundred and twenty-eight feet. There are some small fresh-water tarns.

The islands take their name from the old Silurian inhabitants, to whom they served as a last refuge where they could maintain their independence, just as the Arran Isles answered the same purpose to their kindred, the Firbolgs, in Ireland. But the general notion is that they take their designation from the conger eels, locally called *selli*. It is remarkable that they must at one time have contained a much larger population than at present, as the remains of hedges and houses in ruins indicate.

In 993 Olaf Trygvason, of Norway, with Sweyn Forkbeard, of Denmark, together with a fleet of ninety-three ships, came a-harrying the coasts of England. They sailed up the Thames and attacked

London, but the citizens behaved with great valour, and beat them off. Then they ravaged the east coast of England, took and burnt Sandwich and Ipswich; next they entered the Blackwater and attacked Maldon. There a great fight ensued. The Saxons were under the command of the eorlderman Britnoth. The Norsemen gained the day, and Britnoth was slain. It is with this battle that one of the earliest remains of Anglo-Saxon poetry deals. It is, unhappily, but a fragment. After recording the fall of the eorlderman, the poet concludes:--

"I am old of age, hence will I not stir;
I will sit by the side of my dead master;
I think to lay me down and die by him I loved."

On the doors of some of the churches in the East of England were formerly "Danes' skins" and the remains of these still exist. When the Anglo-Saxons did succeed in killing a Norseman they flayed him, and nailed his tanned skin against the church door.

Olaf stormed the Castle of Bamborough, then harried the Scottish coast, the Western Isles and the Isle of Man, then Ireland, where "he burned far and wide, wherever inhabited."

Not yet content with blood and flame, he crossed to Wales and ravaged there, then sailed to France to do there what mischief he could. After a while he turned back, and sighted the Scilly Isles, and then ran his fleet into the harbour of S. Mary's, the largest of the isles. Here Olaf heard tell of a hermit who lived in a cell among the granite crags, and who was believed to have the gift of prophecy.

"I will test his powers," said Olaf.

Then he dressed up one of his men in his armour, gave him his spear and red-cross shield, and sent him to consult the old man.

But no sooner did the hermit see the fellow than he said, "Thou art not King Olaf, thou art a servant. Beware that thou be not false to him, that is my rede to thee." No more would he say.

Then the party returned to the ship and told Olaf. He was highly pleased, and went ashore in a boat with a small following, that he might consult the anchorite as to the prospect of his being able to recover the kingdom of his ancestors.

The hermit was undoubtedly a Cornish Briton, and Olaf was obliged to hold communication with him through an interpreter from Ireland or Wales.

The old man said to him, "There is a great future in store for thee, Olaf. Thou wilt have to pass through much conflict, but in the end wilt reign in thine own land; and when that comes to pass remember to advance the faith, and to use every opportunity to turn men from their idols."

Now the interpreter knew that there was discontent simmering among the followers of the prince. They wanted to return to their homes with the plunder they had acquired, but Olaf set his face against this.

The interpreter, knowing that the men were mutinous, said a few words in Welsh or Irish to the hermit. He was afraid of himself giving warning to Olaf, lest the mutineers should wreak their resentment on him. So the anchorite told the king that there were those amongst his followers who plotted, and purposed seizing the opportunity of his being on land to execute their design of revolt.

Olaf precipitately returned to his ships, and found that the mutineers were making off with some of the ships. He hurried on board, gave chase, and a fight ensued. Finally the mutiny was quelled, but not without Olaf being wounded. His vessel then put into Tresco harbour, where were monks to whom Athelstan had granted land in 936. He was carried into the monastery, carefully tended, and was induced to receive baptism. Hitherto, though convinced that Christianity was the true religion, Olaf had never formally been enrolled in the Church. Unhappily, Olaf could not speak Cornish, and the abbot was ignorant of the Norse tongue, so that all communication had to go on through the interpreter, and Olaf did not receive much religious instruction. Nevertheless, as far as his lights went, he was sincere.

Then he returned to Norway to proclaim his right to the throne.

"To avenge his fathers slain,
And reconquer realm and reign,
Came the youthful Olaf home,
Through the midnight sailing, sailing,
Listening to the wild wind's wailing,
And the dashing of the foam.
"To his thoughts the sacred name
Of his mother, Astrid, came;
And the tale she oft had told
Of her flight by secret passes,
Through the mountains and morasses,
To the home of Hakon old.
"Then his cruisings o'er the seas,
Westward to the Hebrides,

And to Scilly's rocky shore,
And the hermit's cavern dismal,
Christ's great name and rites baptismal,
In the ocean's rush and roar."

S. Mary's is the largest of the islands, and it has a population of over 1600 people; Tresco is the second; then S. Agnes, pronounced S. Anne's; then S. Martin's; next Bryher; after this comes S. Sampson, no longer inhabited; and the remainder are very small. The original population was doubtless Silurian or Ivernian; the traces, however, of this early race are few. The population now is less pure than on the mainland. Not only were there Irish colonists, but it is said that in the Civil Wars a Bedfordshire regiment was sent there--and forgotten; so the soldiers looked about for comely Scilly maids, married, and were content to be no more remembered in the adjacent island of Great Britain. In 1649 Sir John Grenville employed Scilly as a great nursery for privateers, and so swept the seas that the Channel trade was seriously injured. Parliament at length fitted out and despatched an expedition under Blake, and in June, 1651, compelled Sir John Grenville to surrender.

The islands belong to the Duchy of Cornwall, and thereby leased to the late Mr. Augustus Smith, who, firmly imbued with the notion that men must be manufactured by education rather than allowed to bring themselves up in independence, transported the population from the smaller islands and planted them about the schools. No doubt that the native originality, freshness, and force will be drilled out of the new generation, and they will all spell and think, and write and act alike. It is, however, sad to notice on islands now deserted the ruins of ancient farms.

The Scilly Isles are a great seat of the flower trade; previously early potatoes were grown there, but now these are imported.

Of flowers, narcissi and anemones are chiefly grown, and in the open, though large numbers of flowers are now under glass. As soon as the blooms show colour they are picked, and placed in water under cover. One may see in the interior of a cottage all the furniture stacked in a corner of the room, and the entire floor covered with pots and jars of water full of flower buds. If the blossoms need forcing to make them expand, they are put in warm water.

It is rare to see a field of flowers in full bloom. The damage caused by rain and wind is so great, that rather than run the risk they are picked when in bud.

One feature of the flower fields is that they are hedged about with escalonia, with its pretty shining leaves and pink flower. This shrub delights in wind, and it also serves to shelter the crop from the gales, as it stands clipping and grows vigorously.

Fishing is not much carried on, but anyone with a steam launch will be able to find good shelter in case of rough weather, and he can manage to catch as many fish as he desires. One prolific ground is round the Seven Stones Lightship, north-east of the isles.

It is a curious fact that little flotsam and jetsam comes up on the isles. The Atlantic tides divide and run up on each side of the tides that course along the shores of the islands.

Formerly Scilly was a favourite breeding-place for birds, but now they no longer employ it for this purpose, or do so to a very minor degree.

There are traces of streaming for tin in some of the isles, but no mineral veins are now known to run through the Scilly granite. Ferns abound, but the islands are a little disappointing to the botanist, though to a florist they are a paradise.

To give a true idea of Scilly I must quote from *Armorel*, for such as have not the book:--

"The visitor who comes by one boat and goes away by the next thinks he has seen this archipelago. As well stand inside a cathedral for half an hour and then go away thinking you have seen all. It takes many days to see these fragments of Lyonesse and to get a true sense of the place."

By the way, the idea that Scilly represents the peaks of a submerged realm of Lyonesse is altogether baseless. Lyonesse is the realm of Leon in Brittany, so-called because founded by colonists from Caerleon, who fled from the swords of the Saxons. It remained a little independent principality till at the close of the sixth century it became incorporated with the principality of Domnonia, in Brittany.

"Everywhere in Scilly there are the same features: here a hill strewn with boulders; there a little down with fern and gorse and heath; here a bay in which the water, on such days as it can be approached, peacefully laps a smooth white beach; here dark caves and holes in which the water always, even in the calmest days of summer, grumbles and groans, and, when the least sea rises, begins to roar and bellow--in time of storm it shrieks and howls.... All round the rocks at low tide hangs the long seaweed, undisturbed since the days when they manufactured kelp, like the rank growth of a tropical creeper: at high tide it stands up erect, rocking to and fro in the wash and sway of the water like the tree-tops of the forest in the breeze. Everywhere, except in the rare places where men come and go, the wild sea-birds make their nests; the shags stand on the ledges of the highest rocks in silent rows gazing upon the water below; the sea-gulls fly, shrieking in sea-gullic rapture--there is surely no life quite so joyous as the seagull's; the curlews call; the herons sail across the sky; and in spring millions of puffins swim and dive and fly about the rocks and lay their eggs in the hollow places of these wild and lonely islands."

Is not that beautiful writing? But it is not fanciful; it is beautiful because true, absolutely true. Go and see if it be not so.

Have you ever made acquaintance with the horrors of Lowestoft, a flat insipid shore, where the sea is always charged with mud and no breakers thunder, where the land scene is as dull and insipid as is the sea-scape? I was there last summer. It was a dismal place, made the more dismal by being invaded and pervaded, spread out, exposed, devoted to the "tripper." And I fled to the west coast to see the Atlantic, with the water crystal clear, through which you look down into infinity, and to the glorious cliffs about which that transparent water tosses, shakes its silver mane, curls its waves blue and iridescent as a peacock's neck, and I wondered that any should ever visit the east coast of England.

"All the islands, except the bare rocks, are covered with down and moorland, bounded in every direction by rocky headlands and slopes covered with granite boulders. And always, day after day, they came continually upon unexpected places: strange places, beautiful places: beaches of dazzling white; wildly-heaped carns; here a cromlech, a logan stone, a barrow; a new view of sea and sky and white-footed rock. I believe that there does not live any single man who has actually explored all the isles of Scilly, stood upon every rock, climbed every hill, and searched on every island for its treasures of ancient barrows, plants, birds, carns, and headlands. Once there was a worthy person who came here as chaplain to S. Martin's. He started with the excellent intention of seeing everything. Alas! he never saw a single island properly: he never walked round one exhaustively. He wrote a book about them, to be sure; but he saw only half."

There are numerous cairns, barrows, kistvaens, and circles of stones in the islands, and Giant's Castle, in S. Mary's, is a good example of a cliff-camp of the Irish Firbolg type. A local guide attributes it to the Danes, but that is nonsense.

In Porth Hellick Bay Sir Cloudesley Shovel was washed ashore and buried.

In 1707 Sir Cloudesley in the *Association*, Captain Hancock in the *Eagle*, Sir George Byng in the *Royal Anne*, Captain Coney in the *Romney*, Lord Dudley in the *St. George*, Captain Piercy in the *Firebrand*, and a captured fireship, the *Phœnix*, were returning from Toulon after the capture of Gibraltar. On the morning of the 22nd October, the weather being thick and dirty, they came into soundings of nineteen fathoms. There is a tradition that a seaman on the admiral's ship warned the officer of the watch that unless the ship's course were altered they would soon be on the rocks of Scilly. This was reported to Sir Cloudesley, who was very angry. He had the man brought before him, and attempted to browbeat him, but the man stuck to his opinion. The admiral lost his temper, as he considered it a breach of decorum for a common mariner to dictate the course of the vessel to a superior officer, and he ordered the man to be hanged at the yard-arm. One request was granted to the sailor--that he should be allowed to read aloud a psalm to the assembled crew. This was permitted, and he read out Psalm cix.:--

"Hold not Thy tongue, O God of my praise: for the mouth of the ungodly, yea, the mouth of the deceitful, is opened upon us."

That night the ship was lost. At six in the evening the admiral, who had brought the fleet to during the afternoon, made sail again, and stood away under canvas. Directly after he made signals of distress, which were returned by several of the fleet. Sir George Byng in the *Royal Anne*, who was a mile to windward of him, saw the breakers, and saved his vessel with difficulty.

The *Association*, Sir Cloudesley's vessel, had struck at eight o'clock upon the Gilstones, a cluster of rocks of what are called the Western Isles, and in about two minutes went down with all on board save one. He clung to a piece of the wreck, and was swept on to the Hellweathers, where he remained for some time till rescued. The *Eagle* and the *Romney* were also lost with all hands. The *Firebrand* was lost as well, but the captain and some of the crew were rescued. The *Phœnix* ran ashore, but was got off again. The *Royal Anne* was saved. So was the *S. George* by the merest accident. She struck the same rock as the *Association* and about the same time, but the wave which sank the admiral's ship floated the *S. George* from the rocks.

The body of Sir Cloudesley Shovel was picked up at Porth Hellick by a soldier and his wife, who gave it decent burial in the sand. It was afterwards conveyed at Lady Shovel's desire to Westminster Abbey and laid there. She rewarded the soldier with a pension for life. The diamond ring stolen from the body was sent to Lady Shovel by the thief, when he was dying.

Finally, with its amount of sunshine, with its equable temperature, and its air charged with ozone, I believe Scilly will be the sanatorium of the future.

NOTE.--Book to be consulted:--

TONKIN (J. C. and R. W.), *Guide to the Isles of Scilly*. Penzance, *n.d.* A capital little book.

FOOTNOTES:

1. *Irish Nennius*, ed. Todd and Herbert (Dublin, 1848), p. 237.

2. Misses Couch were misled when they visited S. Mawes, and they give a photograph of a well which is not the holy well. The latter is among the houses opposite the post office, and had an arched entrance, now walled up.

3. MATTHEWS, *History of the Parishes of S. Ives, Lelant, Towednack, and Zennor* (London, 1892), p. 40.

4. *Archæologia Cambrensis*, January, 1899. See also A. J. Langdon, "The Ornament of the Early Crosses of Cornwall," *Journal of the Royal Institution of Cornwall*, vol. x. (1890-1).

5. Not to be confounded with S. Clether of Clodock, in Herefordshire, son of Gwynnar, and from whom the poet Taliesin was descended. The invasion of Carmarthen by Dyfnwal from the north had much to do with Clether's departure.

6. Tremendous confusion has been made of his life, as he has been confounded with a S. Paternus, who was Bishop of Vannes in 462 or 465; and the Cornish Venedotia has been construed as Venettia, Vannes. Nearly a century intervened between the two saints.

7. *The Cornish Magazine*, 1899.

8. GUEST, *Mabinogion*, p. 227.

9. *Celtic Scotland.* Edinburgh, 1876-80.

10. "Cornish Choughs," in the *Journals of the Roy. Inst. of Cornwall*, x. (1890-1).

11. New Edition, 1893, vol. i. p. 136.

12. "The earthwork, of which a great part is still in existence, does not command the steep part of the slope on the other three sides, though the guns would be available against an enemy after he had once established himself on the plateau."

13. Lord Tenterden in the summing up of Rowe *v.* Brenton, 1830.

14. After the Armada the Corporation of Saltash raised the harbour due to seven shillings for a Spanish ship. This sum is still paid by Trinity House, which, however, exacts two shillings only from the Spaniards, the same as from a French or German vessel.

15. I have given them in my *Garland of Country Song*. Methuen, 1895.

16. There are two rivers Lew in West Devon and two in Wales. There is a Loue that flows into the Vézère. There is also Loe Pool by Helston; the root enters into lough or loch.

17. A new edition was published by Longmans in 1845.

18. Madoc and Madan are the same name; *oc* and *an* are diminutives. The real name was Aed. It became Mo-aedoc. *Mo* is a term of endearment--"my"--given to many Irish and Welsh saints.

19. I must caution the visitor against the blunders that crowd the pages of a little local guide to Golant. Amongst other misstatements is this, that the capitals are Norman and the arches of Moorish design. The four-centred arch is quite common in all third-pointed work.

20. Reprinted in Preb. HINGESTON-RANDOLPH'S *Registers of Bishop Grandisson*. Exeter, 1897, p. 608.

21. The arch over door and window is decisive against sixth-century work. All the earliest Irish churches have a stone slab thrown across from the jambs, and no arch with key.

22. The church without, as outside of the camp.

23. Not Witherne in Galway, nor Ty Gwyn âr Daf. See Mrs. DAWSON'S article in *Archæol. Cambr.*, 1898.

24. SULLIVAN, Introduction to O'Curry's *Lectures on the Manners and Customs of the Ancient Irish*, 1873, i. p. cliv.

25. Quite the best monograph on the colonisation of Brittany is by DOM PLAINE, *La Colonisation de l'Armorique par les Bretons insulaires*. Paris: Picard, 1899. See also LOTH (M. J.), *Emigration Bretonne en Armorique*. Rennes, 1883.

26. Figured in WOOD-MARTIN, *The Rude Stone Monuments of Ireland*, 1888, p. 154.

27. MATTHEWS, *A History of St. Ives*. London, 1892.

28. JAGO (F. W. P.), *Glossary of the Cornish Dialect*. Truro, 1882.

Freeriver is a community project working to create a place for people to visit and potentially live, long-term, in peace, free from the normal stresses of modern life.

We aim to provide a place where people can spend time discovering themselves and discovering nature. We aim to focus on creativity, health and wellbeing. We plan to provide events and classes for people in the local area and enhance the community.

Please visit our website for more details

www.freerivercommunity.com
freerivercommunity@hotmail.com

240

Printed in Great Britain
by Amazon

53666435R00138